4 –
Jan ?

PUFFIN **CLASSICS**

A Tale of Two Cities

D1014023

It was the best of times, it was the worst of times, it was the age of wisdom, it was the age of foolishness, it was the spring of hope, it was the winter of despair, we had everything before us, we had nothing before us, we were all going direct to Heaven, we were all going direct the other way.

There were a king with a large jaw and a queen with a plain face, on the throne of England; there were a king with a large jaw and a queen with a fair face, on the throne of France.

It was the year of Our Lord one thousand seven hundred and seventy-five.

CHARLES DICKENS

A Tale of Two Cities

INTRODUCED BY
RODDY DOYLE

Abridged by LINDA JENNINGS

PUFFIN

PUFFIN BOOKS

Published by the Penguin Group
Penguin Books Ltd, 80 Strand, London WC2R ORL, England
Penguin Group (USA) Inc., 375 Hudson Street, New York, New York 10014, USA
Penguin Group (Canada), 90 Eglinton Avenue East, Suite 700, Toronto, Ontario, Canada M4P 2Y3
(a division of Pearson Penguin Canada Inc.)
Penguin Ireland, 25 St Stephen's Green, Dublin 2, Ireland (a division of Penguin Books Ltd)
Penguin Group (Australia), 250 Camberwell Road, Camberwell, Victoria 3124, Australia
(a division of Pearson Australia Group Pty Ltd)
Penguin Books India Pvt Ltd, 11 Community Centre, Panchsheel Park, New Delhi – 110 017, India
Penguin Group (NZ), 67 Apollo Drive, Rosedale, North Shore 0632, New Zealand
(a division of Pearson New Zealand Ltd)
Penguin Books (South Africa) (Pty) Ltd, 24 Sturdee Avenue, Rosebank, Johannesburg 2196, South Africa

Penguin Books Ltd, Registered Offices: 80 Strand, London WC2R ORL, England

puffinbooks.com

First published 1859
This abridgement first published in Puffin Books 1995
Reissued in this edition 2009
1

This abridgement copyright © Linda Jennings, 1995
Introduction copyright © Roddy Doyle, 2009
Endpages copyright © Penguin Books, 2009
All rights reserved

Set in 11.5/15 pt Minion by Palimpsest Book Production Limited, Grangemouth, Stirlingshire
Printed in the UK by Clays Ltd, St Ives plc

British Library Cataloguing in Publication Data
A CIP catalogue record for this book is available from the British Library

ISBN: 978-0-141-32554-5

www.greenpenguin.co.uk

Penguin Books is committed to a sustainable future
for our business, our readers and our planet.
The book in your hands is made from paper
certified by the Forest Stewardship Council.

INTRODUCTION BY
RODDY DOYLE

Charles Dickens wrote *A Tale of Two Cities* when he was forty-seven. More importantly, I read it when I was eleven. I remember it clearly – I think.

That's the problem with memory; we *think* we remember. But how can we be certain that we're not just making it up? I remember – I think – telling a friend of mine about a fight I'd seen outside a fish and chip shop near where I lived. I was halfway through describing the fight when I realized that I hadn't actually seen the fight at all, or not really. It was something I'd seen in a film, something so vivid and frightening it had gone into my head and become mine. Things we imagine, or things we see in films, the books we read, the stories we hear – these can become as real to us as the 'real' things that actually happen to us.

Charles Dickens was born in 1812. *A Tale of Two Cities* is set in London and Paris in the years just before, and during, the French Revolution, which started in Paris in 1789. Dickens wasn't there; he wasn't even born. The descriptions of the rioting and terror, the prisons, the guillotine, the nasty and the noble characters – he made them up. I think that's amazing. But I didn't think that when I was eleven, when I was reading *A Tale of Two Cities* – not at first. I didn't care who'd written the book. It was so vivid and brilliant, so dramatic and scary, I wasn't aware that anyone had written it. There was just me and the story. The characters were real people who were being carried to a real guillotine and their real heads were being chopped off. It was great. Heads were being chopped off – in a book! Like all good Irish boys, I loved a good execution. And death by guillotine was as good as it got, as exciting and as absolutely terrifying. Carts – *tumbrils* – full of people were being pulled through the crowded streets of Paris to the guillotine. Women sat knitting while they watched. Knitting! Like my mother! And that wasn't all. Graves were robbed, spies spied on other spies, coaches full of frightened men and women charged across the countryside – in much the same way that I charged through the book. I felt I had no choice. Somehow, if I finished the book in one sitting without going to the toilet or going outside to play football (badly), fewer people would die. The faster I read, the fewer heads would roll. I saved hundreds of lives that day but, by the time I had finished the book, I was bursting to go the toilet.

A Tale of Two Cities had a huge impact on me. When

I'd finished it I paid proper attention to the name of the writer, Charles Dickens. I wanted to read more of his books: *Oliver Twist, Great Expectations, David Copperfield.* I read them, and Dickens became my favourite writer.

And then there was the knitting. Before I read *A Tale of Two Cities* knitting was something that mothers did, like cooking and ironing. My mother knitted. But after *A Tale of Two Cities* knitting became much more sinister. One of the book's best characters, Madame Defarge, knits while she watches the guillotine slice through the necks of hundreds of men and women. (To be fair to my mother, she never knitted while she watched heads being chopped off – as far as I know.) Earlier in the book, she – Madame Defarge, not my mother – knits the names of her enemies into whatever garment she's knitting. She even knits the name of a spy, John Barsad, as she's talking to him. The knitting is a code, a death sentence. Hidden in the wool is a list of people who are going to go to the guillotine. Something as innocent as knitting has become secret and frightening and absolutely brilliant.

It was then I realized that the story had actually been written, that a writer had invented the idea of the code in the wool, because it was too brilliant to be true. The plot, the characters, the big events and the tiny details had all been created by Charles Dickens, by writing words, by putting them on to a page, one after the other. It seemed as simple and as inviting as that. *A Tale of Two Cities* isn't

Dickens's best book but it's still great, and it's the book that made me want to be a writer – I think.

Knitting still scares me. When I asked my wife to marry me I asked her another question first:

'Do you like knitting?'

'No.'

'Will you marry me?'

'OK.'

She doesn't know it, but she was the fifteenth woman I asked to marry me that day. Knitting is very popular in Ireland. It's a frightening place to live in. But at least it never rains.

Contents

BOOK THREE: THE TRACK OF A STORM

BOOK ONE

RECALLED TO LIFE

1

The Period

It was the best of times, it was the worst of times, it was the age of wisdom, it was the age of foolishness, it was the spring of hope, it was the winter of despair, we had everything before us, we had nothing before us, we were all going direct to Heaven, we were all going direct the other way.

There were a king with a large jaw and a queen with a plain face, on the throne of England; there were a king with a large jaw and a queen with a fair face, on the throne of France.

It was the year of Our Lord one thousand seven hundred and seventy-five.

France rolled with exceeding smoothness down hill, making paper money and spending it. Under the guidance of her Christian pastors, she entertained herself, besides, with such humane achievements as sentencing a youth to have his hands cut off, his tongue torn out with pincers, and his body burned alive, because he had not kneeled down in the rain to do honour to a dirty procession of monks. It is likely enough that, rooted in the woods of France and Norway, there were growing trees, when that sufferer was put to death, already marked by the woodman, Fate, to come down and be sawn into boards, to make a certain movable framework with a sack and a knife in it, terrible in history. It is likely enough that in the rough outhouses of some tillers of the heavy lands adjacent to Paris, there were sheltered from the weather that very day, rude carts, which the Farmer, Death, had already set apart to be his tumbrils of the Revolution.

In England, daring burglaries by armed men, and highway robberies, took place in the capital itself every night; families were publicly cautioned not to go out of town without removing their furniture to upholsterers' warehouses for security; thieves snipped off diamond crosses from the necks of noble lords at Court drawing-rooms; musketeers went into St Giles's, to search for contraband goods, and the mob fired on the musketeers, and the musketeers fired on the mob; and nobody thought any of these occurrences much out of the common way.

These things, and a thousand like them, came to pass in and close upon the dear old year one thousand seven hundred and seventy-five. Environed by them, while the Woodman and the Farmer worked unheeded, those two of the large jaws, and those other two of the plain and the fair faces, trod with stir enough, and carried their divine rights with a high hand. Thus did the year one

'There's two on you,' said the man, thrusting the candle farther out, and shading his eyes with his hand. 'Who's the t'other one?'

'A new pal,' replied Jack Dawkins, pulling Oliver forward. 'Is Fagin upstairs?'

'Yes, he's a sortin' the wipes. Up with you!' The candle was drawn back, and the face disappeared.

Oliver, groping his way with one hand, and having the other firmly grasped by his companion, ascended with much difficulty the dark and broken stairs, which his conductor mounted with an ease and expedition that showed he was well acquainted with them. He threw open the door of a back-room, and drew Oliver in after him.

Oliver Twist is available in Puffin Classics

impregnated with filthy odours. There were a good many small shops; but the only stock in trade appeared to be heaps of children, who, even at that time of night, were crawling in and out at the doors, or screaming from the inside. The sole places that seemed to prosper amid the general blight of the place, were the public-houses; and in them, the lowest orders of Irish were wrangling with might and main. Covered ways and yards, which here and there diverged from the main street, disclosed little knots of houses, where drunken men and women were positively wallowing in filth; and from several of the doorways, great ill-looking fellows were cautiously emerging, bound, to all appearance, on no very well-disposed or harmless errands.

Oliver was just considering whether he hadn't better run away, when they reached the bottom of the hill. His conductor, catching him by the arm, pushed open the door of a house near Field Lane; and, drawing him into the passage, closed it behind them.

'Now, then!' cried a voice from below, in reply to a whistle from the Dodger.

'Plummy and slam!' was the reply.

This seemed to be some watchword or signal that all was right; for the light of a feeble candle gleamed on the wall at the remote end of the passage; and a man's face peeped out, from where a balustrade of the old kitchen staircase had been broken away.

from which Oliver discovered that his friend's name was Jack Dawkins, and that he was a peculiar pet and *protégé* of the elderly gentleman before mentioned.

Mr Dawkins's appearance did not say a vast deal in favour of the comforts which his patron's interest obtained for those whom he took under his protection; but, as he had a rather flighty and dissolute mode of conversing, and furthermore avowed that among his intimate friends he was better known by the *sobriquet* of 'The artful Dodger', Oliver concluded that, being of a dissipated and careless turn, the moral precepts of his benefactor had hitherto been thrown away upon him. Under this impression, he secretly resolved to cultivate the good opinion of the old gentleman as quickly as possible; and, if he found the Dodger incorrigible, as he more than half suspected he should, to decline the honour of his further acquaintance.

As John Dawkins objected to their entering London before nightfall, it was nearly eleven o'clock when they reached the turnpike at Islington, and then progressed by several streets into Saffron Hill the Great, along which the Dodger scudded at a rapid pace, directing Oliver to follow close at his heels.

Although Oliver had enough to occupy his attention in keeping sight of his leader, he could not help bestowing a few hasty glances on either side of the way, as he passed along. A dirtier or more wretched place he had never seen. The street was very narrow and muddy, and the air was

If you have enjoyed *A Tale of Two Cities* **you may
like to read** *Oliver Twist*, **in which young orphan
Oliver finds himself living on the streets of London:**

'Going to London?' said the strange boy, when Oliver
had at length concluded.

'Yes.'

'Got any lodgings?'

'No.'

'Money?'

'No.'

The strange boy whistled; and put his arms into his
pockets, as far as the big coat-sleeves would let them go.

'Do you live in London?' inquired Oliver.

'Yes. I do, when I'm at home,' replied the boy. 'I suppose
you want some place to sleep in tonight, don't you?'

'I do, indeed,' answered Oliver. 'I have not slept under a
roof since I left the country.'

'Don't fret your eyelids on that score,' said the young
gentleman. 'I've got to be in London tonight; and I know
a 'spectable old genelman as lives there, wot'll give you
lodgings for nothink, and never ask for the change.'

This led to a more friendly and confidential dialogue;

postilion – a man who rides on the nearside leading horse of a team drawing a coach to guide them in the absence of a coachman

Sessions – meetings of legal officials working in court

shoe – a type of brake under a carriage

Solicitor-General – a legal officer, ranking below Attorney-General

Temple Bar – a London landmark, located near Tellson's Bank

tumbril – a crude, two-wheeled cart used to carry prisoners to execution

turnkey – a person in charge of the keys of a prison

flambeau – a flaming torch

Hackney coach – a coach for hire; an old-fashioned taxi

jackal – someone who performs menial tasks for another

lamplighter – a person whose job it was to light and extinguish gas street-lamps

laudanum – a solution of opium in alcohol or wine used as a painkiller

lettre de cachet – a document containing a royal warrant for the imprisonment without trial of a particular person

mail-coach – before the building of the railways there were two types of coach on English roads: the mail-coach and the stage-coach. The mail-coaches were subsidized by the Post Office, whereas stage-coaches were privately owned

Old Bailey – London's historic Central Criminal Court on Old Bailey Street

packet – a boat that travels a regular route, carrying passengers, mail and freight

parley – a conference to discuss points in dispute with an enemy

GLOSSARY

adieu – French for 'farewell'

affidavit – a statement written under oath for use as proof in a court of law

arm-chest – a chest containing weapons

Attorney-General – the chief legal officer of a nation

Bastille – a state prison in Paris that held many prisoners indefinitely without trial. It was stormed and destroyed during the French Revolution in 1789 and its destruction is commemorated on Bastille Day (14 July)

blunderbuss – a musket with a large gun barrel and a broad muzzle, accurate only at close range

chain of the shoe – a chain beneath a carriage, attached to the brake

château – a large country house

coach and six – a coach drawn by six horses

farmer-general – a member of a rich organization that made a living from collecting taxes

* There are stories that the eyes and mouths of the decapitated heads still moved seconds after having been cut off! Charlotte Corday, for example, is said to have stared angrily at a man who slapped her cheek. Maybe the guillotine was not as painless as Mr Guillotin hoped . . .

* The guillotine was used not only in France, but also in Greece, Switzerland and Sweden. It was particularly popular with the Nazis in Germany, who killed 16,000 people with the guillotine. Capital punishment is now outlawed in Europe. In France, the last person died under the guillotine in 1977.

* The first guillotine was modelled on a decapitating machine called the Halifax Gibbet, which was used in England between 1286 and 1650. The guillotine was built in 1792, painted blood-red and had a bucket to catch the head. Later versions also had a metal tray to catch blood.

* Before the French Revolution, how a convict was executed depended on his social status. Commoners were worst off. They were burnt or hanged, drawn through the city by a horse or cut into pieces while still alive. But even noblemen, who were beheaded by axe or sword, had a hard time. Many strokes could be needed to sever the head from the body.

* The guillotine was not actually invented by its name source, Joseph-Ignace Guillotin. Mr Guillotin had merely demanded a form of capital punishment that was less painful and that could be applied to *all* convicted criminals, regardless of their status.

* Between the years 1792 and 1799 more than 15,000 people died on the guillotine. The executioners could not keep up with the physically tough job of cutting off heads with an axe, but the guillotine made their work much easier. It became so notorious that there were even toy guillotines for children and guillotine earrings for women.

A Tale of Two Cities takes place during the French Revolution, which began in 1789. The French people were tired of the social and economic inequalities forced upon them by the ruling monarchy. The rich aristocracy and members of the clergy lived a life of luxury while the ordinary peasants were made to pay high taxes and forced into military service. Many were extremely poor and starving to death because they weren't allowed to hunt or fish on the nobles' estates.

Take a look at the story of the French Revolution on the internet or read about it in the library to find out more about this terrible period of France's history. What happened to King Louis XVI and his famous consort, Marie Antoinette? Who was Maximilien Robespierre? What role did he play during the Revolution? Find out why the years 1793–4 became known as the 'Reign of Terror'.

Imagine you are a young man or woman living at the time of Louis XVI of France. What clothes would you have worn? Study the paintings and drawings of the extraordinary clothes of that period and write or draw a portrait.

A Tale of Two Cities, with its highly suspenseful plot, has been made into many films and stage plays. Imagine you are asked to cast a new movie. Who would you choose for the roles of the main characters from today's actors, and why?

Draw a map of England and France and plot the route from London to Paris.

Although Sydney Carton and Charles Darnay look very much alike, they are two very different men. What was your first impression of Sydney Carton and why do you think he resents Charles?

One of the many themes in *A Tale of Two Cities* is resurrection – that if you die, you will somehow return. Dickens uses many metaphors for this notion. For example, Doctor Manette is 'recalled to life' after his long incarceration in the Bastille. Can you think of any other characters in the story who have been 'resurrected'? And why do you think Jerry Cruncher is referred to as 'The Resurrection Man'?

Who do you think is the most memorable character in the story, and why?

Bastille Day is one of the most important dates in French history. Why do you think the French people celebrate it?

The opening line of *A Tale of Two Cities* is one of the most famous lines in English literature. Can you think of any other famous first lines?

Jeremiah (Jerry) Cruncher – the porter at Tellson's Bank. He makes extra money by robbing graves and selling the corpses to medical schools for scientific research.

C. J. Stryver – works with Sydney Carton at the law firm.

Miss Pross – Lucie's nurse and companion.

Solomon Pross – brother of Miss Pross, Lucie Manette's nurse. He works as a spy under the name John Barsad, first for the English and then for the French government.

Gaspard – a resident of Saint Antoine who is executed for assassinating Charles Darnay's uncle, the Marquis.

Sydney Carton – a lawyer who drinks too much for his own good. He is in love with Lucie Manette. Carton bears a strong resemblance to Lucie's husband, Charles Darnay. His devotion to Lucie is the main reason for his decision to take Darnay's place in prison and to be sent to the guillotine.

Jarvis Lorry – an agent of Tellson's Bank. It was Mr Lorry who had rescued the young Lucie Manette and took her to safety in England after her father was arrested and her mother died. Mr Lorry reunites Lucie and her father after his eighteen years in prison.

Ernest Defarge – a former servant of Doctor Manette before he was sent to prison. He helps to plot the French Revolution from his wine-shop in the Parisian suburb of Saint Antoine.

Madame Thérèse Defarge – Monsieur Defarge's ruthless wife and the leader of the town's female revolutionaries. She seeks revenge for crimes against her family and knits a register of the people who deserve to die at the hands of the Revolution.

The Vengeance – a friend of Madame Defarge and a fellow revolutionary.

Jacques Three – a member of the corrupt Tribunal that sentences Charles Darnay to execution. He operates as a bloodthirsty sidekick to Madame Defarge and The Vengeance.

Doctor Manette – Doctor Manette is one of the central characters in the story. Wrongfully imprisoned in France for eighteen years and virtually insane, he is eventually freed and makes his home in England with his loving daughter, Lucie. There he begins to regain his sanity but relapses when he discovers his son-in-law, Charles Darnay, is a member of the wicked Evrémonde family.

Lucie Manette – Doctor Manette's beautiful daughter who, up until the age of seventeen, believed she was an orphan. She learns that her father has been in a French prison and travels with her ward, Mr Lorry, to rescue him. Later she marries Charles Darnay.

Charles Darnay – the nephew and heir of the wicked aristocrat Marquis St Evrémonde. Working as a French tutor in England, he is arrested as a spy and placed on trial. There he meets Doctor Manette's daughter, Lucie, and marries her. When he goes back to France he is caught trying to help a former family servant. He is put in prison and sentenced to death, but is saved by his 'double', Sydney Carton.

Marquis St Evrémonde (Monseigneur) – he was responsible for the imprisonment of Doctor Manette and for crimes against Thérèse Defarge's family. He is also responsible for the death of Gaspard's young son, whom he runs down in his coach.

***Where did he get the idea for* A Tale of Two Cities?**
Dickens became fascinated by the subject of the French
Revolution after reading a history of the Revolution by
his friend Thomas Carlyle. Many incidents in Dickens's
story are based on actual events as described by Carlyle
in his book.

***What did people think of* A Tale of Two Cities *when it was
first published?***
A Tales of Two Cities was Dickens's twelfth novel, published
in 1859. It was originally published in weekly instalments in
Dickens's own magazine called *All the Year Round*. At first
the book received mixed reviews, but nevertheless people
enjoyed the characters in the story and the fast-paced action,
set against the exciting, historical background of the French
Revolution.

What other books did he write?
Starting with *The Pickwick Papers* in 1836, Dickens wrote over
twenty novels, including *A Christmas Carol*, *David Copperfield*,
Great Expectations, *Nicholas Nickleby*, and *Oliver Twist* (also
available in Puffin Classics), all of which are still read today.

couple who enjoyed parties and family gatherings, but the cost of entertaining and raising a large family put them into financial difficulties.

When Dickens was twelve, his father was sent to Marshalsea Prison for debt and so Charles was sent out to work in Warren's Blacking Factory – a boot-polish factory – for two years in order to support the family. (While employed there he met a man named Bob Fagin. Charles later used the name in *Oliver Twist*.) Charles never forgot the hard labour or the appalling conditions. He went on to become a dedicated social campaigner and an administrator for several charitable organizations.

What did he do apart from writing books?
At first Dickens worked as a clerk in a law firm, with the intention of training as a barrister. This taught him about the law in detail and provided him with his knowledge of judicial injustices against the poor, which he used extensively in his later books.

The next job that Dickens took was as a political journalist. Although he moved on to become a full-time novelist, he continued to write for, and edit, journals throughout his life.

Dickens enjoyed travelling, particularly in North America. His involvement in public speaking meant that he toured widely both at home and abroad, pouring his boundless energy into lecturing on subjects such as the abolition of slavery, as well as giving numerous readings of his own works.

Another of Dickens's passions was the theatre, for which he wrote a number of plays as well as performing on stage himself.

NAME: Charles John Huffam Dickens
BORN: 7 February 1812 in Portsmouth, England
DIED: 9 June 1870 in Gad's Hill, Kent, England (but he is
    buried in Poets' Corner in Westminster Abbey)
NATIONALITY: English
LIVED: mainly in and around London
MARRIED: to Catherine (Kate) Thomson Hogarth, in 1836;
    separated 1858
CHILDREN: ten: Charles, Mary, Kate, Walter, Francis, Alfred,
    Sydney, Henry, Dora and Edward

What was he like?

Charles Dickens was a very likeable character. He had a lively
sense of humour, a vivid imagination and a tremendous
amount of energy and enthusiasm. He was also very caring
and throughout his life demonstrated empathy for his fellow
man. In 1865 Dickens was on board the train involved in the
Staplehurst rail crash, in which the first seven carriages of the
train plunged off a bridge that was being repaired. The
carriage he was travelling in was not critically damaged and
he was lucky enough to emerge unscathed, so he immediately
set about tending to the injured and dying. The incident had a
profound and lasting effect on his life.

Where did he grow up?

Dickens spent his early childhood in Portsmouth and London.
He was the second of eight children. His parents were a lively

CONTENTS

PUFFIN 🐧 CLASSICS

A Tale of Two Cities

With Puffin Classics, the adventure isn't
over when you reach the final page.
Want to discover more about your favourite
characters, their creators and their worlds?
Read on . . .

thousand seven hundred and seventy-five conduct their Greatnesses, and myriads of small creatures – the creatures of this chronicle among the rest – along the roads that lay before them.

2

The Mail

It was the Dover road that lay, on a Friday night late in November, before the first of the persons with whom this history has business. The Dover road lay, as to him, beyond the Dover mail, as it lumbered up Shooter's Hill. He walked up-hill in the mire by the side of the mail, as the rest of the passengers did; because the hill, and the harness, and the mud, and the mail, were all so heavy, that the horses had three times already come to a stop.

Two other passengers, besides the one, were plodding up the hill by the side of the mail. Not one of the three could have said, from anything he saw, what either of the other two was like; and each was hidden under almost as many wrappers from the eyes of the mind, as from the eyes of the body, of his two companions. In those days, travellers were very shy of being confidential on a short notice, for anybody on the road might be a robber or in league with robbers.

The Dover mail was in its usual genial position that the guard suspected the passengers, the passengers

suspected one another and the guard, they all suspected everybody else, and the coachman was sure of nothing but the horses.

'Wo-ho!' said the coachman. 'So, then! One more pull and you're at the top and be damned to you, for I have had trouble enough to get you to it!'

The emphatic horse made a decided scramble for it, and the three other horses followed suit.

The last burst carried the mail to the summit of the hill. The horses stopped to breathe again, and the guard got down to skid the wheel for the descent, and open the coach-door to let the passengers in.

'Tst! Joe!' cried the coachman in a warning voice, looking down from his box. 'What do you say, Tom?' They both listened. 'I say a horse at a canter coming up.'

'*I* say a horse at a gallop, Tom,' returned the guard, leaving his hold of the door, and mounting nimbly to his place. 'Gentlemen! In the king's name, all of you!'

With this hurried adjuration, he cocked his blunderbuss, and stood on the offensive.

The passenger booked by this history, was on the coach-step, getting in; the two other passengers were close behind him, and about to follow. He remained on the step, half in the coach and half out of it; they remained in the road below him.

The sound of a horse at a gallop came fast and furiously up the hill.

'So-ho!' the guard sang out, as loud as he could roar. 'Yo there! Stand! I shall fire!'

The pace was suddenly checked, and, with much splashing and floundering, a man's voice called from the mist, 'Is that the Dover mail?'

'Why do you want to know?'

'I want a passenger, if it is.'

'What passenger?'

'Mr Jarvis Lorry.'

Our booked passenger showed in a moment that it was his name. The guard, the coachman, and the two other passengers eyed him distrustfully.

'Keep where you are,' the guard called to the voice in the mist, 'because, if I should make a mistake, it could never be set right in your lifetime. Gentleman of the name of Lorry answer straight.'

'What is the matter?' asked the passenger, then, with mildly quavering speech. 'Who wants me? Is it Jerry?'

'Yes, Mr Lorry.'

'What is the matter?'

'A despatch sent you from over yonder. T. and Co.'

'I know this messenger, guard,' said Mr Lorry, getting down into the road. 'He may come close; there's nothing wrong.'

'I hope there ain't, but I can't make so 'Nation sure of that,' said the guard, in gruff soliloquy. 'Hallo you!'

'Well! And hallo you!' said Jerry.

The figures of a horse and rider came slowly through the eddying mist, and came to the side of the mail, where the passenger stood. The rider stooped and handed the passenger a small folded paper.

'Guard!' said the passenger, in a tone of quiet business confidence. 'There is nothing to apprehend. I belong to Tellson's Bank. I am going to Paris on business. A crown to drink. I may read this?'

'If so be as you're quick, sir.'

He opened it in the light of the coach-lamp on that side and read – first to himself and then aloud: ' "Wait at Dover for Mam'selle." It's not long, you see, guard. Jerry, say that my answer was, RECALLED TO LIFE.'

Jerry started in his saddle. 'That's a Blazing strange answer, too,' said he, at his hoarsest.

'Take that message back, and they will know that I received this, as well as if I wrote. Make the best of your way. Good night.'

With those words the passenger opened the coach-door and got in; not at all assisted by his fellow-passengers, who had expeditiously secreted their watches and purses in their boots, and were now making a general pretence of being asleep.

The coach lumbered on again, with heavier wreaths of mist closing round it as it began the descent and the guard soon replaced his blunderbuss in his arm-chest.

Jerry, left alone in the mist and darkness, dismounted

meanwhile, not only to ease his spent horse, but to wipe the mud from his face, and shake the wet out of his hat-brim. After standing with the bridle over his heavily-splashed arm, until the wheels of the mail were no longer within hearing and the night was quite still again, he turned to walk down the hill.

'After that there gallop from Temple-bar, old lady, I won't trust your fore-legs till I get you on the level,' said this messenger, glancing at his mare. '"Recalled to life." That's a Blazing strange message. You'd be in a Blazing bad way, if recalling to life was to come into fashion, Jerry!'

3

The Night Shadows

A wonderful fact to reflect upon, that every human creature is constituted to be that profound secret and mystery to every other.

With the three passengers shut up in the narrow compass of one lumbering old mail-coach; they were mysteries to one another, as complete as if each had been in his own coach and six, or his own coach and sixty, with the breadth of a county between him and the next.

The messenger rode back at an easy trot, stopping pretty often at ale-houses by the way to drink, but evincing a tendency to keep his own counsel, and to keep his hat cocked over his eyes. He had eyes that assorted very well with that decoration, being of a surface black, with no depth in the colour or form, and much too near together. They had a sinister expression, under an old cocked-hat like a three-cornered spittoon, and over a great muffler for the chin and throat, which descended nearly to the wearer's knees.

'No, Jerry, no!' said the messenger, harping on one theme

as he rose. 'It wouldn't do for you, Jerry. Jerry, you honest tradesman, it wouldn't suit *your* line of business! Recalled – ! Bust me if I don't think he'd been a drinking!'

His message perplexed his mind to that degree that he was fain, several times, to take off his hat to scratch his head.

While he trotted back with the message he was to deliver to the night watchman in his box at the door of Tellson's Bank, by Temple-bar, who was to deliver it to greater authorities within, the shadows of the night took such shapes to him as arose out of the message. They seemed to be numerous, for she shied at every shadow on the road.

What time, the mail-coach lumbered, jolted, rattled, and bumped upon its tedious way, with its three fellow-inscrutables inside.

Tellson's Bank had a run upon it in the mail. As the bank passenger – with an arm drawn through the leathern strap – nodded in his place, with half-shut eyes, the little coach-windows, and the coach-lamp dimly gleaming through them, and the bulky bundle of opposite passenger, became the bank, and did a great stroke of business. The rattle of the harness was the chink of money, and more drafts were honoured in five minutes that even Tellson's, with all its foreign and home connexion, ever paid in thrice the time.

But, though the bank was almost always with him, and though the coach was always with him, there was another

current of impression that never ceased to run, all through the night. He was on his way to dig some one out of a grave.

Now, which of the multitude of faces that showed themselves before him was the true face of the buried person, the shadows of the night did not indicate; but they were all the faces of a man of five-and-forty by years, and they differed principally in the passions they expressed, and in the ghastliness of their worn and wasted state. A hundred times the dozing passenger inquired of this spectre:

'Buried how long?'

The answer was always the same. 'Almost eighteen years.'

'You had abandoned all hope of being dug out?'

'Long ago.'

'You know that you are recalled to life?'

'They tell me so.'

'I hope you care to live?'

'I can't say.'

'Shall I show her to you? Will you come and see her?'

The answers to this question were various and contradictory. Sometimes the broken reply was, 'Wait! It would kill me if I saw her too soon.' Sometimes, it was given in a tender rain of tears, and then it was 'Take me to her.' Sometimes it was staring and bewildered, and then it was, 'I don't know her. I don't understand.'

After such imaginary discourse, the passenger in his

fancy would dig, and dig, dig – now, with a spade, now with his hands – to dig this wretched creature out. The passenger would then start to himself, and lower the window, to get the reality of mist and rain on his cheek.

Yet even when his eyes were opened on the mist and rain, the night shadows outside the coach would fall into the train of the night shadows within. The real Banking-house by Temple-bar, the real business of the past day, and the real message returned, would all be there. Out of the midst of them, the ghostly face would rise, and he would accost it again.

'Buried how long?'

'Almost eighteen years.'

'I hope you care to live?'

'I can't say.'

Dig – dig – dig – until an impatient movement from one of the two passengers would admonish him to pull up the window.

The words were still in his hearing as just spoken when the weary passenger started to the consciousness of daylight, and found that the shadows of the night were gone.

'Eighteen years!' said the passenger, looking at the sun. 'Gracious Creator of day! To be buried alive for eighteen years!'

4

The Preparation

When the mail got successfully to Dover, in the course of the forenoon, the head drawer at the Royal George Hotel opened the coach-door as his custom was.

By that time, there was only one adventurous traveller left, for the two others had been set down at their respective roadside destinations. Mr Lorry, the passenger, shaking himself out of the coach in chains of straw, a tangle of shaggy wrapper, flapping hat, and muddy legs, was rather like a dog.

'There will be a packet to Calais, tomorrow, drawer?'

'Yes, sir, if the weather holds and the wind sets tolerable fair. Bed, sir?'

'I shall not go to bed till night; but I want a bedroom, and a barber.'

'And then breakfast, sir? Yes sir. That way, sir, if you please. Show Concord! Gentleman's valise and hot water to Concord.'

The Concord bed-chamber being always assigned to a

passenger by the mail, and passengers by the mail being always heavily wrapped up from head to foot, the room had the odd interest for the establishment of the Royal George, that although but one kind of man was seen to go into it, all kinds and varieties of men came out of it. Consequently, another drawer, and two porters, and several maids, and the landlady, were all loitering by accident at various points of the road between the Concord and the coffee-room, when a gentleman of sixty, formally dressed in a brown suit of clothes, passed along on his way to his breakfast.

The coffee-room had no other occupant, that forenoon, than the gentleman in brown. His breakfast-table was drawn before the fire, and as he sat, with its light shining on him, waiting for the meal, he sat so still, that he might have been sitting for his portrait.

He wore an odd little sleek crisp flaxen wig, setting very close to his head. A face, habitually suppressed and quieted, was still lighted up under the quaint wig by a pair of moist bright eyes that it must have cost their owner, in years gone by, some pains to drill to the composed and reserved expression of Tellson's Bank. He had a healthy colour in his cheeks, and his face, though lined, bore few traces of anxiety. But, perhaps the confidential bachelor clerks in Tellson's Bank were principally occupied with the cares of other people; and perhaps second-hand cares, like second-hand clothes, come easily off and on.

Completing his resemblance to a man who was sitting for his portrait, Mr Lorry dropped off to sleep. The arrival of his breakfast roused him, and he said to the drawer, as he moved his chair to it:

'I wish accommodation prepared for a young lady who may come here at any time today. She may ask for Mr Jarvis Lorry, or she may only ask for a gentleman from Tellson's Bank.'

'We have oftentimes the honour to entertain your gentlemen in their travelling backwards and forwards betwixt London and Paris, sir.'

'Yes. We are quite a French House, as well as an English one.'

'Yes, sir. Not much in the habit of such travelling yourself, I think, sir?'

'Not of late years. It is fifteen years since we – since I – came last from France.'

'Indeed, sir? That was before my time here, sir.'

The waiter shifted his napkin from his right arm to his left, dropped into a comfortable attitude, and stood surveying the guest while he ate and drank, as from an observatory or watch-tower.

When Mr Lorry had finished his breakfast, he went out for a stroll on the beach. It was a desert of heaps of sea and stones tumbling wildly about, and the sea thundered at the town, and thundered at the cliffs, and brought the coast down, madly. A little fishing was done in the port,

and a quantity of strolling about by night, and looking seaward: particularly at those times when the tide made, and was near flood. Small tradesmen, who did no business whatever, sometimes unaccountably realised large fortunes, and it was remarkable that nobody in the neighbourhood could endure a lamplighter.

As the day declined into the afternoon, and the air became again charged with mist and vapour, Mr Lorry's thoughts seemed to cloud too. When it was dark, and he sat before the coffee-room fire, awaiting his dinner as he had awaited his breakfast, his mind was busily digging, digging, digging, in the live red coals.

Mr Lorry had just poured out his last glassful of wine, when a rattling of wheels came up the narrow street, and rumbled into the inn-yard.

In a very few minutes the waiter came in to announce that Miss Manette had arrived from London.

'So soon?'

Miss Manette had taken some refreshment on the road, and required none then, and was extremely anxious to see the gentleman from Tellson's immediately, if it suited his pleasure and convenience.

The gentleman from Tellson's followed the waiter to Miss Manette's apartment. It was a large, dark room, furnished in a funereal manner with black horsehair, and loaded with heavy dark tables.

The obscurity was so difficult to penetrate that Mr

Lorry, picking his way over the well-worn Turkey carpet, supposed Miss Manette to be, for the moment, in some adjacent room, until he saw standing to receive him by the table between candles and the fire, a young lady of not more than seventeen, in a riding-cloak, and still holding her straw travelling-hat by its ribbon, in her hand. As his eyes rested on a short, slight, pretty figure, a quantity of golden hair, a pair of blue eyes that met his own with an inquiring look, and a forehead with a singular capacity of lifting and knitting itself into an expression of a bright fixed attention, a sudden vivid likeness passed before him, of a child whom he had held in his arms on the passage across that very Channel, one cold time, when the hail drifted heavily and the sea ran high. The likeness passed away, and he made his formal bow to Miss Manette.

'Pray take a seat, sir.' In a very clear and pleasant young voice; a little foreign in its accent, but a very little indeed.

'I kiss your hand, miss,' said Mr Lorry, with the manners of an earlier date, as he made his formal bow again, and took his seat.

'I received a letter from the Bank, sir, yesterday, informing me that some intelligence – or discovery – respecting the small property of my poor father, whom I never saw – so long dead – rendered it necessary that I should go to Paris, there to communicate with a gentleman of the Bank, so good as to be despatched to Paris for the purpose.'

'Myself.'

She curtseyed to him with a pretty desire to convey to him that she felt how much older and wiser he was than she. He made her another bow.

'I replied to the Bank, sir, that as it was considered necessary that I should go to France, I should esteem it highly if I might be permitted to place myself, during the journey, under that worthy gentleman's protection. The gentleman had left London, but I think a messenger was sent after him to beg the favour of his waiting for me here.'

'I was happy,' said Mr Lorry, 'to be entrusted with the charge.'

'Sir, I thank you indeed. I thank you very gratefully. It was told me by the Bank that the gentleman would explain to me the details of the business, and that I must prepare myself to find them of a surprising nature.'

Mr Lorry settled the crisp flaxen wig at the ears:

'It is very difficult to begin.'

He did not begin, but, in his indecision, met her glance. The young forehead lifted itself into that singular expression, and she raised her hand.

'Are you quite a stranger to me, sir?'

'Am I not?' Mr Lorry opened his hands, and extended them outwards with an argumentative smile.

Between the eyebrows and just over the little feminine nose, the expression deepened itself as she took her seat

thoughtfully in the chair by which she had hitherto remained standing. He went on:

'In your adopted country, I presume, I cannot do better than address you as a young English lady, Miss Manette?'

'If you please, sir.'

'Miss Manette, I have a business charge to acquit myself of. In your reception of it, don't heed me any more than if I was a speaking machine. I will, with your leave, relate to you, miss, the story of one of our customers.'

'Story!'

He seemed wilfully to mistake the word she had repeated, when he added, in a hurry, 'Yes, customers; in the banking business we usually call our connexion our customers. He was a French gentleman; a scientific gentleman; a Doctor.'

'Not of Beauvais?'

'Why, yes, of Beauvais. Like Monsieur Manette, your father, the gentleman was of Beauvais. Like Monsieur Manette, your father, the gentleman was of repute in Paris. I had the honour of knowing him there. Our relations were business relations, but confidential. I speak, miss, of twenty years ago. He married – an English lady – and I was one of the trustees. His affairs were entirely in Tellson's hands. These are mere business relations, miss; there is no friendship in them, no particular interest, nothing like sentiment. In short, I have no feelings; I am a mere machine. To go on –'

'But this is my father's story, sir; and I begin to think that when I was left an orphan through my mother's surviving my father only two years, it was you who brought me to England.'

Mr Lorry took the hesitating little hand that confidingly advanced to take his, and he put it with some ceremony to his lips.

'Miss Manette, it *was* I. And you will see how truly I spoke of myself just now, in saying I had no feelings, and that all the relations I hold with my fellow-creatures are mere business relations, when you reflect that I have never seen you since. No; you have been the ward of Tellson's House since, and I have been busy with the other business of Tellson's House since.'

Mr Lorry flattened his flaxen wig upon his head with both hands, and resumed.

'So far, miss, this is the story of your regretted father. Now comes the difference. If your father had not died when he did – Don't be frightened! How you start!'

She did, indeed, start. And she caught his wrist with both her hands.

'Pray,' said Mr Lorry, in a soothing tone, 'pray control your agitation.'

Her look so discomposed him that he stopped, wandered, and began anew:

'As I was saying; if Monsieur Manette had not died; if he had suddenly and silently disappeared; if he had been

spirited away; if it had not been difficult to guess to what dreadful place, though no art could trace him; if he had an enemy in some compatriot who could exercise a privilege that I in my own time have known the boldest people afraid to speak of in a whisper, across the water, there; if his wife had implored the king, the queen, the court, the clergy, for any tidings of him, and all quite in vain; – then the history of your father would have been the history of this unfortunate gentleman, the Doctor of Beauvais.'

'I entreat you to tell me more, sir.'

'I will. I am going to. You can bear it?'

'I can bear anything but the uncertainty you leave me in at this moment.'

'You speak collectedly, and you – *are* collected. That's good! Now if this doctor's wife, though a lady of great courage and spirit, had suffered so intensely from this cause before her little child was born –'

'The little child was a daughter, sir?'

'A daughter. Miss, if the poor lady had suffered so intensely before her little child was born, that she came to the determination of sparing the poor child the inheritance of any part of the agony she had known the pains of, by rearing her in the belief that her father was dead – No, don't kneel! In Heaven's name why should you kneel to me?'

'For the truth. O dear, good, compassionate sir, for the truth!'

'Let us be clear-headed. If you could kindly mention now, for instance, what nine times ninepence are, it would be so encouraging. I should be so much more at my ease about your state of mind.'

Without directly answering to this appeal, she sat so still when he had very gently raised her, and the hands that had not ceased to clasp his wrists were so much more steady than they had been, that she communicated some reassurance to Mr Jarvis Lorry.

'That's right, that's right. Courage! Miss Manette, your mother took this course with you. And when she died, she left you, at two years old, to grow to be blooming, beautiful, and happy, without the dark cloud upon you of living in uncertainty whether your father soon wore his heart out in prison, or wasted there through many lingering years.'

As he said the words he looked down, with an admiring pity, on the flowing golden hair; as if he pictured to himself that it might have been already tinged with grey.

'You know that your parents had no great possession, and that what they had was secured to your mother and to you. There has been no new discovery, of money, or of any other property; but –'

He felt his wrist held closer, and he stopped. The expression in the forehead, which had so particularly attracted his notice, had deepened into one of pain and horror.

'But he has been – been found. He is alive. Greatly

changed, it is too probable; almost a wreck, it is possible. Still, alive. Your father has been taken to the house of an old servant in Paris, and we are going there: I, to identify him if I can: you, to restore him to life, love, duty, rest, comfort.'

A shiver ran through her frame, and from it through his. She said, in a low, distinct, awe-stricken voice, as if she were saying it in a dream,

'I am going to see his Ghost! It will be his Ghost – not him!'

Mr Lorry quietly chafed the hands that held his arm. 'There, there, there! See now, see now! The best and the worst are known to you, now.'

She repeated in the same tone, sunk to a whisper, 'I have been free, I have been happy, yet his Ghost has never haunted me!'

'Only one thing more,' said Mr Lorry, 'he has been found under another name; his own, long forgotten or long concealed. It would be worse than useless now to inquire which. It would be worse than useless now to make any inquiries, because it would be dangerous. Better not to mention the subject, anywhere or in any way, and to remove him – for a while at all events – out of France. Even I, safe as an Englishman, and even Tellson's, important as they are to French credit, avoid all naming of the matter. My credentials, entries, and memoranda, are all comprehended in the one line, "Recalled to Life;" which may mean

anything. But what is the matter? She doesn't notice a word! Miss Manette!'

Perfectly still and silent, and not even fallen back in her chair, she sat under his hand, utterly insensible. So close was her hold upon his arm, that he feared to detach himself lest he should hurt her; therefore he called out loudly for assistance without moving.

A wild-looking woman, whom even in his agitation, Mr Lorry observed to have red hair, and to have on her head a most wonderful bonnet like a Grenadier wooden measure, came running into the room in advance of the inn servants, and soon settled the question of his detachment from the poor young lady, by laying a brawny hand upon his chest, and sending him flying back against the nearest wall.

'Why, look at you all!' bawled this figure, addressing the inn servants. 'Why don't you go and fetch things, instead of standing there staring at me? I'll let you know, if you don't bring smelling-salts, cold water, and vinegar, quick, I will.'

There was an immediate dispersal for these restoratives, and she softly laid the patient on a sofa, and tended her with great skill and gentleness.

'And you in brown!' she said, indignantly turning to Mr Lorry; 'couldn't you tell her what you had to tell her, without frightening her to death?'

Mr Lorry was so exceedingly disconcerted by a question

so hard to answer, that he could only look on, while the strong woman recovered her charge by a regular series of gradations, and coaxed her to lay her drooping head upon her shoulder.

'I hope she will do well now,' said Mr Lorry.

'No thanks to you in brown, if she does. My darling pretty!'

'I hope,' said Mr Lorry, after another pause of feeble sympathy and humility, 'that you accompany Miss Manette to France?'

'A likely thing, too!' replied the strong woman. 'If it was ever intended that I should go across salt water, do you suppose Providence would have cast my lot in an island?'

This being another question hard to answer, Mr Jarvis Lorry withdrew to consider it.

5

The Wine-shop

A large cask of wine had been dropped and broken, in the street. The cask had tumbled out with a run, the hoops had burst, and it lay on the stones just outside the door of the wine-shop, shattered like a walnut-shell.

All the people within reach had suspended their business, or their idleness, to run to the spot and drink the wine. Some men kneeled down, made scoops of their two hands joined, and sipped, or tried to help women, who bent over their shoulders, to sip, before the wine had all run out between their fingers. Others, men and women, dipped in the puddles with little mugs of mutilated earthenware, or even with handkerchiefs from women's heads, which were squeezed dry into infants' mouths.

A shrill sound of laughter and of amused voices – voices of men, women, and children – resounded in the street while this wine game lasted. There was little roughness in the sport, and much playfulness. There was a special companionship in it, an observable inclination on the part of every one to join some other one, which led, especially

among the luckier or lighter-hearted, to frolicsome embraces, drinking of healths, shaking of hands, and even joining of hands and dancing, a dozen together. When the wine was gone, these demonstrations ceased, as suddenly as they had broken out. The woman who had left on a door-step the little pot of hot-ashes, at which she had been trying to soften the pain in her own starved fingers and toes, or in those of her child, returned to it; men with bare arms, matted locks, and cadaverous faces, who had emerged into the winter light from cellars, moved away to descend again; and a gloom gathered on the scene that appeared more natural to it than sunshine.

The wine was red wine, and had stained the ground of the narrow street in the suburb of Saint Antoine, in Paris, where it was spilled. It had stained many hands, too, and many faces, and many naked feet, and many wooden shoes. Those who had been greedy with the staves of the cask, had acquired a tigerish smear about the mouth; and one tall joker so besmirched, his head more out of a long squalid bag of a night-cap than in it, scrawled upon a wall with his finger dipped in muddy wine-lees–BLOOD.

The time was to come, when that wine too would be spilled on the street-stones, and when the stain of it would be red upon many there.

And now that the cloud settled on Saint Antoine, which a momentary gleam had driven from his sacred countenance, the darkness of it was heavy – cold, dirt, sickness,

ignorance, and want, were the lords in waiting on the saintly presence – nobles of great power all of them; but, most especially the last. Samples of a people that had undergone a terrible grinding and re-grinding in the mill: the mill which had worked them down, was the mill that grinds young people old; the children had ancient faces and grave voices; and upon them, and upon the grown faces, and ploughed into every furrow of age and coming up afresh, was the sign, Hunger. It was prevalent everywhere. Hunger was pushed out of the tall houses, in the wretched clothing that hung upon poles and lines; Hunger was patched into them with straw and rag and wood and paper; Hunger was the inscription on the baker's shelves, written in every small loaf of his scanty stock of bad bread; at the sausage-shop, in every dead-dog preparation that was offered for sale.

The trade signs were, all, grim illustrations of Want. The butcher and the porkman painted up, only the leanest scrags of meat; the baker, the coarsest of meagre loaves. Nothing was represented in a flourishing condition, save tools and weapons; but, the cutler's knives and axes were sharp and bright, the smith's hammers were heavy, and the gunmaker's stock was murderous. Across the streets, at wide intervals, one clumsy lamp was slung by a rope and pulley; at night, when the lamplighter had let these down, and lighted, and hoisted them again, a feeble grove of dim wicks swung in a sickly manner overhead, as if they were at sea.

The time was to come, when the gaunt scarecrows of

that region should have watched the lamplighter, in their idleness and hunger, so long, as to conceive the idea of improving on his method, and hauling up men by those ropes and pulleys, to flare upon the darkness of their condition. But, the time was not come yet; and every wind that blew over France shook the rags of the scarecrows in vain, for the birds, fine of song and feather, took no warning.

The wine-shop was a corner shop, better than most others in its appearance and degree, and the master of the wine-shop had stood outside it, in a yellow waistcoat and green breeches, looking on at the struggle for the lost wine. 'It's not my affair,' said he, 'the people from the market did it. Let them bring another.'

There, his eyes happening to catch the tall joker writing up his joke, he called to him across the way:

'Say, then, my Gaspard, what do you do there?'

The fellow pointed to his joke with immense significance, as is often the way with his tribe. It missed its mark, and completely failed, as is often the way with his tribe too.

'What now? Are you a subject for the mad hospital?' said the wine-shop keeper, crossing the road, and obliterating the jest with a handful of mud. 'Why do you write in the public streets?'

In his expostulation he dropped his cleaner hand (perhaps accidentally, perhaps not) upon the joker's heart. The joker rapped it with his own, took a nimble spring

upward, and came down in a fantastic dancing attitude, with one of his stained shoes jerked off his foot into his hand, and held out.

'Put it on, put it on,' said the other. 'Call wine, wine; and finish there.' With that advice, he wiped his soiled hand upon the joker's dress, then recrossed the road and entered the wine-shop.

This wine-shop keeper was a bull-necked, martial-looking man of thirty. He wore no coat, but carried one slung over his shoulder. His shirt-sleeves were rolled up, too, and his brown arms were bare to the elbows. He was a dark man, with good eyes and a good bold breadth between them. Good-humoured-looking on the whole, but implacable-looking, too; evidently a man of a strong resolution and a set purpose.

Madame Defarge, his wife, sat in the shop behind the counter as he came in. Madame Defarge was a stout woman of about his own age, with a watchful eye that seldom seemed to look at anything, a large hand heavily ringed, a steady face, strong features, and great composure of manner. Her knitting was before her, but she had laid it down to pick her teeth with a toothpick. Thus engaged, with her right elbow supported by her left hand, Madame Defarge said nothing when her lord came in, but coughed just one grain of cough. This, in combination with the lifting of her darkly defined eyebrows over her toothpick by the breadth of a line, suggested to her husband that he would do well

to look around the shop among the customers, for any new customer who had dropped in while he stepped over the way.

The wine-shop keeper accordingly rolled his eyes about, until they rested upon an elderly gentleman and a young lady, who were seated in a corner. As he passed behind the counter, he took notice that the elderly gentleman said in a look to the young lady, 'This is our man.'

'What the devil do *you* do in that galley there?' said Monsieur Defarge to himself; 'I don't know you.'

But, he feigned not to notice the two strangers, and fell into discourse with the triumvirate of customers who were drinking at the counter.

'How goes it, Jacques?' said one of these three to Monsieur Defarge. 'Is all the spilt wine swallowed?'

'Every drop, Jacques,' answered Monsieur Defarge.

When this interchange of christian name was effected, Madame Defarge raised her eyebrows by the breadth of another line.

'It is not often,' said the second of the three, addressing Monsieur Defarge, 'that many of these miserable beasts know the taste of wine, or of anything but black bread and death. Is it not so, Jacques?'

'It is so, Jacques,' Monsieur Defarge returned.

At this second interchange of the christian name, Madame Defarge raised her eyebrows by the breadth of another line.

The last of the three now said his say.

'Ah! So much the worse! A bitter taste it is that such poor cattle always have in their mouths, and hard lives they live, Jacques.'

'You are right, Jacques,' was the response of Monsieur Defarge.

This third interchange of the christian name was complete at the moment when Madame Defarge put her toothpick by, kept her eyebrows up, and slightly rustled in her seat.

'Hold then! True!' muttered her husband. 'Gentlemen – my wife!'

The three customers pulled off their hats to Madame Defarge, with three flourishes. She acknowledged their homage by bending her head, and giving them a quick look. Then she glanced in a casual manner round the wine-shop, took up her knitting with great apparent calmness and repose of spirit, and became absorbed in it.

'Gentlemen,' said her husband. 'The chamber, furnished bachelor-fashion, that you wished to see, is on the fifth floor. I remember, one of you has already been there, and can show the way. Gentlemen, adieu!'

They paid for their wine, and left the place. The eyes of Monsieur Defarge were studying his wife at her knitting when the elderly gentleman advanced from his corner, and begged the favour of a word.

'Willingly, sir,' said Monsieur Defarge.

Their conference was very short, but very decided. Almost at the first word, Monsieur Defarge started and became deeply attentive. It had not lasted a minute, when he nodded and went out. The gentleman then beckoned to the young lady, and they, too, went out. Madame Defarge knitted with nimble fingers and steady eyebrows, and saw nothing.

Mr Jarvis Lorry and Miss Manette, emerging from the wine-shop thus, joined Monsieur Defarge in the doorway to which he had directed his other company just before. In the gloomy tile-paved entry to the gloomy tile-paved staircase, Monsieur Defarge bent down on one knee to the child of his old master, and put her hand to his lips. It was a gentle action, but not at all gently done; a very remarkable transformation had come over him in a few seconds. He had no good-humour in his face, nor any openness of aspect left, but had become a secret, angry, dangerous man.

'It is very high; it is little difficult. Better to begin slowly.'

'Is he alone?' whispered Mr Lorry.

'Alone! God help him, who should be with him?'

'Of his own desire?'

'Of his own necessity. As he was, when I first saw him after they found me and demanded to know if I would take him, and, at my peril, be discreet – as he was then, so he is now.'

'He is greatly changed?'

'Changed!'

The keeper of the wine-shop stopped to strike the wall with his hand, and mutter a tremendous curse. No direct answer could have been half so forcible. Mr Lorry's spirits grew heavier and heavier, as he and his two companions ascended higher and higher.

Yielding to his own disturbance of mind, and to his young companion's agitation, which became greater every instant, Mr Jarvis Lorry twice stopped to rest. Each of these stoppages was made at a doleful grating, by which any languishing good airs that were left uncorrupted, seemed to escape, and all spoilt and sickly vapours seemed to crawl in.

At last, the top of the staircase was gained, and they stopped for the third time. There was yet an upper staircase, of a steeper inclination and of contracted dimensions, to be ascended, before the garret story was reached. The keeper of the wine-shop, always going a little in advance, turned himself about here, and, carefully feeling in the pockets of the coat he carried over his shoulder, took out a key.

'The door is locked then, my friend?' said Mr Lorry, surprised.

'Ay. Yes,' was the grim reply of Monsieur Defarge.

'You think it necessary to keep the unfortunate gentleman so retired?'

'I think it necessary to turn the key.'

'Why?'

'Why! Because he has lived so long, locked up, that he

would be frightened – rave – tear himself to pieces – die – come to I know not what harm – if his door was left open.'

'Is it possible?' exclaimed Mr Lorry.

'Is it possible?' repeated Defarge, bitterly. 'Yes. And a beautiful world we live in, when it *is* possible, and when many other such things are possible.'

This dialogue had been held in so very low a whisper, that not a word of it had reached the young lady's ears. But, by this time she trembled under such strong emotion, and her face expressed such deep anxiety, and, above all, such dread and terror, that Mr Lorry felt it incumbent on him to speak a word or two of reassurance.

'Courage, dear miss! Courage! The worst will be over in a moment. Then, all the good you bring to him, all the relief, all the happiness you bring to him, begin.'

They went up slowly and softly. The staircase was short, and they were soon at the top. There, as it had an abrupt turn in it, they came all at once in sight of three men, whose heads were bent down close together at the side of a door, and who were intently looking into the room to which the door belonged, through some chinks or holes in the wall. On hearing footsteps close at hand, these three turned, and rose, and showed themselves to be the three of one name who had been drinking in the wine-shop.

The three glided by, and went silently down.

There appearing to be no other door on that floor, and

the keeper of the wine-shop going straight to this one when they were left alone, Mr Lorry asked him in a whisper, with a little anger:

'Do you make a show of Monsieur Manette?'

'I show him, in the way you have seen, to a chosen few.'

'Who are the few? How do you choose them?'

'I choose them as real men, of my name – Jacques is my name – to whom the sight is likely to do good. Enough; you are English; that is another thing. Stay there, if you please, a little moment.'

With an admonitory gesture to keep them back, he stooped, and looked in through the crevice in the wall. Soon raising his head again, he struck twice or thrice upon the door – evidently with no other object than to make a noise there. With the same intention, he drew the key across it, three or four times, before he put it clumsily into the lock, and turned it as heavily as he could.

The door slowly opened inward under his hand, and he looked into the room and said something. A faint voice answered something.

He looked back over his shoulder, and beckoned them to enter. Mr Lorry got his arm securely round the daughter's waist, and held her; for he felt that she was sinking.

'A – a – a – business, business!' he urged, with a moisture that was not of business shining on his cheek. 'Come in, come in!'

'I am afraid of it,' she answered, shuddering.

'Of it? What?'

'I mean of him. Of my father.'

He drew over his neck the arm that shook upon his shoulder, lifted her a little, and hurried her into the room. He set her down just within the door, and held her, clinging to him.

Defarge drew out the key, closed the door, locked it on the inside, took out the key again, and held it in his hand.

The garret was dim and dark: for, the window of dormer shape, was in truth a door in the roof, with a little crane over it for the hoisting up of stores from the street: unglazed, and closing up the middle in two pieces, like any other door of French construction. To exclude the cold, one half of this door was fast closed, and the other was opened but a very little way. Such a scanty portion of light was admitted through these means, that it was difficult, on first coming in, to see anything; and long habit alone could have slowly formed in any one, the ability to do any work requiring nicety in such obscurity. Yet, work of that kind was being done in the garret; for, with his back towards the door, and his face towards the window where the keeper of the wine-shop stood looking at him, a white-haired man sat on a low bench, stooping forward and very busy, making shoes.

6

The Shoemaker

'Good day!' said Monsieur Defarge, looking down at the white head that bent low over the shoemaking. 'You are still hard at work, I see?'

After a long silence, the head was lifted and the voice replied, 'Yes – I am working.'

The faintness of the voice was pitiable and dreadful. Its deplorable peculiarity was, that it was the faintness of solitude and disuse. So entirely had it lost the life and resonance of the human voice, that it affected the senses like a once beautiful colour faded away into a poor weak stain. So expressive it was, of a hopeless and lost creature, that a famished traveller, wearied out by lonely wandering in a wilderness, would have remembered home and friends in such a tone before lying down to die.

'I want,' said Defarge, who had not removed his gaze from the shoemaker, 'to let in a little more light here. You can bear a little more?'

The shoemaker stopped his work; looked with a vacant air of listening, at the floor on one side of him; then

similarly, at the floor on the other side of him; then, upward at the speaker.

'What did you say?'

'You can bear a little more light?'

'I must bear it, if you let it in.'

The opened half-door was opened a little further, and secured at that angle for the time. A broad ray of light fell into the garret, and showed the workman with an unfinished shoe upon his lap, pausing in his labour. He had a white beard, raggedly cut, but not very long, a hollow face, and exceedingly bright eyes. His yellow rags of shirt lay open at the throat, and showed his body to be withered and worn. He, and his old canvas frock, and his loose stockings, and all his poor tatters of clothes, had, in a long seclusion from direct light and air, faded down to such a dull uniformity of parchment-yellow, that it would have been hard to say which was which.

He sat, with a steadfastly vacant gaze, pausing in his work. He never looked at the figure before him, without first looking down on this side of himself, then on that, as if he had lost the habit of associating place with sound; he never spoke, without first wandering in this manner, and forgetting to speak.

Mr Lorry came silently forward, leaving the daughter by the door. When he had stood, for a minute or two, by the side of Defarge, the shoemaker looked up. He showed no surprise at seeing another figure, but the unsteady

fingers of one of his hands strayed to his lips as he looked at it, and then the hand dropped to his work, and he once more bent over the shoe.

'You have a visitor, you see,' said Monsieur Defarge.

The shoemaker looked up as before, but without removing a hand from his work.

'Come!' said Defarge. 'Here is monsieur, who knows a well-made shoe when he sees one. Show him that shoe you are working at. Take it, monsieur.'

Mr Lorry took it in his hand.

'Tell monsieur what kind of shoe it is, and the maker's name.'

There was a longer pause than usual, before the shoemaker replied:

'I forget what it was you asked me. What did you say?'

'I said, couldn't you describe the kind of shoe, for monsieur's information?'

'It is a lady's shoe. It is a young lady's walking-shoe.' He glanced at the shoe with some little passing touch of pride.

'And the maker's name?' said Defarge.

The task of recalling him from the vacancy into which he always sank when he had spoken, was like recalling some very weak person from a swoon.

'Did you ask me for my name?'

'Assuredly I did.'

'One Hundred and Five, North Tower.'

With a weary sound that was not a sigh, nor a groan, he bent to work again, until the silence was again broken.

'You are not a shoemaker by trade?' said Mr Lorry.

'I am not a shoemaker by trade? No, I was not a shoemaker by trade. I – I learnt it here. I asked leave to teach myself, and I got it with much difficulty after a long while, and I have made shoes ever since.'

As he held out his hand for the shoe that had been taken from him, Mr Lorry said, still looking steadfastly in his face:

'Monsieur Manette, do you remember nothing of me?'

The shoe dropped to the ground, and he sat looking fixedly at the questioner.

'Monsieur Manette,' Mr Lorry laid his hand upon Defarge's arm; 'do you remember nothing of this man? Look at him. Look at me. Is there no old banker, no old business, no old servant, no old time, rising in your mind, Monsieur Manette?'

As the captive of many years sat looking fixedly, by turns, at Mr Lorry and at Defarge, some long obliterated marks of an actively intent intelligence in the middle of the forehead, gradually forced themselves through the black mist that had fallen on him. They were overclouded again, they were fainter, they were gone; but they had

been there. And so exactly was the expression repeated on the fair young face of her who had crept along the wall to a point where she could see him, and where she now stood looking at him, with hands which at first had been only raised in frightened compassion, but which were now extending towards him, trembling with eagerness to lay the spectral face upon her warm young breast, and love it back to life and hope, that it looked as though it had passed like a moving light, from him to her.

Darkness had fallen on him in its place. He looked at the two, less and less attentively, and his eyes in gloomy abstraction sought the ground and looked about him in the old way. Finally, with a deep long sigh, he took the shoe up, and resumed his work.

'Have you recognised him, monsieur?' asked Defarge in a whisper.

'Yes; for a moment. At first I thought it quite hopeless, but I have unquestionably seen, for a single moment, the face that I once knew so well. Hush! Let us draw further back. Hush!'

She had moved from the wall of the garret, very near to the bench on which he sat.

Not a word was spoken, not a sound was made. She stood, like a spirit, beside him, and he bent over his work.

It happened, at length, that he had occasion to change the instrument in his hand, for his shoemaker's knife. He

had taken it up, and was stooping to work again, when his eyes caught the skirt of her dress. He raised them, and saw her face.

He stared at her with a fearful look, and after a while his lips began to form some words, though no sound proceeded from them. By degrees, in the pauses of his quick and laboured breathing, he was heard to say:

'What is this?'

With the tears streaming down her face, she put her two hands to her lips, and kissed them to him; then clasped them on her breast, as if she laid his ruined head there.

'You are not the gaoler's daughter?'

She sighed 'No.'

'Who are you?'

Not yet trusting the tones of her voice, she sat down on the bench beside him. He recoiled, but she laid her hand upon his arm. A strange thrill struck him when she did so, and visibly passed over his frame; he laid the knife down softly, as he sat staring at her.

Her golden hair, which she wore in long curls, had been hurriedly pushed aside, and fell down over her neck. Advancing his hand by little and little, he took it up and looked at it.

Releasing his arm, she laid her hand upon his shoulder. After looking doubtfully at it, two or three times, as if to be sure that it was really there, he put his hand to his neck, and took off a blackened string with a scrap of

folded rag attached to it. He opened this, carefully, on his knee, and it contained a very little quantity of hair: not more than one or two long golden hairs, which he had, in some old day, wound off upon his finger.

He took her hair into his hand again, and looked closely at it. 'It is the same. How can it be! When was it! How was it!'

As the concentrating expression returned to his forehead, he seemed to become conscious that it was in hers too.

'She had laid her head upon my shoulder, that night when I was summoned out and when I was brought to the North Tower they found these upon my sleeve. "You will leave me them? They can never help me to escape in the body, though they may in the spirit."'

He formed this speech with his lips many times before he could utter it. But when he did find spoken words for it, they came to him coherently, though slowly.

'How was this? – *Was it you?* No, no, no; you are too young, too blooming. It can't be. See what the prisoner is. These are not the hands she knew, this is not the face she knew, this is not a voice she ever heard. What is your name, my gentle angel?'

Hailing his softened tone and manner, his daughter fell upon her knees before him, with her appealing hands upon his breast.

'O, sir, at another time you shall know my name, and

who my mother was, and who my father, and how I never knew their hard, hard history. But I cannot tell you here. All that I may tell you is, that I pray to you to touch me and to bless me. Kiss me, kiss me! O my dear, my dear!'

His cold white head mingled with her radiant hair, which warmed and lighted it as though it were the light of Freedom shining on him.

'If you hear in my voice any resemblance to a voice that once was sweet music in your ears, weep for it! If you touch, in touching my hair, anything that recalls a beloved head that lay in your breast when you were young and free, weep for it! If, when I hint to you of a Home there is before us, where I will be true to you with all my duty and with all my faithful service, I bring back the remembrance of a Home long desolate, while your poor heart pined away, weep for it!'

She held him closer round the neck, and rocked him on her breast like a child.

'If, when I tell you, dearest dear, that your agony is over, and that I have come here to take you from it, and that we go to England to be at peace and at rest, I cause you to think of your useful life laid waste, and of our native France so wicked to you, weep for it! And if, when I shall tell you of my name, and of my father who is living, and of my mother who is dead, you learn that I have to kneel to my honoured father, and implore his pardon for having never for his sake striven all day and lain awake and wept

all night, because the love of my poor mother hid his torture from me, weep for it!'

He had sunk in her arms, and his face dropped on her breast: a sight so touching, yet so terrible in the tremendous wrong and suffering which had gone before it, that the two beholders covered their faces.

When the quiet of the garret had been long undisturbed, and his heaving breast and shaken form had long yielded to the calm that must follow all storms, they came forward to raise the father and daughter from the ground.

'If, without disturbing him,' she said, raising her hand to Mr Lorry, 'all could be arranged for our leaving Paris at once.'

'But, consider. Is he fit for the journey?' asked Mr Lorry.

'More fit for that, I think, than to remain in this city.'

'It is true,' said Defarge, who was kneeling to look on and hear. 'More than that; Monsieur Manette is, for all reasons, best out of France. Say, shall I hire a carriage and post-horses?'

'That's business,' said Mr Lorry, resuming on the shortest notice his methodical manners; 'and if business is to be done, I had better do it.'

'Then be so kind,' urged Miss Manette, 'as to leave us here. If you will lock the door to secure us from interruption, I do not doubt that you will find him, when you

come back, as quiet as you leave him. In any case, I will take care of him until you return, and then we will remove him straight.'

Both Mr Lorry and Defarge were rather disinclined to this course, and in favour of one of them remaining. But, as there were not only carriage and horses to be seen to, but travelling papers; it came at last to their hastily dividing the business that was necessary to be done, and hurrying away to do it.

Then, as the darkness closed in, the daughter laid her head down on the hard ground close at the father's side, and watched him. The darkness deepened and deepened, and they both lay quiet, until a light gleamed through the chinks in the wall.

Mr Lorry and Monsieur Defarge had made all ready for the journey, and had brought with them, besides travelling cloaks and wrappers, bread and meat, wine, and hot coffee. Monsieur Defarge put his provender, and the lamp he carried, on the shoemaker's bench and he and Mr Lorry roused the captive, and assisted him to his feet.

No human intelligence could have read the mysteries of his mind, in the scared blank wonder of his face. He had a wild, lost manner of occasionally clasping his head in his hands, that had not been seen in him before; yet, he had some pleasure in the mere sound of his daughter's voice, and invariably turned to it when she spoke.

They began to descend; Monsieur Defarge going first

with the lamp, Mr Lorry closing the little procession. They had not traversed many steps of the long main staircase when he stopped, and stared at the roof and round at the walls.

'You remember the place, my father? You remember coming up here?'

'Remember? No, I don't remember. It was so very long ago.'

That he had no recollection whatever of his having been brought from his prison to that house, was apparent to them. They heard him mutter, 'One Hundred and Five, North Tower,' and when he looked about him, it evidently was for the strong fortress-walls which had long encompassed him.

No crowd was about the door; no people were discernible at any of the many windows; not even a chance passer-by was in the street. An unnatural silence and desertion reigned there. Only one soul was to be seen, and that was Madame Defarge – who leaned against the door-post, knitting, and saw nothing.

The prisoner had got into a coach, and his daughter had followed him, when Mr Lorry's feet were arrested on the step by his asking, miserably, for his shoemaking tools and the unfinished shoes. Madame Defarge immediately called to her husband that she would get them, and went, knitting, out of the lamplight, through the court-yard. She quickly brought them down and handed them in.

Defarge got upon the box, and gave the word 'To the Barrier!' The postilion cracked his whip, and they clattered away under the feeble over-swinging lamps.

Under the over-swinging lamps and by lighted shops, gay crowds, illuminated coffee-houses, and theatre-doors, to one of the city gates. Soldiers with lanterns, at the guard-house there. 'Your papers, travellers!' 'See here then. Monsieur the Officer,' said Defarge, getting down, and taking him gravely apart, 'these are the papers of monsieur inside, with the white head. They were consigned to me, with him, at the –' He dropped his voice, there was a flutter among the military lanterns, and one of them being handed into the coach by an arm in uniform, the eyes connected with the arm looked, not an every day or an every night look, at monsieur with the white head. 'It is well. Forward!' from the uniform. 'Adieu!' from Defarge.

All through the cold and restless interval, until dawn, they once more whispered in the ears of Mr Jarvis Lorry – sitting opposite the buried man who had been dug out, and wondering what subtle powers were for ever lost to him, and what were capable of restoration – the old inquiry:

'I hope you care to be recalled to life?'

And the old answer:

'I can't say.'

THE END OF BOOK ONE

THE GOLDEN THREAD

1

Five Years Later

Tellson's Bank by Temple-bar was an old-fashioned place, even in the year one thousand seven hundred and eighty. It was very small, very dark, very ugly, very incommodious. After bursting open a door of idiotic obstinacy with a weak rattle in its throat, you fell into Tellson's down two steps, and came to your senses in a miserable little shop, with two little counters, where the oldest of men made your cheque shake as if the wind rustled it, while they examined the signature by the dingiest of windows. If your business necessitated your seeing 'the House,' you were put into a species of Condemned Hold at the back, where you meditated on a misspent life, until the House came with its hands in its pockets, and you could hardly blink at it in the dismal twilight. Your money came out of, or went into, wormy old wooden drawers, particles of which flew up your nose and down your throat when they were opened and shut. Your deeds got into extemporised strong-rooms made of kitchens and sculleries. Your lighter boxes of family papers

went up-stairs into a Barmecide room, that always had a great dining-table in it and never had a dinner, and where, even in the year one thousand seven hundred and eighty, the first letters written to you by your old love, or by your little children, were but newly released from the horror of being ogled through the windows, by the heads exposed on Temple-bar with an insensate brutality and ferocity worthy of Abyssinia or Ashantee.

But indeed, at that time, putting to death was a recipe much in vogue with all trades and professions, and not least of all with Tellson's. Accordingly, the forger was put to Death; the utterer of a bad note was put to Death; the purloiner of forty shillings and sixpence was put to Death; the holder of a horse at Tellson's door, who made off with it, was put to Death. Not that it did the least good in the way of prevention, but, it cleared off the trouble of each particular case, and left nothing else connected with it to be looked after. Thus, Tellson's, in its day, like greater places of business, its contemporaries, had taken so many lives, that, if the heads laid low before it had been ranged on Temple-bar instead of being privately disposed of, they would probably have excluded what little light the ground floor had, in a rather significant manner.

Outside Tellson's was an odd-job-man, an occasional porter and messenger, who served as the live sign of the house. He was never absent during business hours, unless upon an errand, and then he was represented by his son:

a grisly urchin of twelve, who was his express image. People understood that Tellson's, in a stately way, tolerated the odd-job-man. His surname was Cruncher, and on the youthful occasion of his renouncing by proxy the works of darkness, in the easterly parish church of Houndsditch, he had received the added appellation of Jerry.

The scene was Mr Cruncher's private lodging in Hanging-sword-alley, Whitefriars; the time, half-past seven of the clock on a windy March morning, Anno Domini seventeen hundred and eighty.

Mr Cruncher's apartments were not in a savoury neighbourhood, but they were very decently kept. Early as it was, on the windy March morning, the room in which he lay a-bed was already scrubbed throughout; and between the cups and saucers arranged for breakfast, and the lumbering deal table, a very clean white cloth was spread.

Mr Cruncher reposed under a patchwork counterpane, like a Harlequin at home. At first, he slept heavily, but, by degrees, began to roll and surge in bed, until he rose above the surface, with his spiky hair looking as if it must tear the sheets to ribbons. At which juncture, he exclaimed, in a voice of dire exasperation:

'Bust me, if she ain't at it agin!'

A woman of orderly and industrious appearance rose from her knees in a corner.

'What!' said Mr Cruncher, looking out of bed for a boot. 'You're at it agin, are you?'

After hailing the morn with this second salutation, he threw a boot at the woman as a third.

'What,' said Mr Cruncher, varying his apostrophe after missing his mark – 'what are you up to, Aggerawayter?'

'I was only saying my prayers.'

'Saying your prayers! You're a nice woman! What do you mean by flopping yourself down and praying agin me?'

'I was not praying against you; I was praying for you.'

'Here! your mother's a nice woman, young Jerry, going a praying agin your father's prosperity. You've got a dutiful mother, you have, my son. You've got a religious mother, you have, my boy: going and flopping herself down, and praying that the bread-and-butter may be snatched out of the mouth of her only child. And what do you suppose, you conceited female, that the worth of *your* prayers may be? Name the price that you put *your* prayers at!'

'They only come from the heart, Jerry. They are worth no more than that.'

'Worth no more than that,' repeated Mr Cruncher. 'They ain't worth much, then. If you must go flopping yourself down, flop in favour of your husband and child, and not in opposition to 'em. If I had had any but a unnat'ral wife, and this poor boy had had any but a unnat'ral mother, I might had made some money last week instead of being counter-prayed and counter-mined and religiously circum-

wented into the worst of luck. B-u-u-ust me!' said Mr Cruncher, who all this time had been putting on his clothes, 'if I ain't, what with piety and one blowed thing and another, been choused this last week into as bad luck as ever a poor devil of a honest tradesman met with! Young Jerry, dress yourself, my boy, and while I clean my boots keep a eye upon your mother now and then, and if you see any signs of more flopping, give me a call.'

Growling, in addition, such phrases as 'Ah! yes! You're religious, too. You wouldn't put yourself in opposition to the interests of your husband and child, would you? Not you!' and throwing off other sarcastic sparks from the whirling grindstone of his indignation, Mr Cruncher betook himself to his boot-cleaning and his general preparations for business. In the mean time, his son kept the required watch upon his mother. He greatly disturbed that poor woman at intervals, by darting out of his sleeping closet, where he made his toilet, with a suppressed cry of 'You are going to flop, mother. – Halloa, father!' and, after raising this fictitious alarm, darting in again with an undutiful grin.

Mr Cruncher's temper was not at all improved when he came to his breakfast. He resented Mrs Cruncher's saying grace with particular animosity.

'Now, Aggerawayter! What are you up to? At it agin?'

His wife explained that she had merely 'asked a blessing'.

'Don't do it!' said Mr Cruncher, looking about, as if he rather expected to see the loaf disappear under the efficacy of his wife's petitions. 'I ain't a going to be blest out of house and home. I won't have my wittles blest off my table. Keep still!'

Towards nine o'clock he smoothed his ruffled aspect, and, presenting as respectful and business-like an exterior as he could overlay his natural self with, issued forth to the occupation of the day.

It could scarcely be called a trade, in spite of his favourite description of himself as 'a honest tradesman.' His stock consisted of a wooden stool, made out of a broken-backed chair cut down, which stool, young Jerry, walking at his father's side, carried every morning to beneath the banking-house window that was nearest Temple-bar: where it formed the encampment for the day.

Encamped at a quarter before nine, in good time to touch his three-cornered hat to the oldest of men as they passed in to Tellson's, Jerry took up his station on this windy March morning, with young Jerry standing by him. Father and son, extremely like each other, looking silently on at the morning traffic in Fleet-street, with their two heads as near to one another as the two eyes of each were, bore a considerable resemblance to a pair of monkeys.

The head of one of the regular indoor messengers attached to Tellson's establishment was put through the door, and the word was given.

'Porter wanted!'

'Hooray, father! Here's an early job to begin with!'

Having thus given his parent God speed, young Jerry seated himself on the stool.

'Al-ways rusty! His fingers is al-ways rusty!' muttered young Jerry. 'Where does my father get all that iron rust from? He don't get no iron rust here!'

2

A Sight

'You know the Old Bailey well, no doubt?' said one of the oldest of clerks to Jerry the messenger.

'Ye-es, sir,' returned Jerry, in something of a dogged manner. 'I *do* know the Bailey.'

'Just so. And you know Mr Lorry.'

'I know Mr Lorry, sir, much better than I know the Bailey. Much better,' said Jerry.

'Very well. Find the door where the witnesses go in, and show the door-keeper this note for Mr Lorry. He will then let you in.'

'Am I to wait in the court, sir?' he asked.

'I am going to tell you. The door-keeper will pass the note to Mr Lorry, and do you make any gesture that will attract Mr Lorry's attention, and show him where you stand. Then what you have to do, is, to remain there until he wants you.'

As the ancient clerk deliberately folded and superscribed the note, Mr Cruncher remarked:

'I suppose they'll be trying Forgeries this morning?'

'Treason!'

'That's quartering,' said Jerry. 'Barbarous!'

'It is the law,' remarked the ancient clerk, turning his surprised spectacles upon him. 'It is the law.'

'It's hard in the law to spile a man, I think. It's hard enough to kill him, but it's wery hard to spile him, sir.'

'Not at all,' returned the ancient clerk. 'Speak well of the law. Here is the letter. Go along.'

Jerry took the letter, informed his son, in passing, of his destination, and went his way.

The gaol was a vile place, in which most kinds of debauchery and villainy were practised, and where dire diseases were bred, that came into court with the prisoners, and sometimes rushed straight from the dock at my Lord Chief Justice himself, and pulled him off the bench. It had more than once happened, that the Judge in the black cap pronounced his own doom as certainly as the prisoner's. For the rest, the Old Bailey was famous as a kind of deadly inn-yard, from which pale travellers set out continually, in carts and coaches, on a violent passage into the other world. It was famous, too, for the pillory, a wise old institution, that inflicted a punishment of which no one could foresee the extent; also, for the whipping-post, another dear old institution, very humanising and softening to behold in action. Altogether, the Old Bailey, at that date, was a choice illustration of the precept, that 'Whatever is is right;' an aphorism that would be as final

as it is lazy, did it not include the troublesome consequence, that nothing that ever was, was wrong.

Making his way through the tainted crowd, the
messenger found out the door he sought, and handed in
his letter through a trap in it.

After some delay and demur, the door grudgingly
turned on its hinges a very little way, and allowed Mr
Jerry Cruncher to squeeze himself into court.

'What's on?' he asked, in a whisper, of the man he found
himself next to.

'Nothing yet.'

'What's coming on?'

'The Treason case.'

'The quartering one, eh?'

'Ah!' returned the man, with a relish; 'he'll be drawn
on a hurdle to be half hanged, and then he'll be taken
down and sliced before his own face, and then his inside
will be taken out and burnt while he looks on, and then
his head will be chopped off, and he'll be cut into quarters.
That's the sentence.'

'If he's found Guilty, you mean to say?' Jerry added, by
way of proviso.

'Oh! they'll find him guilty,' said the other. 'Don't you
be afraid of that.'

Mr Cruncher's attention was here diverted to the door-
keeper, whom he saw making his way to Mr Lorry, with
the note in his hand. Mr Lorry sat at a table, among the

gentlemen in wigs: not far from a wigged gentleman, the prisoner's counsel, who had a great bundle of papers before him: and nearly opposite another wigged gentleman with his hands in his pockets, whose whole attention seemed to be concentrated on the ceiling of the court. After some gruff coughing and rubbing of his chin and signing with his hand, Jerry attracted the notice of Mr Lorry, who had stood up to look for him, and who quietly nodded and sat down again.

'What's *he* got to do with the case?' asked the man he had spoken with.

'Blest if I know,' said Jerry.

'What have *you* got to do with it, then, if a person may inquire?'

'Blest if I know that either,' said Jerry.

The entrance of the Judge stopped the dialogue. Presently, the dock became the central point of interest. Two gaolers, who had been standing there, went out, and the prisoner was brought in, and put to the bar.

Everybody present stared at him. Eager faces strained round pillars and corners, to get a sight of him; people on the floor of the court, laid their hands on the shoulders of the people before them, to help themselves, at anybody's cost, to a view of him. Conspicuous among these latter, Jerry stood: aiming at the prisoner the beery breath of a whet he had taken as he came along.

The object of all this staring and blaring, was a young

man of about five-and-twenty, well-grown and well-looking, with a sunburnt cheek and a dark eye. He was plainly dressed in black, or very dark grey, and his hair, which was long and dark, was gathered in a ribbon at the back of his neck. As an emotion of the mind will express itself through any covering of the body, so the paleness which his situation engendered came through the brown upon his cheek, showing the soul to be stronger than the sun. He was otherwise quite self-possessed, bowed to the Judge, and stood quiet.

The sort of interest with which this man was stared and breathed at, was not a sort that elevated humanity. Had he stood in peril of a less horrible sentence – had there been a chance of any one of its savage details being spared – by just so much would he have lost in his fascination. The form that was to be doomed to be so shamefully mangled, was the sight. Whatever gloss the various spectators put upon the interest, the interest was, at the root of it, Ogreish.

Silence in the court! Charles Darnay had yesterday pleaded Not Guilty to an indictment denouncing him for that he was a false traitor to our serene, illustrious, excellent, and so forth, prince, our Lord the King, by reason of his having, on divers occasions, assisted Lewis, the French King, in his wars against our said serene, illustrious, excellent, and so forth; that was to say, by coming and going, between the dominions of our said serene, illustrious,

excellent, and so forth, and those of the said French Lewis, and wickedly, falsely, traitorously, and otherwise evil-adverbiously, revealing to the said French Lewis what forces our said serene, illustrious, excellent, and so forth, had in preparation to send to Canada and North America. This much, Jerry made out with huge satisfaction, and so arrived circuitously at the understanding that the afore-said, Charles Darnay, stood there before him upon his trial; that the jury were swearing in; and that Mr Attorney-General was making ready to speak.

The accused, who was being mentally hanged, beheaded, and quartered, by everybody there, neither flinched from the situation, nor assumed any theatrical air in it. He watched the opening proceeding with a grave interest; and stood with his hands resting on the slab of wood before him, so composedly, that they had not displaced a leaf of the herbs with which it was strewn. The court was all bestrewn with herbs and sprinkled with vinegar, as a precaution against gaol air and gaol fever.

Over the prisoner's head there was a mirror, to throw the light down upon him. Crowds of the wicked and the wretched had been reflected in it, and had passed from its surface and this earth's together. Some passing thought of the infamy and disgrace for which it had been reserved, may have struck the prisoner's mind. Be that as it may, a change in his position making him conscious of a bar of light across his face, he looked up; and when he saw the

glass his face flushed, and his right hand pushed the herbs away.

About on a level with his eyes, there sat, in that corner of the Judge's bench, two persons upon whom his look immediately rested; so immediately, and so much to the changing of his aspect, that all the eyes that were turned upon him, turned to them.

The spectators saw in the two figures, a young lady of little more than twenty, and a gentleman who was evidently her father; a man of very remarkable appearance in respect of the absolute whiteness of his hair, and a certain indescribable intensity of face.

His daughter had one of her hands drawn through his arm, as she sat by him, and the other pressed upon it. She had drawn close to him, in her dread of the scene, and in her pity for the prisoner. Her forehead had been strikingly expressive of an engrossing terror and compassion that saw nothing but the peril of the accused. This had been so very noticeable, so very powerfully and naturally shown, that starers who had had no pity for him were touched by her; and the whisper went about, 'Who are they?'

Jerry, the messenger, stretched his neck to hear who they were.

'Witnesses.'

'For which side?'

'Against.'

'Against what side?'

'The prisoner's.'

The Judge, whose eyes had gone in the general direction, recalled them, leaned back in his seat, and looked steadily at the man whose life was in his hand, as Mr Attorney-General rose to spin the rope, grind the axe, and hammer the nails into the scaffold.

3

A Disappointment

Mr Attorney-General had to inform the jury, that the prisoner before them, though young in years, was old in the treasonable practices which claimed the forfeit of his life. That, it was certain the prisoner had been in the habit of passing and repassing between France and England, on secret business of which he could give no honest account. That, if it were in the nature of traitorous ways to thrive, the real wickedness and guilt of his business might have remained undiscovered. That Providence, however, had put it into the heart of a person who was beyond fear and beyond reproach, to ferret out the nature of the prisoner's schemes, and to disclose them to his Majesty's Chief Secretary of State and most honourable Privy Council. That this patriot would be produced before them. That, he had been the prisoner's friend, but had resolved to immolate the traitor he could no longer cherish in his bosom, on the sacred altar of his country. That, the lofty example of this immaculate and unimpeachable witness for the Crown, to refer to whom however un-

worthily was an honour, had communicated itself to the prisoner's servant, and had engendered in him a holy determination to examine his master's table-drawers and pockets, and secrete his papers. That, he (Mr Attorney-General) was prepared to hear some disparagement attempted of this admirable servant; but that, in a general way, he preferred him to his (Mr Attorney-General's) brothers and sisters, and honoured him more than his (Mr Attorney-General's) father and mother. That, the evidence of these two witnesses, coupled with the documents of their discovering that would be produced, would show the prisoner to have been furnished with lists of his Majesty's forces, and of their disposition and preparation, both by sea and land, and would leave no doubt that he had habitually conveyed such information to a hostile power. That, these lists could not be proved to be in the prisoner's handwriting; but that it was all the same; that, indeed, it was rather the better for the prosecution, as showing the prisoner to be artful in his precautions. That, the proof would go back five years, and would show the prisoner already engaged in these pernicious missions, within a few weeks before the date of the very first action fought between the British troops and the Americans. That, for these reasons, the jury, being a loyal jury, and being a responsible jury, must positively find the prisoner Guilty, and make an end of him, whether they liked it or not. That, they never could lay their heads upon their pillows, unless

the prisoner's head was taken off. That head Mr Attorney-General concluded by demanding of them, in the name of everything he could think of with a round turn in it, and on the faith of his solemn asseveration that he already considered the prisoner as good as dead and gone.

When the Attorney-General ceased, a buzz arose in the court as if a cloud of great blue-flies were swarming about the prisoner, in anticipation of what he was soon to become. When toned down again, the unimpeachable patriot appeared in the witness-box.

Mr Solicitor-General then, following his leader's lead, examined the patriot: John Barsad, gentleman, by name. The story of his pure soul was exactly what Mr Attorney-General had described it to be – perhaps, if it had a fault, a little too exactly. Having released his noble bosom of its burden, he would have modestly withdrawn himself, but that the wigged gentleman with the papers before him, sitting not far from Mr Lorry, begged to ask him a few questions. The wigged gentleman sitting opposite, still looking at the ceiling of the court.

Had he ever been a spy himself? No, he scorned the base insinuation. What did he live upon? His property. What was it? No business of anybody's. Had he inherited it? Yes, he had. From whom? Distant relation. Very distant? Rather. Ever been in prison? Certainly not. Never in a debtors' prison? Didn't see what that had to do with it. Never in a debtor's prison? – Come, once again. Never?

Yes. How many times? Two or three times. Of what profession? Gentleman. Ever been kicked? Might have been. Frequently? No. Ever kicked down-stairs? Decidedly not; once received a kick on the top of a staircase, and fell down-stairs of his own accord. Kicked on that occasion for cheating at dice? Something to that effect was said by the intoxicated liar who committed the assault, but it was not true. Ever live by cheating at play? Never. Ever borrow money of the prisoner? Yes. Ever pay him? No. Was not this intimacy with the prisoner, in reality a very slight one, forced upon the prisoner in coaches, inns, and packets? No. Sure he saw the prisoner with these lists? Certain. Knew no more about the lists? No. Had not procured them himself, for instance? No. Expect to get anything by this evidence? No. Not in regular government pay and employment, to lay traps? Oh dear no. Swear that? Over and over again. No motives but motives of sheer patriotism? None whatever.

The virtuous servant, Roger Cly, swore his way through the case at a great rate. He had taken service with the prisoner, in good faith and simplicity, four years ago. He had asked the prisoner, aboard the Calais packet, if he wanted a handy fellow, and the prisoner had engaged him. He began to have suspicions of the prisoner, and to keep an eye upon him, soon afterwards. In arranging his clothes, while travelling, he had seen similar lists to these in the prisoner's pockets, over and over again. He had taken these

lists from the drawer of the prisoner's desk. He had not put them there first. He had seen the prisoner show these identical lists to French gentlemen both at Calais and Boulogne. He loved his country, and couldn't bear it, and had given information. He had known the last witness seven or eight years; that was merely a coincidence. He didn't call it a particularly curious coincidence; most coincidences were curious. Neither did he call it a curious coincidence that true patriotism was *his* only motive too.

The blue-flies buzzed again, and Mr Attorney-General called Mr Jarvis Lorry.

'Mr Jarvis Lorry, are you a clerk in Tellson's bank?'

'I am.'

'On a certain Friday night in November one thousand seven hundred and seventy-five, did business occasion you to travel between London and Dover by the mail?'

'It did.'

'Were there any other passengers in the mail?'

'Two.'

'Did they alight on the road in the course of the night?'

'They did.'

'Mr Lorry, look upon the prisoner. Was he one of those two passengers?'

'I cannot undertake to say that he was.'

'Does he resemble either of these two passengers?'

'Both were so wrapped up, that I cannot undertake to say even that.'

'Mr Lorry, look again upon the prisoner. Supposing him wrapped up as those two passengers were, is there anything in his bulk and stature to render it unlikely that he was one of them?'

'No.'

'You will not swear, Mr Lorry, that he was not one of them?'

'No.'

'Mr Lorry, look once more upon the prisoner. Have you seen him, to your certain knowledge, before?'

'I have.'

'When?'

'I was returning from France a few days afterwards, and, at Calais, the prisoner came on board the packet-ship in which I returned, and made the voyage with me.'

'At what hour did he come on board?'

'At a little after midnight.'

'In the dead of the night. Was he the only passenger who came on board at that untimely hour?'

'He happened to be the only one.'

'Were you travelling alone, Mr Lorry, or with any companion?'

'With two companions. A gentleman and lady. They are here.'

'They are here. Had you any conversation with the prisoner?'

'Hardly any. The weather was stormy, and the passage

long and rough, and I lay on a sofa, almost from shore to shore.'

'Miss Manette!'

The young lady, to whom all eyes had been turned before, and were now turned again, stood up where she had sat. Her father rose with her, and kept her hand drawn through his arm.

'Miss Manette, look upon the prisoner.'

To be confronted with such pity, and such earnest youth and beauty, was far more trying to the accused than to be confronted with all the crowd. His hurried right hand parcelled out the herbs before him into imaginary beds of flowers in a garden; and his efforts to control and steady his breathing shook the lips from which the colour rushed to his heart. The buzz of the great flies was loud again.

'Miss Manette, have you seen the prisoner before?'

'Yes, sir.'

'Where?'

'On board of the packet-ship just now referred to, sir, and on the same occasion.'

'Miss Manette, had you any conversation with the prisoner on that passage across the Channel?'

'Yes, sir.'

'Recall it.'

In the midst of a profound stillness, she faintly began:

'When the gentleman came on board –'

'Do you mean the prisoner?' inquired the Judge, knitting his brows.

'Yes, my Lord.'

'Then say the prisoner.'

'When the prisoner came on board, he noticed that my father,' turning her eyes lovingly to him as he stood beside her, 'was much fatigued and in a very weak state of health. My father was so reduced, that I was afraid to take him out of the air, and I had made a bed for him on the deck near the cabin steps. The prisoner was so good as to beg permission to advise me how I could shelter my father from the wind and weather, better than I had done. I had not known how to do it well, not understanding how the wind would set when we were out of the harbour. He did it for me. He expressed great gentleness and kindness for my father's state, and I am sure he felt it.'

'Let me interrupt you for a moment. Had he come on board alone?'

'No.'

'How many were with him?'

'Two French gentlemen.'

'Had they conferred together?'

'They had conferred together until the last moment, when it was necessary for the French gentlemen to be landed in their boat.'

'Had any papers been handed about among them, similar to these lists?'

'Some papers had been handed about among them, but I don't know what papers.'

'Like these in shape and size?'

'Possibly, but indeed I don't know, although they stood whispering very near to me: because they stood at the top of the cabin steps to have the light of the lamp that was hanging there; it was a dull lamp, and they spoke very low, and I did not hear what they said, and saw only that they looked at papers.'

'Now, to the prisoner's conversation, Miss Manette.'

'The prisoner was as open in his confidence with me – which arose out of my helpless situation – as he was kind, and good, and useful to my father. I hope,' bursting into tears, 'I may not repay him by doing him harm today.'

'Miss Manette, if the prisoner does not perfectly understand that you give the evidence which it is your duty to give with great unwillingness, he is the only person present in that condition. Please to go on.'

'He told me that he was travelling on business of a delicate and difficult nature, which might get people into trouble, and that he was therefore travelling under an assumed name. He said that this business had, within a few days, taken him to France, and might, at intervals, take him backwards and forwards between France and England for a long time to come.'

'Did he say anything about America, Miss Manette? Be particular.'

'He tried to explain to me how that quarrel had arisen, and he said that, so far as he could judge, it was a wrong and foolish one on England's part. He added, in a jesting way, that perhaps George Washington might gain almost as great a name in history as George the Third. But there was no harm in his way of saying this: it was said laughingly, and to beguile the time.'

Her forehead was painfully anxious and intent as she gave this evidence, and, in the pauses when she stopped for the Judge to write it down, watched its effect upon the Counsel for and against. Among the lookers-on there was the same expression in all quarters of the court; insomuch, that a great majority of the foreheads there, might have been mirrors reflecting the witness, when the Judge looked up from his notes to glare at that tremendous heresy about George Washington.

Mr Attorney-General now signified to my Lord, that he deemed it necessary, as a matter of precaution and form, to call the young lady's father, Doctor Manette. Who was called accordingly.

'Doctor Manette, look upon the prisoner. Have you ever seen him before?'

'Once. When he called at my lodgings in London. Some three years, or three years and a half ago.'

'Can you identify him as your fellow-passenger on board the packet, or speak to his conversation with your daughter?'

'Sir, I can do neither.'

'Is there any particular and special reason for your being unable to do either?'

He answered, in a low voice, 'There is.'

'Has it been your misfortune to undergo a long imprisonment, without trial, or even accusation, in your native country, Doctor Manette?'

He answered, in a tone that went to every heart, 'A long imprisonment.'

'Were you newly released on the occasion in question?'

'They tell me so.'

'Have you no remembrance of the occasion?'

'None. My mind is a blank, from some time when I employed myself, in my captivity, in making shoes, to the time when I found myself living in London with my dear daughter here.'

Mr Attorney-General sat down, and the father and daughter sat down together.

A singular circumstance then arose in the case. The object in hand, being, to show that the prisoner went down, with some fellow-plotter untracked, in the Dover mail on that Friday night in November five years ago, and got out of the mail in the night, as a blind, at a place where he did not remain, but from which he travelled back some dozen miles or more, to a garrison and dockyard, and there collected information; a witness was called to identify him as having been at the precise time required,

in the coffee-room of an hotel in that garrison-and-dock-yard town, waiting for another person. The prisoner's counsel was cross-examining this witness with no result, except that he had never seen the prisoner on any other occasion, when the wigged gentleman who had all this time been looking at the ceiling of the court, wrote a word or two on a little piece of paper, screwed it up, and tossed it to him. Opening this piece of paper in the next pause, the counsel looked with great attention and curiosity at the prisoner.

'You say again you are quite sure that it *was* the prisoner?'

The witness was quite sure.

'Did you ever see anybody very like the prisoner?'

Not so like (the witness said) as that he could be mistaken.

'Look well upon that gentleman, my learned friend there,' pointing to him who had tossed the paper over, 'and then look well upon the prisoner. How say you? Are they very like each other?'

Allowing for my learned friend's appearance being care-less and slovenly if not debauched, they were sufficiently like each other to surprise, not only the witness, but every-body present. My Lord being prayed to bid my learned friend lay aside his wig, the likeness became much more remarkable. My Lord inquired of Mr Stryver (the prison-er's counsel), whether they were next to try Mr Carton

(name of my learned friend) for treason? But, Mr Stryver replied to my Lord, no; but he would ask the witness to tell him whether what happened once, might happen twice; whether he would have been so confident if he had seen this illustration of his rashness sooner, whether he would be so confident, having seen it; and more. The upshot of which was, to smash this witness like a crockery vessel, and shiver his part of the case to useless lumber.

Mr Cruncher had now to attend while Mr Stryver fitted the prisoner's case on the jury, showing them how the patriot, Barsad, was a hired spy and traitor. How the virtuous servant, Cly, was his friend and partner, how the watchful eyes of those forgers and false swearers had rested on the prisoner as a victim, because some family affairs in France, he being of French extraction, did require his making those passages across the Channel – though what those affairs were, a consideration for others who were near and dear to him, forbad him, even for his life, to disclose. How the evidence that had been warped and wrested from the young lady came to nothing, involving the mere little innocent gallantries and politenesses likely to pass between any young gentleman and young lady so thrown together.

Mr Stryver then called his few witnesses, and Mr Cruncher had next to attend while Mr Attorney-General turned the whole suit of clothes Mr Stryver had fitted on the jury, inside out; showing how Barsad and Cly were even a hundred times better than he had thought them,

and the prisoner a hundred times worse. Lastly, came my Lord himself, turning the suit of clothes, now inside out, now outside in, but on the whole decidedly trimming and shaping them into grave-clothes for the prisoner.

And now, the jury turned to consider, and the great flies swarmed again.

Mr Carton, who had so long sat looking at the ceiling of the court, changed neither his place nor his attitude, even in this excitement. He sat leaning back, with his torn gown half off him, his untidy wig put on just as it had happened to light on his head after its removal, his hands in his pockets, and his eyes on the ceiling as they had been all day. Something especially reckless in his demeanour, not only gave him a disreputable look, but so diminished the strong resemblance he undoubtedly bore to the prisoner, that many of the lookers-on, taking note of him now, said to one another they would hardly have thought the two were so alike.

Yet, this Mr Carton took in more of the details of the scene than he appeared to take in; for now, when Miss Manette's head dropped upon her father's breast, he was the first to see it, and to say audibly: 'Officer! look to that young lady. Help the gentleman to take her out. Don't you see she will fall!'

There was much commiseration for her as she was removed, and much sympathy with her father. It had evidently been a great distress to him, to have the days of

his imprisonment recalled. He had shown strong internal agitation when he was questioned, and that pondering or brooding look which made him old, had been upon him, like a heavy cloud, ever since. As he passed out, the jury, who had turned back and paused a moment, spoke, through their foreman.

They were not agreed, and wished to retire. The trial had lasted all day, and the lamps in the court were now being lighted. It began to be rumoured that the jury would be out a long while.

Mr Lorry, who had gone out when the young lady and her father went out, now reappeared, and beckoned to Jerry: who, in the slackened interest, could easily get near him.

'Jerry, you will be sure to hear when the jury come in. Don't be a moment behind them, for I want you to take the verdict back to the bank.'

Jerry had just enough forehead to knuckle, and he knuckled it in acknowledgement of this communication and a shilling. Mr Carton came up at the moment, and touched Mr Lorry on the arm.

'How is the young lady?'

'She is greatly distressed; but her father is comforting her, and she feels the better for being out of court.'

'I'll tell the prisoner so. It won't do for a respectable bank gentleman like you, to be seen speaking to him publicly, you know.' Mr Carton made his way to the

outside of the bar. The way out of court lay in that direction, and Jerry followed him, all eyes, ears, and spikes.

'Mr Darnay!'

The prisoner came forward directly.

'You will naturally be anxious to hear of the witness, Miss Manette. She will do very well. You have seen the worst of her agitation.'

'I am deeply sorry to have been the cause of it. Could you tell her so for me.'

'Yes, I could. I will, if you ask it.'

Mr Carton's manner was so careless as to be almost insolent. He stood, half turned from the prisoner, lounging with his elbow against the bar.

'I do ask it. Accept my cordial thanks.'

'What,' said Carton, 'do you expect, Mr Darnay?'

'The worst.'

'It's the wisest thing to expect, and the likeliest. But I think their withdrawing is in your favour.'

An hour and a half limped heavily away in the thief-and-rascal crowded passages below, even though assisted off with mutton pies and ale. The messenger, uncomfortably seated on a form after taking that refection, had dropped into a doze, when a loud murmur and a rapid tide of people setting up the stairs that led to the court, carried him along with them.

'Jerry! Jerry!' Mr Lorry was already calling at the door when he got there.

'Here, sir! It's a fight to get back again. Here I am, sir!'

Mr Lorry handed him a paper through the throng. 'Quick! Have you got it?'

'Yes, sir!'

Hastily written on the paper was the word 'ACQUITTED.'

'If you had sent the message, "Recalled to Life," again,' muttered Jerry, as he turned, 'I should have known what you meant, this time.'

4

Congratulatory

From the dimly-lighted passages of the court, the last sediment of the human stew that had been boiling there all day, was straining off, when Doctor Manette, Lucie Manette his daughter, Mr Lorry, the solicitor for the defence, and its counsel Mr Stryver, stood gathered round Mr Charles Darnay – just released – congratulating him on his escape from death.

It would have been difficult by a far brighter light, to recognise in Doctor Manette, intellectual of face and upright of bearing, the shoemaker of the garret in Paris. Yet, no one could have looked at him twice, without looking again: even though the opportunity of observation had not extended to the mournful cadence of his low grave voice, and to the abstraction that overclouded him fitfully, without any apparent reason. While one external cause, and that a reference to his long lingering agony, would always – as on the trial – evoke this condition from the depths of his soul, it was also in its nature to arise of itself, and to draw a gloom over him.

Only his daughter had the power of charming this black brooding from his mind. The sound of her voice, the light of her face, the touch of her hand, had a strong beneficial influence with him almost always.

Mr Darnay had kissed her hand fervently and gratefully, and had turned to Mr Stryver, whom he warmly thanked. Mr Stryver still had his wig and gown on, and he said: 'I am glad to have brought you off with honour, Mr Darnay. It was an infamous prosecution, grossly infamous; but not the less likely to succeed on that account.'

'You have laid me under an obligation to you for life – in two senses,' said his late client, taking his hand.

'I have done my best for you, Mr Darnay; and my best is as good as another man's, I believe.'

It clearly being incumbent on some one to say, 'Much better,' Mr Lorry said it.

'You think so?' said Mr Stryver. 'Well you have been present all day, and you ought to know. You are a man of business, too.'

'And as such,' quoth Mr Lorry, 'I will appeal to Doctor Manette, to break up this conference and order us all to our homes. Miss Lucie looks ill, Mr Darnay has had a terrible day, we are worn out.'

'Speak for yourself, Mr Lorry,' said Stryver; 'I have a night's work to do yet. Speak for yourself.'

'I speak for myself,' answered Mr Lorry, 'and for Mr

Darnay, and for Miss Lucie, and – Miss Lucie, do you not think I may speak for us all?' He asked her the question pointedly, and with a glance at her father.

His face had become frozen, as it were, in a very curious look at Darnay: an intent look, deepening into a frown of dislike and distrust, not even unmixed with fear.

'My father,' said Lucie, softly laying her hand on his.

He slowly shook the shadow off, and turned to her.

'Shall we go home, my father?'

With a long breath, he answered 'Yes'.

The friends of the acquitted prisoner had dispersed, under the impression that he would not be released that night. The iron gates were being closed with a jar and a rattle, and the dismal place was deserted until tomorrow morning's interest of gallows, pillory, whipping-post, and branding-iron, should re-people it. Walking between her father and Mr Darnay, Lucie Manette passed into the open air. A hackney-coach was called, and the father and daughter departed in it.

Mr Stryver had left them in the passages, to shoulder his way back to the robing-room. Another person, who had not joined the group, or interchanged a word with any one of them, but who had been leaning against the wall where its shadow was darkest, had silently strolled out after the rest, and had looked on until the coach drove away. He now stepped up to where Mr Lorry and Mr Darnay stood upon the pavement.

'So, Mr Lorry! Men of business may speak to Mr Darnay now?'

Nobody had made any acknowledgement of Mr Carton's part in the day's proceedings; nobody had known of it.

'If you knew what a conflict goes on in the business mind, when the business mind is divided between good-natured impulse and business appearances, you would be amused, Mr Darnay.'

Mr Lorry reddened, and said, warmly, 'You have mentioned that before, sir. We men of business, who serve a House, are not our own masters.'

'*I* know, *I* know,' rejoined Mr Carton, carelessly. 'Don't be nettled, Mr Lorry. You are as good as another, I have no doubt.'

'And indeed, sir,' pursued Mr Lorry, not minding him, 'I really don't know what you have to do with the matter. If you'll excuse me, I really don't know that it is your business.'

'Business! Bless you, *I* have no business,' said Mr Carton.

'If you had,' pursued Mr Lorry, 'perhaps you would attend to it.'

'Lord love you, no! – I shouldn't,' said Mr Carton.

'Well, sir!' cried Mr Lorry, thoroughly heated by his indifference, 'business is a very good thing, and a very respectable thing. And, sir, if business imposes its restraints

and its silences and impediments, Mr Darnay as a young gentleman of generosity knows how to make allowance for that circumstance. Mr Darnay, good-night, God bless you, sir! I hope you have been this day preserved for a prosperous and happy life. – Chair there!'

Mr Lorry bustled into the chair, and was carried off to Tellson's. Carton, who smelt of port wine, and did not appear to be quite sober, laughed then, and turned to Darnay:

'This must be a strange night to you, standing alone here with your counterpart on these street stones?'

'I hardly seem yet,' returned Charles Darnay, 'to belong to this world again.'

'I don't wonder at it; it's not so long since you were pretty far advanced on your way to another. You speak faintly.'

'I begin to think I *am* faint.'

'Then why the devil don't you dine?'

Drawing his arm through his own, he took him down Ludgate-hill to Fleet-street, and so, up a covered way, into a tavern. Here, they were shown into a little room, where Charles Darnay was soon recruiting his strength with a good plain dinner and good wine: while Carton sat opposite to him at the same table, with his separate bottle of port before him.

'Do you feel, yet, that you belong to this terrestrial scheme again, Mr Darnay?'

'I am frightfully confused regarding time and place; but I am so far mended as to feel that.'

'It must be an immense satisfaction!'

He said it bitterly, and filled up his glass again.

'As to me, the greatest desire I have, is to forget that I belong to it. It has no good in it for me – except wine like this – nor I for it. So we are not much alike in that particular.'

Feeling his being there with this Double of coarse deportment, to be like a dream, Charles Darnay was at a loss how to answer; finally, answered not at all.

'Now your dinner is done,' Carton presently said, 'why don't you give your toast?'

'What toast?'

'Why, it's on the tip of your tongue. It ought to be, it must be, I'll swear it's there.'

'Miss Manette, then!'

'Miss Manette, then!'

Looking his companion full in the face while he drank the toast, Carton flung his glass over his shoulder against the wall, where it shivered to pieces; then, rang the bell, and ordered in another.

'That's a fair young lady to be pitied by and wept for by! How does it feel? Is it worth being tried for one's life, to be the object of such sympathy and compassion, Mr Darnay?'

Again Darnay answered not a word.

'She was mightily pleased to have your message, when I gave it her.'

The allusion served as a timely reminder to Darnay that this disagreeable companion had, of his own free will, assisted him in the strait of the day. He thanked him for it.

'I neither want any thanks, nor merit any,' was the careless rejoinder. 'I don't know why I did it. Mr Darnay, let me ask you a question.'

'Willingly, and a small return for your good offices.'

'Do you think I particularly like you?'

'You have acted as if you do; but I don't think you do.'

'*I* don't think I do,' said Carton.

'Nevertheless,' pursued Darnay, rising to ring the bell, 'there is nothing in that, I hope, to prevent my calling the reckoning, and our parting without ill-blood on either side.'

Carton rejoining, 'Nothing in life!' Darnay rang. 'Do you call the whole reckoning?' said Carton. On his answering in the affirmative, 'Then bring me another pint of this same wine, drawer, and come and wake me at ten.'

The bill being paid, Charles Darnay rose and wished him good-night. Without returning the wish, Carton rose too, with something of a threat of defiance in his manner, and said, 'A last word, Mr Darnay: you think I am drunk?'

'I think you have been drinking, Mr Carton.'

'Then you shall likewise know why. I am a disappointed

drudge, sir. I care for no man on earth, and no man on earth cares for me.'

'Much to be regretted. You might have used your talents better.'

'May be so, Mr Darnay; may be not. Don't let your sober face elate you, however; you don't know what it may come to. Good-night!'

When he was left alone, this strange being took up a candle, went to a glass that hung against the wall, and surveyed himself minutely in it.

'Do you particularly like the man?' he muttered, at his own image; 'why should you particularly like a man who resembles you? Change places with him, and would you have been looked at by those blue eyes as he was, and commiserated by that agitated face as he was? Come on, and have it out in plain words! You hate the fellow.'

He resorted to his pint of wine for consolation, drank it all in a few minutes, and fell asleep on his arms.

5

The Jackal

A favourite at the Old Bailey, and eke at the Sessions, Mr Stryver had begun cautiously to hew away the lower staves of the ladder on which he mounted. Sessions and Old Bailey had now to summon their favourite, specially, to their longing arms; and shouldering itself towards the visage of the Lord Chief Justice in the Court of King's Bench, the florid countenance of Mr Stryver might be daily seen, bursting out of the bed of wigs, like a great sunflower pushing its way at the sun from among a rank garden-full of flaring companions.

It had once been noted at the Bar, that while Mr Stryver was a glib man, and an unscrupulous, and a ready, and a bold, he had not that faculty of extracting the essence from a heap of statements, which is among the most striking and necessary of the advocate's accomplishments. But a remarkable improvement came upon him as to this. The more business he got, the greater his power seemed to grow of getting at its pith and marrow; and however late at night he sat carousing with Sydney Carton, he

always had his points at his fingers' ends in the morning.

Sydney Carton, idlest and most unpromising of men, was Stryver's great ally. Stryver never had a case in hand, anywhere, but Carton was there, with his hands in his pockets, staring at the ceiling of the court; they went the same Circuit, and even there they prolonged their usual orgies late into the night. At last, it began to get about, among such as were interested in the matter, that although Sydney Carton would never be a lion, he was an amazingly good jackal, and that he rendered suit and service to Stryver in that humble capacity.

'Ten o'clock, sir,' said the man at the tavern, whom he had charged to wake him – 'ten o'clock, sir.'

'What do you mean? Ten o'clock at night?'

'Yes, sir. Your honour told me to call you.'

'Oh! I remember. Very well, very well.'

After a few dull efforts to get to sleep again, he got up, tossed his hat on, and walked out. He turned into the Temple, and, having revived himself by twice pacing the pavements of King's Bench-walk and Paper-buildings, turned into the Stryver chambers.

The Stryver clerk, who never assisted at these conferences, had gone home, and the Stryver principal opened the door. He had that rather wild, strained, seared marking about the eyes, which may be observed in all free livers of his class, from the portrait of Jeffries downward, and

which can be traced, under various disguises of Art, through the portraits of every Drinking Age.

'You are a little late, Memory,' said Stryver.

They went into a dingy room lined with books and littered with papers, where there was a blazing fire. A kettle steamed upon the hob, and in the midst of the wreck of papers a table shone, with plenty of wine upon it, and brandy, and rum, and sugar, and lemons.

'You have had your bottle, I perceive, Sydney.'

'Two tonight, I think. I have been dining with the day's client.'

'That was a rare point, Sydney, that you brought to bear upon the identification. When did it strike you?'

'I thought he was rather a handsome fellow, and I thought I should have been much the same sort of fellow, if I had had any luck.'

Mr Stryver laughed till he shook his precocious paunch. 'You and your luck, Sydney! Get to work, get to work.'

Sullenly enough, the jackal loosened his dress, went into an adjoining room, and came back with a large jug of cold water, a basin, and a towel or two. Steeping the towels in the water, and partially wringing them out, he folded them on his head in a manner hideous to behold, sat down at the table, and said, 'Now I am ready!'

'Not much boiling down to be done tonight, Memory,' said Mr Stryver, gaily, as he looked among his papers.

'How much?'

'Only two sets of them.'

'Give me the worst first.'

'There they are, Sydney. Fire away!'

The lion then composed himself on his back on a sofa on one side of the drinking-table, while the jackal sat at his own paper-bestrewn table proper, on the other side of it, with the bottles and glasses ready to his hand. Both resorted to the drinking-table without stint.

At length the jackal had got together a compact repast for the lion, and proceeded to offer it to him. The lion took it with care and caution, made his selections from it, and his remarks upon it, and the jackal assisted both. When the repast was fully discussed, the lion put his hands in his waistband, and lay down to meditate. The jackal then applied himself to the collection of a second meal; this was not disposed of until the clocks struck three in the morning.

'And now we have done, Sydney, fill a bumper of punch,' said Mr Stryver.

The jackal shook himself, yawned, shivered, and complied.

'You were very sound, Sydney, in the matter of those crown witnesses today. Every question told.'

'I always am sound; am I not?'

'I don't gainsay it. What has roughened your temper? Put some punch to it and smooth it again.'

With a deprecatory grunt, the jackal again complied.

'The old Sydney Carton of old Shrewsbury School,' said Stryver. 'Up one minute and down the next; now in spirits and now in despondency!'

'Ah!' returned the other, sighing: 'yes! The same Sydney, with the same luck. Even then, I did exercises for other boys, and seldom did my own.'

'And why not?'

'God knows. It was my way, I suppose.'

'Carton,' said his friend, squaring himself at him with a bullying air, 'your way is, and always was, a lame way. You summon no energy and purpose. Look at me.'

'Oh, botheration!' returned Sydney, with a lighter and more good-humoured laugh, 'don't *you* be moral!'

'How have I done what I have done?' said Stryver.

'Partly through paying me to help you, I suppose. What you want to do, you do. You were always in the front rank, and I was always behind.'

'I had to get into the front rank; I was not born there, was I?'

'I was not present at the ceremony; but my opinion is you were,' said Carton.

'Before Shrewsbury, and at Shrewsbury, and ever since Shrewsbury,' pursued Carton, 'you have fallen into your rank, and I have fallen into mine. You were always somewhere, and I was always – nowhere.'

'And whose fault was that?'

'Upon my soul, I am not sure that it was not yours.

You were always driving and riving and shouldering and pressing, to that restless degree that I had no chance for my life but in rust and repose. It's a gloomy thing, however, to talk about one's own past, with the day breaking. Turn me in some other direction before I go.'

'Well then! Pledge me to the pretty witness,' said Stryver, holding up his glass.

'Pretty witness,' Carton muttered, looking down into his glass. 'Who's your pretty witness?'

'The picturesque doctor's daughter, Miss Manette.'

'*She* pretty?'

'Why, man alive, she was the admiration of the whole Court!'

'Rot the admiration of the Court! She was a golden-haired doll!'

'Do you know, Sydney,' said Mr Stryver, 'I rather thought, at the time, that you sympathised with the golden-haired doll, and were quick to see what happened to the golden-haired doll?'

'Quick to see what happened! If a girl, doll or no doll, swoons within a yard or two of a man's nose, he can see it without a perspective-glass.'

When his host followed him out on the staircase with a candle, to light him down the stairs, the day was coldly looking in through its grimy windows. When he got out of the house, the air was cold and sad, the river dark and dim, the whole scene like a lifeless desert.

Waste forces within him, and a desert all around, this man stood still on his way across a silent terrace, and saw for a moment a mirage of honourable ambition, self-denial, and perseverance. In the fair city of this vision, there were airy galleries from which the loves and graces looked upon him, gardens in which the fruits of life hung ripening, waters of Hope that sparkled in his sight. A moment, and it was gone. Climbing to a high chamber in a well of houses, he threw himself down in his clothes on a neglected bed, and its pillow was wet with wasted tears.

6

Hundreds of People

The quiet lodgings of Doctor Manette were in a quiet street-corner not far from Soho-square. On the afternoon of a certain fine Sunday when the waves of four months had rolled over the trial for treason, Mr Jarvis Lorry walked along the sunny streets from Clerkenwell where he lived, on his way to dine with the Doctor.

A quainter corner than the corner where the Doctor lived, was not to be found in London. There was no way through it, and the front windows of the Doctor's lodgings commanded a pleasant little vista of street that had a congenial air of retirement on it.

It was a cool spot, staid but cheerful, a wonderful place for echoes, and a very harbour from the raging streets.

The Doctor occupied two floors of a large still house, where several callings purported to be pursued by day, but whereof little was audible any day, and which was shunned by all of them at night. In a building at the back, attainable by a courtyard where a plane-tree rustled its green leaves, church-organs claimed to be made, and

silver to be chased. Very little of these trades, or of a lonely lodger rumoured to live upstairs, or of a dim coach-trimming maker asserted to have a counting-house below, was ever heard or seen.

Doctor Manette received such patients here as his old reputation, and its revival in the floating whispers of his story, brought him. His scientific knowledge, and his vigilance and skill in conducting ingenious experiments, brought him otherwise into moderate request, and he earned as much as he wanted.

These things were within Mr Jarvis Lorry's knowledge, thoughts, and notice, when he rang the door-bell of the tranquil house in the corner, on the fine Sunday afternoon.

'Doctor Manette at home?'

Expected home.

'Miss Lucie at home?'

Expected home.

'Miss Pross at home?'

Possibly at home, but of a certainty impossible for handmaid to anticipate intentions of Miss Pross, as to admission or denial of the fact.

'As I am at home myself,' said Mr Lorry, 'I'll go upstairs.'

There were three rooms on a floor, and, the doors by which they communicated being put open that the air might pass freely through them all, Mr Lorry walked from one to

another. The first was the best room, and in it were Lucie's birds, and flowers, and books, and desk, and work-table, and box of water-colours; the second was the Doctor's consulting-room, used also as the dining-room; the third, changingly speckled by the rustle of the plane-tree in the yard, was the Doctor's bedroom – and there, in a corner, stood the disused shoemaker's bench and tray of tools, much as it had stood on the fifth floor of the dismal house by the wine-shop, in the suburb of Saint Antoine in Paris.

'I wonder,' said Mr Lorry, pausing in his looking about, 'that he keeps that reminder of his sufferings about him!'

'And why wonder at that?' was the abrupt inquiry that made him start.

It proceeded from Miss Pross, the wild red woman, strong of hand, whose acquaintance he had first made at the Royal George Hotel at Dover, and had since improved.

'I should have thought –' Mr Lorry began.

'Pooh! You'd have thought!' said Miss Pross; and Mr Lorry left off.

'How do you do?' inquired that lady then.

'I am pretty well, I thank you,' answered Mr Lorry, with meekness; 'how are you?'

'Nothing to boast of,' said Miss Pross.

'Indeed?'

'Ah! indeed!' said Miss Pross. 'I am very much put out about my Ladybird.'

'May I ask the cause?'

'I don't want dozens of people who are not at all worthy of Ladybird, to come here looking after her,' said Miss Pross.

'*Do* dozens come for that purpose?'

'Hundreds,' said Miss Pross.

It was characteristic of this lady that whenever her original proposition was questioned, she exaggerated it.

'I have lived with the darling – or the darling has lived with me, and paid me for it; which she certainly should never have done, you may take your affidavit, if I could have afforded to keep either myself or her for nothing – since she was ten years old. And it's really very hard,' said Miss Pross.

Not seeing with precision what was very hard, Mr Lorry shook his head.

'All sorts of people who are not in the least degree worthy of the pet, are always turning up,' said Miss Pross. 'When you began it –'

'*I* began it, Miss Pross?'

'Didn't you? Who brought her father to life?'

'Oh! If *that* was beginning it –' said Mr Lorry.

'It wasn't ending it, I suppose? I say, when you began it, it was hard enough: not that I have any fault to find with Doctor Manette, except that he is not worthy of such a daughter. But it really is doubly and trebly hard to have crowds and multitudes of people turning up after him, to take Ladybird's affections away from me.'

Mr Lorry knew Miss Pross to be very jealous, but he also knew her by this time to be, beneath the surface of her eccentricity, one of those unselfish creatures who will, for pure love and admiration, bind themselves willing slaves, to youth when they have lost it, to beauty that they never had, to bright hopes that never shone upon their own sombre lives.

'There never was, nor will be, but one man worthy of Ladybird,' said Miss Pross; 'and that was my brother Solomon, if he hadn't made a mistake in life.'

Here again: Mr Lorry's inquiries into Miss Pross's personal history had established the fact that her brother Solomon was a heartless scoundrel who had stripped her of everything she possessed, as a stake to speculate with, and had abandoned her in her poverty for evermore. Miss Pross's fidelity of belief in Solomon was quite a serious matter with Mr Lorry, and had its weight in his good opinion of her.

'As we happen to be alone for the moment, and are both people of business,' he said, 'let me ask you – does the Doctor, in talking with Lucie, never refer to the shoe-making time, yet?'

'Never.'

'And yet keeps that bench and those tools beside him?'

'Ah!' returned Miss Pross, shaking her head. 'But I don't say he don't refer to it within himself.'

'Do you suppose,' Mr Lorry went on, 'that Doctor Manette has any theory of his own, preserved through all those years, relative to the cause of his being so oppressed; perhaps, even to the name of his oppressor?'

'I don't suppose anything about it but what Ladybird tells me.'

'And that is –?'

'That she thinks he has.'

'Now don't be angry at my asking all these questions; because I am a mere dull man of business, and you are a woman of business. Is it not remarkable that Doctor Manette, unquestionably innocent of any crime as we are all well assured he is, should never touch upon that question? I will not say with me, though he had business relations with me many years ago, and we are now intimate; I will say with the fair daughter to whom he is so devotedly attached, and who is so devotedly attached to him?'

'Well! To the best of my understanding, and bad's the best, you'll tell me,' said Miss Pross, softened by the tone of the apology, 'he is afraid of the whole subject.'

'Afraid?'

'It's plain enough, I should think, why he may be. It's a dreadful remembrance. Besides that, his loss of himself grew out of it. Not knowing how he lost himself, or how he recovered himself, he may never feel certain of not losing himself again.'

It was a profounder remark than Mr Lorry had looked for. 'True,' said he, 'and fearful to reflect upon. Yet, a doubt lurks in my mind, Miss Pross, whether it is good for Doctor Manette to have that suppression always shut up within him.'

'Can't be helped,' said Miss Pross, shaking her head. 'Better leave it alone. Sometimes, he gets up in the dead of the night, and will be heard, by us overhead there, walking up and down, walking up and down, in his room. Ladybird hurries to him, and they go on together, walking up and down, walking up and down, until he is composed. But he never says a word of the true reason of his restlessness, to her, and she finds it best not to hint at it to him.'

The corner has been mentioned as a wonderful corner for echoes; it had begun to echo so resoundingly to the tread of coming feet, that it seemed as though the very mention of that weary pacing to and fro had set it going.

'Here they are!' said Miss Pross, rising to break up the conference; 'and now we shall have hundreds of people pretty soon!'

It was such a curious corner in its acoustical properties, that as Mr Lorry stood at the open window, looking for the father and daughter whose steps he heard, he fancied they would never approach. Not only would the echoes die away, as though the steps had gone; but, echoes of other steps that never came would be heard in their stead, and would die away for good when they seemed close at

hand. However, father and daughter did at last appear, and Miss Pross was ready at the street door to receive them.

Miss Pross was a pleasant sight, albeit wild, and red, and grim, taking off her darling's bonnet when she came upstairs, and touching it up with the ends of her handkerchief, and smoothing her rich hair. Her darling was a pleasant sight too, embracing her and thanking her, and protesting against her taking so much trouble for her. The Doctor was a pleasant sight too, looking on at them, and telling Miss Pross how she spoilt Lucie, in accents and with eyes that had as much spoiling in them as Miss Pross had, and would have had more if it were possible. Mr Lorry was a pleasant sight too, beaming at all this in his little wig, and thanking his bachelor stars for having lighted him in his declining years to a Home. But, no Hundreds of people came to see the sights, and Mr Lorry looked in vain for the fulfilment of Miss Pross's prediction.

Dinner-time, and still no Hundreds of people. In the arrangements of the little household, Miss Pross took charge of the lower regions, and always acquitted herself marvellously. Her dinners, of a very modest quality, were so well cooked and so well served, and so neat in their contrivances, half English and half French, that nothing could be better.

On Sundays, Miss Pross dined at the Doctor's table, but on other days persisted in taking her meals at unknown

periods, either in the lower regions, or in her own room on the second floor. On this occasion, Miss Pross, responding to Ladybird's pleasant face and pleasant efforts to please her, unbent exceedingly; so the dinner was very pleasant, too.

It was an oppressive day, and, after dinner, Lucie proposed that the wine should be carried out under the plane-tree, and they should sit there in the air. As everything turned upon her, and revolved about her, they went out under the plane-tree, and she carried the wine down for the special benefit of Mr Lorry.

Still, the Hundreds of people did not present themselves. Mr Darnay presented himself while they were sitting under the plane-tree, but he was only One.

Doctor Manette received him kindly, and so did Lucie. But, Miss Pross suddenly became afflicted with a twitching in the head and body, and retired into the house. She was not unfrequently the victim of this disorder, and she called it, in familiar conversation, 'a fit of the jerks.'

The Doctor was in his best condition, and looked specially young.

He had been talking all day, on many subjects, and with unusual vivacity. 'Pray, Doctor Manette,' said Mr Darnay, as they sat under the plane-tree, 'have you seen much of the Tower?'

'Lucie and I have been there; but only casually. We have seen enough of it, to know that it teems with interest; little more.'

'*I* have been there, as you remember,' said Darnay, with a smile, though reddening a little angrily, 'in another character, and not in a character that gives facilities for seeing much of it. They told me a curious thing when I was there.'

'What was that?' Lucie asked.

'In making some alterations, the workmen came upon an old dungeon, which had been, for many years, built up and forgotten. Upon a corner stone in an angle of the wall, one prisoner, who seemed to have gone to execution, had cut as his last work, three letters. At first, they were read as D. I. C.; but, on being more carefully examined, the last letter was found to be G. At length, it was suggested that the letters were not initials, but the complete word, D I G. The floor was examined very carefully under the inscription, and, in the earth beneath a stone were found the ashes of a paper, mingled with the ashes of a small leathern case or bag. What the unknown prisoner had written will never be read, but he had written something, and hidden it away to keep it from the gaoler.'

'My father,' exclaimed Lucie, 'you are ill!'

He had suddenly started up, with his hand to his head.

'No, my dear, not ill. There are large drops of rain falling, and they made me start. We had better go in.'

He recovered himself almost instantly. Rain was really falling in large drops, and he showed the back of his hand

with rain-drops on it. But, he said not a single word in reference to the discovery that had been told of, and, as they went into the house, the business eye of Mr Lorry either detected, or fancied it detected, on his face, as it turned towards Charles Darnay, the same singular look that had been upon it when it turned towards him in the passages of the Court House.

Tea-time, and Miss Pross making tea, with another fit of the jerks upon her, and yet no Hundreds of people. Mr Carton had lounged in, but he made only Two.

When the tea-table was done with, they all moved to one of the windows, and looked out into the heavy twilight. Lucie sat by her father; Darnay sat beside her; Carton leaned against a window.

'The rain-drops are still falling, large, heavy, and few,' said Doctor Manette. 'It comes slowly.'

'It comes surely,' said Carton.

They spoke low, as people in a dark room, watching and waiting for Lightning, always do.

There was a great hurry in the streets, of people speeding away to get shelter before the storm broke; the wonderful corner for echoes resounded with the echoes of footsteps coming and going, yet not a footstep was there.

'Is it not impressive, Mr Darnay?' asked Lucie. 'Sometimes, I have sat here of an evening, until I have fancied – but even the shade of a foolish fancy makes me shudder tonight, when all is so black and solemn –'

'Let us shudder too. We may know what it is.'

'It will seem nothing to you. I have sometimes sat alone here of an evening, listening, until I have made the echoes out to be the echoes of all the footsteps that are coming by-and-by into our lives.'

'There is a great crowd coming one day into our lives, if that be so,' Sydney Carton struck in, in his moody way.

The corner echoed and re-echoed with the tread of feet; some, as it seemed, under the windows; some, as it seemed, in the room; some coming, some going, some breaking off, some stopping altogether; all in the distant streets, and not one within sight.

'Are all these footsteps destined to come to all of us, Miss Manette, or are we to divide them among us?'

'I don't know, Mr Darnay. When I have yielded myself to it, I have been alone, and then I have imagined them the footsteps of the people who are to come into my life, and my father's.'

'I take them into mine!' said Carton. '*I* ask no questions and make no stipulations. There is a great crowd bearing down upon us, Miss Manette, and I see them! – by the Lightning.' He added the last words, after there had been a vivid flash which had shown him lounging in the window.

'And I hear them!' he added again, after a peal of thunder. 'Here they come, fast, fierce, and furious!'

It was the rush and roar of rain that he typified, and

it stopped him, for no voice could be heard in it. A memorable storm of thunder and lightning broke with that sweep of water, and there was not a moment's interval in crash, and fire, and rain, until after the moon rose at midnight.

The great bell of Saint Paul's was striking One in the cleared air, when Mr Lorry, escorted by Jerry, high-booted and bearing a lantern, set forth on his return-passage to Clerkenwell.

'What a night it has been! Almost a night, Jerry,' said Mr Lorry, 'to bring the dead out of their graves.'

'I never see the night myself, master – nor yet I don't expect to see it – what would do that,' answered Jerry.

'Good-night, Mr Carton,' said the man of business.

'Good-night, Mr Darnay. Shall we ever see such a night again, together!'

Perhaps. Perhaps, see the great crowd of people with its rush and roar, bearing down upon them, too.

7

Monseigneur in Town

Monseigneur, one of the great lords in power at the Court, held his fortnightly reception in his grand hotel in Paris. Monseigneur was about to take his chocolate. Monseigneur could swallow a great many things with ease, and was by some few sullen minds supposed to be rather rapidly swallowing France; but, his morning's chocolate could not so much as get into the throat of Monseigneur, without the aid of four strong men besides the Cook.

Monseigneur had been out at a little supper last night, where the Comedy and the Grand Opera were charmingly represented. So polite and so impressible was Monseigneur, that the Comedy and the Grand Opera had far more influence with him in the tiresome articles of state affairs and state secrets, than the needs of all France.

Monseigneur had one truly noble idea of general public business, which was, to let everything go on in its own way; of particular public business, Monseigneur had the other truly noble idea that it must all go his way – tend

to his own power and pocket. Of his pleasures, general and particular, Monseigneur had the other truly noble idea, that the world was made for them.

Yet, Monseigneur had slowly found that vulgar embarrassments crept into his affairs, both private and public; and he had, as to both classes of affairs, allied himself perforce with a Farmer-General. As to finances public, because Monseigneur could not make anything at all of them, and must consequently let them out to somebody who could; as to finances private, because Farmer-Generals were rich, and Monseigneur, after generations of great luxury and expense, was growing poor. Hence Monseigneur had taken his sister from a convent, while there was yet time to ward off the impending veil, the cheapest garment she could wear, and had bestowed her as a prize upon a very rich Farmer-General, poor in family. Which Farmer-General, carrying an appropriate cane with a golden apple on the top of it, was now among the company in the outer rooms, much prostrated before by mankind.

A sumptuous man was the Farmer-General. Thirty horses stood in his stables, twenty-four male domestics sat in his halls, six body-women waited on his wife. As one who pretended to do nothing but plunder and forage where he could, the Farmer-General was the greatest reality among the personages who attended at the hotel of Monseigneur that day.

For, the rooms, though a beautiful scene to look at, were,

in truth, not a sound business; considered with any reference to the scarecrows in the rags and nightcaps elsewhere, they would have been an exceedingly uncomfortable business at the house of Monseigneur. Military officers destitute of military knowledge; naval officers with no idea of a ship; brazen ecclesiastics, of the worst world worldly, with sensual eyes, loose tongues, and looser lives; all totally unfit for their several callings, all lying horribly in pretending to belong to them, but all nearly or remotely of the order of Monseigneur, and therefore foisted on all public employments from which anything was to be got; these were to be told off by the score and the score. People not immediately connected with Monseigneur or the State, yet equally unconnected with anything that was real, or with lives passed in travelling by any straight road to any true earthly end, were no less abundant. Doctors who made great fortunes out of dainty remedies for imaginary disorders that never existed, smiled upon their courtly patients in the antechambers of Monseigneur. Unbelieving Philosophers who were remodelling the world with words, and making card-towers of Babel to scale the skies with, talked with Unbelieving Chemists who had an eye on the transmutation of metals, at this wonderful gathering accumulated by Monseigneur. Exquisite gentlemen of the finest breeding, which was at that remarkable time to be known by its fruits of indifference to every natural subject of human interest, were in the most exemplary state of exhaustion,

at the hotel of Monseigneur. Such homes had these various notabilities left behind them in the fine world of Paris, that the spies among the assembled devotees of Monseigneur would have found it hard to discover among the angels of that sphere one solitary wife, who, in her manners and appearance, owned to being a Mother. Indeed, except for the mere act of bringing a troublesome creature into this world – there was no such thing known to the fashion. Peasant women kept the unfashionable babies close, and brought them up, and charming grandmammas of sixty dressed and supped as at twenty.

The leprosy of unreality disfigured every human creature in attendance upon Monseigneur. In the outermost room were half a dozen exceptional people who had had, for a few years, some vague misgiving in them that things in general were going rather wrong. As a promising way of setting them right, half of the half-dozen had become members of a fantastic sect of Convulsionists, and were even then considering within themselves whether they should foam, rage, roar, and turn cataleptic on the spot – thereby setting up a highly intelligible finger-post to the Future, for Monseigneur's guidance. Besides these Dervishes, were other three who had rushed into another sect, which mended matters with a jargon about 'the Centre of Truth:' holding that Man had got out of the Centre of Truth but had not got out of the Circumference, and that he was to be kept from flying out of the Circum-

ference, and was even to be shoved back into the Centre, by fasting and seeing of spirits.

All the company at the grand hotel of Monseigneur were perfectly dressed. Such frizzling and powdering and sticking up of hair, such delicate complexions artificially preserved and mended, such gallant swords to look at, and such delicate honour to the sense of smell, would surely keep anything going, for ever and ever.

Dress was the one unfailing talisman and charm used for keeping all things in their places. Everybody was dressed for a Fancy Ball that was never to leave off. From the Palace of the Tuileries, through Monseigneur and the whole Court, through the Chambers, the Tribunals of Justice, and all society (except the scarecrows), the Fancy Ball descended to the common Executioner: who, in pursuance of the charm, was required to officiate 'frizzled, powdered, in a gold-laced coat, pumps, and white silk stockings.' And who among the company at Monseigneur's reception in that seventeen hundred and eightieth year of our Lord, could possibly doubt, that a system rooted in a frizzled hangman, powdered, gold-laced, pumped, and white-silk stockinged, would see the very stars out!

Monseigneur having eased his four men of their burdens and taken his chocolate, caused the doors to be thrown open, and issued forth.

Bestowing a word of promise here and a smile there, Monseigneur affably passed through his rooms to the

remote region of the Circumference of Truth. There, Monseigneur turned, and came back again, and so in due course of time got himself shut up in his sanctuary by the chocolate sprites, and was seen no more.

There was soon but one person left of all the crowd, and he, with his hat under his arm and his snuff-box in his hand, slowly passed among the mirrors on his way out.

'I devote you,' said this person, stopping at the last door on his way, and turning in the direction of the sanctuary, 'to the Devil!'

With that, he shook the snuff from his fingers as if he had shaken the dust from his feet, and quietly walked down stairs.

He was a man of about sixty, handsomely dressed, haughty in manner, and with a face like a fine mask. The nose, beautifully formed otherwise, was very slightly pinched at the top of each nostril. In those two compressions, or dints, the only little change that the face ever showed, resided. They persisted in changing colour sometimes, and they would be occasionally dilated and contracted by something like a faint pulsation; then, they gave a look of treachery, and cruelty, to the whole countenance.

The man went down stairs into the court-yard, got into his carriage, and drove away. It appeared rather agreeable to him to see the common people dispersed before his horses, and often barely escaping from being run down. His man drove as if he were charging an enemy, and the

furious recklessness of the man brought no check into the face, or to the lips, of the master.

With a wild rattle and clatter, and an inhuman abandonment of consideration not easy to be understood in these days, the carriage dashed through streets and swept round corners, with women screaming before it, and men clutching each other and clutching children out of its way. At last, swooping at a street corner by a fountain, one of its wheels came to a sickening little jolt, and there was a loud cry from a number of voices, and the horses reared and plunged.

But for the latter inconvenience, the carriage probably would not have stopped; carriages were often known to drive on, and leave their wounded behind, and why not? But the frightened valet had got down in a hurry, and there were twenty hands at the horses' bridles.

'What has gone wrong?' said Monsieur, calmly looking out.

A tall man in a nightcap had caught up a bundle from among the feet of the horses, and had laid it on the basement of the fountain, and was down in the mud and wet, howling over it like a wild animal.

'Pardon, Monsieur the Marquis!' said a ragged and submissive man, 'it is a child.'

'Why does he make that abominable noise? Is it his child?'

'Excuse me, Monsieur the Marquis – it is a pity – yes.'

The fountain was a little removed; for the street opened,

where it was, into a space some ten or twelve yards square. As the tall man suddenly got up from the ground, and came running at the carriage, Monsieur the Marquis clapped his hand for an instant on his sword-hilt.

'Killed!' shrieked the man, in wild desperation, extending both arms at their length above his head, and staring at him. 'Dead!'

The people closed round, and looked at Monsieur the Marquis. There was nothing revealed by the many eyes that looked at him but watchfulness and eagerness; there was no visible menacing or anger. Monsieur the Marquis ran his eyes over them all, as if they had been mere rats come out of their holes.

He took out his purse.

'It is extraordinary to me,' said he, 'that you people cannot take care of yourselves and your children. One or the other of you is for ever in the way. How do I know what injury you have done my horses? See! Give him that.'

He threw out a gold coin for the valet to pick up, and all the heads craned forward that all the eyes might look down at it as it fell. The tall man called out again with a most unearthly cry, 'Dead!'

He was arrested by the quick arrival of another man. On seeing him, the miserable creature fell upon his shoulder, sobbing and crying, and pointing to the fountain, where some women were stooping over the motionless bundle, and moving gently about it.

'I know all, I know all,' said that last comer. 'Be a brave man, my Gaspard! It is better for the poor little plaything to die so, than to live. It has died in a moment without pain. Could it have lived an hour as happily?'

'You are a philosopher, you there,' said the Marquis, smiling. 'How do they call you?'

'They call me Defarge.'

'Of what trade?'

'Monsieur the Marquis, vendor of wine.'

'Pick up that, philosopher and vendor of wine,' said the Marquis throwing him another gold coin, 'and spend it as you will.'

Without deigning to look at the assemblage a second time, Monsieur the Marquis leaned back in his seat, and was just being driven away when his ease was suddenly disturbed by a coin flying into his carriage, and ringing on its floor.

'Hold!' said Monsieur the Marquis. 'Who threw that?'

He looked to the spot where Defarge the vendor of wine had stood, a moment before; but the wretched father was grovelling on his face on the pavement in that spot, and the figure that stood beside him was the figure of a dark stout woman, knitting.

'You dogs!' said the Marquis, but smoothly, and with an unchanged front, except as to the spots on his nose: 'I would ride over any of you very willingly, and exterminate you from the earth. If I knew which rascal threw at the

carriage, and if that brigand were sufficiently near it, he should be crushed under the wheels.'

So cowed was their condition, and so long and hard their experience of what such a man could do to them, within the law and beyond it, that not a voice, or a hand, or even an eye was raised. But the woman who stood knitting looked up steadily, and looked the Marquis in the face. It was not for his dignity to notice it; his contemptuous eyes passed over her, and over all the other rats; and he leaned back in his seat again, and gave the word 'Go on!'

He was driven on, and other carriages came whirling by in quick succession; the Minister, the Farmer-General, the Doctor, the Lawyer, the Ecclesiastic, the Grand Opera, the Comedy, the whole Fancy Ball in a bright continuous flow, came whirling by. The father had long ago taken up his bundle and hidden himself away with it, when the one woman who had stood conspicuous, knitting, still knitted on with the steadfastness of Fate. The water of the fountain ran, the swift river ran, the day ran into evening, so much life in the city ran into death according to rule, time and tide waited for no man, the rats were sleeping close together in their dark holes again, the Fancy Ball was lighted up at supper, all things ran their course.

8

Monseigneur in the Country

Monsieur the Marquis in his travelling carriage, conducted by four post-horses and two postilions, fagged up a steep hill.

The sunset struck so brilliantly into the travelling carriage when it gained the hill-top, that its occupant was steeped in crimson. 'It will die out,' said Monsieur the Marquis, glancing at his hands, 'directly.'

In effect, the sun was so low that it dipped at the moment. When the heavy drag had been adjusted to the wheel, and the carriage slid down hill, with a cinderous smell, in a cloud of dust, the red glow departed quickly.

But, there remained a broken country, bold and open, a little village at the bottom of the hill, a broad sweep and rise beyond it, a church-tower, a windmill, a forest for the chase, and a crag with a fortress on it used as a prison. Round upon all these darkening objects as the night drew on, the Marquis looked, with the air of one who was coming near home.

The village had its one poor street, with its poor

brewery, poor tannery, poor tavern, poor stable-yard for relay of post-horses, poor fountain, all usual poor appointments. All its people were poor, and many of them were sitting at their doors, shredding spare onions and the like for supper. Expressive signs of what made them poor, were not wanting; the tax for the state, the tax for the church, the tax for the lord, tax local and tax general, were to be paid here and to be paid there, according to solemn inscription in the little village, until the wonder was, that there was any village left unswallowed.

Few children were to be seen, and no dogs. As to the men and women, their choice on earth was stated in the prospect – Life on the lowest terms that could sustain it, down in the little village under the mill; or captivity and Death in the dominant prison on the crag.

Monsieur the Marquis drew up in his travelling carriage at the posting-house gate. It was hard by the fountain, and the peasants suspended their operations to look at him.

Monsieur the Marquis cast his eyes over the submissive faces that drooped before him, as the like of himself had drooped before Monseigneur of the Court – only the difference was, that these faces drooped merely to suffer and not to propitiate – when a grizzled mender of the roads joined the group.

'Bring me hither that fellow!' said the Marquis to the courier.

The fellow was brought, cap in hand, and the other fellows closed round to look and listen.

'I passed you on the road?'

'Monseigneur, it is true. I had the honour of being passed on the road.'

'What did you look at, so fixedly?'

'Monseigneur, I looked at the man.'

He stooped a little, and with his tattered blue cap pointed under the carriage. All his fellows stooped to look under the carriage.

'What man, pig? And why look there?'

'Pardon, Monseigneur; he swung by the chain of the shoe – the drag.'

'Swinging by the chain? To be suffocated?'

'With your gracious permission, that was the wonder of it, Monseigneur. His head hanging over – like this!'

He turned himself sideways to the carriage, and leaned back, with his face thrown up to the sky, and his head hanging down.

'What was he like?'

'Monseigneur, he was whiter than the miller. All covered with dust, white as a spectre, tall as a spectre!'

The picture produced an immense sensation in the little crowd; but all eyes, without comparing notes with other eyes, looked at Monsieur the Marquis.

'Truly, you did well,' said the Marquis, felicitously sensible that such vermin were not to ruffle him, 'to see a thief

accompanying my carriage, and not open that great mouth of yours. Bah! Put him aside, Monsieur Gabelle!'

Monsieur Gabelle was the Postmaster, and some other taxing functionary united; he had come out with great obsequiousness to assist at this examination.

'Bah! Go aside!' said Monsieur Gabelle.

'Lay hands on this stranger if he seeks to lodge in your village tonight, and be sure that his business is honest, Gabelle.'

'Monseigneur, I am flattered to devote myself to your orders.'

'Did he run away, fellow? – where is that Accursed?'

The accursed was already under the carriage with some half-dozen particular friends, pointing out the chain with his blue cap. Some half-dozen other particular friends promptly hauled him out, and presented him breathless to Monsieur the Marquis.

'Did the man run away, Dolt, when we stopped for the drag?'

'Monseigneur, he precipitated himself over the hill-side, head first, as a person plunges into the river.'

'See to it, Gabelle. Go on!'

The half-dozen who were peering at the chain were still among the wheels, like sheep; the wheels turned so suddenly that they were lucky to save their skins and bones.

The burst with which the carriage started out of the village and up the rise beyond, was soon checked by the

steepness of the hill. Gradually, it subsided to a foot pace, swinging and lumbering upward among the many sweet scents of a summer night.

At the steepest point of the hill there was a little burial-ground, with a Cross and a new large figure of Our Saviour on it; it was a poor figure in wood, done by some inexperienced rustic carver, but he had studied the figure from the life – his own life, maybe – for it was dreadfully spare and thin.

To this distressful emblem of a great distress that had long been growing worse, and was not at its worst, a woman was kneeling. She turned her head as the carriage came up to her, rose quickly, and presented herself at the carriage-door.

'It is you, Monseigneur! Monseigneur, a petition.'

With an exclamation of impatience, but with his unchangeable face, Monseigneur looked out.

'How, then! What is it? Always petitions!'

'Monseigneur. For the love of God! My husband, the forester.'

'What of your husband, the forester? Always the same with you people. He cannot pay something?'

'He has paid all, Monseigneur. He is dead.'

'Well! He is quiet. Can I restore him to you?'

'Alas, no, Monseigneur! But he lies yonder, under a little heap of poor grass.'

'Well?'

'Monseigneur, there are so many little heaps of poor grass?'

She looked an old woman, but was young. Her manner was one of passionate grief; by turns she clasped her veinous and knotted hands together with wild energy, and laid one of them on the carriage-door – tenderly, caressingly, as if it had been a human breast, and could be expected to feel the appealing touch.

'Monseigneur, hear me! Monseigneur, hear my petition! My husband died of want; so many more will die of want.'

'Again, well? Can I feed them?'

'Monseigneur, the good God knows; but I don't ask it. My petition is, that a morsel of stone or wood, with my husband's name, may be placed over him to show where he lies. Otherwise, the place will be quickly forgotten, it will never be found when I am dead of the same malady, I shall be laid under some other heap of poor grass. Monseigneur, they are so many, they increase so fast, there is so much want. Monseigneur! Monseigneur!'

The valet had put her away from the door, the carriage had broken into a brisk trot, the postilions had quickened the pace, she was left far behind, and Monseigneur was rapidly diminishing the league or two of distance that remained between him and his château.

The sweet scents of the summer night rose all around him, and rose, as the rain falls, impartially, on the dusty,

ragged, and toil-worn group at the fountain not far away; to whom the mender of roads still enlarged upon his man like a spectre, as long as they could bear it. By degrees, as they could bear no more, they dropped off one by one, and lights twinkled in little casements.

The shadow of a large high-roofed house, and of many over-hanging trees, was upon Monsieur the Marquis by that time; and the shadow was exchanged for the light of a flambeau, as his carriage stopped, and the great door of his château was opened to him.

'Monsieur Charles, whom I expect; is he arrived from England?'

'Monseigneur, not yet.'

9

The Gorgon's Head

It was a heavy mass of building, that château of Monsieur the Marquis, with a large stone court-yard before it, and two stone sweeps of staircase meeting in a stone terrace before the principal door. A stony business altogether, with heavy stone balustrades, and stone urns, and stone flowers, and stone faces of men, and stone heads of lions, in all directions. As if the Gorgon's head had surveyed it, when it was finished, two centuries ago.

The great door clanged behind him, and Monsieur the Marquis crossed a hall grim with certain old boar-spears, swords, and knives of the chase; grimmer with certain heavy riding-rods and riding-whips, of which many a peasant, gone to his benefactor Death, had felt the weight when his lord was angry.

Avoiding the larger rooms, which were dark and made fast for the night, Monsieur the Marquis, with his flambeau-bearer going on before, went up the staircase to a door in a corridor. This thrown open, admitted him

to his own private apartment of three rooms: his bed-chamber and two others.

A supper-table was laid for two, in the third of the rooms; a round room, in one of the château's four extinguisher-topped towers. A small lofty room, with its window wide open, and the wooden jalousie-blinds closed, so that the dark night only showed in slight horizontal lines of black, alternating with their broad lines of stone colour.

'My nephew,' said the Marquis, glancing at the supper preparation; 'they said he was not arrived.'

Nor was he; but, he had been expected with Monseigneur.

'Ah! It is not probable he will arrive tonight; nevertheless, leave the table as it is.'

In a quarter of an hour Monseigneur was ready, and sat down alone to his sumptuous and choice supper. His chair was opposite to the window, and he had taken his soup, and was raising his glass of Bordeaux to his lips, when he put it down.

'What is that?' he calmly asked, looking with attention at the horizontal lines of black and stone colour.

'Monseigneur? That?'

'Outside the blinds. Open the blinds.'

It was done.

'Well?'

'Monseigneur, it is nothing. The trees and the night are all that are here.'

'Good,' said the imperturbable master. 'Close them again.'

The Marquis was half-way through his supper when he again stopped with his glass in his hand, hearing the sound of wheels.

'Ask who is arrived.'

It was the nephew of Monseigneur. He had been some few leagues behind Monseigneur, early in the afternoon. He had diminished the distance rapidly, but not so rapidly as to come up with Monseigneur on the road. He had heard of Monseigneur, at the posting-houses, as being before him. He had been known in England as Charles Darnay.

Monseigneur received him in a courtly manner, but they did not shake hands.

'You left Paris yesterday, sir?' he said to Monseigneur, as he took his seat at table.

'Yesterday. And you?'

'I come direct from London.'

'You have been a long time coming,' said the Marquis, with a smile.

'On the contrary; I come direct.'

'Pardon me! I mean, not a long time on the journey; a long time intending the journey.'

'I have been detained by' – the nephew stopped a moment in his answer – 'various business.'

When coffee had been served, the nephew, looking at

the uncle and meeting the eyes of the face that was like a fine mask, opened a conversation.

'I have come back, sir, as you anticipate, pursuing the object that took me away. It carried me into great and unexpected peril; but it is a sacred object, and if it had carried me to death I hope it would have sustained me.'

'Not to death,' said the uncle; 'it is not necessary to say, to death.'

'I doubt, sir,' returned the nephew, 'whether, if it had carried me to the utmost brink of death, you would have cared to stop me there.'

The deepened marks in the nose, and the lengthening of the fine straight lines in the cruel face, looked ominous as to that; the uncle made a graceful gesture of protest, which was so clearly a slight form of good breeding that it was not reassuring.

'Indeed, sir,' pursued the nephew, 'for anything I know, you may have expressly worked to give a more suspicious appearance to the suspicious circumstances that surrounded me. I know that your diplomacy would stop me by any means, and would know no scruple as to means.'

'My friend, I told you so,' said the uncle, with a fine pulsation in the two marks. 'Do me the favour to recall that I told you so, long ago.'

'I recall it.'

'Thank you,' said the Marquis – very sweetly indeed.

'In effect, sir,' pursued the nephew, 'I believe it to be at

once your bad fortune, and my good fortune, that has kept me out of a prison in France here.'

'I do not quite understand,' returned the uncle, sipping his coffee. 'Dare I ask you to explain?'

'I believe that if you were not in disgrace with the Court, and had not been overshadowed by that cloud for years past, a letter *de cachet* would have sent me to some fortress indefinitely.'

'It is possible,' said the uncle, with great calmness. 'For the honour of the family, I could even resolve to incommode you to that extent. Pray excuse me!'

'I perceive that, happily for me, the Reception of the day before yesterday was, as usual, a cold one,' observed the nephew.

'I would not say happily, my friend,' returned the uncle, with refined politeness. 'A good opportunity for consideration, surrounded by the advantages of solitude, might influence your destiny to far greater advantage than you influence it for yourself. But it is useless to discuss the question. I am, as you say, at a disadvantage. These little instruments of correction, these gentle aids to the power and honour of families, are only to be obtained now by interest and importunity. We have lost many privileges; a new philosophy has become the mode; and the assertion of our station, in these days, might cause us real inconvenience. All very bad, very bad!'

'We have so asserted our station, both in the old time

and in the modern time also,' said the nephew, gloomily, 'that I believe our name to be more detested than any name in France.'

'Let us hope so,' said the uncle. 'Detestation of the high is the involuntary homage of the low.'

'There is not,' pursued the nephew, in his former tone, 'a face I can look at, in all this country round about us, which looks at me with any deference on it but the dark deference of fear and slavery.'

'A compliment,' said the Marquis, 'to the grandeur of the family, merited by the manner in which the family has sustained its grandeur. Hah!'

But, when his nephew, leaning an elbow on the table, covered his eyes thoughtfully and dejectedly with his hand, the fine mask looked at him sideways with a stronger concentration of keenness, closeness, and dislike, than was comportable with its wearer's assumption of indifference.

'The dark deference of fear and slavery, my friend,' observed the Marquis, 'will keep the dogs obedient to the whip, as long as this roof,' looking up to it, 'shuts out the sky.'

That might not be so long as the Marquis supposed. If a picture of the château as it was to be a very few years hence could have been shown to him that night, he might have been at a loss to claim his own from the ghastly, fire-charred, plunder-wrecked ruins. As for the roof he vaunted, he might have found *that* shutting out the sky

in a new way – to wit, for ever, from the eyes of the bodies into which its lead was fired, out of the barrels of a hundred thousand muskets.

'Meanwhile,' said the Marquis, 'I will preserve the honour and repose of the family, if you will not.'

'Sir,' said the nephew, 'we have done wrong, and are reaping the fruits of wrong.'

'*We* have done wrong?' repeated the Marquis, with an inquiring smile, and delicately pointing, first to his nephew, then to himself.

'Our family; our honourable family, whose honour is of so much account to both of us, in such different ways. Even in my father's time, we did a world of wrong, injuring every human creature who came between us and our pleasure, whatever it was. This has left me,' said the nephew, 'bound to a system that is frightful to me, responsible for it, but powerless in it; seeking to execute the last request of my dear mother's lips, and obey the last look of my dear mother's eyes, which implored me to have mercy and to redress; and tortured by seeking assistance and power in vain.'

'Seeking them from me, my nephew,' said the Marquis, 'you will for ever seek them in vain, be assured.'

Every fine straight line in the clear whiteness of his face, was cruelly, craftily, and closely compressed, while he stood looking quietly at his nephew, with his snuff-box in his hand. Once again he touched him on the breast, as

though his finger were the fine point of a small sword, with which, in delicate finesse, he ran him through the body, and said,

'My friend, I will die, perpetuating the system under which I have lived. Better to be a rational creature, and accept your natural destiny. But you are lost, Monsieur Charles, I see.'

'This property and France are lost to me,' said the nephew, sadly; 'I renounce them.'

'Are they both yours to renounce? France may be, but is the property?'

'I had no intention, in the words I used, to claim it yet. If it passed to me from you, tomorrow –'

'Which I have the vanity to hope is not probable.'

'– I would abandon it, and live otherwise and elsewhere. It is little to relinquish. What is it but a wilderness of misery and ruin?'

'Hah!' said the Marquis, glancing round the luxurious room.

'To the eye it is fair enough, here; but seen in its integrity, under the sky, and by the daylight, it is a crumbling tower of waste, mismanagement, extortion, debt, mortgage, oppression, hunger, nakedness, and suffering. If it ever becomes mine, it shall be put into some hands better qualified to free it slowly from the weight that drags it down, so that the miserable people who cannot leave it and who have been long wrung to the last point of

endurance, may, in another generation, suffer less; but it is not for me.'

'And you?' said the uncle. 'Forgive my curiosity; do you, under your new philosophy, graciously intend to live?'

'I must do, to live, what others of my countrymen, even with nobility at their backs, may have to do some day – work.'

'In England, for example?'

'Yes. The family honour, sir, is safe from me in this country. The family name can suffer from me in no other, for I bear it in no other.'

The ringing of the bell had caused the adjoining bed-chamber to be lighted. It now shone brightly, through the door of communication. The Marquis looked that way, and listened for the retreating step of his valet.

'England is very attractive to you, seeing how indifferently you have prospered there,' he observed then.

'I have already said, that for my prospering there, I am sensible I may be indebted to you, sir. For the rest, it is my Refuge.'

'They say, those boastful English, that it is the Refuge of many. You know a compatriot who has found a Refuge there? A Doctor?'

'Yes.'

'With a daughter?'

'Yes.'

'Yes,' said the Marquis. 'You are fatigued. Good-night!'

As he bent his head in his most courtly manner, there was a secrecy in his smiling face, and he conveyed an air of mystery to those words, which struck the eyes and ears of his nephew forcibly. At the same time, the thin straight lines of the setting of the eyes, and the thin straight lips, and the markings in the nose, curved with a sarcasm that looked handsomely diabolic.

'Yes,' repeated the Marquis. 'A Doctor with a daughter. Yes. So commences the new philosophy! Good-night! I look to the pleasure of seeing you again in the morning. Good repose! Light Monsieur my nephew to his chamber there! – And burn Monsieur my nephew in his bed, if you will,' he added to himself.

Monsieur the Marquis walked to and fro in his loose chamber-robe, to prepare himself gently for sleep, that hot still night.

He moved from end to end of his voluptuous bedroom, looking again at the scraps of the day's journey that came unbidden into his mind; the slow toil up the hill at sunset, the mill, the prison on the crag, the little village in the hollow, the peasants at the fountain, and the mender of roads with his blue cap pointing out the chain under the carriage. That fountain suggested the Paris fountain, the little bundle lying on the step, the women bending over it, and the tall man with his arms up, crying, 'Dead!'

'I am cool now,' said Monsieur the Marquis, 'and may go to bed.'

So, leaving only one light burning on the large hearth, he let his thin gauze curtains fall around him, and heard the night break its silence with a long sigh as he composed himself to sleep.

For three heavy hours, the stone faces of the château, lion and human, stared blindly at the night. Dead darkness lay on all the landscape, dead darkness added its own hush to the hushing dust on all the roads. In the village, taxers and taxed were fast asleep. Dreaming, perhaps, of banquets, as the starved usually do, and of ease and rest, as the driven slave and the yoked ox may, its lean inhabitants slept soundly, and were fed and freed.

The fountain in the village flowed unseen and unheard, and the fountain at the château dropped unseen and unheard – both melting away, like the minutes that were falling from the spring of Time – through three dark hours. Then, the grey water of both began to be ghostly in the light, and the eyes of the stone faces of the château were opened.

Lighter and lighter, until at last the sun touched the tops of the still trees, and poured its radiance over the hill. In the glow, the water of the château fountain seemed to turn to blood, and the stone faces crimsoned.

Now, the sun was full up, and movement began in the village, and people came forth shivering – chilled, as yet, by the new sweet air. Then began the rarely lightened toil of the day among the village population. Some, to the

fountain; some, to the fields; men and women here, to dig and delve; men and women there, to see to the poor live stock, and lead the bony cows out, to such pasture as could be found by the roadside.

The château awoke later, as became its quality, but awoke gradually and surely. Doors and windows were thrown open, horses in their stables looked round over their shoulders at the light and freshness pouring in at doorways, leaves sparkled and rustled at iron-grated windows, dogs pulled hard at their chains, and reared impatient to be loosed.

All these trivial incidents belonged to the routine of life, and the return of morning. Surely, not so the ringing of the great bell of the château, nor the running up and down the stairs; nor the hurried figures on the terrace; nor the booting and tramping here and there and everywhere, nor the quick saddling of horses and riding away?

What winds conveyed this hurry to the grizzled mender of roads? Had the birds, carrying some grains of it to a distance, dropped one over him as they sow chance seeds? Whether or no, the mender of roads ran, on the sultry morning, as if for his life, down the hill, knee-high in dust, and never stopped till he got to the fountain.

All the people of the village were at the fountain, standing about in their depressed manner, and whispering low, but showing no other emotions than grim curiosity and surprise. Some of the people of the château, and some

of those of the posting-house, and all the taxing authorities, were armed more or less, and were crowded on the
other side of the little street in a purposeless way, that
was highly fraught with nothing. Already, the mender of
roads had penetrated into the midst of a group of fifty
particular friends, and was smiting himself in the breast
with his blue cap. What did all this portend, and what
portended the swift hoisting-up of Monsieur Gabelle
behind a servant on horseback, and the conveying away
of the said Gabelle at a gallop.

It portended that there was one stone face too many,
up at the château.

It lay back on the pillow of Monsieur the Marquis. It
was like a fine mask, suddenly startled, made angry, and
petrified. Driven home into the heart of the stone figure
attached to it, was a knife. Round its hilt was a frill of
paper, on which was scrawled:

'*Drive him fast to his tomb. This, from* JACQUES.'

10

Two Promises

More months, to the number of twelve, had come and gone, and Mr Charles Darnay was established in England as a higher teacher of the French language who was conversant with French literature. He read with young men who could find any leisure and interest for the study of a living tongue spoken all over the world, and he cultivated a taste for its stores of knowledge and fancy. He could write of them, besides, in sound English, and render them into sound English. He was well acquainted, moreover, with the circumstances of his country, and those were of ever-growing interest. So, with great perseverance and untiring industry, he prospered.

A certain portion of his time was passed at Cambridge, where he read with undergraduates as a sort of tolerated smuggler who drove a contraband trade in European languages, instead of conveying Greek and Latin through the Custom-house. The rest of his time he passed in London.

Now, from the days when it was always summer in

Eden, to these days when it is mostly winter in fallen latitudes, the world of a man has invariably gone one way – Charles Darnay's way – the way of the love of a woman.

He had loved Lucie Manette from the hour of his danger. He had never heard a sound so sweet and dear as the sound of her compassionate voice; he had never seen a face so tenderly beautiful, as hers when it was confronted with his own on the edge of the grave that had been dug for him. But, he had not yet spoken to her on the subject; the assassination at the deserted château far away beyond the heaving water and the long, long, dusty roads had been done a year, and he had never yet, by so much as a single spoken word, disclosed to her the state of his heart.

That he had his reasons for this, he knew full well. It was again a summer day when, lately arrived in London from his college occupation, he turned into the quiet corner in Soho, bent on seeking an opportunity of opening his mind to Doctor Manette.

He found the Doctor reading in his arm-chair at a window. The energy which had at once supported him under his old sufferings and aggravated their sharpness, had been gradually restored to him. He was now a very energetic man indeed, with great firmness of purpose, strength of resolution, and vigour of action.

He studied much, slept little, sustained a great deal of

fatigue with ease, and was equally cheerful. To him, now entered Charles Darnay, at sight of whom he laid aside his book and held out his hand.

'Charles Darnay! I rejoice to see you. We have been counting on your return these three or four days past. Mr Stryver and Sydney Carton were both here yesterday, and both made you out to be more than due.'

'I am obliged to them for their interest in the matter,' he answered, a little coldly as to them, though very warmly as to the Doctor. 'Miss Manette –'

'Is well,' said the Doctor, as he stopped short, 'and your return will delight us all. She has gone out on some household matters, but will soon be home.'

'Doctor Manette, I knew she was from home. I took the opportunity of her being from home, to beg to speak to you.'

'Yes?' said the Doctor, with evident constraint. 'Bring your chair here, and speak on.'

He complied as to the chair, but appeared to find the speaking on less easy.

'I have had the happiness, Doctor Manette, of being so intimate here,' so he at length began, 'for some year and a half, that I hope the topic on which I am about to touch may not –'

'Is Lucie the topic?'

'She is.'

'It is hard for me to speak of her, at any time. It is very

hard for me to hear her spoken of in that tone of yours, Charles Darnay.'

'It is a tone of fervent admiration, true homage, and deep love, Doctor Manette!' he said deferentially.

There was blank silence before her father rejoined:

'I believe it. I do you justice; I believe it.'

'Shall I go on, sir?'

Another blank.

'Yes, go on.'

'You anticipate what I would say, though you cannot know how earnestly I say it. Dear Doctor Manette, I love your daughter fondly, dearly, disinterestedly, devotedly. You have loved yourself; let your old love speak for me!'

The Doctor sat with his face turned away, and his eyes bent on the ground. At the last words, he stretched out his hand again, hurriedly, and cried:

'Not that, sir! Let that be! I adjure you, do not recall that!'

His cry was so like a cry of actual pain, that it rang in Charles Darnay's ears long after he had ceased. He motioned with the hand he had extended, and it seemed to be an appeal to Darnay to pause. The latter so received it, and remained silent.

'I ask your pardon,' said the Doctor, in a subdued tone, after some moments. 'I do not doubt your loving Lucie; you may be satisfied of it.'

He turned towards him in his chair, but did not look at him, or raise his eyes.

'Have you spoken to Lucie?'

'No.'

'Nor written?'

'Never.'

'It would be ungenerous to affect not to know that your self-denial is to be referred to your consideration for her father. Her father thanks you.'

He offered his hand; but his eyes did not go with it.

'I know,' said Darnay, respectfully, 'how can I fail to know, Doctor Manette, I who have seen you together from day to day, that between you and Miss Manette there is an affection so unusual, so touching, that it can have few parallels, even in the tenderness between a father and child. I know, Dr Manette, that, mingled with the affection and duty of a daughter who has become a woman, there is, in her heart, towards you, all the love and reliance of infancy itself. I know perfectly well that if you had been restored to her from the world beyond this life, you could hardly be invested, in her sight, with a more sacred character than that in which you are always with her. I know that in loving you she sees and loves her mother at her own age, sees and loves you at my age, loves her mother broken-hearted, loves you through your dreadful trial and in your blessed restoration. I have known this, night and day, since I have known you in your home.'

Her father sat silent, with his face bent down. His breathing was a little quickened; but he repressed all other signs of agitation.

'Dear Doctor Manette, always knowing this, always seeing her and you with this hallowed light about you, I have forborne, and forborne, as long as it was in the nature of man to do it. I have felt, and do even now feel, that to bring my love – even mine – between you, is to touch your history with something not quite so good as itself. But I love her. Heaven is my witness that I love her!'

'I believe it,' answered her father, mournfully. 'I have thought so before now. I believe it.'

'But, do not believe,' said Darnay, upon whose ear the mournful voice struck with a reproachful sound, 'that if my fortune were so cast as that, being one day so happy as to make her my wife, I must at any time put any separation between her and you, I could or would breathe a word of what I now say. If I had any such possibility, even at a remote distance of years, harboured in my thoughts, and hidden in my heart, I could not now touch this honoured hand.'

He laid his own upon it as he spoke.

'No, dear Doctor Manette. I look only to sharing your fortunes, sharing your life and home, and being faithful to you to the death.'

His touch still lingered on her father's hand. Answering the touch for a moment, but not coldly, her father rested his hands upon the arms of his chair, and looked up for

the first time since the beginning of the conference. A struggle was evidently in his face; a struggle with that occasional look which had a tendency in it to dark doubt and dread.

'You speak so feelingly and so manfully, Charles Darnay, that I thank you with all my heart, and will open all my heart – or nearly so. Have you any reason to believe that Lucie loves you?'

'None. As yet, none.'

'Do you seek any promise from me?'

'I do seek that.'

'What is it?'

'I well understand that, without you, I could have no hope. I well understand that, even if Miss Manette held me at this moment in her innocent heart I could retain no place in it against her love for her father.'

'If that be so, do you see what, on the other hand, is involved in it?'

'I understand equally well, that a word from her father in any suitor's favour, would outweigh herself and all the world. For which reason, Doctor Manette,' said Darnay, modestly but firmly, 'I would not ask that word, to save my life.'

'I am sure of it. Charles Darnay, mysteries arise out of close love, as well as out of wide division. My daughter Lucie is, in this one respect, such a mystery to me; I can make no guess at the state of her heart.'

'May I ask, sir, if you think she is –'

'Is sought by any other suitor?'

'It is what I meant to say.'

Her father considered a little before he answered:

'You have seen Mr Carton here, yourself. Mr Stryver is here too, occasionally. If it be at all, it can only be by one of these.'

'Or both,' said Darnay.

'I had not thought of both; I should not think either, likely. You want a promise from me. Tell me what it is.'

'It is, that if Miss Manette should bring to you at any time, on her own part, such a confidence as I have ventured to lay before you, you will bear testimony to what I have said, and to your belief in it. I hope you may be able to think so well of me, as to urge no influence against me.'

'I give the promise,' said the Doctor, 'without any condition. I believe your object to be, purely and truthfully, as you have stated it. If she should ever tell me that you are essential to her perfect happiness, I will give her to you. If there were – Charles Darnay, if there were any fancies, any reasons, any apprehensions, anything whatsoever, new or old, against the man she really loved, they should all be obliterated for her sake. She is everything to me; more to me than suffering, more to me than wrong, more to me – Well! This is idle talk.'

So strange was the way in which he faded into silence, and so strange his fixed look when he had ceased to speak,

that Darnay felt his own hand turn cold in the hand that slowly released and dropped it.

'You said something to me,' said Doctor Manette, breaking into a smile. 'What was it you said to me?'

He was at a loss how to answer, until he remembered having spoken of a condition. Relieved as his mind reverted to that, he answered:

'Your confidence in me ought to be returned with full confidence on my part. My present name, though but slightly changed from my mother's, is not, as you will remember, my own. I wish to tell you what that is, and why I am in England.'

'Stop!' said the Doctor of Beauvais.

'I wish it, that I may the better deserve your confidence, and have no secret from you.'

'Stop! Tell me when I ask you, not now. If your suit should prosper, if Lucie should love you, you shall tell me on your marriage morning. Do you promise?'

'Willingly.'

'Give me your hand. She will be home directly, and it is better she should not see us together tonight. Go! God bless you!'

It was dark when Charles Darnay left him, and it was an hour later and darker when Lucie came home; she hurried into the room alone and was surprised to find his reading-chair empty.

'My father!' she called to him. 'Father dear!'

Nothing was said in answer, but she heard a low hammering sound in his bedroom. Passing lightly across the intermediate room, she looked in at his door and came running back frightened, crying to herself, with her blood all chilled, 'What shall I do!'

Her uncertainty lasted but a moment; she hurried back, and tapped at his door, and softly called to him. The noise ceased at the sound of her voice, and he presently came out to her, and they walked up and down together for a long time.

She came down from her bed, to look at him in his sleep that night. He slept heavily, and his tray of shoemaking tools, and his old unfinished work, were all as usual.

11

A Companion Picture

'Sydney,' said Mr Stryver, on that self-same night, or morning, to his jackal; 'mix another bowl of punch; I have something to say to you.'

Sydney had been making a grand clearance among Mr Stryver's papers before the setting in of the long vacation. The clearance was effected at last; the Stryver arrears were handsomely fetched up; everything was got rid of until November should come with its fogs atmospheric and fogs legal, and bring grist to the mill again.

Sydney was none the livelier and none the soberer for so much application. It had taken a deal of extra wet-towelling to pull him through the night; a correspondingly extra quantity of wine had preceded the towelling; and he was in a very damaged condition.

'Are you mixing that other bowl of punch?' said Stryver.

'I am.'

'Now, look here! I am going to tell you something that will rather surprise you, and that perhaps will make you

think me not quite as shrewd as you usually do think me. I intend to marry.'

'*Do* you?'

'Yes. And not for money. What do you say now?'

'I don't feel disposed to say much. Who is she?'

'Guess.'

'I am not going to guess, at five o'clock in the morning, with my brains frying and sputtering in my head.'

'Well then, I'll tell you,' said Stryver, coming slowly into a sitting posture. 'Sydney, I rather despair of making myself intelligible to you, because you are such a insensible dog.'

'And you,' returned Sydney, busy concocting the punch, 'are such a sensitive and poetical spirit.'

'Come!' rejoined Stryver, laughing boastfully, 'though I don't prefer any claim to being the soul of Romance (for I hope I know better), still I am a tenderer sort of fellow than *you*.'

'You are a luckier, if you mean that.'

'My meaning is that I am a man who cares more to be agreeable, who takes more pains to be agreeable, who knows better how to be agreeable, in a woman's society, than you do.'

'Go on,' said Sydney Carton.

'No; but before I go on,' said Stryver, shaking his head in his bullying way, 'I'll have this out with you. You've been at Dr Manette's house as much as I have, or more

than I have. Why, I have been ashamed of your moroseness there!'

'It should be very beneficial to a man in your practice at the bar, to be ashamed of anything,' returned Sydney; 'you ought to be much obliged to me.'

'You shall not get off in that way,' rejoined Stryver, shouldering the rejoinder at him; 'no, Sydney, it's my duty to tell you that you are a de-vilish ill-conditioned fellow in that sort of society.'

Sydney drank a bumper of the punch he had made, and laughed.

'Look at me?' said Stryver, squaring himself; 'I have less need to make myself agreeable than you have, being more independent in circumstances. Why do I do it?'

'I never saw you do it yet,' muttered Carton.

'I do it because it's politic. And look at me! I get on.'

'You don't get on with your account of your matrimonial intentions,' answered Carton, with a careless air; 'I wish you would keep to that. As to me – will you never understand that I am incorrigible?'

'You have no business to be incorrigible,' was his friend's answer, delivered in no very soothing tone.

'I have no business to be, at all, that I know of,' said Sydney Carton. 'Who is the lady?'

'Now, don't let my announcement of the name make you uncomfortable, Sydney,' said Mr Stryver, 'because I know you don't mean half you say; and if you meant it

all, it would be of no importance. I make this little preface, because you once mentioned the young lady to me in slighting terms.'

'I did?'

'Certainly; and in these chambers.'

Sydney Carton drank his punch and looked at his complacent friend.

'You made mention of the young lady as a golden-haired doll. The young lady is Miss Manette. If you had been a fellow of any sensitiveness or delicacy of feeling in that kind of way, Sydney, I might have been a little resentful of your employing such a designation; but you are not.'

Sydney Carton drank the punch at a great rate; drank it by bumpers, looking at his friend.

'Now you know all about it, Syd,' said Mr Stryver. 'I don't care about fortune: she is a charming creature, and I have made up my mind to please myself. She will have in me a man already pretty well off, and a rapidly rising man, and a man of some distinction: it is a piece of good fortune for her, but she is worthy of good fortune. Are you astonished?'

Carton, still drinking the punch, rejoined, 'Why should I be astonished?'

'You approve?'

Carton, still drinking the punch, rejoined, 'Why should I not approve?'

'Well!' said his friend Stryver, 'you take it more easily than I fancied you would. Yes, Sydney, I have had enough of this style of life, with no other as a change from it; I feel that it is a pleasant thing for a man to have a home when he feels inclined to go to it and I feel that Miss Manette will tell well in any station, and will always do me credit. And now, Sydney, old boy, I want to say a word to *you* about *your* prospects. You are in a bad way, you know; you really are in a bad way. You don't know the value of money, you live hard, you'll knock up one of these days, and be ill and poor; you really ought to think about a nurse.'

The prosperous patronage with which he said it, made him look twice as big as he was, and four times as offensive.

'Now, let me recommend you,' pursued Stryver, 'to look it in the face. Marry. Provide somebody to take care of you. Find out somebody. Find out some respectable woman with a little property – somebody in the landlady way, or lodging-letting way – and marry her, against a rainy day. That's the kind of thing for *you*. Now think of it, Sydney.'

'I'll think of it,' said Sydney.

12

The Fellow of Delicacy

M r Stryver having made up his mind to that magnanimous bestowal of good fortune on the Doctor's
daughter, resolved to make her happiness known to her
before he left town for the Long Vacation. After some mental
debating of the point, he came to the conclusion that it
would be as well to get all the preliminaries done with, and
they could then arrange at their leisure whether he should
give her his hand a week or two before Michaelmas Term,
or in the little Christmas vacation between it and Hilary.

Accordingly, Mr Stryver inaugurated the Long Vacation
with a formal proposal to take Miss Manette to Vauxhall
Gardens; that failing, to Ranelagh; that unaccountably
failing too, it behoved him to present himself in Soho,
and there declare his noble mind.

Towards Soho, therefore, Mr Stryver shouldered his
way from the Temple, while the bloom of the Long Vacation's infancy was still upon it.

His way taking him past Tellson's, and he both banking
at Tellson's and knowing Mr Lorry as the intimate friend

of the Manettes, it entered Mr Stryver's mind to enter the bank, and reveal to Mr Lorry the brightness of the Soho horizon. So, he pushed open the door with the weak rattle in its throat, stumbled down the two steps, got past the two ancient cashiers, and shouldered himself into the musty back closet where Mr Lorry sat at great books ruled for figures, with perpendicular iron bars to his window as if that were ruled for figures too, and everything under the clouds were a sum.

'Halloa!' said Mr Stryver. 'How do you do? I hope you are well?'

The discreet Mr Lorry said, in a sample tone of the voice he would recommend under the circumstances, 'How do you do, Mr Stryver? How do you do, sir?' and shook hands. 'Can I do anything for you?'

'Why, no, thank you; this is a private visit to yourself, Mr Lorry; I have come for a private word.'

'Oh indeed!' said Mr Lorry, bending down his ear, while his eye strayed to the House afar off.

'I am going,' said Mr Stryver, leaning his arms confidently on the desk, 'I am going to make an offer of myself in marriage to your agreeable little friend, Miss Manette, Mr Lorry.'

'Oh dear me!' cried Mr Lorry, rubbing his chin, and looking at his visitor dubiously.

'Oh dear me, sir?' repeated Stryver, drawing back. 'Oh dear you, sir? What may your meaning be, Mr Lorry?'

'My meaning,' answered the man of business, 'is, of course, friendly and appreciative, and that it does you the greatest credit, and – in short, my meaning is everything you could desire. But –' Mr Lorry paused, and shook his head at him in the oddest manner, as if he were compelled against his will to add, internally, 'you know there really is so much too much of you!'

'Well!' said Stryver, slapping the desk with his contentious hand, opening his eyes wider, and taking a long breath, 'if I understand you, Mr Lorry, I'll be hanged!'

Mr Lorry adjusted his little wig at both ears as a means towards the end, and bit the feather of a pen.

'D—n it all, sir!' said Stryver, staring at him, 'am I not eligible?'

'Oh dear yes! Yes. Oh yes, you're eligible!' said Mr Lorry.

'Am I not prosperous?' asked Stryver.

'Oh! if you come to prosperous, you are prosperous,' said Mr Lorry.

'Then what on earth is your meaning, Mr Lorry?' demanded Stryver, perceptibly crestfallen.

'Well! I – Were you going there now?' asked Mr Lorry.

'Straight!' said Stryver, with a plump of his fist on the desk.

'Then I think I wouldn't, if I was you.'

'Why?' said Stryver. 'Now, I'll put you in a corner,' forensically shaking a forefinger at him. 'You are a man

of business and bound to have a reason. State your reason. Why wouldn't you go?'

'Because,' said Mr Lorry, 'I wouldn't go on such an object without having some cause to believe that I should succeed.'

'D—n ME!' cried Stryver, 'but this beats everything.'

Mr Lorry glanced at the distant House, and glanced at the angry Stryver.

'Here's a man of business – a man of years – a man of experience – *in* a Bank,' said Stryver; 'and having summed up three leading reasons for complete success, he says there's no reason at all!'

'When I speak of success, I speak of success with the young lady. The young lady, my good sir,' said Mr Lorry, mildly tapping the Stryver arm, 'goes before all.'

'Then you mean to tell me, Mr Lorry,' said Stryver, squaring his elbows, 'that it is your deliberate opinion that the young lady at present in question is a mincing Fool?'

'Not exactly so. I mean to tell you, Mr Stryver,' said Mr Lorry, reddening, 'that I will hear no disrespectful word of that young lady from any lips; and that if I knew any man whose taste was so coarse, and whose temper was so over-bearing, that he could not restrain himself from speaking disrespectfully of that young lady at this desk, not even Tellson's should prevent my giving him a piece of my mind.'

The necessity of being angry in a suppressed tone had

put Mr Stryver's blood-vessels into a dangerous state when it was his turn to be angry; Mr Lorry's veins, methodical as their courses could usually be, were in no better state now it was his turn.

'That is what I mean to tell you, sir,' said Mr Lorry.

Mr Stryver sucked the end of a ruler for a little while, and then stood hitting a tune out of his teeth with it, which probably gave him the toothache. He broke the awkward silence by saying:

'This is something new to me, Mr Lorry. You deliberately advise me not to go up to Soho and offer myself – *my*self, Stryver of the King's Bench bar?'

'Now understand me,' pursued Mr Lorry. 'As an old fellow, who has carried Miss Manette in his arms, who is the trusted friend of Miss Manette and of her father too, and who has a great affection for them both, I have spoken. The confidence is not of my seeking, recollect. Now, you think I may not be right?'

'Not I!' said Stryver, whistling. 'I can't undertake to find third parties in common sense; I can only find it for myself. I suppose sense in certain quarters; you suppose mincing bread-and-butter nonsense. It's new to me, but you are right, I dare say.'

'What I suppose, Mr Stryver, I claim to characterise for myself. And understand me, sir,' said Mr Lorry, quickly flushing again, 'I will not – not even at Tellson's – have it characterised for me by any gentleman breathing.'

'There! I beg your pardon!' said Stryver.

'Granted. Thank you. Well, Mr Stryver, I was about to say: – it might be painful to you to find yourself mistaken, it might be painful to Doctor Manette to have the task of being explicit with you, it might be very painful to Miss Manette to have the task of being explicit with you. You know the terms upon which I have the honour and happiness to stand with the family. If you please, I will undertake to correct my advice by the exercise of a little new observation and judgment expressly brought to bear upon it. If you should then be dissatisfied with it, you can but test its soundness for yourself; if, on the other hand, you should be satisfied with it, it may spare all sides what is best spared. What do you say?'

'How long would you keep me in town?'

'Oh! It is only a question of a few hours. I could go to Soho in the evening, and come to your chambers afterwards.'

'Then I say yes,' said Stryver: 'I won't go up there now.'

Then Mr Stryver turned and burst out of the Bank, causing such a concussion of air on his passage through, that to stand up against it bowing behind the two counters, required the utmost remaining strength of the two ancient clerks.

The barrister was keen enough to divine that the banker would not have gone so far in his expression of opinion on any less solid ground than moral certainty. Unprepared

as he was for the large pill he had to swallow, he got it down. 'And now,' said Mr Stryver, shaking his forensic forefinger at the Temple in general, when it was down, 'my way out of this, is, to put you all in the wrong.'

Accordingly, when Mr Lorry called that night as late as ten o'clock, Mr Stryver, among a quantity of books and papers littered out for the purpose, seemed to have nothing less on his mind than the subject of the morning. He even showed surprise when he saw Mr Lorry, and was altogether in an absent and preoccupied state.

'Well!' said that good-natured emissary, after a full half-hour of bootless attempts to bring him round to the question. 'I have been to Soho.'

'To Soho?' repeated Mr Stryver, coldly. 'Oh, to be sure! What am I thinking of!'

'And I have no doubt,' said Mr Lorry, 'that I was right in the conversation we had. My opinion is confirmed, and I reiterate my advice.'

'I assure you,' returned Mr Stryver, in the friendliest way, 'that I am sorry for it on your account, and sorry for it on the poor father's account. I know this must always be a sore subject with the family; let us say no more about it.'

'I don't understand you,' said Mr Lorry.

'I dare say not,' rejoined Stryver, nodding his head in a smoothing and final way; 'no matter, no matter.'

'But it does matter,' Mr Lorry urged.

'No it doesn't; I assure you it doesn't. Having supposed that there was sense where there is no sense, and a laudable ambition where there is not a laudable ambition, I am well out of my mistake, and no harm is done. Young women have committed similar follies often before, and have repented them in poverty and obscurity often before. I have not proposed to the young lady, and, between ourselves, I am by no means certain, on reflection, that I ever should have committed myself to that extent. Now, pray say no more about it. I tell you, I regret it on account of others, but I am satisfied on my own account. And I am really very much obliged to you for allowing me to sound you, and for giving me your advice; you were right, it never would have done.'

Mr Lorry was so taken aback, that he looked quite stupidly at Mr Stryver shouldering him towards the door, with an appearance of showering generosity, forbearance, and goodwill, on his erring head. 'Make the best of it, my dear sir,' said Stryver; 'say no more about it; thank you again for allowing me to sound you; good-night!'

Mr Lorry was out in the night, before he knew where he was. Mr Stryver was lying back on his sofa, winking at his ceiling.

13

The Fellow of No Delicacy

If Sydney Carton ever shone anywhere, he certainly never shone in the house of Doctor Manette. He had been there often, during a whole year, and had always been the same moody and morose lounger there. When he cared to talk, he talked well; but, the cloud of caring for nothing, which overshadowed him with such a fatal darkness, was very rarely pierced by the light within him.

And yet he did care something for the streets that environed that house, and for the senseless stones that made their pavements. Many a night he vaguely and unhappily wandered there, when wine had brought no transitory gladness to him; many a dreary daybreak revealed his solitary figure lingering there, and still lingering there when the first beams of the sun brought into strong relief, removed beauties of architecture in spires of churches and lofty buildings, as perhaps the quiet time brought some sense of better things, else forgotten and unattainable, into his mind.

On a day in August, when Mr Stryver had carried his

delicacy into Devonshire, and when the sight and scent of flowers in the City streets had some waifs of goodness in them for the worst, of health for the sickliest, and of youth for the oldest, Sydney's feet still trod those stones. From being irresolute and purposeless, his feet became animated by an intention, and, in the working out of that intention, they took him to the Doctor's door.

He was shown upstairs, and found Lucie at her work, alone. She had never been quite at her ease with him, and received him with some little embarrassment as he seated himself near her table. But, looking up at his face in the interchange of the first few common-places, she observed a change in it.

'I fear you are not well, Mr Carton!'

'No. But the life I lead, Miss Manette, is not conducive to health.'

'Is it not – forgive me; I have begun the question on my lips – a pity to live no better life?'

'God knows it is a shame!'

'Then why not change it?'

Looking gently at him again, she was surprised and saddened to see that there were tears in his eyes.

'It is too late for that. I shall never be better than I am.'

He leaned an elbow on her table, and covered his eyes with his hand.

'Pray forgive me, Miss Manette. I break down before

the knowledge of what I want to say to you. Will you hear me?'

'If it will do you any good, Mr Carton, if it would make you happier, it would make me very glad!'

'God bless you for your sweet compassion!'

He unshaded his face after a little while, and spoke steadily.

'Don't be afraid to hear me. I am like one who died young. All my life might have been.'

'No, Mr Carton. I am sure that the best part of it might still be; I am sure that you might be much, much worthier of yourself.'

'Say of you, Miss Manette, and although I know better I shall never forget it!'

She was pale and trembling. He came to her relief with a fixed despair of himself which made the interview unlike any other that could have been holden.

'If it has been possible, Miss Manette, that you could have returned the love of the man you see before you – he would have been conscious this day and hour, in spite of his happiness, that he would bring you to misery, bring you to sorrow and repentance, blight you, disgrace you, pull you down with him. I know very well that you can have no tenderness for me; I ask for none; I am even thankful that it cannot be.'

'Without it, can I not save you, Mr Carton? Can I not recall you – forgive me again! – to a better course? I know

this is a confidence,' she modestly said, after a little hesitation, and in earnest tears, 'I know you would say this to no one else. Can I turn it to no good account for yourself, Mr Carton?'

He shook his head.

'To none. No, Miss Manette, to none. I wish you to know that you have been the last dream of my soul. In my degradation I have not been so degraded but that the sight of you with your father, and of this home made such a home by you, has stirred old shadows that I thought had died out of me. I have had unformed ideas of striving afresh, beginning anew, shaking off sloth and sensuality, and fighting out the abandoned fight. A dream, all a dream, that ends in nothing, and leaves the sleeper where he lay down, but I wish you to know that you inspired it.'

'Will nothing of it remain? O Mr Carton, think again! Try again!'

'No, Miss Manette; all through it, I have known myself to be quite undeserving. And yet I have had the weakness, and have still the weakness, to wish you to know with what a sudden mastery you kindled me, heap of ashes that I am, into fire.'

'Since it is my misfortune, Mr Carton, to have made you more unhappy than you were before you knew me –'

'Don't say that, Miss Manette, for you would have reclaimed me, if anything could. You will not be the cause of my becoming worse.'

'Since the state of your mind that you describe, is, at all events, attributable to some influence of mine, can I use no influence to serve you? Have I no power for good, with you, at all?'

'The utmost good that I am capable of now, Miss Manette, I have come here to realise. Let me carry through the rest of my misdirected life, the remembrance that I opened my heart to you, last of all the world; and that there was something left in me at this time which you could deplore and pity. I draw fast to an end. Will you let me believe, when I recall this day, that the last confidence of my life was reposed in your pure and innocent breast, and that it lies there alone, and will be shared by no one?'

'If that will be a consolation to you, yes.'

'Thank you. And again, God bless you.'

He put her hand to his lips, and moved towards the door.

'Be under no apprehension, Miss Manette, of my ever resuming this conversation by so much as a passing word. I will never refer to it again. In the hour of my death, I shall hold sacred the one good remembrance that my last avowal of myself was made to you, and that my name, and faults, and miseries were gently carried in your heart.'

He was so unlike what he had ever shown himself to be, and it was so sad to think how much he had thrown away, and how much he every day kept down and perverted,

that Lucie Manette wept mournfully for him as he stood looking back at her.

'Be comforted!' he said, 'I am not worth such feeling, Miss Manette. But, within myself, I shall always be, towards you, what I am now, though outwardly I shall be what you have heretofore seen me. The last supplication but one I make to you, is, that you will believe this of me.'

'I will, Mr Carton.'

'My last supplication of all, is this; and with it, I will relieve you of a visitor with whom I well know you have nothing in unison, and between whom and you there is an impassable space. For you, and for any dear to you, I would do anything. If my career were of that better kind that there was any opportunity or capacity of sacrifice in it, I would embrace any sacrifice for you and for those dear to you. Try to hold me in your mind, at some quiet times, as ardent and sincere in this one thing. O Miss Manette, when the little picture of a happy father's face looks up in yours, when you see your own bright beauty springing up anew at your feet, think now and then that there is a man who would give his life, to keep a life you love beside you!'

He said, 'Farewell!' said 'A last God bless you!' and left her.

14

The Honest Tradesman

To the eyes of Mr Jeremiah Cruncher, sitting on his stool in Fleet-street with his grisly urchin beside him, a vast number and variety of objects in movement were every day presented. Who could sit upon anything in Fleet-street during the busy hours of the day, and not be dazed and deafened by two immense processions, one ever tending westward with the sun, the other ever tending eastward from the sun, both ever tending to the plains beyond the range of red and purple where the sun goes down!

Time was, when a poet sat upon a stool in a public place, and mused in the sight of men. Mr Cruncher, sitting on a stool in a public place, but not being a poet, mused as little as possible, and looked about him.

It fell out that he was thus engaged in a season when his affairs in general were so unprosperous as to awaken a strong suspicion in his breast that Mrs Cruncher must have been 'flopping' in some pointed manner, when an unusual concourse pouring down Fleet Street westward,

attracted his attention. Looking that way, Mr Cruncher made out that some kind of funeral was coming along, and that there was popular objection to this funeral, which engendered uproar.

'Young Jerry,' said Mr Cruncher, turning to his offspring, 'it's a buryin'.'

'Hooroar, father!' cried Young Jerry.

'What d'ye mean? What are you hooroaring at? What do you want to conwey to your own father, you young Rip?' said Mr Cruncher, surveying him. 'Don't let me hear no more of you, or you shall feel some more of me. D'ye hear?'

'I warn't doing no harm,' Young Jerry protested.

'Drop it then,' said Mr Cruncher; 'I won't have none of *your* no harms. Get atop of that there seat, and look at the crowd.'

His son obeyed, and the crowd approached; they were bawling and hissing round a dingy hearse and dingy mourning coach, in which mourning coach there was only one mourner, dressed in the dingy trappings that were considered essential to the dignity of the position.

Funerals had at all times a remarkable attraction for Mr Cruncher. Naturally, therefore, a funeral with this uncommon attendance excited him greatly, and he asked of the first man who ran against him:

'What is it, brother? What's it about?'

'*I* don't know,' returned the man, clapping his hands

to his mouth nevertheless, and vociferating in a surprising heat and with the greatest ardour, 'Spies! Yaha! Tst, tst! Spi-ies!'

At length, a person better informed on the merits of the case, tumbled against him, and from this person he learned that the funeral was the funeral of one Roger Cly.

'Was He a spy?' asked Mr Cruncher.

'Old Bailey spy,' returned his informant. 'Yaha! Tst! Yah! Old Bailey Spi-i-es!'

'Why, to be sure!' exclaimed Jerry, recalling the Trial at which he had assisted. 'I've seen him. Dead, is he?'

'Dead as mutton,' returned the other, 'and can't be too dead. Have 'em out, there! Spies! Pull 'em out, there! Spies!'

The idea was so acceptable in the prevalent absence of any idea, that the crowd mobbed the two vehicles so closely that they came to a stop. On the crowd's opening the coach doors, the one mourner scuffled out of himself and was in their hands for a moment; but he was so alert, and made such good use of his time, that in another moment he was scouring away up a by-street, after shedding his cloak, hat, long hatband, white pocket-handkerchief, and other symbolical tears.

These, the people tore to pieces and scattered far and wide with great enjoyment, while the tradesmen hurriedly shut up their shops; for a crowd in those times stopped

at nothing, and was a monster much dreaded. They had already got the length of opening the hearse to take the coffin out, when some brighter genius proposed instead, its being escorted to its destination amidst general rejoicing. Among the first of these volunteers was Jerry Cruncher himself.

The remodelled procession started, with a chimney-sweep driving the hearse and with a pieman, also attended by his cabinet minister, driving the mourning coach. A bear-leader, a popular street character of the time, was impressed as an additional ornament, before the cavalcade had gone far down the Strand; and his bear, who was black and very mangy, gave quite an Undertaking air to that part of the procession in which he walked.

The disorderly procession went its way. Its destination was the old church of Saint Pancras, far off in the fields. It got there in course of time; insisted on pouring into the burial-ground; finally, accomplished the interment of the deceased Roger Cly in its own way, and highly to its own satisfaction.

The dead man disposed of, and the crowd being under the necessity of providing some other entertainment for itself, another brighter genius conceived the humour of impeaching casual passers-by, as Old Bailey spies, and wreaking vengeance on them. Chase was given to some score of inoffensive persons who had never been near the Old Bailey in their lives, and they were roughly hustled

and maltreated. At last, after several hours, when sundry summer-houses had been pulled down, and some area-railings had been torn up, to arm the more belligerent spirits, a rumour got about that the Guards were coming. Before this rumour, the crowd gradually melted away, and perhaps the Guards came, and perhaps they never came, and this was the usual progress of a mob.

Mr Cruncher did not assist at the closing sports, but had remained behind in the churchyard, to confer and condole with the undertakers.

'Jerry,' said Mr Cruncher, apostrophising himself in his usual way, 'you see that there Cly that day, and you see with your own eyes that he was a young 'un and a straight made 'un.'

Having ruminated a little longer, he turned himself about, that he might appear, before the hour of closing, on his station at Tellson's. Whether his meditations on mortality had touched his liver, or whether his general health had been previously at all amiss, or whether he desired to show a little attention to an eminent man, is not so much to the purpose, as that he made a short call upon his medical adviser on his way back.

Young Jerry relieved his father with dutiful interest, and reported No job in his absence. The bank closed, the ancient clerks came out, the usual watch was set, and Mr Cruncher and his son went home to tea.

'Now, I tell you where it is!' said Mr Cruncher to his

wife, on entering. 'If, as a honest tradesman, my wenturs goes wrong tonight, I shall make sure that you've been praying again me, and I shall work you for it just the same as if I seen you do it.'

The dejected Mrs Cruncher shook her head.

'Why, you're at it afore my face!' said Mr Cruncher.

'I am saying nothing.'

'Well, then; don't meditate nothing. You might as well flop as meditate. You may as well go again me one way as another. Drop it altogether.'

'Yes, Jerry.'

Mr Cruncher had no particular meaning in these sulky corroborations, but made use of them, as people not unfrequently do, to express general ironical dissatisfaction.

'You are going out tonight?' asked his decent wife, when he took another bite.

'Yes, I am.'

'May I go with you, father?' asked his son, briskly.

'No, you mayn't. I'm a going fishing.'

'Shall you bring any fish home, father?'

'If I don't, you'll have short commons, tomorrow,' returned that gentleman, shaking his head.

He devoted himself during the remainder of the evening to keeping a most vigilant watch on Mrs Cruncher, and sullenly holding her in conversation that she might be prevented from meditating any petitions to his disadvantage. With this view, he urged his son to hold her in

conversation also, and led the unfortunate woman a hard life by dwelling on any causes of complaint he could bring against her. The devoutest person could have rendered no greater homage to the efficacy of an honest prayer than he did in this distrust of his wife.

'And mind you!' said Mr Cruncher. 'No games tomorrow! If I, as a honest tradesman, succeed in providing a jinte of meat or two, none of your not touching of it, and sticking to bread.'

Then he began grumbling again:

'With your flying into the face of your own wittles and drink! Look at your boy: he *is* you'rn, ain't he? He's as thin as a lath. Do you call yourself a mother, and not know that a mother's first duty is to blow her boy out?'

Thus the evening wore away with the Cruncher family, until Young Jerry was ordered to bed, and his mother, laid under similar injunctions, obeyed them. Mr Cruncher beguiled the earlier watches of the night with solitary pipes, and did not start upon his excursion until nearly one o'clock. Towards that small and ghostly hour, he rose up from his chair, took a key out of his pocket, opened a locked cupboard, and brought forth a sack, a crowbar of convenient size, a rope and chain, and other fishing tackle of that nature. Disposing these articles about him in skilful manner, he bestowed a parting defiance on Mrs Cruncher, extinguished the light, and went out.

Young Jerry, who had only made a feint of undressing

when he went to bed, was not long after his father. Under cover of the darkness he followed down the stairs, followed out into the streets.

Impelled by a laudable ambition to study the art and mystery of his father's honest calling, Young Jerry, keeping as close to house-fronts, walls, and doorways, as his eyes were close to one another, held his honoured parent in view. The honoured parent steering Northward, had not gone far, when he was joined by another, and the two trudged on together.

Within half an hour from the first starting, they were beyond the winking lamps, and the more than winking watchmen, and were out upon a lonely road. Another fisherman was picked up here – and that so silently, that if Young Jerry had been superstitious, he might have supposed the second follower of the gentle craft to have, all of a sudden, split himself in two.

The three went on, and Young Jerry went on, until the three stopped under a bank overhanging the road. Upon the top of the bank was a low brick wall, surmounted by an iron railing. In the shadow of bank and wall the three turned out of the road, and up a blind lane. Crouching down in a corner, peeping up the lane, the next object that Young Jerry saw, was the form of his honoured parent, pretty well defined against a watery and clouded moon, nimbly scaling an iron gate. He was soon over, and then the second fisherman got over, and then the third.

It was now Young Jerry's turn to approach the gate: which he did, holding his breath. Crouching down again in a corner there, and looking in, he made out the three fishermen creeping through some rank grass, and all the gravestones in the churchyard looking on like ghosts in white, while the church tower itself looked on like the ghost of a monstrous giant.

They fished with a spade, at first. Presently the honoured parent appeared to be adjusting some instrument like a great corkscrew. Whatever tools they worked with, they worked hard, until the awful striking of the church clock so terrified Young Jerry, that he made off, with his hair as stiff as his father's.

But, his long-cherished desire to know more about these matters, not only stopped him in his running away, but lured him back again. They were still fishing persever-ingly, when he peeped in at the gate for the second time. There was a screwing and complaining sound down below, and their bent figures were strained, as if by a weight. By slow degrees the weight broke away the earth upon it, and came to the surface. Young Jerry very well knew what it would be; but, when he saw it, and saw his honoured parent about to wrench it open, he was so frightened, being new to the sight, that he made off again, and never stopped until he had run a mile or more.

He had a strong idea that the coffin he had seen was running after him; and, pictured as hopping on behind

him, bolt upright, upon its narrow end, always on the point of overtaking him and hopping on at his side. It got into shadows on the road, and lay cunningly on its back to trip him up. All this time it was incessantly hopping on behind and gaining on him, so that when the boy got to his own door he had reason for being half dead. And even then it would not leave him, but followed him up-stairs with a bump on every stair, scrambled into bed with him, and bumped down, dead and heavy, on his breast when he fell asleep.

From his oppressed slumber, Young Jerry in his closet was awakened after daybreak and before sunrise, by the presence of his father in the family room. Something had gone wrong with him; at least, so Young Jerry inferred, from the circumstance of his holding Mrs Cruncher by the ears, and knocking the back of her head against the head board of the bed.

'I told you I would,' said Mr Cruncher, 'and I did. You oppose yourself to the profit of the business, and me and my partners suffer. You was to honour and obey; why the devil don't you?'

'I try to be a good wife, Jerry,' the poor woman protested.

'Is it being a good wife to oppose your husband's business? Is it obeying your husband to disobey him on the wital subject of his business?'

'You hadn't taken to the dreadful business then, Jerry.'

'It's enough for you,' retorted Mr Cruncher, 'to be the wife of a honest tradesman, and not to occupy your female mind with calculations when he took to his trade or when he didn't. You have no more nat'ral sense of duty than the bed of this here Thames river has of a pile, and similarly it must be knocked into you.'

There was no fish for breakfast next morning, and not much of anything else. Mr Cruncher was out of spirits, and out of temper, and kept an iron pot-lid by him as a projectile for the correction of Mrs Cruncher, in case he should observe any symptoms of her saying Grace. He was brushed and washed at the usual hour, and set off with his son to pursue his ostensible calling.

Young Jerry, walking with the stool under his arm at his father's side along sunny and crowded Fleet-street, was a very different Young Jerry from him of the previous night, running home through darkness and solitude from his grim pursuer. His cunning was fresh with the day, and his qualms were gone with the night.

'Father,' said Young Jerry, as they walked along: taking care to keep at arm's length and to have the stool well between them: 'what's a Resurrection-Man?'

Mr Cruncher came to a stop on the pavement before he answered, 'How should I know?'

'I thought you knowed everything, father,' said the artless boy.

'Hem! Well,' returned Mr Cruncher, going on again,

and lifting off his hat to give his spikes free play, 'he's a tradesman.'

'What's his goods, father?' asked the brisk Young Jerry.

'His goods,' said Mr Cruncher, after turning it over in his mind, 'is a branch of Scientific goods.'

'Persons' bodies, ain't it, father?' asked the lively boy.

'I believe it is something of that sort,' said Mr Cruncher.

'Oh, father, I should so like to be a Resurrection-Man when I'm quite growed up!'

Mr Cruncher was soothed, but shook his head in a dubious and moral way. 'It depends upon how you dewelop your talents. Be careful to dewelop your talents, and never to say no more than you can help to nobody, and there's no telling at the present time what you may not come to be fit for.' As Young Jerry, thus encouraged, went on a few yards in advance, to plant the stool in the shadow of the Bar, Mr Cruncher added to himself: 'Jerry, you honest tradesman, there's hopes wot that boy will yet be a blessing to you, and a recompense to you for his mother!'

15
Knitting

There had been earlier drinking than usual in the wine-shop of Monsieur Defarge. He sold a very thin wine at the best of times, but it would seem to have been an unusually thin wine that he sold at this time.

It had begun on Monday, and here was Wednesday come. There had been more of early brooding than drinking; for, many men had listened and whispered and slunk about there from the time of the opening of the door, who could not have laid a piece of money on the counter to save their souls. These were to the full as interested in the place, however, as if they could have commanded whole barrels of wine; and they glided from seat to seat, and from corner to corner, swallowing talk in lieu of drink, with greedy looks.

Notwithstanding an unusual flow of company, the master of the wine-shop was not visible. He was not missed; for, nobody who crossed the threshold looked for him, nobody asked for him, nobody wondered to see only Madame Defarge in her seat, presiding over the distribution of wine.

A suspended interest and a prevalent absence of mind, were perhaps observed by the spies who looked in at the wine-shop, as they looked in at every place, high and low, from the king's palace to the criminal's gaol. Games at cards languished, drinkers drew figures on the tables with spilt drops of wine, Madame Defarge herself picked out the pattern on her sleeve with her toothpick, and saw and heard something inaudible and invisible a long way off.

Thus, Saint Antoine in this vinous feature of his, until midday. It was high noontide, when two dusty men passed through his streets and under his swinging lamps: of whom, one was Monsieur Defarge: the other a mender of roads in a blue cap. All adust and athirst, the two entered the wine-shop. Their arrival had lighted a kind of fire in the breast of Saint Antoine, fast spreading as they came along, which stirred and flickered in flames of faces at most doors and windows.

'Good-day, gentlemen!' said Monsieur Defarge.

It may have been a signal for loosening the general tongue. It elicited an answering chorus of 'Good-day!'

It is bad weather, gentlemen,' said Defarge, shaking his head.

Upon which, every man looked at his neighbour, and then all cast down their eyes and sat silent. Except one man, who got up and went out.

'My wife,' said Defarge aloud, addressing Madame

Defarge; 'I have travelled certain leagues with this good mender of roads, called Jacques. Give him to drink, my wife!'

A second man got up and went out. Madame Defarge set wine before the mender of roads called Jacques, who doffed his blue cap to the company, and drank. In the breast of his blouse he carried some coarse dark bread; he ate of this between whiles, and sat munching and drinking near Madame Defarge's counter. A third man got up and went out.

Defarge looked at no one present, and no one now looked at him; not even Madame Defarge, who had taken up her knitting, and was at work.

'Have you finished your repast, friend?' he asked, in due season.

'Yes, thank you.'

'Come, then! You shall see the apartment that I told you you could occupy. It will suit you to a marvel.'

Out of the wine-shop into the street, out of the street into a court-yard, out of the court-yard up a steep staircase, out of the staircase into a garret, – formerly the garret where a white-haired man sat on a low bench, stooping forward and very busy, making shoes.

No white-haired man was there now; but, the three men were there who had gone out of the wine-shop singly.

Defarge closed the door carefully, and spoke in a subdued voice:

'Jacques One, Jacques Two, Jacques Three! This is the witness encountered by appointment, by me, Jacques Four. He will tell you all. Speak, Jacques Five!'

'I saw him then, messieurs,' began the mender of roads, 'a year ago this running summer, underneath the carriage of the Marquis, hanging by the chain.'

Jacques One struck in, and asked if he had ever seen the man before?

'Never,' answered the mender of roads.

Jacques Three demanded how he afterwards recognised him then?

'By his tall figure,' said the mender of roads, softly, and with his finger at his nose. 'When Monsieur the Marquis demands that evening, "Say, what is he like?" I make response, "Tall as a spectre."'

'You should have said, short as a dwarf,' returned Jacques Two.

'But what did I know? The deed was not then accomplished, neither did he confide in me. Monsieur the Marquis indicates me with his finger, standing near our little fountain, and says, "To me! Bring that rascal!" My faith, messieurs, I offer nothing.'

'He is right there, Jacques,' murmured Defarge, to him who had interrupted. 'Go on!'

'Good!' said the mender of roads, with an air of mystery. 'The tall man is lost, and he is sought – how many months? Nine, ten, eleven?'

'No matter, the number,' said Defarge. 'He is well hidden, but at last he is unluckily found. Go on!'

'I am again at work upon the hill-side, when I raise my eyes, and see coming over the hill six soldiers. In the midst of them is a tall man with his arms bound – tied to his sides. I stand aside, messieurs, by my heap of stones, to see the soldiers and their prisoner pass and at first, as they approach, I see no more than that they are six soldiers with a tall man bound, and that they are almost black to my sight – except on the side of the sun going to bed, where they have a red edge, messieurs. But when they advance quite near to me, I recognise the tall man, and he recognises me. I do not show the soldiers that I recognise the tall man; he does not show the soldiers that he recognises me; we do it, and we know it, with our eyes. "Come on!" says the chief of that company, pointing to the village, "bring him fast to his tomb!" and they bring him faster. I follow. His arms are swelled because of being bound so tight, and he is lame. Because he is lame, and consequently slow, they drive him with their guns. As they descend the hill like madmen running a race, he falls. They laugh and pick him up again. They bring him into the village; all the village runs to look; they take him past the mill, and up to the prison; all the village sees the prison gate open in the darkness of the night, and swallow him – like this!'

He opened his mouth as wide as he could, and shut it with a sounding snap of his teeth. Observant of his

unwillingness to mar the effect by opening it again, Defarge said, 'Go on, Jacques.'

'All the village,' pursued the mender of roads, 'withdraws; all the village whispers by the fountain; all the village sleeps; all the village dreams of that unhappy one, within the locks and bars of the prison on the crag, and never to come out of it, except to perish. In the morning, I make a circuit by the prison, on my way to my work. There I see him, high up, behind the bars of a lofty iron cage, bloody and dusty as last night, looking through. He has no hand free, to wave to me; I dare not call to him; he regards me like a dead man.'

Defarge and the three glanced darkly at one another. The looks of all of them were dark, repressed, and revengeful, as they listened to the countryman's story; They had the air of a rough tribunal.

'Go on, Jacques,' said Defarge.

'He remains up there in his iron cage some days. The village looks at him by stealth, for it is afraid. But it always looks up, from a distance, at the prison on the crag. They whisper at the fountain, that although condemned to death he will not be executed; they say that petitions have been presented in Paris, showing that he was enraged and made mad by the death of his child; they say that a petition has been presented to the King himself. What do I know? It is possible.'

'Listen then, Jacques,' Number One of that name sternly

interposed. 'Know that a petition was presented to the King and Queen. All here, yourself excepted, saw the King take it, in his carriage in the street, sitting beside the Queen. It is Defarge whom you see here, who, at the hazard of his life, darted out before the horses, with the petition in his hand.'

'And once again listen, Jacques!' said Number Three; 'the guard, horse and foot, surrounded the petitioner, and struck him blows. You hear?'

'I hear, messieurs.'

'Go on then,' said Defarge.

'Again; on the other hand, they whisper at the fountain,' resumed the countryman, 'that he is brought down into our country to be executed on the spot, and that he will very certainly be executed. They even whisper that because he has slain Monseigneur, and because Monseigneur was the father of his tenants – serfs – what you will – he will be executed as a parricide. Some whisper this, some whisper that; they speak of nothing else; even the fountain appears to fall to that tune. At length, on Sunday night when all the village is asleep, come soldiers, winding down from the prison, and their guns ring on the stones of the little street. Workmen dig, workmen hammer, soldiers laugh and sing; in the morning, by the fountain, there is raised a gallows forty feet high, poisoning the water.'

The mender of roads looked *through* rather than *at* the low ceiling, and pointed as if he saw the gallows somewhere in the sky.

'All work is stopped, all assemble there. At midday, the roll of drums. Soldiers have marched into the prison in the night, and he is in the midst of many soldiers. He is bound as before, and in his mouth there is a gag – tied so, with a tight string, making him look almost as if he laughed. On the top of the gallows is fixed the knife, blade upwards, with its point in the air. He is hanged there forty feet high – and is left hanging, poisoning the water.'

They looked at one another, as he used his blue cap to wipe his face, on which the perspiration had started afresh while he recalled the spectacle.

'It is frightful, messieurs. How can the women and the children draw water! Who can gossip of an evening, under that shadow! That's all, messieurs. I left at sunset and I walked on, that night and half next day, until I met this comrade.'

After a gloomy silence, the first Jacques said, 'Good! You have acted and recounted faithfully. Will you wait for us a little, outside the door?'

'Very willingly,' said the mender of roads. Whom Defarge escorted to the top of the stairs, and, leaving seated there, returned.

The three had risen, and their heads were together when he came back to the garret.

'How say you, Jacques?' demanded Number One. 'To be registered?'

'To be registered, as doomed to destruction,' returned Defarge.

'Magnificent!' croaked Jacques Three.

'The château and all the race?' inquired the first.

'The château and all the race,' returned Defarge. 'Extermination.'

'Are you sure,' asked Jacques Two, of Defarge, 'that no embarrassment can arise from our manner of keeping the register? Without doubt it is safe, for no one beyond ourselves can decipher it; but shall we always be able to decipher it – or, I ought to say, will she?'

'Jacques,' returned Defarge, drawing himself up, 'if madame my wife undertook to keep the register in her memory alone, she would not lose a word of it – not a syllable of it. Knitted, in her own stitches and her own symbols, it will always be as plain to her as the sun.'

There was a murmur of confidence and approval, and then the man who hungered, asked: 'Is this rustic to be sent back soon? I hope so. He is very simple; is he not a little dangerous?'

'He knows nothing,' said Defarge; 'let him remain with me; I will take care of him, and set him on his road. He wishes to see the fine world – the King, the Queen, and Court; let him see them on Sunday.'

'What?' exclaimed Jacques Three, staring. 'Is it a good sign, that he wishes to see Royalty and Nobility?'

'Jacques,' said Defarge; 'judiciously show a cat milk, if

you wish her to thirst for it. Judiciously show a dog his natural prey, if you wish him to bring it down one day.'

Nothing more was said, and the mender of roads, being found already dozing on the topmost stair, was advised to lay himself down on the pallet-bed and take some rest.

Worse quarters than Defarge's wine-shop, could easily have been found in Paris for a provincial slave of that degree. Saving for a mysterious dread of madame by which he was constantly haunted, his life was very new and agreeable. But, madame sat all day at her counter, so particularly determined not to perceive that his being there had any connexion with anything below the surface, that he shook in his wooden shoes whenever his eye lighted on her. For, he contended with himself that it was impossible to foresee what that lady might pretend next; and he felt assured that if she should take it into her head to pretend that she had seen him do a murder and afterwards flay the victim, she would infallibly go through with it until the play was played out.

Therefore, when Sunday came, the mender of roads was not enchanted to find that madame was to accompany monsieur and himself to Versailles. It was additionally disconcerting to have madame knitting all the way there, in a public conveyance; it was additionally disconcerting yet, to have madame in the crowd in the afternoon, still with her knitting in her hands as the crowd waited to see the carriage of the King and Queen.

'You work hard, madame,' said a man near her.

'Yes,' answered Madame Defarge; 'I have a good deal to do.'

'What do you make, madame?'

'Many things.'

'For instance –'

'For instance,' returned Madame Defarge, composedly, 'shrouds.'

The man moved a little further away, as soon as he could, and the mender of roads fanned himself with his blue cap: feeling it mightily close and oppressive. If he needed a King and Queen to restore him, he was fortunate in having his remedy at hand; for, soon the large-faced King and the fair-faced Queen came in their golden coach, attended by the shining Bull's Eye of their Court, a glittering multitude of laughing ladies and fine lords; and in jewels and silks and powder and splendour, the mender of roads bathed himself, so much to his temporary intoxication, that he cried Long live the King, Long live the Queen, Long live everybody and everything! as if he had never heard of ubiquitous Jacques in his time. Then, there were gardens, court-yards, terraces, fountains, green banks, more King and Queen, more Bull's Eye, more lords and ladies, more Long live they all! until he absolutely wept with sentiment.

'You are the fellow we want,' said Defarge, in his ear; 'you make these fools believe that it will last for ever. Then, they are the more insolent, and it is the nearer ended.'

'Hey!' cried the mender of roads, reflectively; 'that's true.'

'These fools know nothing. While they despise your breath, and would stop it for ever and ever, in you or in a hundred like you rather than in one of their own horses or dogs, they only know what your breath tells them. Let it deceive them, then, a little longer.'

Madame Defarge looked superciliously at the client, and nodded in confirmation.

'As to you,' said she, 'you would shout and shed tears for anything, if it made a show and a noise. Say! Would you not?'

'Truly, madame, I think so. For the moment.'

'If you were shown a great heap of dolls, and were set upon them to pluck them to pieces and despoil them for your own advantage, you would pick out the richest and gayest. Say! Would you not?'

'Truly yes, madame.'

'Yes. And if you were shown a flock of birds, unable to fly, and were set upon them to strip them of their feathers for your own advantage, you would set upon the birds of the finest feathers; would you not?'

'It is true, madame.'

'You have seen both dolls and birds today,' said Madame Defarge, with a wave of her hand towards the place where they had last been apparent; 'now, go home!'

16

Still Knitting

Madame Defarge and monsieur her husband returned amicably to the bosom of Saint Antoine, while a speck in a blue cap toiled through the darkness, towards that point of the compass where the château of Monsieur the Marquis, now in his grave, listened to the whispering trees. Such ample leisure had the stone faces, now, for listening to the trees and to the fountain, that the few village scarecrows who, in their quest for herbs to eat and fragments of dead stick to burn, strayed within sight of the great stone court-yard and terrace staircase, had it borne in upon their starved fancy that the expression of the faces was altered. A rumour just lived in the village that when the knife struck home, the faces changed, from faces of pride to faces of anger and pain; also, that when that dangling figure was hauled up forty feet above the fountain, they changed again, and bore a cruel look of being avenged.

Château and hut, stone face and dangling figure, the red stain on the stone floor, and the pure water in the

village well – thousands of acres of land – a whole province of France – all France itself – lay under the night sky, concentrated into a faint hair-breadth line.

The Defarges, husband and wife, came lumbering under the starlight, in their public vehicle, to that gate of Paris whereunto their journey naturally tended. Monsieur Defarge alighted: knowing one or two of the soldiery there, and one of the police. The latter he was intimate with, and affectionately embraced.

When Saint Antoine had again enfolded the Defarges in his dusky wings, and they, having finally alighted near the Saint's boundaries, were picking their way on foot through the black mud and offal of his streets, Madame Defarge spoke to her husband:

'Say then, my friend; what did Jacques of the police tell thee?'

'Very little tonight, but all he knows. There is another spy commissioned for our quarter.'

'Eh well!' said Madame Defarge, raising her eyebrows with a cool business air. 'It is necessary to register him. How do they call that man?'

'He is English.'

'So much the better. His name?'

'Barsad,' said Defarge, making it French by pronunciation.

'Barsad,' repeated madame. 'Good. Christian name?'

'John.'

'John Barsad,' repeated madame, after murmuring it once to herself. 'Good. His appearance; is it known?'

'Age, about forty years; height, about five feet nine; black hair; complexion dark; generally, rather handsome visage; eyes dark, face thin, long, and sallow; nose aquiline, having a peculiar inclination towards the left cheek; expression, therefore, sinister.'

'Eh my faith. It is a portrait!' said madame, laughing. 'He shall be registered tomorrow.'

They turned into the wine-shop, which was closed and where Madame Defarge immediately took her post at her desk, counted the small moneys that had been taken during her absence, examined the stock, checked the serving man in every possible way, and finally dismissed him to bed. Then she turned out the contents of the bowl of money for the second time, and began knotting them up in her handkerchief. All this while, Defarge walked up and down, complacently admiring, but never interfering; in which condition, indeed, as to the business and his domestic affairs, he walked up and down through life.

'You are fatigued,' said madame, raising her glance as she knotted the money.

'I am a little tired,' her husband acknowledged.

'You are a little depressed, too,' said madame, whose quick eyes had never been so intent on the accounts, but they had had a ray or two for him. 'Oh, the men, the men!'

'Well, then,' said Defarge, as if a thought were wrung out of his breast, 'it *is* a long time.'

'It is a long time,' repeated his wife. 'Vengeance and retribution require a long time; it is the rule.'

'It does not take a long time to strike a man with Lightning,' said Defarge.

'How long,' demanded madame, composedly, 'does it take to make and store the lightning? Tell me.'

Defarge raised his head thoughtfully, as if there were something in that too.

'It does not take a long time,' said madame, 'for an earthquake to swallow a town. Eh well! Tell me how long it takes to prepare the earthquake?'

'A long time, I suppose,' said Defarge.

'But when it is ready, it takes place, and grinds to pieces everything before it. In the meantime, it is always preparing, though it is not seen or heard. That is your consolation. Keep it.'

She tied a knot with flashing eyes, as if it throttled a foe.

'I tell thee,' said madame, extending her right hand, for emphasis, 'that although it is a long time on the road, it is on the road and coming. I tell thee it never retreats, and never stops.'

'My brave wife,' returned Defarge, 'I do not question all this. But it has lasted a long time, and it is possible that it may not come, during our lives.'

'Eh well! How then?' demanded madame.

'Well!' said Defarge, with a half-complaining and half-apologetic shrug. 'We shall not see the triumph.'

'We shall have helped it,' returned madame, 'nothing that we do, is done in vain. I believe, with all my soul, that we shall see the triumph. But even if not, even if I knew certainly not, show me the neck of an aristocrat and tyrant, and still I would –'

Then madame, with her teeth set, tied a very terrible knot indeed.

'Hold!' cried Defarge, reddening a little as if he felt charged with cowardice; 'I too, my dear, will stop at nothing.'

'Yes! But it is your weakness that you sometimes need to see your victim and your opportunity, to sustain you. Sustain yourself without that. When the time comes, let loose a tiger and a devil; but wait for the time with the tiger and the devil chained – not shown yet always ready.'

Next noontide saw the admirable woman in her usual place in the wine-shop, knitting away assiduously. There were a few customers, drinking or not drinking, standing or seated, sprinkled about.

A figure entering at the door threw a shadow on Madame Defarge which she felt to be a new one. She laid down her knitting.

'Good day, madame,' said the new comer.

'Good day, monsieur.'

She said it aloud, but added to herself, as she resumed her knitting: 'Hah! Good day, age about forty, height about five feet nine, black hair, generally rather handsome visage, complexion dark, eyes dark, thin long and sallow face, aquiline nose but not straight, having a peculiar inclination towards the left cheek which imparts a sinister expression! Good day, one and all!'

'Have the goodness to give me a little glass of old cognac, and a mouthful of cool fresh water, madame.'

Madame complied with a polite air.

'You knit with great skill, madame.'

'I am accustomed to it.'

'A pretty pattern too! May one ask what it is for?'

'Pastime,' said madame, still looking at him with a smile, while her fingers moved nimbly.

'Not for use?'

'That depends. I may find a use for it one day. If I do – well,' said madame, drawing a breath and nodding her head with a stern kind of coquetry, 'I'll use it!'

'JOHN,' she thought, checking off her work as her fingers knitted, and her eyes looked at the stranger. 'Stay long enough, and I shall knit "BARSAD" before you go.'

'You have a husband, madame?'

'I have.'

'Business seems bad?'

'Business is very bad; the people are so poor.'

'Ah, the unfortunate, miserable people! So oppressed, too – as you say.'

'As *you* say,' madame retorted, correcting him, and deftly knitting an extra something into his name that boded him no good.

'Pardon me; certainly it was I who said so, but you naturally think so. Of course.'

'*I* think?' returned madame, in a high voice. 'I and my husband have enough to do to keep this wine-shop open, without thinking. All we think, here, is how to live. *I* think for others? No, no.'

The spy, who was there to pick up any crumbs he could find or make, did not allow his baffled state to express itself in his sinister face; but, stood with an air of gossiping gallantry, leaning his elbow on Madame Defarge's little counter, and occasionally sipping his cognac.

'A bad business this, madame, of Gaspard's execution. Ah! the poor Gaspard!' With a sigh of great compassion.

'My faith!' returned madame, coolly and lightly, 'if people use knives for such purposes, they have to pay for it.'

'I believe,' said the spy, dropping his soft voice to a tone that invited confidence, 'I believe there is much compassion and anger in this neighbourhood, touching the poor fellow?'

'Is there?' asked madame, vacantly.

'Is there not?'

'– Here is my husband!' said Madame Defarge.

As the keeper of the wine-shop entered at the door, the spy saluted him by touching his hat, and saying, with an engaging smile, 'Good day, Jacques!' Defarge stopped short, and stared at him.

'Good day, Jacques!' the spy repeated; with not quite so much confidence, or quite so easy a smile under the stare.

'You deceive yourself, monsieur,' returned the keeper of the wine-shop. 'That is not my name. I am Ernest Defarge.'

'It is all the same,' said the spy, airily, but discomfited too: 'good day!'

'Good day!' answered Defarge, drily.

'I was saying to madame, that they tell me there is – and no wonder! – much sympathy and anger in Saint Antoine, touching the unhappy fate of poor Gaspard.'

'No one has told me so,' said Defarge, shaking his head. 'I know nothing of it.'

The spy, well used to his business, did not change his unconscious attitude, but drained his little glass of cognac, took a sip of fresh water, and asked for another glass of cognac. Madame Defarge poured it out for him, took to her knitting again, and hummed a little song over it.

'You seem to know this quarter well; that is to say, better than I do?' observed Defarge.

'Not at all, but I hope to know it better. I am so profoundly interested in its miserable inhabitants.'

'Hah!' muttered Defarge.

'The pleasure of conversing with you, Monsieur Defarge, recalls to me,' pursued the spy, 'that I have the honour of cherishing some interesting associations with your name.'

'Indeed!' said Defarge, with much indifference.

'Yes, indeed. When Dr Manette was released, you, his old domestic, had the charge of him, I know. He was delivered to you.'

'Such is the fact, certainly,' said Defarge.

'It was to you,' said the spy, 'that his daughter came; and it was from your care that his daughter took him, accompanied by a neat brown monsieur; how is he called? – in a little wig – Lorry – of the bank of Tellson and Company – over to England.'

'Such is the fact,' repeated Defarge.

'Very interesting remembrances!' said the spy. 'I have known Dr Manette and his daughter, in England.'

'Yes?' said Defarge.

'You don't hear much about them now?' said the spy.

'No,' said Defarge.

'In effect,' madame struck in, looking up from her work and her little song, 'we never hear about them. We received the news of their safe arrival, but we have held no correspondence.'

'Perfectly so, madame,' replied the spy. 'She is going to be married.'

'Going?' echoed madame. 'She was pretty enough to have been married long ago. You English are cold, it seems to me.'

'Oh! You know I am English.'

'I perceive your tongue is,' returned madame; 'and what the tongue is, I suppose the man is.'

He did not take the identification as a compliment; but he made the best of it, and turned it off with a laugh. After sipping his cognac to the end, he added:

'Yes, Miss Manette is going to be married. But not to an Englishman; to one who, like herself, is French by birth. And speaking of Gaspard, it is a curious thing that she is going to marry the nephew of Monsieur the Marquis, for whom Gaspard was exalted to that height of so many feet. But he lives unknown in England, he is no Marquis there; he is Mr Charles Darnay.'

Madame Defarge knitted steadily, but the intelligence had a palpable effect upon her husband. He was troubled, and his hand was not trustworthy. The spy would have been no spy if he had failed to see it, or to record it in his mind.

Having made, at least, this one hit, Mr Barsad paid for what he had drunk, and took his leave: taking occasion to say, in a genteel manner, before he departed, that he looked forward to the pleasure of seeing Monsieur and Madame Defarge again.

'Can it be true,' said Defarge, in a low voice after he had left, 'what he has said of Ma'amselle Manette?'

'As he has said it,' returned madame, lifting her eyebrows a little, 'it is probably false. But it may be true.'

'If it is –' Defarge began, and stopped.

'If it is?' repeated his wife.

'– And if it does come, while we live to see it triumph – I hope, for her sake, Destiny will keep her husband out of France.'

'Her husband's destiny,' said Madame Defarge, with her usual composure, 'will take him where he is to go.'

'But it is very strange,' said Defarge, 'that, after all our sympathy for Monsieur her father, and herself, her husband's name should be proscribed under your hand at this moment, by the side of that infernal dog's who has just left us?'

'Stranger things than that will happen when it does come,' answered madame.

In the evening, at which season of all others Saint Antoine turned himself inside out, and sat on door-steps and window-ledges, Madame Defarge with her work in her hand was accustomed to pass from place to place and from group to group: a Missionary – there were many like her – such as the world will do well never to breed again. All the women knitted. They knitted worthless things; but, the mechanical work was a mechanical substitute for eating and drinking; the hands moved for the jaws and the digestive apparatus: if the bony fingers had been still, the stomachs would have been more famine-pinched.

But, as the fingers went, the eyes went, and the thoughts. And as Madame Defarge moved on from group to group, all three went quicker and fiercer among every little knot of women that she had spoken with, and left behind.

Her husband smoked at his door, looking after her with admiration. 'A great woman,' said he, 'a strong woman.'

Darkness closed around, and then came the ringing of church bells and the distant beating of the military drums of the Royal Guard, as the women sat knitting, knitting. Another darkness was closing in as surely, when the church bells, then ringing pleasantly, should be melted into thundering cannon; when the military drums should be beating to drown a wretched voice, that night all potent as the voice of Power and Plenty, Freedom and Life. So much was closing in about the women who sat knitting, knitting, that they their very selves were closing in around a structure yet unbuilt, where they were to sit knitting, knitting, counting dropping heads.

17

One Night

Never did the sun go down with a brighter glory on the quiet corner in Soho, than one memorable evening when the Doctor and his daughter sat under the plane-tree together. Never did the moon rise with a milder radiance over great London, than on that night when it found them still seated under the tree, and shone upon their faces through its leaves.

Lucie was to be married tomorrow. She had reserved this last evening for her father, and they sat alone under the plane-tree.

'You are happy, my dear father?'

'Quite, my child.'

'And I am very happy tonight, dear father. I am deeply happy in my love for Charles, and Charles's love for me. But, if my life were not to be still consecrated to you, or if my marriage were so arranged as that it would part us, even by the length of a few of these streets, I should be more unhappy and self-reproachful now than I can tell you.'

In the sad moonlight, she clasped him by the neck, and laid her face upon his breast.

'Dearest dear! Can you tell me, this last time, that you feel quite, quite sure, no new affections of mine, and no new duties of mine, will ever interpose between us? *I* know it well, but do you know it?'

Her father answered, with a cheerful firmness of conviction he could scarcely have assumed, 'Quite sure, my darling! More than that,' he added, as he tenderly kissed her: 'my future is far brighter, Lucie, seen through your marriage, than it could have been – nay, than it ever was – without it.'

'If I could hope *that*, my father! –'

'Believe it, love! Indeed it is so. You, devoted and young, cannot fully appreciate the anxiety I have felt that your life should not be wasted –'

She moved her hand towards his lips, but he took it in his, and repeated the word.

'– wasted, my child, for my sake. Your unselfishness cannot entirely comprehend how much my mind has gone on this; but, only ask yourself, how could my happiness be perfect, while yours was incomplete?'

'If I had never seen Charles, my father, I should have been quite happy with you.'

'My child, you did see him, and it is Charles. If it had not been Charles, it would have been another. Or, if it had been no other, I should have been the cause, and then

the dark part of my life would have cast its shadow beyond myself, and would have fallen on you.'

It was the first time, except at the trial, of her ever hearing him refer to the period of his suffering. It gave her a strange and new sensation while his words were in her ears; and she remembered it long afterwards.

'See!' said the Doctor of Beauvais, raising his hand towards the moon. 'I have looked at her from my prison-window, when I could not bear her light. I have looked at her, in a state so dull and lethargic, that I have thought of nothing but the number of horizontal lines I could draw across her at the full, and the number of perpendicular lines with which I could intersect them.'

The strange thrill with which she heard him go back to that time, deepened as he dwelt upon it; but, there was nothing to shock her in the manner of his reference. He only seemed to contrast his present cheerfulness and felicity with the dire endurance that was over.

'I have looked at her, speculating thousands of times upon the unborn child from whom I had been rent. Whether it had been born alive, or the poor mother's shock had killed it. Whether it was a son who would never know his father's story; who might even live to weigh the possibility of his father's having disappeared of his own will and act. Whether it was a daughter who would grow to be a woman.'

She drew closer to him, and kissed his cheek and his hand.

'I have pictured my daughter, to myself, altogether unconscious of me. I have seen her married to a man who knew nothing of my fate. I have altogether perished from the remembrance of the living, and in the next generation my place was a blank.'

'My father! Even to hear that you had such thoughts of a daughter who never existed, strikes to my heart as if I had been that child.'

'You, Lucie? It is out of the consolation and restoration you have brought to me, that these remembrances arise, and pass between us and the moon on this last night. – What did I say just now?'

'She knew nothing of you. She cared nothing for you.'

'So! But on other moonlight nights, when the sadness and the silence have touched me in a different way I have imagined her as coming to me in my cell, and leading me out into the freedom beyond the fortress. But, you understand that that was not the child I am speaking of?'

'The figure was not; the – the – image; the fancy?'

'No. That was another thing. The phantom that my mind pursued, was another and more real child. Of her outward appearance I know no more than that she was like her mother. The other had that likeness too – as you have – but was not the same. Can you follow me, Lucie? Hardly, I think? I doubt you must have been a solitary prisoner to understand these perplexed distinctions.'

His collected and calm manner could not prevent her blood from running cold, as he thus tried to anatomise his old condition.

'In that more peaceful state, I have imagined her, in the moonlight, coming to me and taking me out to show me that the home of her married life was full of her loving remembrance of her lost father. Her life was active, cheerful, useful; but my poor history pervaded it all.'

'I was that child, my father. I was not half so good, but in my love that was I.'

'And she showed me her children,' said the Doctor of Beauvais, 'and they had heard of me, and had been taught to pity me. She could never deliver me; I imagined that she always brought me back after showing me such things. But then, blessed with the relief of tears, I fell upon my knees, and blessed her.'

'I am that child, I hope, my father. O my dear, my dear, will you bless me as fervently tomorrow?'

'Lucie, my thoughts, when they were wildest, never rose near the happiness that I have known with you, and that we have before us.'

He embraced her, and humbly thanked Heaven for having bestowed her on him. By-and-by, they went into the house.

There was no one bidden to the marriage but Mr Lorry. The marriage was to make no change in their place of residence; they had been able to extend it, by taking to

themselves the upper rooms formerly belonging to the apocryphal invisible lodger.

Doctor Manette was very cheerful at the little supper. He regretted that Charles was not there; was more than half disposed to object to the loving little plot that kept him away; and drank to him affectionately.

So, the time came for him to bid Lucie good-night, and they separated. But, in the stillness of the third hour of the morning, Lucie came down stairs again, and stole into his room: not free from unshaped fears, beforehand.

All things, however, were in their places; all was quiet; and he lay asleep, his white hair picturesque on the untroubled pillow, and his hands lying quiet on the coverlet. She put her needless candle in the shadow at a distance, crept up to his bed, and put her lips to his; then, leaned over him, and looked at him.

Into his handsome face, the bitter waters of captivity had worn; but, he covered up their tracks with a determination so strong, that he held the mastery of them, even in his sleep. A more remarkable face in its quiet, resolute, and guarded struggle with an unseen assailant, was not to be beheld in all the wide dominions of sleep, that night.

She timidly laid her hand on his dear breast, and put up a prayer that she might ever be as true to him as her love aspired to be, and as his sorrows deserved. Then, she withdrew her hand, and kissed his lips once more, and went away.

18

Nine Days

The marriage-day was shining brightly, and they were ready outside the closed door of the Doctor's room, where he was speaking with Charles Darnay. They were ready to go to church; the beautiful bride, Mr Lorry, and Miss Pross.

'And so,' said Mr Lorry, 'it was for this, my sweet Lucie, that I brought you across the Channel, such a baby! Lord bless me! How lightly I valued the obligation I was conferring on my friend Mr Charles!'

'You didn't mean it,' remarked the matter-of-fact Miss Pross, 'and therefore how could you know it? Nonsense!'

'Really? Well; but don't cry,' said the gentle Mr Lorry.

'I am not crying,' said Miss Pross; '*you* are.'

'I, my Pross?' (By this time, Mr Lorry dared to be pleasant with her, on occasion.)

'You were, just now; I saw you do it, and I don't wonder at it. Such a present of plate as you have made 'em, is enough to bring tears into anybody's eyes.'

'I am highly gratified,' said Mr Lorry, 'though, upon

my honour, I had no intention of rendering those trifling articles of remembrance, invisible to any one. This is an occasion that makes a man speculate on all he has lost. To think that there might have been a Mrs Lorry, any time these fifty years almost!'

'Pooh!' rejoined Miss Pross; 'you were a bachelor in your cradle.'

'Well!' observed Mr Lorry, beamingly adjusting his little wig, 'that seems probable, too.'

'And you were cut out for a bachelor,' pursued Miss Pross, 'before you were put in your cradle.'

'Then, I think,' said Mr Lorry, 'that I was very unhandsomely dealt with, and that I ought to have had a voice in the selection of my pattern. Enough! Now, my dear Lucie,' drawing his arm soothingly round her waist, 'I hear them moving in the next room, and Miss Pross and I are anxious not to lose the final opportunity of saying something to you that you wish to hear. You leave your good father, my dear, in hands as earnest and as loving as your own; he shall be taken every conceivable care of; during the next fortnight, while you are in Warwickshire, even Tellson's shall go to the wall before him. And when, at the fortnight's end, he comes to join you and your beloved husband, on your other fortnight's trip in Wales, you shall say that we have sent him to you in the best health and in the happiest frame. Let me kiss my dear girl with an old-fashioned bachelor blessing, before Somebody comes to claim his own.'

The door of the Doctor's room opened, and he came out with Charles Darnay. He was so deadly pale that no vestige of colour was to be seen in his face. But, in the composure of his manner he was unaltered, except that to the shrewd glance of Mr Lorry it disclosed some shadowy indication that the old air of avoidance and dread had lately passed over him, like a cold wind.

He gave his arm to his daughter, and took her downstairs to the chariot which Mr Lorry had hired in honour of the day. The rest followed in another carriage, and soon, in a neighbouring church, where no strange eyes looked on, Charles Darnay and Lucie Manette were happily married.

They returned home to breakfast, and all went well, and in due course, the golden hair that had mingled with the poor shoemaker's white locks in the Paris garret, were mingled with them again in the morning sunlight, on the threshold of the door at parting.

It was a hard parting, though it was not for long. But her father cheered her, and said at last, gently disengaging himself from her enfolding arms, 'Take her, Charles! She is yours!' And her agitated hand waved to them from a chaise window, and she was gone.

The preparations having been very simple and few, the Doctor, Mr Lorry, and Miss Pross, were left quite alone. It was when they turned into the welcome shade of the cool old hall, that Mr Lorry observed a great change to

have come over the Doctor; as if the golden arm uplifted there, had struck him a poisoned blow.

It was the old scared lost look that troubled Mr Lorry; and through his absent manner of clasping his head and drearily wandering away into his own room when they got upstairs, Mr Lorry was reminded of Defarge the wine-shop keeper, and the starlight ride.

'I think,' he whispered to Miss Pross, after anxious consideration, 'I think we had best not speak to him just now, or at all disturb him. I must look in at Tellson's; so I will go there at once and come back presently.'

It was easier for Mr Lorry to look in at Tellson's, than to look out of Tellson's. He was detained two hours. When he came back he ascended the old staircase alone, having asked no question of the servant; going thus into the Doctor's rooms, he was stopped by a low sound of knocking.

Miss Pross, with a terrified face, was at his ear. 'O me, O me! All is lost!' cried she, wringing her hands. 'What is to be told to Ladybird? He doesn't know me, and is making shoes!'

Mr Lorry said what he could to calm her, and went himself into the Doctor's room. The bench was turned towards the light, as it had been when he had seen the shoemaker at his work before, and his head was bent down, and he was very busy.

'Doctor Manette. My dear friend, Doctor Manette!'

The Doctor looked at him for a moment and bent over his work again.

Mr Lorry glanced at the work in his hand, and observed that it was a shoe of the old size and shape. He took up another that was lying by him, and asked what it was?

'A young lady's walking shoe,' he muttered, without looking up. 'It ought to have been finished long ago. Let it be.'

'But, Doctor Manette. Look at me!'

He obeyed, in the old mechanically submissive manner, without pausing in his work.

'You know me, my dear friend? Think again. This is not your proper occupation. Think, dear friend!'

Nothing would induce him to speak more. He looked up, for an instant at a time, when he was requested to do so; but, no persuasion would extract a word from him. The only ray of hope that Mr Lorry could discover, was, that he sometimes furtively looked up without being asked. In that, there seemed a faint expression of curiosity or perplexity – as though he were trying to reconcile some doubts in his mind.

Two things at once impressed themselves on Mr Lorry, as important above all others; the first, that this must be kept secret from Lucie; the second that it must be kept secret from all who knew him. In conjunction with Miss Pross, he took immediate steps towards the latter precaution, by giving out that the Doctor was not well, and

required a few days of complete rest. In aid of the kind deception to be practised on his daughter, Miss Pross was to write, describing his having been called away professionally, and referring to an imaginary letter of two or three hurried lines in his own hand, represented to have been addressed to her by the same post.

In the hope of his recovery, Mr Lorry resolved to watch him attentively, with as little appearance as possible of doing so. He therefore made arrangements to absent himself from Tellson's for the first time in his life, and took his post by the window in the same room.

Doctor Manette took what was given him to eat and drink, and worked on, that first day, until it was too dark to see – worked on, half an hour after Mr Lorry could not have seen, for his life, to read or write. When he put his tools aside as useless, until morning, Mr Lorry rose and said to him:

'Will you go out?'

'Out?'

'Yes; for a walk with me. Why not?'

He made no effort to say why not, and said not a word more. But, Mr Lorry thought he saw, as he leaned forward on his bench in the dusk, with his elbows on his knees and his head in his hands, that he was in some misty way asking himself, 'Why not?'

Miss Pross and he divided the night into two watches, and observed him at intervals from the adjoining room.

He paced up and down for a long time before he lay down; but, when he did finally lay himself down, he fell asleep. In the morning, he was up betimes, and went straight to his bench and to work.

On this second day, Mr Lorry saluted him cheerfully by his name, and spoke to him on topics that had been of late familiar to them. He returned no reply, but it was evident that he heard what was said, and that he thought about it, however confusedly. This encouraged Mr Lorry to have Miss Pross in with her work, several times during the day; at those times, they quietly spoke of Lucie, and of her father then present, precisely in the usual manner, and as if there were nothing amiss.

When it fell dark again, Mr Lorry asked him as before:

'Dear Doctor, will you go out?'

As before, he repeated, 'Out?'

'Yes; for a walk with me. Why not?'

This time, Mr Lorry feigned to go out when he could extract no answer from him, and, after remaining absent for an hour, returned. In the meanwhile, the Doctor had removed to the seat in the window, and had sat there looking down at the plane-tree; but, on Mr Lorry's return, he slipped away to his bench.

The time went very slowly on, and Mr Lorry's hope darkened. The third day came and went, the fourth, the fifth. Five days, six days, seven days, eight days, nine days.

With a hope ever darkening, and with a heart always growing heavier and heavier, Mr Lorry passed through this anxious time. The secret was well kept, and Lucie was unconscious and happy; but he could not fail to observe that the shoemaker was growing dreadfully skilful, and that his hands had never been so nimble and expert, as in the dusk of the ninth evening.

19

An Opinion

Worn out by anxious watching, Mr Lorry fell asleep at his post. On the tenth morning of his suspense, he was startled by the shining of the sun into the room where a heavy slumber had overtaken him when it was dark night.

He roused himself; but he doubted, when he had done so, whether he was not still asleep. For, going to the door of the Doctor's room and looking in, he perceived that the shoemaker's bench and tools were put aside again, and that the Doctor himself sat reading at the window. He was in his usual morning dress, and his face, though still very pale, was calmly studious and attentive.

Even when he had satisfied himself that he was awake, Mr Lorry felt giddily uncertain for some few moments whether the late shoemaking might not be a disturbed dream of his own; for, did not his eyes show him his friend before him in his accustomed clothing and aspect, and employed as usual; and was there any sign within

their range, that the change of which he had so strong an impression had actually happened?

It was but the inquiry of his first confusion and astonishment, the answer being obvious. If the impression were not produced by a real corresponding and sufficient cause, how came he, Jarvis Lorry, there? How came he to have fallen asleep, in his clothes, on the sofa in Dr Manette's consulting-room, and to be debating these points outside the Doctor's bedroom door in the early morning?

Within a few minutes, Miss Pross stood whispering at his side. If he had had any particle of doubt left, her talk would of necessity have resolved it; but he was by that time clear-headed, and had none. He advised that they should let the time go by until the regular breakfast-hour, and should then meet the Doctor as if nothing unusual had occurred. If he appeared to be in his customary state of mind, Mr Lorry would then cautiously proceed to seek direction and guidance from the opinion he had been, in his anxiety, so anxious to obtain.

Miss Pross submitting herself to his judgment, the scheme was worked out with care. The Doctor was summoned in the usual way, and came to breakfast.

So far as it was possible to comprehend him without overstepping those delicate and gradual approaches which Mr Lorry felt to be the only safe advance, he at first supposed that his daughter's marriage had taken place

yesterday. An incidental allusion, purposely thrown out, to the day of the week, and the day of the month, set him thinking and counting, and evidently made him uneasy. In all other respects, however, he was so composedly himself, that Mr Lorry determined to have the aid he sought. And that aid was his own.

Therefore, when the breakfast was done and cleared away, and he and the Doctor were left together, Mr Lorry said, feelingly:

'My dear Manette, I am anxious to have your opinion, in confidence, on a very curious case in which I am deeply interested.'

Glancing at his hands, which were discoloured by his late work, the Doctor looked troubled, and listened attentively.

'Doctor Manette,' said Mr Lorry, 'the case is the case of a particularly dear friend of mine. Pray give your mind to it, and advise me well for his sake – and above all, for his daughter's.'

'Be explicit,' said the Doctor. 'Spare no detail.'

Mr Lorry saw that they understood one another, and proceeded.

'My dear Manette, it is the case of an old and a prolonged shock, of great acuteness and severity to the affections, the feelings, the – the – as you express it – the mind. It is the case of a shock from which he has recovered, so completely, as to be a highly intelligent man,

capable of close application of mind, and great exertion of body. But, unfortunately, there has been' – he paused and took a deep breath – 'a slight relapse.'

The Doctor, in a low voice, asked, 'Of how long duration?'

'Nine days and nights.'

'How did it show itself? I infer,' glancing at his hands again, 'in the resumption of some old pursuit connected with the shock?'

'That is the fact.'

'Now, did you ever see him,' asked the Doctor, distinctly and collectedly, though in the same low voice, 'engaged in that pursuit originally?'

'Once.'

'And when the relapse fell on him, was he in most respects – or in all respects – as he was then?'

'I think in all respects.'

'You spoke of his daughter. Does his daughter know of the relapse?'

'No. It has been kept from her.'

The Doctor grasped his hand, and murmured, 'That was very kind. That was very thoughtful!'

'Now, my dear Manette,' said Mr Lorry, at length, in his most considerate and most affectionate way. 'Tell me, how does this relapse come about? Is there danger of another? How should a repetition of it be treated? No man ever can have been more desirous in his heart to serve a friend,

than I am to serve mine, if I knew how. If your sagacity, knowledge, and experience, could put me on the right track, I might be able to do so much; unenlightened and undirected, I can do so little. Pray discuss it with me; pray enable me to see it a little more clearly.'

Doctor Manette sat meditating after these earnest words were spoken, and Mr Lorry did not press him.

'I think it probable,' said the Doctor, breaking silence with an effort, 'that the relapse you have described, my dear friend, was not quite unforeseen by its subject.'

'Was it dreaded by him?' Mr Lorry ventured to ask.

'Very much.' He said it with an involuntary shudder. 'You have no idea how such an apprehension weighs on the sufferer's mind, and how difficult – how almost impossible – it is, for him to force himself to utter a word upon the topic that oppresses him.'

'Would he,' asked Mr Lorry, 'be sensibly relieved if he could prevail upon himself to impart that secret brooding to any one, when it is on him?'

'I think so. But it is, as I have told you, next to impossible.'

'Now,' said Mr Lorry, 'to what would you refer this attack?'

'I believe,' returned Doctor Manette, 'that there had been a strong and extraordinary revival of the train of thought and remembrance that was the first cause of the malady. Some intense associations of a most distressing

nature were vividly recalled, on a particular occasion.'

'Would he remember what took place in the relapse?' asked Mr Lorry, with natural hesitation.

The Doctor looked desolately round the room, shook his head, and answered, in a low voice, 'Not at all.'

'Now, as to the future,' hinted Mr Lorry.

'As to the future,' said the Doctor, recovering firmness, 'I should have great hope. He, yielding under the pressure of a complicated something, long dreaded and long vaguely foreseen and contended against, and recovering after the cloud had burst and passed, I should hope that the worst was over.'

'Well, well! That's good comfort. I am thankful!' said Mr Lorry.

'I am thankful!' repeated the Doctor, bending his head with reverence.

'There are two other points,' said Mr Lorry, 'on which I am anxious to be instructed. I may go on?'

'You cannot do your friend a better service.' The Doctor gave him his hand.

'To the first, then. He is of a studious habit, and un-usually energetic; he applies himself with a great ardour to the acquisition of professional knowledge, to the conducting of experiments, to many things. Now, does he do too much?'

'I think not. It may be the character of his mind, to be always in singular need of occupation. The less it was

occupied with healthy things, the more it would be in danger of turning in the unhealthy direction. He may have observed himself, and made the discovery.'

'You are sure that he is not under too great a strain?'

'I think I am quite sure of it.'

'Excuse me, as a persistent man of business. Assuming for a moment, that he *was* overworked; it would show itself in some renewal of this disorder?'

'I do not think so. I do not think,' said Doctor Manette with the firmness of self-conviction, 'that anything but the one train of association would renew it. After what has happened, and after his recovery, I find it difficult to imagine any such violent sounding of that string again.'

'The occupation resumed under the influence of this passing affliction so happily recovered from,' said Mr Lorry, clearing his throat, 'we will call – Blacksmith's work, Blacksmith's work. We will say, to put a case and for the sake of illustration, that he had been used, in his bad time, to work at a little forge. We will say that he was unexpectedly found at his forge again. Is it not a pity that he should keep it by him?'

The Doctor shaded his forehead with his hand, and beat his foot nervously on the ground.

'He has always kept it by him,' said Mr Lorry, with an anxious look at his friend. 'Now, would it not be better that he should let it go?'

Still, the Doctor, with shaded forehead, beat his foot nervously on the ground.

'You do not find it easy to advise me?' said Mr Lorry.

'You see,' said Doctor Manette, turning to him after an uneasy pause, 'it is very hard to explain, consistently, the innermost workings of this poor man's mind. He once yearned so frightfully for that occupation, and it was so welcome when it came; no doubt it relieved his pain so much, by substituting the perplexity of the fingers for the perplexity of the brain, and by substituting, as he became more practised, the ingenuity of the hands, for the ingenuity of the mental torture; that he has never been able to bear the thought of putting it quite out of his reach. Even now, the idea that he might need that old employment, and not find it, gives him a sudden sense of terror.'

He looked like his illustration, as he raised his eyes to Mr Lorry's face.

'If the thing were gone, my dear Manette, might not the fear go with it? In short, is it not a concession to the misgiving, to keep the forge?'

There was another silence.

'You see, too,' said the Doctor, tremulously, 'it is such an old companion.'

'I would not keep it,' said Mr Lorry, shaking his head; for he gained in firmness as he saw the Doctor disquieted. 'I would recommend him to sacrifice it. Come! Give me

your authority, like a dear good man. For his daughter's sake, my dear Manette!'

Very strange to see what a struggle there was within him!

'In her name, then, let it be done. Let it be removed when he is not there; let him miss his old companion after an absence.'

Mr Lorry readily engaged for that, and the conference was ended. On the three following days the Doctor remained perfectly well, and on the fourteenth day he went away to join Lucie and her husband.

On the night of the day on which he left the house, Mr Lorry went into his room with a chopper, saw, chisel, and hammer, attended by Miss Pross carrying a light. There, with closed doors, and in a mysterious and guilty manner, Mr Lorry hacked the shoemaker's bench to pieces, while Miss Pross held the candle as if she were assisting at a murder. The burning of the body was commenced without delay in the kitchen fire; and the tools, shoes, and leather, were buried in the garden. So wicked do destruction and secrecy appear to honest minds, that Mr Lorry and Miss Pross, while engaged in the commission of their deed and in the removal of its traces, almost felt, and almost looked, like accomplices in a horrible crime.

20

A Plea

When the newly-married pair came home, the first person who appeared, to offer his congratulations, was Sydney Carton.

He watched his opportunity of taking Darnay aside into a window, and of speaking to him when no one overheard.

'Mr Darnay,' said Carton, 'I wish we might be friends.'

'We are already friends, I hope.'

'You are good enough to say so, as a fashion of speech; but, I don't mean any fashion of speech. Indeed, when I say I wish we might be friends, I scarcely mean quite that, either.'

Charles Darnay – as was natural – asked him, in all good-humour and good-fellowship, what he did mean?

'Upon my life,' said Carton, smiling, 'I find that easier to comprehend in my own mind, than to convey to yours. However, let me try. You remember a certain famous occasion when I was more drunk than – than usual?'

'I remember a certain famous occasion when you forced me to confess that you had been drinking.'

'Ah!' said Carton. 'On the drunken occasion in question, I was insufferable about liking you, and not liking you. I wish you would forget it.'

'I forgot it long ago.'

'Fashion of speech again! But, Mr Darnay, oblivion is not so easy to me, as you represent it to be to you. I have by no means forgotten it, and a light answer does not help me to forget it.'

'If it was a light answer,' returned Darnay, 'I beg your forgiveness for it. I had no other object than to turn a slight thing, which, to my surprise, seems to trouble you too much, aside. I declare to you on the faith of a gentleman, that I have long dismissed it from my mind. Have I had nothing more important to remember, in the great service you rendered me that day?'

'As to the great service,' said Carton, 'I am bound to avow to you, when you speak of it in that way, that it was mere professional claptrap.'

'You make light of the obligation,' returned Darnay, 'but I will not quarrel with *your* light answer.'

'Genuine truth, Mr Darnay, trust me! I have gone aside from my purpose; I was speaking about our being friends. Now, you know me as a dissolute dog who has never done any good, and never will.'

'I don't know that you "never will."'

'But I do. Well! If you could endure to have such a worthless fellow, coming and going at odd times, I should ask that I might be permitted to come and go as a privileged person here. I doubt if I should abuse the permission. It is a hundred to one if I should avail myself of it four times in a year. It would satisfy me, I dare say, to know that I had it.'

'Will you try?'

'That is another way of saying that I am placed on the footing I have indicated. I thank you, Darnay. I may use that freedom with your name?'

'I think so, Carton, by this time.'

They shook hands upon it, and Sydney turned away.

When he was gone, and in the course of an evening passed with Miss Pross, the Doctor, and Mr Lorry, Charles Darnay made some mention of this conversation in general terms, and spoke of Sydney Carton as a problem of carelessness and recklessness. He spoke of him, in short, not bitterly or meaning to bear hard upon him, but as anybody might who saw him as he showed himself.

He had no idea that this could dwell in the thoughts of his fair young wife; but, when he afterwards joined her in their own rooms, he found her waiting for him with the old pretty lifting of the forehead strongly marked.

'We are thoughtful tonight!' said Darnay, drawing his arm about her.

'Yes, dearest Charles, we are rather thoughtful tonight, for we have something on our mind tonight.'

'What is it, my Lucie?'

'I think, Charles, poor Mr Carton deserves more consideration and respect than you expressed for him tonight.'

'Indeed, my own? Why so?'

'That is what you are not to ask me. But I think – I know – he does.'

'If you know it, it is enough. What would you have me do, my Life?'

'I would ask you, dearest, to be very lenient on his faults when he is not by. I would ask you to believe that he has a heart he very, very seldom reveals, and that there are deep wounds in it.'

'It is a painful reflection to me,' said Charles Darnay, quite astounded, 'that I should have done him any wrong. I never thought this of him.'

'My husband, it is so. There is scarcely a hope that anything in his character or fortunes is reparable now. But, I am sure that he is capable of good things, gentle things, even magnanimous things.'

She looked so beautiful in the purity of her faith in this lost man, that her husband could have looked at her as she was for hours.

'And, O my dearest Love!' she urged, 'remember how

strong we are in our happiness, and how weak he is in his misery!'

The supplication touched him home. 'I will always remember it, dear Heart! I will remember it as long as I live.'

21

Echoing Footsteps

A wonderful corner for echoes, that corner where the Doctor lived. Ever busily winding the golden thread which bound her husband, and her father, and herself, and her old directress and companion, in a life of quiet bliss, Lucie sat in the still house, listening to the echoing footsteps of years.

At first, there were times, though she was a perfectly happy young wife, when her work would slowly fall from her hands, and her eyes would be dimmed. For, there was something coming in the echoes, something light, afar off, and scarcely audible yet, that stirred her heart too much. Fluttering hopes and doubts divided her breast. Among the echoes then, there would arise the sound of footsteps at her own early grave; and thoughts of the husband who would be left so desolate, and who would mourn for her so much, swelled to her eyes, and broke like waves.

That time passed, and her little Lucie lay on her bosom. Then, among the advancing echoes, there was the tread

of her tiny feet and the sound of her prattling words, and the shady house was sunny with a child's laugh.

Ever busily winding the golden thread that bound them all together, Lucie heard in the echoes of years none but friendly and soothing sounds. Her husband's step was strong and prosperous among them; her father's firm and equal. Lo, Miss Pross, in harness of string, awakening the echoes, as an unruly charger, whip-corrected, snorting and pawing the earth under the plane-tree in the garden!

Even when there were sounds of sorrow among the rest, they were not harsh nor cruel. Even when golden hair, like her own, lay in a halo on a pillow round the worn face of a little boy, those were not tears all of agony that wetted his young mother's cheek, as the spirit departed from her embrace that had been entrusted to it. Suffer them and forbid them not. They see my Father's face. O Father, blessed words!

Thus, the rustling of an Angel's wings got blended with the other echoes. Sighs of the winds that blew over a little garden-tomb were mingled with them also, and both were audible to Lucie, in a hushed murmur, as the little Lucie, comically studious at the task of the morning, or dressing a doll at her mother's footstool, chattered in the tongues of the Two Cities that were blended in her life.

The echoes rarely answered to the actual tread of Sydney Carton. Some half-dozen times a year, at most, he claimed

his privilege of coming in uninvited, and would sit among them through the evening, as he had once done often.

No man ever really loved a woman, lost her and knew her with a blameless though an unchanged mind, when she was a wife and a mother, but her children had a strange sympathy with him – an instinctive delicacy of pity for him. Carton was the first stranger to whom little Lucie held out her chubby arms, and he kept his place with her as she grew. The little boy had spoken of him, almost at the last. 'Poor Carton! Kiss him for me!'

Mr Stryver shouldered his way through the law, like some great engine forcing itself through turbid water, and dragged his useful friend in his wake, like a boat towed astern. As the boat so favoured is usually in a rough plight, and mostly under water, so, Sydney had a swamped life of it. But, easy and strong custom, unhappily so much easier and stronger in him than any stimulating sense of desert or disgrace, made it the life he was to lead. Stryver was rich; had married a florid widow with property and three boys.

These three young gentlemen, Mr Stryver, had walked before him like three sheep to the quiet corner in Soho, and had offered as pupils to Lucie's husband: delicately saying, 'Halloa! here are three lumps of bread-and-cheese towards your matrimonial picnic, Darnay!' The polite rejection of the three lumps of bread-and-cheese had quite bloated Mr Stryver with indignation, which he afterwards turned to account in the training of the young gentlemen,

by directing them to beware of the pride of Beggars, like that tutor-fellow.

These were among the echoes to which Lucie, sometimes pensive, sometimes amused and laughing, listened in the echoing corner, until her little daughter was six years old. How near to her heart the echoes of her child's tread came, and those of her own dear father's, always active and self-possessed, and those of her dear husband's, need not be told.

But, there were other echoes, from a distance, that rumbled menacingly in the corner all through this space of time. And it was now, about little Lucie's sixth birthday, that they began to have an awful sound, as of a great storm in France with a dreadful sea rising.

On a night in mid-July, one thousand seven hundred and eighty-nine, Mr Lorry came in late, from Tellson's, and sat himself down by Lucie and her husband in the dark window. It was a hot, wild night, and they were all three reminded of the old Sunday night when they had looked at the lightning from the same place.

'I began to think,' said Mr Lorry, pushing his brown wig back, 'that I should have to pass the night at Tellson's. We have been so full of business all day, that we have not known what to do first, or which way to turn. There is such an uneasiness in Paris, that we have actually a run of confidence upon us! Our customers over there, seem not to be able to confide their property to us fast enough.'

'That has a bad look,' said Darnay.

'A bad look, you say, my dear Darnay? Yes, but we don't know what reason there is in it. People are so unreasonable! Some of us at Tellson's are getting old, and we really can't be troubled out of the ordinary course without due occasion.'

'Still,' said Darnay, 'you know how gloomy and threatening the sky is.'

'I know that, to be sure,' assented Mr Lorry, 'but I am determined to be peevish after my long day's botheration. Where is Manette?'

'Here he is,' said the Doctor, entering the dark room at the moment.

'I am quite glad you are at home; for these hurries and fore-bodings by which I have been surrounded all day long, have made me nervous without reason. You are not going out, I hope?'

'No; I am going to play backgammon with you, if you like,' said the Doctor.

'I don't think I do like, if I may speak my mind. I am not fit to be pitted against you tonight. Is the tea-board still there, Lucie?'

'Of course, it has been kept for you.'

'Thank ye, my dear. The precious child is safe in bed?'

'And sleeping soundly.'

'That's right; all safe and well! I don't know why anything should be otherwise than safe and well here,

thank God; but I have been so put out all day, and I am not as young as I was! My tea, my dear? Thank ye. Now, let us sit quiet, and hear the echoes about which you have your theory.'

'Not a theory; it was a fancy.'

'A fancy, then, my wise pet,' said Mr Lorry, patting her hand. 'They are very numerous and very loud, though, are they not? Only hear them!'

Headlong, mad, and dangerous footsteps to force their way into anybody's life, footsteps not easily made clean again if once stained red, the footsteps raging in Saint Antoine afar off, as the little circle sat in the dark London window.

Saint Antoine had been, that morning, a vast dusky mass of scarecrows heaving to and fro, with frequent gleams of light above the billowy heads, where steel blades and bayonets shone in the sun. A tremendous roar arose from the throat of Saint Antoine, and a forest of naked arms struggled in the air like shrivelled branches of trees in a winter wind: all the fingers convulsively clutching at every weapon or semblance of a weapon that was thrown up from the depths below, no matter how far off.

Muskets were being distributed – so were cartridges, powder, and ball, bars of iron and wood, knives, axes, pikes, every weapon that distracted ingenuity could discover or devise. Every pulse and heart in Saint Antoine

was on high-fever strain and at high-fever heat. Every living creature there held life as of no account, and was demented with a passionate readiness to sacrifice it.

As a whirlpool of boiling waters has a centre point, so, all this raging circled round Defarge's wine-shop, and every human drop in the caldron had a tendency to be sucked towards the vortex where Defarge himself, already begrimed with gunpowder and sweat, issued orders, issued arms, thrust this man back, dragged this man forward, and strove in the thickest of the uproar.

'Keep near to me, Jacques Three,' cried Defarge; 'and do you, Jacques One and Two, separate and put yourselves at the head of as many of these patriots as you can. Where is my wife?'

'Eh, well! Here you see me!' said madame, composed as ever, but not knitting today. Madame's resolute right hand was occupied with an axe, in place of the usual softer implements, and in her girdle were a pistol and a cruel knife.

'Where do you go, my wife?'

'I go,' said madame, 'with you at present. You shall see me at the head of women, by-and-by.'

'Come, then!' cried Defarge, in a resounding voice. 'Patriots and friends, we are ready! The Bastille!'

With a roar that sounded as if all the breath in France had been shaped into the detested word, the living sea rose, wave on wave, depth on depth, and overflowed the

city to that point. Alarm-bells ringing, drums beating, the sea raging and thundering on its new beach, the attack begun.

Through the fire and through the smoke – in the fire and in the smoke.

Defarge of the wine-shop worked like a manful soldier, two fierce hours.

Deep ditch, single drawbridge; massive stone walls, eight great towers, cannon, muskets, fire and smoke. One drawbridge down! 'Work, comrades all, work! In the name of all the Angels or the Devils – which you prefer – work!' Thus Defarge of the wine-shop, still at his gun, which had long grown hot.

'To me, women!' cried madame his wife. 'What! We can kill as well as the men when the place is taken!'

Cannon, muskets, fire and smoke; but, still the deep ditch, the single drawbridge, the massive stone walls, and the eight great towers. Flashing weapons, blazing torches, smoking waggon-loads of wet straw, hard work at neighbouring barricades in all directions, shrieks, volleys, execrations, bravery without stint, boom, smash and rattle, and the furious sounding of the living sea; but, still the deep ditch, and the single drawbridge, and the massive stone walls, and the eight great towers, and still Defarge of the wine-shop at his gun, grown doubly hot by the service of four fierce hours.

A white flag from within the fortress, and a parley –

suddenly the sea rose immeasurably wider and higher, and swept Defarge of the wine-shop over the lowered drawbridge, past the massive stone outer walls, in among the eight great towers surrendered!

So resistless was the force of the ocean bearing him on, that even to draw his breath or turn his head was as impracticable as if he had been struggling in the surf at the South Sea, until he was landed in the outer court-yard of the Bastille. Jacques Three was nearly at his side; Madame Defarge, still heading some of her women, was visible in the inner distance, and her knife was in her hand. Everywhere was tumult, exultation, deafening and maniacal bewilderment, astounding noise, yet furious dumb-show.

'The Prisoners!'

'The Records!'

'The secret cells!'

'The instruments of torture!'

Of all these cries, and ten thousand incoherencies, 'The Prisoners!' was the cry most taken up by the sea that rushed in, as if there were an eternity of people, as well as of time and space. When the foremost billows rolled past, bearing the prison officers with them, and threatening them all with instant death if any secret nook remained undisclosed, Defarge laid his strong hand on the breast of one of these men, separated him from the rest, and got him between himself and the wall.

'Show me the North Tower!' said Defarge. 'Quick!'

'I will faithfully,' replied the man, 'if you will come with me. But there is no one there.'

'What is the meaning of One Hundred and Five, North Tower?' asked Defarge. 'Quick!'

'The meaning, monsieur?'

'Does it mean a captive, or a place of captivity?'

'Monsieur, it is a cell.'

'Show it me!'

'Pass this way, then.'

Jacques Three, with his usual craving on him, and evidently disappointed by the dialogue taking a turn that did not seem to promise bloodshed, held by Defarge's arm as he held by the turnkey's.

Through gloomy vaults where the light of day had never shone, past hideous doors of dark dens and cages, down cavernous flights of steps, and again up steep rugged ascents of stone and brick, Defarge, the turnkey, and Jacques Three, linked hand and arm, went with all the speed they could make.

The turnkey stopped at a low door, put a key in a clashing lock, swung the door slowly open, and said, as they all bent their heads and passed in:

'One hundred and five, North Tower!'

There was a small, heavily-grated, unglazed window high in the wall, with a stone screen before it, so that the sky could be only seen by stooping low and looking up.

There was a small chimney, heavily barred across, a few feet within. There was a heap of old feathery wood-ashes on the hearth. There was a stool, and table, and a straw bed. There were the four blackened walls, and a rusted iron ring in one of them.

'Pass that torch slowly along these walls, that I may see them,' said Defarge to the turnkey.

The man obeyed, and Defarge followed the light closely with his eyes.

'Stop! – Look here, Jacques!'

'A. M.!' croaked Jacques Three, as he read greedily.

'Alexandre Manette,' said Defarge in his ear, following the letters with his swart forefinger, deeply engrained with gunpowder. 'And here he wrote "a poor physician." And it was he, without doubt, who scratched a calendar on this stone. What is that in your hand? A crowbar? Give it me!'

He had still the linstock of his gun in his own hand. He made a sudden exchange of the two instruments, and turning on the worm-eaten stool and table, beat them to pieces in a few blows.

'Hold the light higher!' he said, wrathfully, to the turnkey. 'Look among those fragments with care, Jacques, Here is my knife,' throwing it to him; 'rip open that bed, and search the straw.'

With a menacing look at the turnkey he crawled upon the hearth, and, peering up the chimney, struck and prised

at its sides with the crowbar, and worked at the iron grating across it. In a few minutes, some mortar and dust came dropping down, and in a crevice in the chimney into which his weapon had slipped or wrought itself, he groped with a cautious touch.

'Nothing in the wood, and nothing in the straw, Jacques?'

'Nothing.'

'Let us collect them together, in the middle of the cell. So! Light them, you!'

The turnkey fired the little pile, which blazed high and hot. Stooping again to come out at the low-arched door, they left it burning, and retraced their way to the court-yard; seeming to recover their sense of hearing as they came down, until they were in the raging flood once more.

They found it surging and tossing, in quest of Defarge himself. Saint Antoine was clamorous to have its wine-shop keeper foremost in the guard upon the governor who had defended the Bastille and shot the people. Other-wise, the governor would not be marched to the Hôtel de Ville for judgment. Otherwise, the governor would escape, and the people's blood be unavenged.

In the howling universe of passion and contention that seemed to encompass this grim old officer conspicuous in his grey coat and red decoration, there was but one quite steady figure, and that was a woman's. She stood

immovable close to the grim old officer, remained immovable close to him through the streets, as Defarge and the rest bore him along; remained immovable close to him when he was got near his destination, and began to be struck at from behind; remained immovable close to him when the long-gathering rain of stabs and blows fell heavy; was so close to him when he dropped dead under it, that, suddenly animated, she put her foot upon his neck, and with her cruel knife – long ready – hewed off his head.

The hour was come, when Saint Antoine was to execute his horrible idea of hoisting up men for lamps to show what he could be and do. Saint Antoine's blood was up, and the blood of tyranny and domination by the iron hand was down – down on the steps of the Hôtel de Ville where the governor's body lay – down on the sole of the shoe of Madame Defarge where she had trodden on the body to steady it for mutilation.

In the ocean of faces where every fierce and furious expression was in vivid life, there were two groups of faces – each seven in number – so fixedly contrasting with the rest, that never did sea roll which bore more memorable wrecks with it. Seven faces of prisoners, suddenly released by the storm that had burst their tomb, were carried high overhead: all scared, all lost, all wondering and amazed, as if the Last Day were come, and those who rejoiced around them were lost spirits. Other seven faces there were, carried higher, seven dead faces, whose drooping

eyelids and half-seen eyes awaited the Last Day. Impassive faces, yet with a suspended – not an abolished – expression on them; faces, rather, in a fearful pause, as having yet to raise the dropped lids of the eyes, and bear witness with the bloodless lips, 'THOU DIDST IT!'

Seven prisoners released, seven gory heads on pikes, the keys of the accursed fortress of the eight strong towers, some discovered letters and other memorials of prisoners of old time, long dead of broken hearts, – such, and suchlike, the loudly echoing footsteps of Saint Antoine escort through the Paris streets in mid-July, one thousand seven hundred and eighty-nine.

22

The Sea Still Rises

Madame Defarge, with her arms folded, sat in the morning light and heat, contemplating the wine-shop and the street. In both, there were several knots of loungers, squalid and miserable, but now with a manifest sense of power enthroned on their distress. The raggedest nightcap, awry on the wretchedest head, had this crooked significance in it: 'I know how hard it has grown for me, the wearer of this, to support life in myself; but do you know how easy it has grown for me, the wearer of this, to destroy life in you!' Every lean bare arm, that had been without work before, had this work always ready for it now, that it could strike. The fingers of the knitting women were vicious, with the experience that they could tear. There was a change in the appearance of Saint Antoine; the image had been hammering into this for hundreds of years, and the last finishing blows had told mightily on the expression.

Madame Defarge sat observing it, with such suppressed approval as was to be desired in the leader of the Saint Antoine women. One of her sisterhood knitted beside her.

The short, rather plump wife of a starved grocer, and the mother of two children withal, this lieutenant had already earned the complimentary name of The Vengeance.

'Hark!' said The Vengeance. 'Listen, then! Who comes?'

'It is Defarge,' said madame. 'Silence, patriots!'

Defarge came in breathless, pulled off a red cap he wore, and looked around him! 'Listen, everywhere!' said madame again. 'Listen to him!' Defarge stood, panting, against a background of eager eyes and open mouths, formed outside the door; all those within the wine-shop had sprung to their feet.

'Say then, my husband. What is it?'

'Does everybody here recall old Foulon, who told the famished people that they might eat grass, and who died, and went to Hell?'

'Everybody!' from all throats.

'The news is of him. He is among us!'

'Among us!' from the universal throat again. 'And dead?'

'Not dead! He feared us so much – and with reason – that he caused himself to be represented as dead, and had a grand mock-funeral. But they have found him alive, hiding in the country, and have brought him in. I have seen him but now, on his way to the Hôtel de Ville, a prisoner. I have said that he had reason to fear us. Say all! *Had* he reason?'

Wretched old sinner of more than threescore years and ten, if he had never known it yet, he would have known

it in his heart of hearts if he could have heard the answering cry.

'Patriots!' said Defarge, in a determined voice, 'are we ready?'

Instantly Madame Defarge's knife was in her girdle; the drum was beating in the streets, as if it and a drummer had flown together by magic; and The Vengeance, uttering terrific shrieks, and flinging her arms about her head like all the forty Furies at once, was tearing from house to house, rousing the women.

The men were terrible, in the bloody-minded anger with which they looked from windows, caught up what arms they had, and came pouring down into the streets; but, the women were a sight to chill the boldest. They ran out with streaming hair, urging one another, and themselves, to madness with the wildest cries and actions. Villain Foulon taken, my sister. Old Foulon taken, my mother. Miscreant Foulon taken, my daughter. Then, a score of others ran into the midst of these, beating their breasts, tearing their hair, and screaming, Foulon alive. Foulon who told the starving people they might eat grass. Foulon who told my old father that he might eat grass, when I had no bread to give him. Husbands, and brothers, and young men, Give us the blood of Foulon, Give us the head of Foulon.

Not a moment was lost; not a moment! This Foulon was at the Hôtel de Ville, and might be loosed. Never, if Saint Antoine knew his own sufferings, insults, and wrongs!

Armed men and women flocked out of the Quarter so fast, and drew even these last dregs after them with such a force of suction, that within a quarter of an hour there was not a human creature in Saint Antoine's bosom but a few old crones and the wailing children.

No. They were all by this time choking the Hall of Examination where this old man, ugly and wicked, was, and over-flowing into the adjacent open space and streets. The Defarges, husband and wife. The Vengeance, and Jacques Three, were in the first press, and at no great distance from him in the Hall.

'See!' cried madame, pointing with her knife. 'See the old villain bound with ropes. That was well done to tie a bunch of grass upon his back. Ha, ha! That was well done.'

The people immediately behind Madame Defarge, explaining the cause of her satisfaction to those behind them, and those again explaining to others, and those to others, the neighbouring streets resounded with the clapping of hands. Similarly, during two or three hours of brawl, and the winnowing of many bushels of words, Madame Defarge's frequent expressions of impatience were taken up, with marvellous quickness, at a distance.

At length the sun rose so high that it struck a kindly ray as of hope or protection, directly down upon the old prisoner's head. The favour was too much to bear; in an instant the barrier of dust and chaff that had stood surprisingly long, went to the winds, and Saint Antoine had got him!

Defarge had but sprung over a railing and a table, and folded the miserable wretch in a deadly embrace – Madame Defarge had but followed and turned her hand in one of the ropes with which he was tied – The Vengeance and Jacques Three were not yet up with them, and the men at the windows had not yet swooped into the Hall, like birds of prey from their high perches – when the cry seemed to go up, all over the city, 'Bring him out! Bring him to the lamp!'

Down, and up, and head foremost on the steps of the building; now, on his back; dragged, and struck at, and stifled by the bunches of grass and straw that were thrust into his face by hundreds of hands; torn, bruised, panting, bleeding, yet always entreating and beseeching for mercy; now full of vehement agony of action, with a small clear space about him as the people drew one another back that they might see; now, a log of dead wood drawn through a forest of legs; he was hauled to the nearest street corner where one of the fatal lamps swung, and there Madame Defarge let him go and silently and composedly looked at him while they made ready, and while he besought her. Once, he went aloft, and the rope broke, and they caught him shrieking; twice, he went aloft, and the rope broke, and they caught him shrieking; then, the rope was merciful, and held him, and his head was soon upon a pike, with grass enough in the mouth for all Saint Antoine to dance at the sight of.

Nor was this the end of the day's bad work, for Saint Antoine, on hearing when the day closed in that the son-in-law of the despatched was coming into Paris under a guard five hundred strong, in cavalry alone. Saint Antoine wrote his crimes on flaring sheets of paper, seized him, set his head and heart on pikes, and carried the three spoils of the day in Wolf-procession through the streets.

Not before dark night did the men and women come back to the children, wailing and breadless. Then, the miserable bakers' shops were beset by long files of them, patiently waiting to buy bad bread; and while they waited with stomachs faint and empty, they beguiled the time by embracing one another on the triumphs of the day, and achieving them again in gossip.

Fathers and mothers who had had their full share in the worst of the day, played gently with their meagre children; and lovers, with such a world around them and before them, loved and hoped.

It was almost morning, when Defarge's wine-shop parted with its last knot of customers, and Monsieur Defarge said to madame his wife, in husky tones, while fastening the door:

'At last it is come, my dear!'

'Eh well!' returned madame. 'Almost.'

Saint Antoine slept, the Defarges slept: even The Vengeance slept with her starved grocer, and the drum was at rest.

23

Fire Rises

There was a change on the village where the fountain fell, and where the mender of roads went forth daily to hammer out of the stones on the highway such morsels of bread as might serve for patches to hold his poor ignorant soul and his poor reduced body together. The prison on the crag was not so dominant as of yore; there were soldiers to guard it, but not many; there were officers to guard the soldiers, but not one of them knew what his men would do – beyond this: that it would probably not be what he was ordered.

Far and wide lay a ruined country, yielding nothing but desolation. Everything was bowed down, dejected, oppressed, and broken. Habitations, fences, domesticated animals, men, women, children, and the soil that bore them – all worn out.

Monseigneur was a national blessing, gave a chivalrous tone to things, was a polite example of luxurious and shining life, and a great deal more to equal purpose; nevertheless, Monseigneur as a class had, somehow or

other, brought things to this. There must be something short-sighted in the eternal arrangements, surely! Thus it was, however; and the last drop of blood having been extracted from the flints, and the last screw of the rack having been turned so often that its purchase crumbled, and it now turned and turned with nothing to bite, Monseigneur began to run away from a phenomenon so low and unaccountable.

But, this was not the change on the village, and on many a village like it. For scores of years gone by, Monseigneur had squeezed it and wrung it, and had seldom graced it with his presence except for the pleasures of the chase. The change consisted in the appearance of strange faces of low caste, rather than in the disappearance of the high-caste, chiselled, and otherwise beatified and beatifying features of Monseigneur.

For, in these times, as the mender of roads worked, solitary, in the dust – in these times, as he raised his eyes from his lonely labour, and viewed the prospect, he would see some rough figure approaching on foot, the like of which was once a rarity in those parts, but was now a frequent presence. As it advanced, the mender of roads would discern without surprise, that it was a shaggy-haired man of almost barbarian aspect, tall, in wooden shoes that were clumsy even to the eyes of a mender of roads, grim, rough, swart, steeped in the mud and dust of many highways.

Such a man came upon him, like a ghost, at noon in the July weather, as he sat on his heap of stones under a bank, taking such shelter as he could get from a shower of hail.

The man looked at him, looked at the village in the hollow, at the mill, and at the prison on the crag. When he had identified these objects in what benighted mind he had, he said, in a dialect that was just intelligible:

'How goes it, Jacques?'

'All well, Jacques.'

'No dinner?'

'Nothing but supper now,' said the mender of roads, with a hungry face.

'It is the fashion,' growled the man. 'I meet no dinner anywhere.'

He took out a blackened pipe, filled it, lighted it with flint and steel, pulled at it until it was in a bright glow: then, suddenly held it from him and dropped something into it from between his finger and thumb, that blazed and went out in a puff of smoke.

'Tonight?' said the mender of roads.

'Tonight,' said the man, putting the pipe in his mouth.

'Where?'

'Here.'

'Show me!' said the traveller then, moving to the brow of the hill.

'See!' returned the mender of roads, with extended

finger. 'You go down here, and straight through the street, and past the fountain –'

'To the Devil with all that!' interrupted the other, rolling his eye over the landscape. '*I* go through no streets and past no fountains. Well?'

'Well! About two leagues beyond the summit of that hill above the village.'

'Good. When do you cease to work?'

'At sunset.'

'Will you wake me, before departing? I have walked two nights without resting. Let me finish my pipe, and I shall sleep like a child. Will you wake me?'

'Surely.'

The wayfarer smoked his pipe out, put it in his breast, slipped off his great wooden shoes, and lay down on his back on the heap of stones. He was fast asleep directly.

As the road-mender plied his dusty labour, and the hail-clouds, rolling away, revealed bright bars and streaks of sky which were responded to by silver gleams upon the landscape, the little man seemed fascinated by the figure on the heap of stones. The bronze face, the shaggy black hair and beard, the powerful frame attenuated by spare living, and the sullen and desperate compression of the lips in sleep, inspired the mender of roads with awe.

The man slept on, indifferent to showers of hail and intervals of brightness, to sunshine on his face and shadow, to the pattering lumps of dull ice on his body and the

diamonds into which the sun changed them, until the sun was low in the west, and the sky was glowing. Then, the mender of roads having got his tools together and all things ready to go down into the village, roused him.

'Good!' said the sleeper, rising on his elbow. 'Two leagues beyond the summit of the hill?'

'About.'

The mender of roads went home, with the dust going on before him according to the set of the wind, and was soon at the fountain, squeezing himself in among the lean kine brought there to drink, and appearing even to whisper to them in his whispering to all the village. When the village had taken its poor supper, it did not creep to bed, as it usually did, but came out of doors again, and remained there. A curious contagion of whispering was upon it, and also, when it gathered together at the fountain in the dark, another curious contagion of looking expectantly at the sky in one direction only. Monsieur Gabelle, chief functionary of the place, became uneasy; went out on his house-top alone, and looked in that direction too; glanced down from behind his chimneys at the darkening faces by the fountain below, and sent word to the sacristan who kept the keys of the church, that there might be need to ring the tocsin by-and-by.

The night deepened. The trees environing the old château, keeping its solitary state apart, moved in a rising wind, as though they threatened the pile of building

massive and dark in the gloom. Up the two terrace flights of steps the rain ran wildly, and beat at the great door, like a swift messenger rousing those within; uneasy rushes of wind went through the hall, and passed lamenting up the stairs, and shook the curtains of the bed where the last Marquis had slept. East, West, North, and South, through the woods, four heavy-treading, unkempt figures crushed the high grass and cracked the branches, striding on cautiously to come together in the court-yard. Four lights broke out there, and moved away in different directions, and all was black again.

But, not for long. Presently, the château began to make itself strangely visible by some light of its own, as though it were growing luminous. Then, a flickering streak played behind the architecture of the front, picking out transparent places, and showing where balustrades, arches, and windows were. Then it soared higher, and grew broader and brighter. Soon, from a score of the great windows, flames burst forth, and the stone faces awakened, stared out of fire.

A faint murmur arose about the house from the few people who were left there, and there was a saddling of a horse and riding away. There was spurring and splashing through the darkness, and bridle was drawn in the space by the village fountain, and the horse in a foam stood at Monsieur Gabelle's door. 'Help, Gabelle! Help, every one!' The tocsin rang impatiently, but other help (if that were

any) there was none. The mender of roads, and two hundred and fifty particular friends, stood with folded arms at the fountain, looking at the pillar of fire in the sky. 'It must be forty feet high,' said they, grimly; and never moved.

The rider from the château, and the horse in a foam, clattered away through the village, and galloped up the stony steep, to the prison on the crag. At the gate, a group of officers were looking at the fire; removed from them, a group of soldiers. 'Help, gentlemen-officers! The château is on fire; valuable objects may be saved from the flames by timely aid! Help, help!' The officers looked towards the soldiers who looked at the fire; gave no orders; and answered, with shrugs and biting of lips, 'It must burn.'

As the rider rattled down the hill again and through the street, the village was illuminating. The mender of roads, and the two hundred and fifty particular friends, inspired as one man and woman by the idea of lighting up, had darted into their houses, and were putting candles in every dull little pane of glass.

The château was left to itself to flame and burn. With the rising and falling of the blaze, the stone faces showed as if they were in torment.

The château burned; the nearest trees, laid hold of by the fire, scorched and shrivelled; trees at a distance, fired by the four fierce figures, begirt the blazing edifice with a new forest of smoke. Molten lead and iron boiled in the

marble basin of the fountain; the water ran dry; the extinguisher tops of the towers vanished like ice before the heat, and trickled down into four rugged wells of flame. Four fierce figures trudged away, East, West, North, and South, along the night-enshrouded roads, guided by the beacon they had lighted, towards their next destination. The illuminated village had seized hold of the tocsin, and, abolishing the lawful ringer, rang for joy.

Not only that; but the village, light-headed with famine, fire, and bell-ringing, and bethinking itself that Monsieur Gabelle had to do with the collection of rent and taxes, became impatient for an interview with him, and, surrounding his house, summoned him to come forth for personal conference. Whereupon, Monsieur Gabelle did heavily bar his door, and retire to hold counsel with himself. The result of that conference was, that Gabelle again withdrew himself to his house-top behind his stack of chimneys: this time resolved, if his door was broken in, to pitch himself head foremost over the parapet, and crush a man or two below.

Probably, Monsieur Gabelle passed a long night up there, with the distant château for fire and candle, and the beating at his door, combined with the joy-ringing, for music; not to mention his having an ill-omened lamp slung across the road before his posting-house gate, which the village showed a lively inclination to displace in his favour. A trying suspense, to be passing a whole summer

night on the brink of the black ocean, ready to take that plunge into it upon which Monsieur Gabelle had resolved! But, the friendly dawn appearing at last, and the rush-candles of the village guttering out, the people happily dispersed, and Monsieur Gabelle came down bringing his life with him for that while.

Within a hundred miles, and in the light of other fires, there were other functionaries less fortunate, that night and other nights, whom the rising sun found hanging across once-peaceful streets, where they had been born and bred; also, there were other villagers and townspeople less fortunate than the mender of roads and his fellows, upon whom the functionaries and soldiery turned with success, and whom they strung up in their turn. But, the fierce figures were steadily wending East, West, North, and South, be that as it would; and whosoever hung, fire burned.

24

Drawn to the Loadstone Rock

In such risings of fire and risings of sea three years of tempest were consumed. Three more birthdays of little Lucie had been woven by the golden thread into the peaceful tissue of the life of her home.

Many a night and many a day had its inmates listened to the echoes in the corner, with hearts that failed them when they heard the thronging feet. For, the footsteps had become to their minds as the footsteps of a people, tumultuous under a red flag and with their country declared in danger, changed into wild beasts, by terrible enchantment long persisted in.

Monseigneur, as a class, had dissociated himself from the phenomenon of his not being appreciated. Like the fabled rustic who raised the Devil with infinite pains, and was so terrified at the sight of him that he could ask the Enemy no question, but immediately fled; so, Monseigneur, after boldly reading the Lord's Prayer backwards for a great number of years, and performing many other potent spells for compelling the Evil One,

no sooner beheld him in his terrors than he took to his noble heels.

The August of the year one thousand seven hundred and ninety-two was come, and Monseigneur was by this time scattered far and wide.

As was natural, the head-quarters and great gathering-place of Monseigneur, in London, was Tellson's Bank. Spirits are supposed to haunt the places where their bodies most resorted, and Monseigneur without a guinea haunted the spot where his guineas used to be. Moreover, it was the spot to which such French intelligence as was most to be relied upon, came quickest. Again: those nobles who had seen the coming storm in time, and anticipating plunder or confiscation, had made provident remittances to Tellson's, were always to be heard of there by their needy brethren. Tellson's was at that time, as to French intelligence, a kind of High Exchange; and this was so well known to the public, and the inquiries made there were in consequence so numerous, that Tellson's sometimes wrote the latest news out in a line or so and posted it in the Bank windows, for all who ran through Temple-bar to read.

On a steaming, misty afternoon, Mr Lorry sat at his desk, and Charles Darnay stood leaning on it, talking with him in a low voice. The penitential den once set apart for interviews with the House, was now the news-Exchange, and was filled to overflowing. It was within half an hour or so of the time of closing.

'But, although you are the youngest man that ever lived,' said Charles Darnay, rather hesitating, 'I must still suggest to you –'

'I understand. That I am too old?' said Mr Lorry.

'Unsettled weather, a long journey, uncertain means of travelling, a disorganised country, a city that may not be even safe for you.'

'My dear Charles,' said Mr Lorry, with cheerful confidence, 'it is safe enough for me; nobody will care to interfere with an old fellow of hard upon four-score when there are so many people there much better worth interfering with. As to its being a disorganised city, if it were not a disorganised city there would be no occasion to send somebody from our House here to our House there. As to the uncertain travelling, the long journey, and the winter weather, if I were not prepared to submit myself to a few inconveniences for the sake of Tellson's, after all these years, who ought to be?'

'I wish I were going myself,' said Charles Darnay, somewhat restlessly, and like one thinking aloud.

'Indeed! You are a pretty fellow to object and advise!' exclaimed Mr Lorry. 'You wish you were going yourself? And you a Frenchman born? You are a wise counsellor.'

'My dear Mr Lorry, it is because I am a Frenchman born, that the thought has passed through my mind often. One cannot help thinking, having had some sympathy for the miserable people, that one might be listened to,

and might have the power to persuade to some restraint. Only last night, after you had left us, when I was talking to Lucie –'

'When you were talking to Lucie,' Mr Lorry repeated. 'Yes. I wonder you are not ashamed to mention the name of Lucie! Wishing you were going to France at this time of day!'

'However, I am not going,' said Charles Darnay, with a smile. 'It is more to the purpose that you say you are.'

'And I am, in plain reality. The truth is, my dear Charles,' Mr Lorry glanced at the distant House, and lowered his voice, 'you can have no conception of the difficulty with which our business is transacted. The Lord above knows what the compromising consequences would be to numbers of people, if some of our documents were seized or destroyed; and they might be, at any time, you know, for who can say that Paris is not set a-fire today, or sacked tomorrow! Now, a judicious selection from these with the least possible delay, and the burying of them, or otherwise getting of them out of harm's way, is within the power (without loss of precious time) of scarcely any one but myself, if any one.'

'How I admire the gallantry of your youthful spirit, Mr Lorry.'

'Tut! Nonsense, sir – And, my dear Charles,' said Mr Lorry, glancing at the House again, 'you are to remember, that getting things out of Paris at this present time, no matter

what things, is next to an impossibility. At another time, our parcels would come and go, as easily as in business-like Old England; but now, everything is stopped.'

'And do you really go tonight?'

'I really go tonight, for the case has become too pressing to admit of delay.'

'And do you take no one with you?'

'I intend to take Jerry. Jerry has been my body-guard on Sunday nights for a long time past, and I am used to him. Nobody will suspect Jerry of being anything but an English bull-dog, or of having any design in his head but to fly at anybody who touches his master.'

This dialogue had taken place at Mr Lorry's usual desk, with Monseigneur swarming within a yard or two of it, boastful of what he would do to avenge himself on the rascal-people before long. It was too much the way of Monseigneur under his reverses as a refugee, and it was much too much the way of native British orthodoxy, to talk of this terrible Revolution as if nothing had ever been done, or omitted to be done, that had led to it. Such vapouring, combined with the extravagant plots of Monseigneur for the restoration of a state of things that had utterly exhausted itself, and worn out Heaven and earth as well as itself, was hard to be endured without some remonstrance by any sane man who knew the truth. And it was such vapouring all about his ears, like a troublesome confusion of blood in his own head, added

to a latent uneasiness in his mind, which had already made Charles Darnay restless, and which still kept him so.

Among the talkers, was Stryver, of the King's Bench Bar, far on his way to state promotion, and, therefore, loud on the theme: broaching to Monseigneur, his devices for blowing the people up and exterminating them from the face of the earth, and doing without them. Him, Darnay heard with a particular feeling of objection; and Darnay stood divided between going away that he might hear no more, and remaining to interpose his word, when the thing that was to be went on to shape itself out.

The House approached Mr Lorry, and laying a soiled and unopened letter before him, asked if he had yet discovered any traces of the person to whom it was addressed? The House laid the letter down so close to Darnay that he saw the direction. The address, turned into English, ran: 'Very pressing. To Monsieur heretofore the Marquis St Evrémonde, of France, Confided to the cares of Messrs. Tellson and Co., Bankers, London, England.'

On the marriage morning, Dr Manette had made it his one urgent and express request to Charles Darnay, that the secret of this name should be kept inviolate between them. Nobody else knew it to be his name; his own wife had no suspicion of the fact; Mr Lorry could have none.

'No,' said Mr Lorry, in reply to the House; 'I have referred it, I think, to everybody now here, and no one can tell me where this gentleman is to be found.'

He held the letter out inquiringly; and Monseigneur looked at it, in the person of this plotting and indignant refugee: all had something disparaging to say, in French or in English, concerning the Marquis who was not to be found.

'Nephew, I believe – but in any case degenerate successor – of the polished Marquis who was murdered,' said one. 'Happy to say, I never knew him.'

'A craven who abandoned his post,' said another – this Monseigneur had been got out of Paris, legs uppermost and half suffocated, in a load of hay – 'some years ago.'

'Infected with the new doctrines,' said a third, eyeing the direction through his glass in passing; 'set himself in opposition to the last Marquis, abandoned the estates when he inherited them, and left them to the ruffian herd. They will recompense him now, I hope, as he deserves.'

'Hey?' cried the blatant Stryver. 'Did he though? Is that the sort of fellow? Let us look at his infamous name. D——n the fellow!'

Darnay, unable to restrain himself any longer, touched Mr Stryver on the shoulder, and said:

'I know the fellow.'

'Do you, by Jupiter?' said Stryver. 'I am sorry for it.'

'Why?'

'I tell you again, Mr Darnay, I am sorry for it. Here is a fellow, who, infected by the most pestilent and blasphemous code of devilry that ever was known, abandoned his property

to the vilest scum of the earth that ever did murder by wholesale, and you ask me why I am sorry that a man who instructs youth knows him? I am sorry because I believe there is contamination in such a scoundrel. That's why.'

Mindful of the secret, Darnay with great difficulty checked himself, and said: 'You may not understand the gentleman.'

'I understand how to put *you* in a corner, Mr Darnay,' said Bully Stryver, 'and I'll do it. If this fellow is a gentleman, I *don't* understand him. You may tell him so, with my compliments. You may also tell him, from me, that after abandoning his worldly goods and position to this butcherly mob, I wonder he is not at the head of them. But, no, gentlemen,' said Stryver, 'he'll always show 'em a clean pair of heels very early in the scuffle, and sneak away.'

With those words, and a final snap of his fingers, Mr Stryver shouldered himself into Fleet-street, amidst the general approbation of his hearers. Mr Lorry and Charles Darnay were left alone at the desk, in the general departure from the Bank.

'Will you take charge of the letter?' said Mr Lorry. 'You know where to deliver it?'

'I do.'

'Will you undertake to explain, that we suppose it to have been addressed here, on the chance of our knowing where to forward it, and that it has been here some time?'

'I will do so. Do you start for Paris from here?'

'From here, at eight.'

'I will come back, to see you off.'

Very ill at ease with himself, and with Stryver and most other men, Darnay made the best of his way into the quiet of the Temple, opened the letter, and read it. These were its contents:

'Prison of the Abbaye, Paris, June 21, 1792.

'Monsieur heretofore the marquis,

'After having long been in danger of my life at the hands of the village, I have been seized, with great violence and indignity, and brought a long journey on foot to Paris. Nor is that all; my house has been destroyed – razed to the ground.

'The crime for which I am imprisoned, Monsieur heretofore the Marquis, and for which I shall be summoned before the tribunal, and shall lose my life (without your so generous help), is, they tell me, treason against the majesty of the people, in that I have acted against them for an emigrant. It is in vain I represent that I have acted for them, and not against, according to your commands. It is in vain I represent that I had collected no rent; that I had had recourse to no process. The only response is, that I have acted for an emigrant, and where is that emigrant?

'Ah! most gracious Monsieur heretofore the Marquis, where is that emigrant? I send my desolate cry across the sea, hoping it may perhaps reach your ears through the great bank of Tilson known at Paris!

'For the love of Heaven, of justice, of generosity, of the honour of your noble name, I supplicate you, Monsieur heretofore the Marquis, to succour and release me. My fault is, that I have been true to you. Oh Monsieur heretofore the Marquis, I pray you be you true to me!

'From this prison here of horror, whence I every hour tend nearer and nearer to destruction, I send you, Monsieur heretofore the Marquis, the assurance of my dolorous and unhappy service.

'Your afflicted
'GABELLE.'

The latent uneasiness in Darnay's mind was roused to vigorous life by this letter. The peril of an old servant and a good one, whose only crime was fidelity to himself and his family, stared him so reproachfully in the face, that, as he walked to and fro in the Temple considering what to do, he almost hid his face from the passers-by.

He knew very well, that in his horror of the deed which had culminated the bad deeds and bad reputation of the

old family house, in his resentful suspicions of his uncle, and in the aversion with which his conscience regarded the crumbling fabric that he was supposed to uphold, he had acted imperfectly. He knew very well, that in his love for Lucie, his renunciation of his social place had been hurried and incomplete. He knew that he ought to have systematically worked it out and supervised it, and that he had meant to do it, and that it had never been done.

The happiness of his own chosen English home, the necessity of being always actively employed, the swift changes and troubles of the time which had followed on one another so fast; he knew very well, that to the force of these circumstances he had yielded. That he had watched the times for a time of action, and that they had shifted and struggled until the time had gone by, and the nobility were trooping from France by every highway and byway, and their property was in course of confiscation and destruction, and their very names were blotting out, was as well known to himself as it could be to any new authority in France that might impeach him for it.

But, he had oppressed no man, he had imprisoned no man; he was so far from having harshly exacted payment of his dues, that he had relinquished them of his own will, thrown himself on a world with no favour in it, won his own private place there, and earned his own bread. Monsieur Gabelle had held the impoverished and involved estate on written instructions, to spare the people, to give

them what little there was to give, and no doubt he had put the fact in plea and proof, for his own safety, so that it could not but appear now.

This favoured the desperate resolution Charles Darnay had begun to make, that he would go to Paris.

Yes. Like the mariner in the old story, the winds and streams had driven him within the influence of the Loadstone Rock, and it was drawing him to itself, and he must go. His latent uneasiness had been, that bad aims were being worked out in his own unhappy land by bad instruments, and that he who could not fail to know that he was better than they, was not there, trying to do something to stay bloodshed, and assert the claims of mercy and humanity.

His resolution was made. He must go to Paris.

Yes. The Loadstone Rock was drawing him, and he must sail on, until he struck. The intention with which he had done what he had done, even although he had left it incomplete, presented it before him in an aspect that would be gratefully acknowledged in France on his presenting himself to assert it.

As he walked to and fro with his resolution made, he considered that neither Lucie nor her father must know of it until he was gone. Lucie should be spared the pain of separation; and her father, always reluctant to turn his thoughts towards the dangerous ground of old, should come to the knowledge of the step, as a step taken, and not in the balance of suspense and doubt.

He walked to and fro, with thoughts very busy, until it was time to return to Tellson's and take leave of Mr Lorry. As soon as he arrived in Paris he would present himself to this old friend, but he must say nothing of his intention now.

A carriage with post-horses was ready at the Bank door, and Jerry was booted and equipped.

'I have delivered that letter,' said Charles Darnay to Mr Lorry. 'I would not consent to your being charged with any written answer, but perhaps you will take a verbal one?'

'That I will, and readily,' said Mr Lorry, 'if it is not dangerous.'

'Not at all. Though it is to a prisoner in the Abbaye.'

'What is his name?' said Mr Lorry.

'Gabelle.'

'Gabelle. And what is the message to the unfortunate Gabelle in prison?'

'Simply, "that he has received the letter, and will come."'

'Any time mentioned?'

'He will start upon his journey tomorrow night.'

'Any person mentioned?'

'No.'

He helped Mr Lorry to wrap himself in a number of coats and cloaks, and went out with him from the warm atmosphere of the old Bank into the misty air of Fleet-street. 'My love to Lucie, and to little Lucie,' said Mr Lorry at parting, 'and take precious care of them till I come back.'

That night – it was the fourteenth of August – he sat up late, and wrote two fervent letters; one was to Lucie, explaining the strong obligation he was under to go to Paris, and showing her, at length, the reasons that he had, for feeling confident that he could become involved in no personal danger there; the other was to the Doctor, confiding Lucie and their dear child to his care, and dwelling on the same topics with the strongest assurances. To both, he wrote that he would despatch letters in proof of his safety, immediately after his arrival.

It was a hard matter to preserve the innocent deceit of which they were profoundly unsuspicious. But, an affectionate glance at his wife, so happy and busy, made him resolute not to tell her what impended, and the day passed quickly away. Early in the evening he embraced her, and her scarcely less dear namesake, pretending that he would return by-and-by (an imaginary engagement took him out, and he had secreted a valise of clothes ready), and so he emerged into the heavy mist of the heavy streets, with a heavier heart.

He left his two letters with a trusty porter, to be delivered half an hour before midnight, and no sooner; took horse for Dover; and began his journey.

THE END OF BOOK TWO

The Track of a Storm

1

In Secret

The traveller fared slowly on his way, who fared towards Paris from England in the autumn of the year one thousand seven hundred and ninety-two. Every town-gate and village taxing-house had its band of citizen-patriots, with their national muskets in a most explosive state of readiness, who stopped all comers and goers, cross-questioned them, inspected their papers, looked for their names in lists of their own, turned them back, or sent them on, or stopped them and laid them in hold, as their capricious judgment or fancy deemed best for the dawning Republic One and Indivisible, of Liberty, Equality, Fraternity, or Death.

A very few French leagues of his journey were accomplished, when Charles Darnay began to perceive that for him along these country roads there was no hope of return until he should have been declared a good citizen at Paris. Not a mean village closed upon him, not a common barrier dropped across the road behind him, but he knew

it to be another iron door in the series that was barred between him and England.

A universal watchfulness stopped him on the highway twenty times in a stage, and retarded his progress twenty times in a day, by riding after him and taking him back, riding before him and stopping him by anticipation, riding with him and keeping him in charge. He had been days upon his journey in France alone, when he went to bed tired out, in a little town on the high road, still a long way from Paris.

Nothing but the production of the afflicted Gabelle's letter from his prison of the Abbaye would have got him on so far. His difficulty at the guard-house in this small place had been such, that he felt his journey to have come to a crisis. And he was, therefore, as little surprised as a man could be, to find himself awakened at the small inn to which he had been remitted until morning, in the middle of the night.

Awakened by a timid local functionary and three armed patriots in rough red caps and with pipes in their mouths, who sat down on the bed.

'Emigrant,' said the functionary, 'I am going to send you on to Paris, under an escort.'

'Citizen, I desire nothing more than to get to Paris, though I could dispense with the escort.'

'Silence!' growled a red-cap, striking at the coverlet with the butt-end of his musket. 'Peace, aristocrat!'

'It is as the good patriot says,' observed the timid func-

tionary. 'You are an aristocrat, and must have an escort – and must pay for it.'

'I have no choice,' said Charles Darnay.

'Choice! Listen to him!' cried the same scowling red-cap. 'As if it was not a favour to be protected from the lamp-iron!'

Darnay was taken back to the guard-house, where other patriots in rough red caps were smoking, drinking, and sleeping, by a watch-fire. Here he paid a heavy price for his escort, and hence he started with it on the wet, wet roads at three o'clock in the morning.

The escort were two mounted patriots in red caps and tricoloured cockades, armed with national muskets and sabres, who rode one on either side of him. The escorted governed his own horse, but a loose line was attached to his bridle, the end of which one of the patriots kept girded round his wrist.

Charles Darnay did not allow the restraint that was laid upon him to awaken any serious fears in his breast; for, he reasoned with himself that it could have no reference to the merits of an individual case that was not yet stated, and of representations, confirmable by the prisoner in the Abbaye, that were not yet made.

But when they came to the town of Beauvais an ominous crowd gathered to see him dismount at the posting-yard, and many voices called out loudly, 'Down with the emigrant!'

He stopped in the act of swinging himself out of his saddle, and, resuming it as his safest place, said:

'Emigrant, my friends! Do you not see me here, in France, of my own will?'

'You are a cursed emigrant,' cried a farrier, making at him in a furious manner through the press, hammer in hand; 'and you are a cursed aristocrat!'

The postmaster interposed himself between this man and the rider's bridle, and soothingly said, 'Let him be; let him be! He will be judged at Paris.'

'Judged!' repeated the farrier, swinging his hammer. 'Ay! and condemned as a traitor.' At this the crowd roared approval.

Darnay said, as soon as he could make his voice heard: 'Friends, you deceive yourselves, or you are deceived. I am not a traitor.'

'He lies!' cried the smith. 'He is a traitor since the decree. His life is forfeit to the people. His cursed life is not his own!'

At the instant when Darnay saw a rush in the eyes of the crowd, which another instant would have brought upon him, the postmaster turned his horse into the yard, the escort rode in close upon his horse's flanks, and the postmaster shut and barred the crazy double gates.

'What is this decree that the smith spoke of?' Darnay asked the postmaster, when he had thanked him.

'Truly, a decree for selling the property of emigrants.'

'When passed?'

'On the fourteenth.'

'The day I left England!'

'Everybody says there will be others, banishing all emigrants, and condemning all to death who return.'

'But there are no such decrees yet?'

'What do I know!' said the postmaster, shrugging his shoulders.

They rested on some straw in a loft until the middle of the night, and then rode forward again when all the town was asleep. They passed on once more into solitude and loneliness: jingling through the untimely cold and wet, among impoverished fields that had yielded no fruits of the earth that year, diversified by the blackened remains of burnt houses, and by the sudden emergence from ambuscade, and sharp reining up across their way, of patriot patrols on the watch on all the roads.

Daylight at last found them before the wall of Paris. The barrier was closed and strongly guarded when they rode up to it.

'Where are the papers of this prisoner?' demanded a resolute-looking man in authority, who was summoned out by the guard.

Naturally struck by the disagreeable word, Charles Darnay requested the speaker to take notice that he was a free traveller and French citizen, in charge of an escort

which the disturbed state of the country had imposed upon him, and which he had paid for.

'Where,' repeated the same personage, without taking any heed of him whatever, 'are the papers of this prisoner?'

One of the patriots had them in his cap, and produced them. Casting his eyes over Gabelle's letter, the same personage in authority showed some disorder and surprise, and looked at Darnay with a close attention.

He left escort and escorted without saying a word, however, and went into the guard-room; meanwhile, they sat upon their horses outside the gate. Looking about him while in this state of suspense, Charles Darnay observed that the gate was held by a mixed guard of soldiers and patriots, the latter far outnumbering the former; and that while ingress into the city for peasants' carts bringing in supplies, and for similar traffic and traffickers, was easy enough, egress, even for the homeliest people, was very difficult.

When he had sat in his saddle some half-hour, taking note of these things, Darnay found himself confronted by the same man in authority, who directed the guard to open the barrier. Then he delivered to the escort a receipt for the escorted, and requested him to dismount. He did so, and the two patriots, leading his tired horse, turned and rode away without entering the city.

He accompanied his conductor into a guard-room,

smelling of common wine and tobacco, where certain soldiers and patriots, asleep and awake, drunk and sober, and in various neutral states between sleeping and waking, drunkenness and sobriety, were standing and lying about. Some registers were lying open on a desk, and an officer of a coarse, dark aspect, presided over these.

'Citizen Defarge,' said he to Darnay's conductor, as he took a slip of paper to write on. 'Is this the emigrant Evrémonde?'

'This is the man.'

'Your age, Evrémonde?'

'Thirty-seven.'

'Married, Evrémonde?'

'Yes.'

'Where married?'

'In England.'

'Without doubt. Where is your wife, Evrémonde?'

'In England.'

'Without doubt. You are consigned, Evrémonde, to the prison of La Force.'

'Just Heaven!' exclaimed Darnay. 'Under what law, and for what offence?'

The officer looked up from his slip of paper for a moment.

'We have new laws, and new offences, since you were here.'

'I entreat you to observe that I have come here voluntarily,

in response to that written appeal of a fellow-countryman which lies before you. I demand no more than the opportunity to do so without delay. Is not that my right?'

'Emigrants have no rights, Evrémonde,' was the stolid reply. The officer wrote until he had finished, read over to himself what he had written, sanded it, and handed it to Defarge, with the words 'In secret.'

Defarge motioned with the paper to the prisoner that he must accompany him. The prisoner obeyed, and a guard of two armed patriots attended them.

'Is it you,' said Defarge, in a low voice, as they went down the guard-house steps and turned into Paris, 'who married the daughter of Doctor Manette, once a prisoner in the Bastille that is no more?'

'Yes,' replied Darnay, looking at him with surprise.

'My name is Defarge, and I keep a wine-shop in the Quarter Saint Antoine. Possibly you have heard of me.'

'My wife came to your house to reclaim her father? Yes!'

The word 'wife' seemed to serve as a gloomy reminder to Defarge, to say with sudden impatience, 'In the name of that sharp female newly-born, and called La Guillotine, why did you come to France?'

'You heard me say why, a minute ago. Do you not believe it is the truth?'

'A bad truth for you,' said Defarge.

'Indeed I am lost here. All here is so unprecedented, so

changed, so sudden and unfair, that I am absolutely lost. Will you render me a little help?'

'None.' Defarge spoke, always looking straight before him.

'Will you answer me a single question?'

'Perhaps. According to its nature. You can say what it is.'

'In this prison that I am going to so unjustly, shall I have some free communication with the world outside?'

'You will see.'

'I am not to be buried there, prejudged, and without any means of presenting my case?'

'You will see. But, what then? Other people have been similarly buried in worse prisons, before now.'

'But never by me, Citizen Defarge.'

Defarge glanced darkly at him for answer, and walked on in a steady and set silence. The deeper he sank into this silence, the fainter hope there was – or so Darnay thought – of his softening in any slight degree. He, therefore, made haste to say:

'It is of the utmost importance to me that I should be able to communicate to Mr Lorry of Tellson's Bank, an English gentleman who is now in Paris, the simple fact, without comment, that I have been thrown into the prison of La Force. Will you cause that to be done for me?'

'I will do,' Defarge doggedly rejoined, 'nothing for you. My duty is to my country and the People.'

Charles Darnay felt it hopeless to entreat him further, and his pride was touched besides. As they walked on in silence, he could not but see how used the people were to the spectacle of prisoners passing along the streets. A man in good clothes should be going to prison, was no more remarkable than that a labourer in working clothes should be going to work. In one narrow, dark, and dirty street through which they passed, an excited orator, mounted on a stool, was addressing an excited audience on the crimes against the people, of the king and the royal family. The few words that he caught from this man's lips, first made it known to Charles Darnay that the king was in prison, and that the foreign ambassadors had one and all left Paris.

That he had fallen among far greater dangers than those which had developed themselves when he left England, he of course knew now. He could not but admit to himself that he might not have made this journey, if he could have foreseen the events of a few days. And yet his misgivings were not so dark as, imagined by the light of this later time, they would appear. The horrible massacre, days and nights long, which within a few rounds of the clock, was to set a great mark of blood upon the blessed garnering time of harvest, was as far out of his knowledge as if it had been a hundred thousand years away. The 'sharp female newly-born, and called La Guillotine,' was hardly known to him, or to the generality of people, by name. The frightful deeds that were to be soon done, were

probably unimagined at that time in the brains of the doers. How could they have a place in the shadowy conceptions of a gentle mind?

Of unjust treatment in detention and hardship, and in cruel separation from his wife and child, he foreshadowed the likelihood, or the certainty; but, beyond this, he dreaded nothing distinctly. With this on his mind, which was enough to carry into a dreary prison court-yard, he arrived at the prison of La Force.

A man with a bloated face opened the strong wicket, to whom Defarge presented 'The Emigrant Evrémonde.'

'What the Devil! How many more of them!' exclaimed the man with the bloated face.

Defarge took his receipt without noticing the exclamation, and withdrew, with his two fellow-patriots.

'In secret, too,' grumbled the gaoler, looking at the written paper. 'As if I was not already full to bursting!'

He stuck the paper on a file, in an ill-humour, and Charles Darnay awaited his further pleasure for half an hour: sometimes, pacing to and fro in the strong arched room: sometimes, resting on a stone seat: in either case detained to be imprinted on the memory of the chief and his subordinates.

'Come!' said the chief, at length taking up his keys, 'come with me, emigrant.'

Through the dismal prison twilight, his new charge accompanied him by corridor and staircase, many doors

clanging and locking behind them, until they came into a large, low, vaulted chamber crowded with prisoners of both sexes.

In the instinctive association of prisoners with shameful crime and disgrace, the new comer recoiled from this company. But the crowning unreality of his long unreal ride, was, their all at once rising to receive him, with every refinement of manner known to the time, and with all the engaging graces and courtesies of life.

So strangely clouded were these refinements by the prison manners and gloom, so spectral did they become in the inappropriate squalor and misery through which they were seen, that Charles Darnay seemed to stand in a company of the dead.

It struck him motionless. The gaoler standing at his side, and the other gaolers moving about, who would have been well enough as to appearance in the ordinary exercise of their functions, looked so extravagantly coarse contrasted with sorrowing mothers and blooming daughters who were there – with the apparitions of the coquette, the young beauty, and the mature woman delicately bred – that the inversion of all experience and likelihood which the scene of shadows presented, was heightened to its utmost.

'In the name of the assembled companions in misfortune,' said a gentleman of courtly appearance and address, coming forward, 'I have the honour of giving you welcome to La Force, and of condoling with you on the calamity

that has brought you among us. May it soon terminate happily! It would be an impertinence elsewhere, but it is not so here, to ask your name and condition?'

Charles Darnay roused himself, and gave the required information, in words as suitable as he could find.

'But I hope,' said the gentleman, following the chief gaoler with his eyes, who moved across the room, 'that you are not in secret?'

'I do not understand the meaning of the term, but I have heard them say so.'

'Ah, what a pity! We so much regret it! But take courage; several members of our society have been in secret, at first, and it has lasted but a short time.'

There was a murmur of commiseration as Charles Darnay crossed the room to a grated door where the gaoler awaited him, and many voices – among which, the soft and compassionate voices of women were conspicuous – gave him good wishes and encouragement. He turned at the grated door, to render the thanks of his heart; it closed under the gaoler's hand; and the apparitions vanished from his sight for ever.

The wicket opened on a stone staircase, leading upward. When they had ascended forty steps, the gaoler opened a low black door, and they passed into a solitary cell. It struck cold and damp, but was not dark.

'Yours,' said the gaoler.

'Why am I confined alone?'

'How do I know!'

'I can buy pen, ink, and paper?'

'Such are not my orders. You will be visited, and can ask then. At present, you may buy your food, and nothing more.'

There were in the cell, a chair, a table, and a straw mattress. When the gaoler was gone, he thought in a wandering way, 'Now am I left, as if I were dead.' Stopping then, to look down at the mattress, he turned from it with a sick feeling, and thought, 'And here in these crawling creatures is the first condition of the body after death.'

'Five paces by four and a half, five paces by four and a half, five paces by four and a half.' The prisoner walked to and fro in his cell, counting its measurement, and the roar of the city arose like muffled drums with a wild swell of voices added to them.

2

The Grindstone

Tellson's bank, established in the Saint Germain
Quarter of Paris, was in a wing of a large house,
approached by a court-yard and shut off from the street
by a high wall and a strong gate. The house belonged to
a great nobleman who had lived in it until he made a
flight from the troubles. He was no other than the same
Monseigneur, the preparation of whose chocolate for
whose lips had once occupied three strong men besides
the cook in question.

Monseigneur's house had been first sequestrated, and
then confiscated. For, all things moved so fast, and decree
followed decree with that fierce precipitation, that now upon
the third night of the autumn month of September, patriot
emissaries of the law were in possession of Monseigneur's
house, and had marked it with the tricolour, and were
drinking brandy in its state apartments.

A place of business in London like Tellson's place of
business in Paris, would soon have driven the House out
of its mind and into the Gazette. For, what would staid

British responsibility and respectability have said to orange-trees in boxes in a Bank court-yard, and even to a Cupid over the counter? Yet such things were.

What money would be drawn out of Tellson's henceforth, and what would lie there, lost and forgotten; what plate and jewels would tarnish in Tellson's hiding-places, while the depositors rusted in prisons, and when they should have violently perished; how many accounts with Tellson's never to be balanced in this world, must be carried over into the next; no man could have said, that night, any more than Mr Jarvis Lorry could, though he thought heavily of these questions. He sat by a newly-lighted wood fire, and on his honest and courageous face there was a deeper shade than the pendent lamp could throw, or any object in the room distortedly reflect – a shade of horror.

He occupied rooms in the Bank, in his fidelity to the House of which he had grown to be a part, like a strong root-ivy. It chanced that they derived a kind of security from the patriotic occupation of the main building, but the true-hearted old gentleman never calculated about that. All such circumstances were indifferent to him, so that he did his duty. On the opposite side of the court-yard, under a colonnade, was extensive standing for carriages – where, indeed, some carriages of Monseigneur yet stood. Against two of the pillars were fastened two great flaring flambeaux, and in the light of these, standing

out in the open air, was a large grindstone: a roughly mounted thing which appeared to have hurriedly been brought there from some neighbouring smithy, or other workshop. Rising and looking out of the window at these harmless objects, Mr Lorry shivered, and retired to his seat by the fire.

From the streets beyond the high wall and the strong gate, there came the usual night hum of the city, with now and then an indescribable ring in it, weird and unearthly, as if some unwonted sounds of a terrible nature were going up to Heaven.

'Thank God,' said Mr Lorry, clasping his hands, 'that no one near and dear to me is in this dreadful town tonight. May He have mercy on all who are in danger!'

Soon afterwards, the bell at the great gate sounded, and he thought, 'They have come back!' and sat listening. But, there was no loud irruption into the court-yard, as he had expected, and he heard the gate clash again, and all was quiet.

The nervousness and dread that were upon him inspired that vague uneasiness respecting the Bank, which a great change would naturally awaken, with such feelings roused. It was well guarded, and he got up to go among the trusty people who were watching it, when his door suddenly opened, and two figures rushed in, at sight of which he fell back in amazement.

Lucie and her father!

'What is this?' cried Mr Lorry, breathless and confused. 'What is the matter? Lucie! Manette! What has happened?'

With the look fixed upon him, in her paleness and wildness, she panted out in his arms, imploringly, 'O my dear friend! My husband!'

'Your husband, Lucie?'

'Charles.'

'What of Charles?'

'Has been here some days. An errand of generosity brought him here unknown to us; he was stopped at the barrier, and sent to prison.'

The old man uttered an irrepressible cry. Almost at the same moment, the bell of the great gate rang again, and a loud noise of feet and voices came pouring into the court-yard.

'What is that noise?' said the Doctor, turning towards the window.

'Don't look!' cried Mr Lorry. 'Don't look out! Manette, for your life, don't touch the blind!'

The Doctor turned, with his hand upon the fastening of the window, and said, with a cool bold smile:

'My dear friend, I have a charmed life in this city. I have been a Bastille prisoner. There is no patriot in Paris – in Paris? In France – who, knowing me to have been a prisoner in the Bastille, would touch me, except to overwhelm me with embraces, or carry me in triumph. My old pain has given me a power that has brought us through

the barrier, and gained us news of Charles there, and brought us here. I knew I could help Charles out of all danger; I told Lucie so. – What is that noise?'

'Don't look!' cried Mr Lorry, absolutely desperate. 'No, Lucie, my dear, nor you!' He got his arm round her, and held her. 'Don't be so terrified, my love. I solemnly swear to you that I know of no harm having happened to Charles. What prison is he in?'

'La Force!'

'La Force! Lucie, my child, if ever you were brave and serviceable in your life – and you were always both – you will compose yourself now, to do exactly as I bid you; for more depends upon it than you can think, or I can say. You must instantly be obedient, still, and quiet. You must let me put you in a room at the back here. You must leave your father and me alone for two minutes, and as there are Life and Death in the world you must not delay.'

'I will be submissive to you. I see in your face that you know I can do nothing else than this. I know you are true.'

The old man kissed her, and hurried her into his room, and turned the key; then, came hurrying back to the Doctor, and opened the window, and looked out with him into the court-yard.

Looked out upon a throng of men and women. The people in possession of the house had let them in at the gate, and they had rushed in to work at the grindstone;

it had evidently been set up there for their purpose, as in a convenient and retired spot.

The grindstone had a double handle, and, turning at it madly were two men, whose faces, as their long hair flapped back when the whirlings of the grindstone brought their faces up, were more horrible and cruel than the visages of the wildest savages in their most barbarous disguise. As these ruffians turned and turned, their matted locks now flung forward over their eyes, now flung backward over their necks, some women held wine to their mouths that they might drink; and what with dropping blood, and what with dropping wine, and what with the stream of sparks struck out of the stone, all their wicked atmosphere seemed gore and fire. Hatchets, knives, bayonets, swords, all brought to be sharpened, were all red with it. Some of the hacked swords were tied to the wrists of those who carried them, with strips of linen and fragments of dress: ligatures various in kind, but all deep of the one colour. And as the frantic wielders of these weapons snatched them from the stream of sparks and tore away into the streets, the same red hue was red in their frenzied eyes.

They drew back from the window, and the Doctor looked for explanation in his friend's ashy face.

'They are,' Mr Lorry whispered the words, glancing fearfully round at the locked room, 'murdering the prisoners. If you really have the power you think you have – make yourself known to these devils, and get taken to La

Force. It may be too late, I don't know, but let it not be a minute later!'

Doctor Manette pressed his hand, hastened bareheaded out of the room, and was in the court-yard when Mr Lorry regained the blind.

His streaming white hair, his remarkable face, and the impetuous confidence of his manner, as he put the weapons aside like water, carried him in an instant to the heart of the concourse at the stone. For a few moments there was a pause, and a hurry, and a murmur, and the unintelligible sound of his voice; and then Mr Lorry saw him, surrounded by all, and in the midst of a line of twenty men long, all linked shoulder to shoulder, and hand to shoulder, hurried out with cries of – 'Live the Bastille prisoner! Help for the Bastille prisoner's kindred in La Force! Save the prisoner Evrémonde at La Force!'

He closed the lattice again with a fluttering heart, closed the window and the curtain, hastened to Lucie, and told her that her father was assisted by the people, and gone in search of her husband. He found her child and Miss Pross with her; but, it never occurred to him to be surprised by their appearance until a long time afterwards, when he sat watching them in such quiet as the night knew.

Lucie had, by that time, fallen into a stupor on the floor at his feet, clinging to his hand. Miss Pross had laid the child down on his own bed, and her head had gradually fallen on the pillow beside her pretty charge.

Twice more in the darkness the bell at the great gate sounded, and the irruption was repeated, and the grindstone whirled and spluttered. 'What is it?' cried Lucie, affrighted. 'Hush! The soldiers' swords are sharpened there,' said Mr Lorry. 'The place is national property now, and used as a kind of armoury, my love.'

The great grindstone, Earth, had turned when Mr Lorry looked out again, and the sun was red on the court-yard. But, the lesser grindstone stood alone there in the calm morning air, with a red upon it that the sun had never given, and would never take away.

3

The Shadow

One of the first considerations which arose in the business mind of Mr Lorry when business hours came round, was this: – that he had no right to imperil Tellson's by sheltering the wife of an emigrant prisoner under the Bank roof. His own possessions, safety, life, he would have hazarded for Lucie and her child, without a moment's demur; but the great trust he held was not his own, and as to that business charge he was a strict man of business.

At first, his mind reverted to Defarge, and he thought of finding out the wine-shop again and taking counsel with its master in reference to the safest dwelling-place in the distracted state of the city. But, the same consideration that suggested him, repudiated him; he lived in the most violent Quarter, and doubtless was influential there, and deep in its dangerous workings.

Noon coming, and the Doctor not returning, and every minute's delay tending to compromise Tellson's, Mr Lorry advised with Lucie. She said that her father had spoken

of hiring a lodging for a short term, in that Quarter, near the Banking-house. Mr Lorry went out in quest of such a lodging, and found a suitable one, high up in a removed by-street where the closed blinds in all the other windows of a high melancholy square of buildings marked deserted homes.

To this lodging he at once removed Lucie and her child, and Miss Pross: giving them what comfort he could, and much more than he had himself. He left Jerry with them, as a figure to fill a doorway that would bear considerable knocking on the head, and returned to his own occupations.

The day wore itself out, and wore him out with it, until the Bank closed. He was again alone in his room of the previous night, considering what to do next, when he heard a foot upon the stair. In a few moments, a man stood in his presence, who, with a keenly observant look at him, addressed him by his name.

'Your servant,' said Mr Lorry. 'Do you know me?'

He was a strongly made man with dark curling hair, from forty-five to fifty years of age. For answer he repeated, without any change of emphasis, the words:

'Do you know me?'

'I have seen you somewhere.'

'Perhaps at my wine-shop?'

Much interested and agitated, Mr Lorry said: 'You come from Doctor Manette?'

'Yes. I come from Doctor Manette.'

'And what says he? What does he send me?'

Defarge gave into his anxious hand, an open scrap of paper. It bore the words in the Doctor's writing:

'Charles is safe, but I cannot safely leave this place yet. I have obtained the favour that the bearer has a short note from Charles to his wife. Let the bearer see his wife.'

It was dated from La Force, within an hour.

'Will you accompany me,' said Mr Lorry, joyfully relieved after reading this note aloud, 'to where his wife resides?'

'Yes,' returned Defarge.

Scarcely noticing as yet, in what a curiously reserved and mechanical way Defarge spoke, Mr Lorry put on his hat and they went down into the court-yard. There, they found two women; one, knitting.

'Madame Defarge, surely!' said Mr Lorry.

'It is she,' observed her husband.

'Does madame go with us?' inquired Mr Lorry.

'Yes. That she may be able to recognise the faces and know the persons. It is for their safety.'

Beginning to be struck by Defarge's manner, Mr Lorry looked dubiously at him, and led the way. Both the women followed; the second woman being The Vengeance.

They passed through the intervening streets as quickly as they might, ascended the staircase of the new domicile, were admitted by Jerry, and found Lucie weeping, alone. She was thrown into a transport by the tidings Mr Lorry gave her of her husband, and clasped the hand that delivered his note – little thinking what it had been doing near him in the night, and might, but for a chance, have done to him.

DEAREST, – Take courage. I am well, and your father has influence around me. You cannot answer this. Kiss our child for me.'

That was all the writing. It was so much, however, to her who received it, that she turned from Defarge to his wife, and kissed one of the hands that knitted. It was a passionate, loving, thankful, womanly action, but the hand made no response – dropped cold and heavy, and took to its knitting again.

There was something in its touch that gave Lucie a check. She stopped in the act of putting the note in her bosom, and, with her hands yet at her neck, looked terrified at Madame Defarge. Madame Defarge met the lifted eyebrows and forehead with a cold, impassive stare.

'My dear,' said Mr Lorry, striking in to explain; 'there are frequent risings in the streets; and, although it is not likely they will ever trouble you, Madame Defarge wishes

to see those whom she has the power to protect at such times, to the end that she may know them. I state the case, Citizen Defarge?'

Defarge looked gloomily at his wife, and gave no other answer than a gruff sound of acquiescence.

'You had better, Lucie,' said Mr Lorry, doing all he could to propitiate, by tone and manner, 'have the dear child here, and our good Pross.'

The lady in question appeared with folded arms, and observed in English to The Vengeance, whom her eyes first encountered, 'Well, I am sure, Boldface! I hope *you* are pretty well!'

'Is that his child?' said Madame Defarge, stopping in her work for the first time, and pointing her knitting-needle at little Lucie as if it were the finger of Fate.

'Yes, madame,' answered Mr Lorry; 'this is our poor prisoner's darling daughter, and only child.'

The shadow attendant on Madame Defarge and her party seemed to fall so threatening and dark on the child, that her mother instinctively kneeled on the ground beside her, and held her to her breast.

'It is enough, my husband,' said Madame Defarge. 'I have seen them. We may go.'

But, the suppressed manner had enough of menace in it – not visible and presented, but indistinct and withheld – to alarm Lucie into saying, as she laid her appealing hand on Madame Defarge's dress:

'You will be good to my poor husband. You will do him no harm. You will help me to see him if you can?'

'Your husband is not my business here,' returned Madame Defarge, looking down at her with perfect composure. 'It is the daughter of your father who is my business here.'

'For my sake, then, be merciful to my husband. For my child's sake! We are more afraid of you than of these others.'

Madame Defarge received it as a compliment, and looked at her husband. Defarge, who had been uneasily biting his thumb-nail and looking at her, collected his face into a sterner expression.

'What is it that your husband says in that little letter?' asked Madame Defarge, with a lowering smile. 'Influence; he says something touching influence?'

'That my father,' said Lucie, hurriedly taking the paper from her breast, but with her alarmed eyes on her questioner and not on it, 'has much influence around him.'

'Surely it will release him!' said Madame Defarge. 'Let it do so.'

'As a wife and mother,' cried Lucie, most earnestly, 'I implore you to have pity on me and not to exercise any power that you possess, against my innocent husband, but to use it in his behalf.'

Madame Defarge looked, coldly as ever, at the suppliant, and said, turning to her friend The Vengeance:

'The wives and mothers we have been used to see, since we were as little as this child, and much less, have not been greatly considered? We have known *their* husbands and fathers laid in prison and kept from them, often enough?'

'We have seen nothing else,' returned The Vengeance.

'We have borne this a long time,' said Madame Defarge, turning her eyes again upon Lucie. 'Judge you! Is it likely that the trouble of one wife and mother would be much to us now?'

She resumed her knitting and went out. The Vengeance followed. Defarge went last, and closed the door.

'Courage, my dear Lucie,' said Mr Lorry, as he raised her. 'Courage, courage! So far all goes well with us.'

'I am not thankless, I hope, but that dreadful woman seems to throw a shadow on me and on all my hopes.'

'Tut, tut!' said Mr Lorry; 'what is this despondency in the brave little breast? A shadow indeed! No substance in it, Lucie.'

But the shadow of the manner of these Defarges was dark upon himself, for all that, and in his secret mind it troubled him greatly.

4

Calm in Storm

Doctor Manette did not return until the morning of the fourth day of his absence. So much of what had happened in that dreadful time as could be kept from the knowledge of Lucie was so well concealed from her, that not until long afterwards, when France and she were far apart, did she know that eleven hundred defenceless prisoners of both sexes and all ages had been killed by the populace, that four days and nights had been darkened by this deed of horror.

To Mr Lorry, the Doctor communicated under an injunction of secrecy on which he had no need to dwell, that the crowd had taken him through a scene of carnage to the prison of La Force. That, in the prison he had found a self-appointed Tribunal sitting, before which the prisoners were brought singly, and by which they were rapidly ordered to be put forth to be massacred, or to be released, or (in a few cases) to be sent back to their cells. That, presented by his conductors to this Tribunal, he had announced himself by name and profession as having

been for eighteen years a secret and unaccused prisoner in the Bastille; that, one of the body so sitting in judgment had risen and identified him, and that this man was Defarge.

That, hereupon he had ascertained, through the registers on the table, that his son-in-law was among the living prisoners, and had pleaded hard to the Tribunal for his life and liberty. That, in the first frantic greetings lavished on himself as a notable sufferer under the over-thrown system, it had been accorded to him to have Charles Darnay brought before the lawless Court, and examined. That, he seemed on the point of being at once released, when the tide in his favour met with some unexplained check, which led to a few words of secret conference. That, the man sitting as President had then informed Doctor Manette that the prisoner must remain in custody, but should, for his sake, be held inviolate in safe custody. That, immediately, on a signal, the prisoner was removed to the interior of the prison again; but, that he, the Doctor, had then so strongly pleaded for permission to remain and assure himself that his son-in-law was, through no malice or mischance, delivered to the concourse whose murderous yells outside the gate had often drowned the proceedings, that he had obtained the permission, and had remained in that Hall of Blood until the danger was over.

The sights he had seen there, with brief snatches of food and sleep by intervals, shall remain untold. One

prisoner there was, he said, who had been discharged into the street free, but at whom a mistaken savage had thrust a pike as he passed out. Being besought to go to him and dress the wound, the Doctor had passed out at the same gate, and had found him in the arms of a company of Samaritans, who were seated on the bodies of their victims. With an inconsistency as monstrous as anything in this awful nightmare, they had helped the healer, and tended the wounded man with the gentlest solicitude, had then caught up their weapons and plunged anew into a butchery so dreadful, that the Doctor had covered his eyes with his hands.

As Mr Lorry received these confidences, and as he watched the face of his friend now sixty-two years of age, a misgiving arose within him that such dread experiences would revive the old danger. But, he had never seen his friend in his present aspect. For the first time the Doctor felt, now, that his suffering was strength and power. 'It all tended to a good end, my friend; it was not mere waste and ruin. As my beloved child was helpful in restoring me to myself, I will be helpful now in restoring the dearest part of herself to her; by the aid of Heaven I will do it!'

Greater things than the Doctor had at that time to contend with, would have yielded before his persevering purpose. While he kept himself in his place, as a physician, whose business was with all degrees of mankind, he used his personal influence so wisely, that he was soon the

inspecting physician of three prisons, and among them of La Force. He could now assure Lucie that her husband was no longer confined alone, but was mixed with the general body of prisoners; he saw her husband weekly, and brought sweet messages to her, straight from his lips; sometimes her husband himself sent a letter to her, but she was not permitted to write to him: for, among the many wild suspicions of plots in the prisons, the wildest of all pointed at emigrants who were known to have made friends or permanent connections abroad.

But, though the Doctor tried hard, and never ceased trying, to get Charles Darnay set at liberty, or at least to get him brought to trial, the public current of the time set too strong and fast for him. The new era began; the king was tried, doomed, and beheaded; the Republic of Liberty, Equality, Fraternity, or Death, declared for victory or death against the world in arms; the black flag waved night and day from the great towers of Notre Dame; three hundred thousand men, summoned to rise against the tyrants of the earth, rose from all the varying soils of France, as if the dragon's teeth had been sown broadcast, and had yielded fruit equally on hill and plain, on rock, in gravel, and alluvial mud, under the bright sky of the South and under the clouds of the North.

There was no pause, no pity, no peace, no interval of relenting rest, no measurement of time. Though days and nights circled as regularly as when time was young, and

the evening and morning were the first day, other count of time there was none. Hold of it was lost in the raging fever of a nation, as it is in the fever of one patient. Now, breaking the unnatural silence of a whole city, the executioner showed the people the head of the king – and now, it seemed almost in the same breath, the head of his fair wife, which had had eight weary months of imprisoned widowhood and misery, to turn it grey.

And yet, observing the strange law of contradiction which obtains in all such cases, the time was long, while it flamed by so fast. A revolutionary tribunal in the capital, and forty or fifty thousand revolutionary committees all over the land; a law of the Suspected which struck away all security for liberty or life, and delivered over any good and innocent person to any bad and guilty one; prisons gorged with people who had committed no offence, and could obtain no hearing; these things became the established order and nature of appointed things. Above all, one hideous figure grew as familiar as if it had been before the general gaze from the foundations of the world – the figure of the sharp female called La Guillotine.

It sheared off heads so many, that it, and the ground it most polluted, were a rotten red. It was taken to pieces, like a toy-puzzle for a young Devil, and was put together again when the occasion wanted it. It hushed the eloquent, struck down the powerful, abolished the beautiful and good. Twenty-two friends of high public mark, twenty-one

living and one dead, it had lopped the heads off, in one morning, in as many minutes, the name of the strong man of Old Scripture had descended to the chief functionary who worked it; but, so armed, he was stronger than his namesake, and blinder, and tore away the gates of God's own Temple every day.

Among these terrors, the Doctor walked with a steady head, never doubting that he would save Lucie's husband at last. Yet the current of the time swept by, so strong and deep, and carried the time away so fiercely, that Charles had lain in prison one year and three months when the Doctor was thus steady and confident. So much more wicked and distracted had the Revolution grown in that December month, that the rivers of the South were encumbered with the bodies of the violently drowned by night, and prisoners were shot in lines and squares under the southern wintry sun. Still, the Doctor walked among the terrors with a steady head. Silent, humane, indispensable in hospital and prison, using his art equally among assassins and victims, he was a man apart. In the exercise of his skill, the appearance and the story of the Bastille Captive removed him from all other men. He was not suspected or brought in question, any more than if he had indeed been recalled to life some eighteen years before, or were a Spirit moving among mortals.

5

The Wood-sawyer

One year and three months. During all that time Lucie was never sure, from hour to hour, but that the Guillotine would strike off her husband's head next day. Every day, through the stony streets, the tumbrils now jolted heavily, filled with Condemned. Lovely girls; bright women, brown-haired, black-haired, and grey; youths; stalwart men and old; gentle born and peasant born; all red wine for La Guillotine, all daily brought into light from the dark cellars of the loathsome prisons, and carried to her through the street to slake her devouring thirst.

If the suddenness of her calamity, and the whirling wheels of the time, had stunned the Doctor's daughter into awaiting the result in idle despair, it would but have been with her as it was with many. But, from the hour when she had taken the white head to her fresh young bosom in the garret of Saint Antoine, she had been true to her duties.

Little Lucie she taught, as regularly, as if they had all been united in their English home. The slight devices with which she cheated herself into the show of a belief that

they would soon be reunited – the little preparations for his speedy return, the setting aside of his chair and his books – these, and the solemn prayer at night for one dear prisoner especially, among the many unhappy souls in prison and the shadow of death – were almost the only outspoken reliefs of her heavy mind.

She lost her colour, and the old and intent expression was a constant, not an occasional, thing; otherwise, she remained very pretty and comely. Sometimes, at night on kissing her father, she would burst into the grief she had repressed all day, and would say that her sole reliance, under Heaven, was on him. He always resolutely answered: 'Nothing can happen to him without my knowledge, and I know that I can save him, Lucie.'

They had not made the round of their changed life many weeks, when her father said to her, on coming home one evening:

'My dear, there is an upper window in the prison, to which Charles can sometimes gain access at three in the afternoon. When he can get to it he might see you in the street, he thinks, if you stood in a certain place that I can show you. But you will not be able to see him, my poor child, and even if you could, it would be unsafe for you to make a sign of recognition.'

'O show me the place, my father, and I will go there every day.'

From that time, in all weathers, she waited there two

hours. When it was not too wet or inclement for her child to be with her, they went together; at other times she was alone; but she never missed a single day.

It was the dark and dirty corner of a small winding street. The hovel of a cutter of wood into lengths for burning, was the only house at that end; all else was wall. On the third day of her being there, he noticed her.

'Good day, citizeness.'

'Good day, citizen.'

This mode of address was now prescribed by decree. It had been established voluntarily some time ago, among the more thorough patriots; but, was now law for everybody.

'Walking here again, citizeness?'

'You see me, citizen!'

The wood-sawyer, who was a little man with a redundancy of gesture (he had once been a mender of roads), cast a glance at the prison, pointed at the prison, and putting his ten fingers before his face to represent bars, peeped through them jocosely.

'But it's not my business,' said he. And went on sawing his wood.

Next day he was looking out for her, and accosted her the moment she appeared.

'What? Walking here again, citizeness?'

'Yes, citizen.'

'Ah! A child too! Your mother, is it not, my little citizeness?'

'Do I say yes, mamma?' whispered little Lucie, drawing close to her.

'Yes, dearest.'

'Yes, citizen.'

'Ah! But it's not my business. My work is my business. See my saw! I call it my Little Guillotine. La, la, la; La, la, la! And off his head comes!'

The billet fell as he spoke, and he threw it into a basket.

'I call myself the Samson of the firewood guillotine. See here again! And off *her* head comes! Now, a child. And off *its* head comes. All the family!'

Lucie shuddered as he threw two more billets into his basket, but it was impossible to be there while the wood-sawyer was at work, and not be in his sight. Thenceforth, to secure his good will, she always spoke to him first, and often gave him drink-money.

In all weathers, Lucie passed two hours of every day at this place; and every day on leaving it, she kissed the prison wall. Her husband saw her, it might be twice or thrice running: it might be, not for a week or a fortnight together. It was enough that he could and did see her when the chances served, and on that possibility she would have waited out the day, seven days a week.

These occupations brought her round to the December month, wherein her father walked among the terrors with a steady head. On a lightly-snowing afternoon she arrived

at the usual corner. It was a day of some wild rejoicing, and a festival. She had seen the houses, as she came along, decorated with little pikes, and with little red caps stuck upon them; also, with tricoloured ribbons; also, with the standard inscription, Republic One and Indivisible. Liberty, Equality, Fraternity, or Death!

The miserable shop of the wood-sawyer was so small, that its whole surface furnished very indifferent space for this legend. He had got somebody to scrawl it up for him, however, who had squeezed Death in with most inappropriate difficulty. On his house-top, he displayed pike and cap, as a good citizen must, and in a window he had stationed his saw inscribed as his 'Little Sainte Guillotine.' His shop was shut and he was not there, which was a relief to Lucie, and left her quite alone.

But, he was not far off, for presently she heard a troubled movement and a shouting coming along, which filled her with fear. A moment afterwards, and a throng of people came pouring round the corner by the prison wall, in the midst of whom was the wood-sawyer hand in hand with The Vengeance. There was no other music than their own singing. They danced to the popular Revolution song, keeping a ferocious time that was like a gnashing of teeth in unison. They advanced, retreated, struck at one another's hands, clutched at one another's heads, spun round alone, caught one another and spun round in pairs, until many of them dropped. While those

were down, the rest linked hand in hand, and all spun round together: then the ring broke, and in separate rings of two and four they turned and turned until they all stopped at once, began again, struck, clutched, and tore, and then reversed the spin, and all spun round another way. Suddenly they stopped again, paused, struck out the time afresh, formed into lines the width of the public way, and, with their heads low down and their hands high up, swooped screaming off. No fight could have been half so terrible as this dance. It was so emphatically a fallen sport – a something, once innocent, delivered over to all devilry – a healthy pastime changed into a means of angering the blood, bewildering the senses, and steeling the heart.

This was the Carmagnole. As it passed, leaving Lucie frightened and bewildered in the doorway of the wood-sawyer's house, the feathery snow fell as quietly and lay as white and soft, as if it had never been.

'O my father!' for he stood before her when she lifted up the eyes she had momentarily darkened with her hand; 'such a cruel, bad sight.'

'I know, my dear, I know. I have seen it many times. Don't be frightened! Not one of them would harm you.'

'I am not frightened for myself, my father. But when I think of my husband, and the mercies of these people –'

'We will set him above their mercies very soon. I left him climbing to the window, and I came to tell you. There

is no one here to see. You may kiss your hand towards that highest shelving roof.'

'I do so, father, and I send him my Soul with it!'

A footstep in the snow. Madame Defarge. 'I salute you, citizeness,' from the Doctor. 'I salute you, citizen.' This in passing. Nothing more. Madame Defarge gone, like a shadow over the white road.

'Give me your arm, my love. Pass from here with an air of cheerfulness and courage, for his sake. That was well done;' they had left the spot; 'it shall not be in vain. Charles is summoned for tomorrow.'

'For tomorrow!'

'There is no time to lose. I am well prepared, but there are precautions to be taken, that could not be taken until he was actually summoned before the Tribunal. You are not afraid?'

She could scarcely answer, 'I trust in you.'

'Do so, implicitly. Your suspense is nearly ended, my darling; he shall be restored to you within a few hours; I have encompassed him with every protection. I must see Lorry.'

It was almost dark when they arrived at the Bank. The stately residence of Monseigneur was altogether blighted and deserted. Above a heap of dust and ashes in the court, ran the letters: National Property. Republic One and Indivisible. Liberty, Equality, Fraternity, or Death.

Who could that be with Mr Lorry – the owner of the

riding-coat upon the chair – who must not be seen? From whom newly arrived, did he come out, agitated and surprised, to take his favourite in his arms? To whom did he appear to repeat her faltering words, when, raising his voice and turning his head towards the door of the room from which he had issued, he said: 'Removed to the Conciergerie, and summoned for tomorrow?'

6

Triumph

The dread Tribunal of five Judges, Public Prosecutor, and determined Jury, sat every day. Their lists went forth every evening, and were read out by the gaolers of the various prisons to their prisoners. The standard gaoler-joke was, 'Come out and listen to the Evening Paper, you inside there!'

'Charles Evrémonde, called Darnay!'

So at last began the Evening Paper at La Force.

When a name was called, its owner stepped apart into a spot reserved for those who were announced as being thus fatally recorded. Charles Evrémonde, called Darnay, had reason to know the usage; he had seen hundreds pass away so.

His bloated gaoler, who wore spectacles to read with, glanced over them to assure himself that he had taken his place, and went through the list, making a similar short pause at each name. The list was read, in the vaulted chamber where Darnay had seen the associated prisoners on the night of his arrival. Every one of those had perished

in the massacre; every human creature he had since cared for and parted with, had died on the scaffold.

The passage to the Conciergerie was short and dark; the night in its vermin-haunted cells was long and cold. Next day, fifteen prisoners were put to the bar before Charles Darnay's name was called. All the fifteen were condemned, and the trials of the whole occupied an hour and a half.

'Charles Evrémonde, called Darnay,' was at length arraigned.

His Judges sat upon the Bench in feathered hats; but the rough red cap and tricoloured cockade was the head-dress otherwise prevailing. Looking at the Jury and the turbulent audience, he might have thought that the usual order of things was reversed, and that the felons were trying the honest men. Of the men, the greater part were armed in various ways; of the women, some wore knives, some daggers, some ate and drank as they looked on, many knitted. Among these last, was one, with a spare piece of knitting under her arm as she worked. She was in a front row, by the side of a man whom he had never seen since his arrival at the Barrier, but whom he directly remembered as Defarge. He noticed that she once or twice whispered in his ear, and that she seemed to be his wife; but, what he most noticed in the two figures was, that although they were posted as close to himself as they could be, they never looked towards him. They seemed

to be waiting for something with a dogged determination, and they looked at the Jury, but at nothing else. Under the President sat Doctor Manette, in his usual quiet dress. As well as the prisoner could see, he and Mr Lorry were the only men there, unconnected with the Tribunal, who wore their usual clothes, and had not assumed the coarse garb of the Carmagnole.

Charles Evrémonde, called Darnay, was accused by the public prosecutor as an emigrant, whose life was forfeit to the Republic, under the decree which banished all emigrants on pain of Death. It was nothing that the decree bore date since his return to France. There he was, and there was the decree; he had been taken in France, and his head was demanded.

'Take off his head!' cried the audience. 'An enemy to the Republic!'

The President rang his bell to silence those cries, and asked the prisoner whether it was not true that he had lived many years in England?

Undoubtedly it was.

Was he not an emigrant then? What did he call himself?

Not an emigrant, he hoped, within the sense and spirit of the law.

Why not? the President desired to know.

Because he had voluntarily relinquished a title that was distasteful to him, and a station that was distasteful to

him, and had left his country to live by his own industry in England, rather than on the industry of the overladen people of France.

What proof had he of this?

He handed in the names of two witnesses: Théophile Gabelle, and Alexandre Manette.

But he had married in England? the President reminded him.

True, but not an English woman.

A citizeness of France?

Yes. By birth.

Her name and family?

'Lucie Manette, only daughter of Doctor Manette, the good physician who sits there.'

This answer had a happy effect upon the audience. Cries in exaltation of the well-known good physician rent the hall. So capriciously were the people moved, that tears immediately rolled down several ferocious countenances which had been glaring at the prisoner a moment before, as if with impatience to pluck him out into the streets and kill him.

The President asked, why had he returned to France when he did, and not sooner?

He had not returned sooner, he replied, simply because he had no means of living in France, save those he had resigned; whereas, in England, he lived by giving instruction in the French language and literature. He had returned

when he did, on the pressing and written entreaty of a French citizen, who represented that his life was endangered by his absence. He had come back, to save a citizen's life. Was that criminal in the eyes of the Republic?

The populace cried enthusiastically, 'No!' and the President rang his bell to quiet them.

The President required the name of that Citizen? The accused explained that the citizen was his first witness. He also referred with confidence to the citizen's letter, which had been taken from him at the Barrier, but which he did not doubt would be found among the papers then before the President.

At this stage of the proceedings it was produced and read. Citizen Gabelle was called to confirm it, and did so. Citizen Gabelle hinted, with infinite delicacy and politeness, that in the pressure of business imposed on the Tribunal by the multitude of enemies of the Republic with which it had to deal, he had been slightly overlooked in his prison of the Abbaye – in fact, had rather passed out of the Tribunal's patriotic remembrance – until three days ago; when he had been summoned before it, and had been set at liberty on the Jury's declaring themselves satisfied that the accusation against him was answered, as to himself, by the surrender of the citizen Evrémonde, called Darnay.

Doctor Manette was next questioned. His high personal popularity, and the clearness of his answers, made a great

impression; but, as he proceeded, as he showed that the Accused was his first friend on his release from his long imprisonment; that, the accused had remained in England, always faithful and devoted to his daughter and himself in their exile; that, so far from being in favour with the Aristocrat government there, he had actually been tried for his life by it, as the foe of England and friend of the United States, the Jury and the populace became one. When he appealed by name to Monsieur Lorry, an English gentleman then and there present, who, like himself, had been a witness on that English trial and could corroborate his account of it, the Jury declared that they had heard enough, and that they were ready with their votes if the President were content to receive them.

At every vote (the Jurymen voted aloud and individually), the populace set up a shout of applause. All the voices were in the prisoner's favour, and the President declared him free.

Then, began one of those extraordinary scenes with which the populace sometimes gratified their fickleness, or their better impulses towards generosity and mercy, or which they regarded as some set-off against their swollen account of cruel rage. No sooner was the acquittal pronounced, than tears were shed as freely as blood at another time, and such fraternal embraces were bestowed upon the prisoner by as many of both sexes as could rush at him, that after his long and unwholesome confinement

he was in danger of fainting from exhaustion; none the less because he knew very well, that the very same people, carried by another current, would have rushed at him with the very same intensity, to rend him to pieces and strew him over the streets.

Five were to be tried together, next, as enemies of the Republic, forasmuch as they had not assisted it by word or deed. So quick was the Tribunal to compensate itself and the nation for a chance lost, that these five came down to him before he left the place, condemned to die within twenty-four hours.

The five had had, it is true, no audience to lengthen their proceedings, for when he and Doctor Manette emerged from the gate, there was a great crowd about it, in which there seemed to be every face he had seen in Court – except two, for which he looked in vain. On his coming out, the concourse made at him anew, weeping, embracing, and shouting, all by turns and all together, until the very tide of the river on the bank of which the mad scene was acted, seemed to run mad, like the people on the shore.

They put him into a great chair they had among them, and which they had taken either out of the Court itself, or one of its rooms or passages. Over the chair they had thrown a red flag, and to the back of it they had bound a pike with a red cap on its top. In this car of triumph, not even the Doctor's entreaties could prevent his being

carried to his home on men's shoulders, with a confused sea of red caps heaving about him, and casting up to sight from the stormy deep such wrecks of faces, that he more than once misdoubted his mind being in confusion, and that he was in the tumbril on his way to the Guillotine.

Reddening the snowy streets with the prevailing Republican colour, in winding and tramping through them, as they had reddened them below the snow with a deeper dye, they carried him thus into the court-yard of the building where she lived. Her father had gone on before, to prepare her, and when her husband stood upon his feet, she dropped insensible in his arms.

As he held her to his heart and turned her beautiful head between his face and the brawling crowd, so that his tears and her lips might come together unseen, a few of the people fell to dancing. Instantly, all the rest fell to dancing, and the court-yard overflowed with the Carmagnole. Then swelling and overflowing out into the adjacent streets, and along the river's bank, and over the bridge, the Carmagnole absorbed them every one and whirled them away.

After grasping the Doctor's hand, and the hand of Mr Lorry, after kissing little Lucie, who was lifted up to clasp her arms round his neck; and after embracing the ever zealous and faithful Pross who lifted her; he took his wife in his arms, and carried her up to their rooms.

'Lucie! My own! I am safe.'

'O dearest Charles, let me thank God for this on my knees as I have prayed to Him.'

They all reverently bowed their heads and hearts. When she was again in his arms, he said to her:

'And now speak to your father, dearest. No other man in all this France could have done what he has done for me.'

She laid her head upon her father's breast, as she had laid his poor head on her own breast, long, long ago. He was happy in the return he had made her, he was recompensed for his suffering, he was proud of his strength. 'You must not be weak, my darling,' he remonstrated; 'don't tremble so. I have saved him.'

7

A Knock at the Door

'I have saved him.' It was not another of the dreams in which he had often come back; he was really here. And yet his wife trembled, and a vague but heavy fear was upon her.

All the air around was so thick and dark, the people were so passionately revengeful and fitful, the innocent were so constantly put to death on vague suspicion and black malice, it was so impossible to forget that many as blameless as her husband and as dear to others as he was to her, every day shared the fate from which he had been clutched, that her heart could not be as lightened of its load as she felt it ought to be.

Their housekeeping was of a very frugal kind: not only because that was the safest way of life, involving the least offence to the people, but because they were not rich, and Charles, throughout his imprisonment, had had to pay heavily for his bad food, and for his guard, and towards the living of the poorer prisoners. Partly on this account, and partly to avoid a domestic spy, they kept no servant,

and Jerry (almost wholly transferred to them by Mr Lorry) had become their daily retainer, and had his bed there every night.

It was an ordinance of the Republic One and Indivisible of Liberty, Equality, Fraternity, or Death, that on the door or doorpost of every house, the name of every inmate must be legibly inscribed in letters of a certain size, at a certain convenient height from the ground. Mr Jerry Cruncher's name, therefore, duly embellished the doorpost down below; and, as the afternoon shadows deepened, the owner of that name himself appeared, from overlooking a painter whom Doctor Manette had employed to add to the list the name of Charles Evrémonde, called Darnay.

For some months past, Miss Pross and Mr Cruncher had discharged the office of purveyors; the former carrying the money; the latter, the basket. Every afternoon at about the time when the public lamps were lighted, they fared forth on this duty, and made and brought home such purchases as were needful.

'Now Mr Cruncher,' said Miss Pross. 'If you are ready, I am.'

Jerry professed himself at Miss Pross's service.

'There's all manner of things wanted,' said Miss Pross, 'and we shall have a precious time of it. We want wine, among the rest. Nice toasts these Redheads will be drinking, wherever we buy it.'

'It will be much the same to your knowledge, miss, I should think,' retorted Jerry, 'whether they drink your health or the Old Un's.'

'Who's he?' said Miss Pross.

Mr Cruncher, with some diffidence, explained himself as meaning 'Old Nick's.'

'Ha!' said Miss Pross, 'it doesn't need an interpreter to explain the meaning of these creatures. They have but one, and it's Midnight Murder, and Mischief.'

'Hush, dear! Pray, pray, be cautious!' cried Lucie.

'Yes, yes, yes, I'll be cautious,' said Miss Pross; 'but I may say among ourselves, that I do hope there will be no oniony and tobaccoey smotherings in the form of embracings all round, going on in the streets. Now, Ladybird, never you stir from that fire till I come back! May I ask a question, Doctor Manette, before I go?'

'I think you may take that liberty,' the Doctor answered, smiling.

'The question, Doctor Manette. Is there' – it was Miss Pross's way to affect to make light of anything that was a great anxiety with them all, and to come at it in this chance manner – 'is there any prospect yet, of our getting out of this place?'

'I fear not yet. It would be dangerous for Charles yet.'

'Heigh-ho-hum!' said Miss Pross, cheerfully repressing a sigh as she glanced at her darling's golden hair in the light of the fire, 'then we must have patience and wait:

that's all. We must hold up our heads and fight low, as my brother Solomon used to say. Now, Mr Cruncher! – Don't you move, Ladybird!'

They went out, leaving Lucie, and her husband, her father, and the child, by a bright fire. Mr Lorry was expected back presently from the Banking House. Little Lucie sat by her grandfather, and he began to tell her a story of a great and powerful Fairy who had opened a prison-wall and let out a captive who had once done the Fairy a service. All was subdued and quiet, and Lucie was more at ease than she had been.

'What is that?' she cried, all at once.

'My dear!' said her father, stopping in his story, and laying his hand on hers, 'command yourself. What a disordered state you are in! The least thing – nothing – startles you!'

'I thought, my father,' said Lucie, excusing herself, with a pale face and in a faltering voice, 'that I heard strange feet upon the stairs.'

'My love, the staircase is as still as Death.'

As he said the word, a blow was struck upon the door.

'Oh father, father. What can this be! Hide Charles. Save him!'

'My child,' said the Doctor, rising, and laying his hand upon her shoulder, 'I *have* saved him. Let me go to the door.'

He took the lamp in his hand, crossed the two inter-

vening outer rooms, and opened it. A rude clattering of feet over the floor, and four rough men in red caps, armed with sabres and pistols, entered the room.

'The Citizen Evrémonde, called Darnay,' said the first.

'Who seeks him?' answered Darnay.

'I seek him. We seek him. I know you, Evrémonde; I saw you before the Tribunal today. You are again the prisoner of the Republic.'

'Tell me how and why am I again a prisoner?'

'It is enough that you return straight to the Conciergerie, and will know tomorrow. You are summoned for tomorrow.'

Dr Manette moved after these words were spoken, put the lamp down, and confronting the speaker, and taking him, not urgently, by the loose front of his red woollen shirt, said:

'You know him, you have said. Do you know me?'

'Yes, I know you, Citizen Doctor.'

'We all know you, Citizen Doctor,' said the other three.

He looked abstractedly from one to another, and said, in a lower voice, after a pause:

'Will you answer his question to me then? How does this happen?'

'Citizen Doctor,' said the first, reluctantly, 'he has been denounced to the Section of Saint Antoine. This citizen,' pointing out the second who had entered, 'is from Saint Antoine.'

The citizen here indicated nodded his head, and added:

'He is accused by Saint Antoine.'

'Of what?' asked the Doctor.

'Citizen Doctor,' said the first, with his former reluctance, 'ask no more. If the Republic demands sacrifices from you, without doubt you as a good patriot will be happy to make them. The Republic goes before all. The People is supreme. Evrémonde, we are pressed.'

'One word,' the Doctor entreated. 'Will you tell me who denounced him?'

'It is against rule,' answered the first; 'but you can ask Him of Saint Antoine here.'

The Doctor turned his eyes upon that man. Who moved uneasily on his feet, rubbed his beard a little, and at length said:

'Well! Truly it is against rule. But he is denounced – and gravely – by the Citizen and Citizeness Defarge. And by one other.'

'What other?'

'Do *you* ask, Citizen Doctor?'

'Yes.'

'Then,' said he of Saint Antoine, with a strange look, 'you will be answered tomorrow. Now, I am dumb!'

8

A Hand at Cards

Happily unconscious of the new calamity at home, Miss Pross threaded her way along the narrow streets and crossed the river by the bridge of the Pont-Neuf, reckoning in her mind the number of indispensable purchases she had to make. Mr Cruncher, with the basket, walked at her side.

Having purchased a few small articles of grocery, and a measure of oil for the lamp, Miss Pross bethought herself of the wine they wanted. After peeping into several wine-shops, she stopped at the sign of The Good Republican Brutus of Antiquity, not far from the National Palace. It had a quieter look than any other place of the same description they had passed, and, though red with patriotic caps, was not so red as the rest. Sounding Mr Cruncher, and finding him of her opinion, Miss Pross resorted to The Good Republican Brutus of Antiquity, attended by her cavalier.

Slightly observant of the smoky lights; of the people, pipe in mouth, playing with limp cards and yellow

dominoes; of the one bare-breasted, bare-armed, soot-begrimed workman reading a journal aloud, and of the others listening to him; of the two or three customers fallen forward asleep; the two outlandish customers approached the counter, and showed what they wanted.

As their wine was measuring out, a man parted from another man in a corner, and rose to depart. In going, he had to face Miss Pross. No sooner did he face her, than Miss Pross uttered a scream, and clapped her hands.

In a moment, the whole company were on their feet. That somebody was assassinated by somebody vindicating a difference of opinion was the likeliest occurrence. Everybody looked to see somebody fall, but only saw a man and a woman standing staring at each other; the man with all the outward aspects of a Frenchman and a thorough Republican; the woman, evidently English.

'What is the matter?' said the man who had caused Miss Pross to scream; speaking in a vexed, abrupt voice and in English.

'Oh, Solomon, dear Solomon!' cried Miss Pross, clapping her hands again. 'After not setting eyes upon you or hearing of you for so long a time, do I find you here!'

'Don't call me Solomon. Do you want to be the death of me?' asked the man, in a furtive, frightened way.

'Brother, brother!' cried Miss Pross, bursting into tears. 'Have I ever been so hard with you that you ask me such a cruel question?'

'Then hold your meddlesome tongue,' said Solomon, 'and come out. Who's this man?'

Miss Pross, shaking her loving and dejected head at her by no means affectionate brother, said through her tears, 'Mr Cruncher.'

'Let him come out too,' said Solomon. 'Does he think me a ghost?'

Apparently, Mr Cruncher did, to judge from his looks. He said not a word, however, and Miss Pross, exploring the depths of her reticule through her tears with great difficulty, paid for her wine.

'Now,' said Solomon, stopping at the dark street corner, 'what do you want?'

'How dreadfully unkind in a brother nothing has ever turned my love away from!' cried Miss Pross, 'to give me such a greeting, and show me no affection.'

'If you expect me to be surprised,' said her brother Solomon, 'I am not surprised; I knew you were here; I know of most people who are here. If you really don't want to endanger my existence – which I half believe you do – go your ways as soon as possible, and let me go mine. I am busy. I am an official.'

'My English brother Solomon,' mourned Miss Pross, casting up her tear-fraught eyes, 'that had the makings in him of one of the best and greatest of men in his native country, an official among foreigners, and such foreigners! I would almost sooner have seen the dear boy lying in his –'

'I said so!' cried her brother, interrupting. 'I knew it. You want to be the death of me. I shall be rendered Suspected, by my own sister. Just as I am getting on!'

'The gracious and merciful Heavens forbid!' cried Miss Pross. 'Far rather would I never see you again, dear Solomon, though I have ever loved you truly, and ever shall. Say but one affectionate word to me, and tell me there is nothing angry or estranged between us, and I will detain you no longer.'

Good Miss Pross! As if the estrangement between them had come of any culpability of her. As if Mr Lorry had not known it for a fact, years ago, in the quiet corner in Soho, that this precious brother had spent her money and left her!

He was saying the affectionate word, however, with a far more grudging condescension and patronage than he could have shown if their relative merits and positions had been reversed, when Mr Cruncher, touching him on the shoulder, hoarsely and unexpectedly interposed with the following singular question:

'I say! Might I ask the favour? As to whether your name is John Solomon, or Solomon John?'

The official turned towards him with sudden distrust. He had not previously uttered a word.

'Come!' said Mr Cruncher. 'John Solomon, or Solomon John? She calls you Solomon, and she must know, being your sister. And *I* know you're John, you know. Which of

the two goes first? And regarding that name of Pross, likewise. That warn't your name over the water.'

'What do you mean?'

'Well, I don't know all I mean, for I can't call to mind what your name was, over the water. I'll swear it was a name of two syllables.'

'Indeed?'

'Yes. T'other one's was one syllable. I know you. You was a spy-witness at the Bailey. What, in the name of the Father of Lies, own father to yourself, was you called at that time?'

'Barsad,' said another voice, striking in.

The speaker who struck in, was Sydney Carton. He stood at Mr Cruncher's elbow as negligently as he might have stood at the Old Bailey itself.

'Don't be alarmed, my dear Miss Pross. I arrived at Mr Lorry's, to his surprise, yesterday evening; we agreed that I would not present myself elsewhere until all was well, or unless I could be useful; I present myself here, to beg a little talk with your brother. I wish you had a better employed brother than Mr Barsad. I wish for your sake Mr Barsad was not a Sheep of the Prisons.'

Sheep was a cant word of the time for a spy, under the gaolers. The spy, who was pale, turned paler, and asked him how he dared –

'I'll tell you,' said Sydney. 'I lighted on you, Mr Barsad, coming out of the prison of the Conciergerie while I was

contemplating the walls, an hour or more ago. Made curious by seeing you in that connection, and having a reason, to which you are no stranger, for associating you with the misfortunes of a friend now very unfortunate, I walked in your direction. I walked into the wine-shop here, close after you, and sat near you. I had no difficulty in deducing from your unreserved conversation, and the rumour openly going about among your admirers, the nature of your calling. And gradually, what I had done at random, seemed to shape itself into a purpose, Mr Barsad.'

'What purpose?' the spy asked.

'It would be troublesome, and might be dangerous, to explain in the street. Could you favour me, in confidence, with some minutes of your company – at the office of Tellson's Bank, for instance?'

'Why should I go there?'

'Really, Mr Barsad, I can't say, if you can't.'

'Do you mean that you won't say, sir?' the spy irresolutely asked.

'You apprehend me very clearly, Mr Barsad. I won't.'

Carton's negligent recklessness of manner came powerfully in aid of his quickness and skill, in such a business as he had in his secret mind, and with such a man as he had to do with. His practised eye saw it, and made the most of it.

'Now, I told you so,' said the spy, casting a reproachful

look at his sister; 'if any trouble comes of this, it's your doing.'

'Come, come, Mr Barsad!' exclaimed Sydney. 'Don't be ungrateful. But for my great respect for your sister, I might not have led up so pleasantly to a little proposal that I wish to make for our mutual satisfaction. Do you go with me to the Bank?'

'I'll hear what you have got to say. Yes, I'll go with you.'

'I propose that we first conduct your sister safely to the corner of her own street. Let me take your arm, Miss Pross.'

Miss Pross recalled soon afterwards, and to the end of her life remembered, that as she pressed her hands on Sydney's arm and looked up in his face, imploring him to do no hurt to Solomon, there was a braced purpose in the arm and a kind of inspiration in the eyes, which not only contradicted his light manner, but changed and raised the man.

They left her at the corner of the street, and Carton led the way to Mr Lorry's, which was within a few minutes' walk. John Barsad, or Solomon Pross, walked at his side.

Mr Lorry had just finished his dinner, and was sitting before a cheery little log or two of fire. He turned his head as they entered, and showed the surprise with which he saw a stranger.

'Miss Pross's brother, sir,' said Sydney. 'Mr Barsad.'

'Barsad?' repeated the old gentleman, 'Barsad? I have an association with the name – and with the face.'

As Carton took a chair, he supplied the link that Mr Lorry wanted, by saying to him with a frown, 'Witness at that trial.' Mr Lorry immediately remembered, and regarded his new visitor with an undisguised look of abhorrence.

'Mr Barsad has been recognised by Miss Pross as the affectionate brother you have heard of,' said Sydney, 'and has acknowledged the relationship. I pass to worse news. Darnay has been arrested again.'

Struck with consternation, the old gentleman exclaimed, 'What do you tell me! I left him safe and free within these two hours, and am about to return to him!'

'Arrested for all that. When was it done, Mr Barsad?'

'Just now, if at all.'

'Mr Barsad is the best authority possible, sir,' said Sydney, 'and I have it from Mr Barsad's communication to a friend that the arrest has taken place. There is no earthly doubt that he is retaken.'

Mr Lorry's business eye read in the speaker's face that it was loss of time to dwell upon the point.

'Now, I trust,' said Sydney to him, 'that the name and influence of Doctor Manette may stand him in as good stead tomorrow – you said he would be before the Tribunal again tomorrow, Mr Barsad? –'

'Yes; I believe so.'

'– In as good stead tomorrow as today. But it may not be so. This is a desperate time, when desperate games are played for desperate stakes. Let the Doctor play the winning game; I will play the losing one. No man's life here is worth purchase. Any one carried home by the people today, may be condemned tomorrow. Now, the stake I have resolved to play for, in case of the worst, is a friend in the Conciergerie. And the friend I purpose to myself to win, is Mr Barsad.'

'You need have good cards, sir,' said the spy.

'I'll run them over. I'll see what I hold. – Mr Lorry, you know what a brute I am; I wish you'd give me a little brandy.'

It was put before him, and he drank off a glassful – drank off another glassful – pushed the bottle thoughtfully away.

'Mr Barsad,' he went on, in the tone of one who really was looking over a hand of cards: 'Sheep of the prisons, emissary of Republican committees, now turnkey, now prisoner, always spy and secret informer, represents himself to his employers under a false name. That's a very good card. Mr Barsad, now in the employ of the republican French government, was formerly in the employ of the aristocratic English government, the enemy of France and freedom. That's an excellent card. Inference clear as day in this region of suspicion, that Mr Barsad, still in the pay of the aristocratic English government, is the spy of Pitt,

the treacherous foe of the Republic. That's a card not to be beaten. Have you followed my hand, Mr Barsad?'

'Not to understand your play,' returned the spy, somewhat uneasily.

'I play my Ace, Denunciation of Mr Barsad to the nearest Section Committee. Look over your hand, Mr Barsad, and see what you have. Don't hurry.'

He drew the bottle near, poured out another glassful of brandy, and drank it off.

'Look over your hand carefully, Mr Barsad. Take time.'

It was a poorer hand than he suspected. Mr Barsad saw losing cards in it that Sydney Carton knew nothing of. Thrown out of his honourable employment in England, through too much unsuccessful hard swearing there, he knew that he had crossed the Channel, and accepted service in France: first, as a tempter and an eavesdropper among his own countrymen there: gradually, as a tempter and an eavesdropper among the natives. He knew that under the overthrown government he had been a spy upon Saint Antoine and Defarge's wine-shop; had received from the watchful police such heads of information concerning Doctor Manette's imprisonment, release, and history, as should serve him for an introduction to familiar conversation with the Defarges; and tried them on Madame Defarge, and had broken down with them signally. He always remembered with fear and trembling, that that terrible woman had knitted when he talked with

her, and had looked ominously at him as her fingers moved. He had since seen her, in the Section of Saint Antoine, over and over again produce her knitted registers, and denounce people whose lives the guillotine then surely swallowed up. Once denounced, and on such grave grounds as had just now been suggested to his mind, he foresaw that the dreadful woman of whose unrelenting character he had seen many proofs, would produce against him that fatal register, and would quash his last chance of life.

'You scarcely seem to like your hand,' said Sydney, with the greatest composure. 'Do you play?'

'I think, sir,' said the spy, in the meanest manner, as he turned to Mr Lorry, 'I may appeal to a gentleman of your years and benevolence, to put it to this other gentleman, so much your junior, whether he can under any circumstances reconcile it to his station to play that Ace of which he has spoken. I admit that *I* am a spy, but this gentleman is no spy, and why should he so demean himself as to make himself one?'

'I play my Ace, Mr Barsad,' said Carton, taking the answer on himself, and looking at his watch, 'without any scruple in a very few minutes.'

'I should have hoped, gentlemen both,' said the spy, always striving to hook Mr Lorry into the discussion, 'that your respect for my sister –'

'I could not better testify my respect for your sister

than by finally relieving her of her brother,' said Sydney Carton.

'You think not, sir?'

'I have thoroughly made up my mind about it.'

The smooth manner of the spy, curiously in dissonance with his ostentatiously rough dress, and probably with his usual demeanour, received such a check from the inscrutability of Carton, that it faltered here and failed him. While he was at a loss, Carton said, resuming his former air of contemplating cards:

'And indeed, now I think again, I have a strong impression that I have another good card here, not yet enumerated. That friend who spoke of himself as pasturing in the country prisons; who was he?'

'French. You don't know him,' said the spy quickly.

'French, eh!' repeated Carton, musing, and not appearing to notice him at all, though he echoed his word. 'Well; he may be.'

'Is, I assure you,' said the spy; 'though it's not important.'

'Though it's not important,' repeated Carton in the same mechanical way. 'No. Yet I know the face.'

'I think not. I am sure not. It can't be,' said the spy.

'It – can't – be,' muttered Sydney Carton, retrospectively, and filling his glass (which fortunately was a small one) again. 'Can't be. Spoke good French. Yet like a foreigner, I thought?'

'Provincial,' said the spy.

'No. Foreign!' cried Carton, striking his open hand on the table, as a light broke clearly on his mind. 'Cly! Disguised, but the same man. We had that man before us at the Old Bailey.'

'Now, there you are hasty, sir,' said Barsad. 'Cly has been dead several years. I attended him in his last illness. He was buried in London, at the church of Saint Pancras-in-the-Fields.'

Here, Mr Lorry became aware, from where he sat, of a most remarkable goblin shadow on the wall. Tracing it to its source, he discovered it to be caused by a sudden extraordinary rising and stiffening of all the risen and stiff hair on Mr Cruncher's head.

'Let us be reasonable,' said the spy. 'To show you how mistaken you are, and what an unfounded assumption yours is, I will lay before you a certificate of Cly's burial, which I happen to have carried in my pocket-book,' with a hurried hand he produced and opened it, 'ever since. You may take it in your hand; it's no forgery.'

Here, Mr Lorry perceived the reflection on the wall to elongate, and Mr Cruncher rose and stepped forward.

Unseen by the spy, Mr Cruncher stood at his side, and touched him on the shoulder like a ghostly bailiff.

'That there Roger Cly, master,' said Mr Cruncher, with a taciturn and iron-bound visage. 'So *you* put him in his coffin?'

'I did.'

'Who took him out of it?'

Barsad leaned back in his chair, and stammered, 'What do you mean?'

'I mean,' said Mr Cruncher, 'that he warn't never in it. No! Not he! I'll have my head took off, if he was ever in it.'

The spy looked round at the two gentlemen; they both looked in unspeakable astonishment at Jerry.

'I tell you,' said Jerry, 'that you buried paving-stones and earth in that there coffin. Don't go and tell *me* that you buried Cly. It was a take in. Me and two more knows it.'

Sydney Carton, who, with Mr Lorry, had been lost in amazement at this turn of the business, here requested Mr Cruncher explain himself.

'At another time, sir,' he returned, evasively, 'the present time is ill-conwenient for explainin'. What I stand to, is, that he knows well wot that there Cly was never in that there coffin. Let him say he was, in so much as a word of one syllable, and I'll either catch hold of his throat and choke him for half a guinea;' Mr Cruncher dwelt upon this as quite a liberal offer; 'or I'll out and announce him.'

'Humph! I see one thing,' said Carton. 'I hold another card, Mr Barsad. Impossible, here in raging Paris, with Suspicion filling the air, for you to outlive denunciation, when you are in communication with another aristocratic

spy of the same antecedents as yourself, who, moreover, has the mystery about him of having feigned death and come to life again! A strong card – a certain Guillotine card! Do you play?'

'No!' returned the spy. 'I throw up. I confess that we were so unpopular with the outrageous mob, that I only got away from England at the risk of being ducked to death, and that Cly was so ferreted up and down, that he never would have got away at all but for that sham. Though how this man knows it was a sham, is a wonder of wonders to me.'

'Never you trouble your head about this man,' retorted the contentious Mr Cruncher; 'you'll have trouble enough with giving your attention to that gentleman.'

The Sheep of the prisons turned from him to Sydney Carton, and said, with more decision, 'It has come to a point. You told me you had a proposal; what is it? Now, it is of no use asking too much of me. Remember! I may denounce you if I think proper, and I can swear my way through stone walls, and so can others. Now, what do you want with me?'

'Not very much. You are a turnkey at the Conciergerie?'

'I am sometimes.'

'You can be when you choose.'

'I can pass in and out when I choose.'

Sydney Carton filled another glass with brandy, poured

it slowly out upon the hearth, and watched it as it dropped. It being all spent, he said, rising:

'So far, we have spoken before these two, because it was as well that the merits of the cards should not rest solely between you and me. Come into the dark room here, and let us have one final word alone.'

9

The Game Made

While Sydney Carton and the Sheep of the prisons were in the adjoining dark room, speaking so low that not a sound was heard, Mr Lorry looked at Jerry in considerable doubt and mistrust.

'Jerry,' said Mr Lorry. 'Come here.'

Mr Cruncher came forward sideways, with one of his shoulders in advance of him.

'What have you been, besides a messenger?'

After some cogitation, accompanied with an intent look at his patron, Mr Cruncher conceived the luminous idea of replying, 'Agricultooral character.'

'My mind misgives me much,' said Mr Lorry, angrily shaking a forefinger at him, 'that you have used the respectable and great house of Tellson's as a blind, and that you have had an unlawful occupation of an infamous description. If you have, don't expect me to keep your secret. Tellson's shall not be imposed upon.'

'I hope, sir,' pleaded the abashed Mr Cruncher, 'that a gentleman like yourself wot I've had the honour of odd

jobbing till I'm grey at it, would think twice about harming of me, even if it wos so – I don't say it is, but even if it wos. There'd be two sides to it. There might be medical doctors at the present hour, a picking up their guineas where a honest tradesman don't pick up his fardens, a banking away like smoke at Tellson's, and a cocking their medical eyes at that tradesman on the sly, a going in and going out to their own carriages. Well, that 'ud be imposing, too, on Tellson's. For you cannot sarse the goose and not the gander. And here's Mrs Cruncher, a floppin' again the business to that degree as is ruinating – stark ruinating! Whereas them medical doctors' wives don't flop – catch 'em at it! Or, if they flop, their floppings goes in favour of more patients, and how can you rightly have one without the t'other? Then, wot with undertakers, and wot with parish clerks, and wot with sextons, and wot with private watchmen (all awaricious and all in it), a man wouldn't get much by it, even if it wos so. And wot little a man did get, would never prosper with him, Mr Lorry.'

'Ugh!' cried Mr Lorry, rather relenting, nevertheless. 'I am shocked at the sight of you.'

'Now, what I would humbly offer to you, sir,' pursued Mr Cruncher, 'would be this. Upon that there stool, at that there Bar, sets that there boy of mine, brought up and growed up to be a man, wot will errand you, message you, general-light-job you, till your heels is where your head is, if such should be your wishes. If it wos so, which I still

don't say it is, let that there boy keep his father's place, and take care of his mother; don't blow upon that boy's father – do not do it, sir – and let that father go into the line of the reg'lar diggin', and make amends for what he would have un-dug – if it wos so – by diggin' of 'em in with a will, and with conwictions respectin' the futur' keepin' of 'em safe. That, Mr Lorry,' said Mr Cruncher, wiping his forehead with his arm, as an announcement that he had arrived at the peroration of his discourse, 'is wot I would respectfully offer to you, sir.'

'Say no more now,' said Mr Lorry. 'It may be that I shall yet stand your friend, if you deserve it, and repent in action – not in words. I want no more words.'

Mr Cruncher knuckled his forehead, as Sydney Carton and the spy returned from the dark room. 'Adieu, Mr Barsad,' said the former; 'our arrangement thus made, you have nothing to fear from me.'

When they were alone, Mr Lorry asked him what he had done?

'Not much. If it should go ill with the prisoner, I have ensured access to him, once. It is all I could do. To propose too much, would be to put this man's head under the axe, and, as he himself said, nothing worse could happen to him if he were denounced. There is no help for it.'

'But access to him,' said Mr Lorry, 'if it should go ill before the Tribunal, will not save him.'

'I never said it would.'

Mr Lorry's eyes gradually sought the fire; his sympathy with his darling, and the heavy disappointment of this second arrest, gradually weakened them; he was an old man now, overborne with anxiety of late, and his tears fell.

'You are a good man and a true friend,' said Carton, in an altered voice. 'Forgive me if I notice that you are affected. And I could not respect your sorrow more, if you were my father. You are free from that misfortune, however.'

Though he said the last words, with a slip into his usual manner, there was a true feeling and respect both in his tone and in his touch, that Mr Lorry, who had never seen the better side of him, was wholly unprepared for. He gave him his hand, and Carton gently pressed it.

'To return to poor Darnay,' said Carton. 'Don't tell Her of this interview, or this arrangement. It would not enable Her to go to see him. She might think it was contrived, in case of the worst, to convey to him the means of anticipating the sentence.'

Mr Lorry had not thought of that, and he looked quickly at Carton to see if it were in his mind. It seemed to be; he returned the look, and evidently understood it.

'She might think a thousand things,' Carton said, 'and any of them would only add to her trouble. Don't speak of me to her. You are going to her, I hope? She must be very desolate tonight.'

'I am going now, directly.'

'I am glad of that. She has such a strong attachment to you and reliance on you. How does she look?'

'Anxious and unhappy, but very beautiful.'

'Ah!'

It was a long, grieving sound, like a sigh – almost like a sob. It attracted Mr Lorry's eyes to Carton's face, which was turned to the fire. A light, or a shade, passed from it as swiftly as a change will sweep over a hill-side on a wild bright day, and he lifted his foot to put back one of the little flaming logs, which was tumbling forward. His indifference to fire was sufficiently remarkable to elicit a word of remonstrance from Mr Lorry; his boot was still upon the hot embers of the flaming log, when it had broken under the weight of his foot.

'I forgot it,' he said.

Mr Lorry's eyes were again attracted to his face. Taking note of the wasted air which clouded the naturally handsome features, and having the expression of prisoners' faces fresh in his mind, he was strongly reminded of that expression.

'And your duties here have drawn to an end, sir?' said Carton.

'Yes. I have at length done all that I can do here. I hoped to have left them in perfect safety, and then to have quitted Paris. I have my Leave to Pass. I was ready to go.'

They were both silent.

'Yours is a long life to look back upon, sir?' said Carton, wistfully.

'I am in my seventy-eighth year.'

'You have been useful all your life; steadily and constantly occupied; trusted, respected, and looked up to?'

'I have been a man of business, ever since I have been a man.'

'See what a place you fill at seventy-eight. How many people will miss you when you leave it empty!'

'A solitary old bachelor,' answered Mr Lorry, shaking his head. 'There is nobody to weep for me.'

'How can you say that? Wouldn't She weep for you? Wouldn't her child?'

'Yes, yes, thank God. I didn't quite mean what I said.'

'If you could say, with truth, to your own solitary heart, tonight, "I have secured to myself the love and attachment, the gratitude or respect, of no human creature; I have won myself a tender place in no regard; I have done nothing good or serviceable to be remembered by!" your seventy-eight years would be seventy-eight heavy curses; would they not?'

'You say truly, Mr Carton; I think they would be.'

'I should like to ask you – do the days when you sat at your mother's knee, seem days of very long ago?'

Responding to his softened manner, Mr Lorry answered:

'Twenty years back, yes; at this time of my life, no. For,

as I draw closer and closer to the end, I travel in the circle, nearer and nearer to the beginning. My heart is touched now, by many remembrances that had long fallen asleep, of my pretty young mother (and I so old!), and by many associations of the days when what we call the World was not so real with me, and my faults were not confirmed in me.'

Carton terminated the conversation here, by rising to help him on with his outer coat; 'but you,' said Mr Lorry, reverting to the theme, 'you are young.'

'Yes,' said Carton. 'I am not old, but my young way was never the way to age. Enough of me. I'll walk with you to her gate. You know my vagabond and restless habits. If I should prowl about the streets a long time, don't be uneasy; I shall reappear in the morning. You go to the Court tomorrow?'

'Yes, unhappily.'

'I shall be there, but only as one of the crowd. My Spy will find a place for me. Take my arm, sir.'

My Lorry did so, and they went downstairs and out in the streets. A few minutes brought them to Mr Lorry's destination. Carton left him there; but lingered at a little distance, and turned back to the gate again when it was shut, and touched it. He had heard of her going to the prison every day. 'She came out here,' he said, looking about him, 'turned this way, must have trod on these stones often. Let me follow in her steps.'

It was ten o'clock at night when he stood before the prison of La Force, where she had stood hundreds of times. A little wood-sawyer, having closed his shop, was smoking his pipe at his shop-door.

'Good night, citizen,' said Sydney Carton, pausing in going by; 'How goes the Republic?'

'You mean the Guillotine. Not ill. Sixty-three today. We shall mount to a hundred soon. Samson and his men complain sometimes, of being exhausted. Ha, ha, ha! He is so droll, that Samson.'

'Do you often go to see him –'

'Shave? Always. Every day. What a barber! Go and see him when he has a good batch. Figure this to yourself, citizen; he shaved the sixty-three today, in less than two pipes! Word of honour!'

As the grinning little man held out the pipe he was smoking, to explain how he timed the executioner, Carton was so sensible of a rising desire to strike the life out of him, that he turned away.

'But you are not English,' said the wood-sawyer, 'though you wear English dress?'

'Yes,' said Carton.

'You speak like a Frenchman.'

'I am an old student here.'

'Aha, a perfect Frenchman! Good night, Englishman.'

'Good night, citizen.'

Sydney had not gone far out of sight, when he stopped

in the middle of the street under a glimmering lamp, and wrote with his pencil on a scrap of paper. Then, traversing with the decided step of one who remembered the way well, several dark and dirty streets, he stopped at a chemist's shop, which the owner was closing with his own hands.

Giving this citizen, too, good night, as he confronted him at his counter, he laid the scrap of paper before him. 'Whew!' the chemist whistled softly, as he read it. 'For you, citizen?'

'For me.'

'You will be careful to keep them separate, citizen? You know the consequences of mixing them?'

'Perfectly.'

Certain small packets were made and given to him. He put them, one by one, in the breast of his inner coat, counted out the money for them, and deliberately left the shop. 'There is nothing more to do,' said he, glancing upward at the moon, 'until tomorrow. I can't sleep.'

It was not a reckless manner, the manner in which he said these words aloud. It was the settled manner of a tired man, who had wandered and struggled and got lost, but who at length struck into his road and saw its end.

Long ago, when he had been famous among his earliest competitors as a youth of great promise, he had followed his father to the grave. His mother had died, years before. These solemn words, which had been read at his father's

grave, arose in his mind as he went down the dark streets, among the heavy shadows, with the moon and the clouds sailing on high above him. 'I am the resurrection and the life, saith the Lord: he that believeth in me, though he were dead, yet shall he live: and whosoever liveth and believeth in me, shall never die.'

In a city dominated by the axe, alone at night, with natural sorrow rising in him for the sixty-three who had been that day put to death, and for tomorrow's victims then awaiting their doom in the prisons, and still of tomorrow's and tomorrow's, the chain of association that brought the words home, like a rusty old ship's anchor from the deep, might have been easily found. He did not seek it, but repeated them and went on.

Few coaches were abroad, for riders in coaches were liable to be suspected, and gentility hid its head in red nightcaps, and put on heavy shoes, and trudged. But, the theatres were all well filled, and the people poured cheerfully out as he passed, and went chatting home. At one of the theatre doors, there was a little girl with a mother, looking for a way across the street through the mud. He carried the child over, and before the timid arm was loosed from his neck asked her for a kiss.

'I am the resurrection and the life, saith the Lord: he that believeth in me, though he were dead, yet shall he live: and whosoever liveth and believeth in me, shall never die.'

Now, that the streets were quiet, and the night wore on, the words were in the echoes of his feet, and were in the air.

The night wore out, and, as he stood upon the bridge listening to the water as it splashed the river-walls of the Island of Paris, where the picturesque confusion of houses and cathedral shone bright in the light of the moon, the day came coldly, looking like a dead face out of the sky. Then, the night, with the moon and the stars, turned pale and died, and for a little while it seemed as if Creation were delivered over to Death's dominion.

But, the glorious sun, rising, seemed to strike those words, that burden of the night, straight and warm to his heart in its long bright rays. And looking along them, with reverently shaded eyes, a bridge of light appeared to span the air between him and the sun, while the river sparkled under it.

Mr Lorry was already out when he got back, and it was easy to surmise where the good old man was gone. Sydney Carton drank nothing but a little coffee, ate some bread, and, having washed and changed to refresh himself, went out to the place of trial.

The court was all astir and a-buzz, when the black sheep – whom many fell away from in dread – pressed him into an obscure corner among the crowd. Mr Lorry was there, and Doctor Manette was there. She was there, sitting beside her father.

When her husband was brought in, she turned a look upon him, so sustaining, so encouraging, so full of admiring love and pitying tenderness, yet so courageous for his sake, that it called the healthy blood into his face, brightened his glance, and animated his heart.

Before that unjust Tribunal, there was little or no order of procedure, ensuring to any accused person any reasonable hearing. There could have been no such Revolution, if all laws, forms, and ceremonies, had not first been so monstrously abused, that the suicidal vengeance of the Revolution was to scatter them all to the winds.

Every eye was turned to the jury. The same determined patriots and good republicans as yesterday and the day before, and tomorrow and the day after. Eager and prominent among them, one man with a craving face, and his fingers perpetually hovering about his lips, whose appearance gave great satisfaction to the spectators. A life-thirsting, cannibal-looking, bloody-minded juryman, the Jacques Three of St Antoine.

Every eye then turned to the five judges and the public prosecutor. No favourable leaning in that quarter today. Every eye then sought some other eye in the crowd, and gleamed at it approvingly; and heads nodded at one another, before bending forward with a strained attention.

Charles Evrémonde, called Darnay. Released yesterday. Re-accused and retaken yesterday. Suspected and Denounced

enemy of the Republic, Aristocrat, one of a family of tyrants, one of a race proscribed, for that they had used their abolished privileges to the infamous oppression of the people. Charles Evrémonde, called Darnay, in right of such proscription, absolutely Dead in Law.

The President asked, was the Accused openly denounced or secretly?

'Openly, President.'

'By whom?'

'Three voices. Ernest Defarge, wine-vendor of St Antoine.'

'Good.'

'Thérèse Defarge, his wife.'

'Good.'

'Alexandre Manette, physician.'

A great uproar took place in the court, and in the midst of it, Doctor Manette was seen, pale and trembling, standing where he had been seated.

'President, I indignantly protest to you that this is a forgery and a fraud. You know the accused to be the husband of my daughter. Who and where is the false conspirator who says that I denounce the husband of my child!'

'Citizen Manette, be tranquil. To fail in submission to the authority of the Tribunal would be to put yourself out of Law. As to what is dearer to you than life, nothing can be so dear to a good citizen as the Republic. If the

Republic should demand of you the sacrifice of your child herself, you would have no duty but to sacrifice her. Listen to what is to follow. In the meanwhile, be silent!'

Doctor Manette sat down, with his eyes looking around, and his lips trembling; his daughter drew closer to him.

Defarge was produced, when the court was quiet enough to admit of his being heard, and rapidly expounded the story of the imprisonment, and of his having been a mere boy in the Doctor's service, and of the release, and of the state of the prisoner when released and delivered to him. This short examination followed, for the court was quick with its work.

'You did good service at the taking of the Bastille, citizen?'

'I believe so.'

'Inform the Tribunal of what you did that day within the Bastille, citizen.'

'I knew,' said Defarge, looking down at his wife, who stood at the bottom of the steps on which he was raised, looking steadily up at him; 'I knew that this prisoner, of whom I speak, had been confined in a cell known as One Hundred and Five, North Tower. I knew it from himself. He knew himself by no other name than One Hundred and Five, North Tower, when he made shoes under my care. As I serve my gun that day, I resolve, when the place shall fall, to examine that cell. It falls. I mount to the cell, with a fellow-citizen who is one of the Jury, directed by

a gaoler. I examine it, very closely. In a hole in the chimney, where a stone has been worked out and replaced, I find a written paper. This is that written paper. I have made it my business to examine some specimens of the writing of Doctor Manette. This is the writing of Doctor Manette. I confide this paper, in the writing of Doctor Manette, to the hands of the President.'

'Let it be read.'

In a dead silence and stillness, the paper was read, as follows.

10

The Substance of the Shadow

'I, Alexandre Manette, write this melancholy paper in my doleful cell in the Bastille, during the last month of the year 1767. I write it at stolen intervals, under every difficulty. I design to secrete it in the wall of the chimney, where I have slowly and laboriously made a place of concealment for it.

'These words are formed by the rusty iron point with which I write with difficulty in scrapings of soot and charcoal from the chimney, mixed with blood, in the last month of the tenth year of my captivity. Hope has quite departed from my breast. I know from terrible warnings I have noted in myself that my reason will not long remain unimpaired, but I solemnly declare that I am at this time in the possession of my right mind – that my memory is exact and circumstantial – and that I write the truth as I shall answer for these my last recorded words, whether they be ever read by men or not, at the Eternal Judgment-seat.

'One cloudy moonlight night, in the third week of December in the year 1757, I was walking on a retired part

of the quay by the Seine, when a carriage came along behind me, driven very fast. As I stood aside to let that carriage pass, apprehensive that it might otherwise run me down, a head was put out at the window, and a voice called to the driver to stop.

'The carriage stopped as soon as the driver could rein in his horses, and the same voice called to me by my name. I answered. The carriage was then so far in advance of me that two gentlemen had time to open the door and alight before I came up with it. As they stood side by side near the carriage door, I observed that they were greatly alike, in stature, manner, voice, and face too.

'"You are Doctor Manette?" said one.

'"I am."'

'"Doctor Manette, formerly of Beauvais," said the other; "the young physician, originally an expert surgeon, who within the last year or two has made a rising reputation in Paris?"

'"Gentlemen," I returned, "I am that Doctor Manette of whom you speak so graciously."

'"We have been to your residence," said the first, "and not being so fortunate as to find you there, and being informed that you were probably walking in this direction, we followed, in the hope of overtaking you. Will you please to enter the carriage?"

'They both moved so as to place me between themselves and the carriage door. They were armed. I was not.

'"Gentlemen," said I, "pardon me; but I usually inquire who does me the honour to seek my assistance, and what is the nature of the case to which I am summoned."

'The reply to this was made by him who had spoken second. "Doctor, your clients are people of condition. As to the nature of the case, our confidence in your skill assures us that you will ascertain it for yourself better than we can describe it. Enough. Will you please to enter the carriage?"

'I could do nothing but comply, and I entered it in silence. They both entered after me.

'The carriage left the streets behind, passed the North Barrier, and emerged upon the country road. At two-thirds of a league from the Barrier – it struck out of the main avenue, and presently stopped at a solitary house. We all three alighted, and walked, by a damp soft footpath in a garden where a neglected fountain had overflowed, to the door of the house. It was not opened immediately, in answer to the ringing of the bell, and one of my two conductors struck the man who opened it, with his heavy riding-glove, across the face.

'There was nothing in this action to attract my particular attention, for I had seen common people struck more commonly than dogs. But, the other of the two, struck the man in like manner with his arm; the look and bearing of the brothers were then so exactly alike, that I then first perceived them to be twin brothers.

'From the time of our alighting at the outer gate, I had heard cries proceeding from an upper chamber. I was conducted to this chamber straight, the cries growing louder as we ascended the stairs, and I found a patient in a high fever of the brain, lying on a bed.

'The patient was a woman of great beauty, and young; assuredly not much past twenty. Her hair was torn and ragged, and her arms were bound to her sides with sashes and handkerchiefs. I noticed that these bonds were all portions of a gentleman's dress. On one of them, which was a fringed scarf for a dress of ceremony, I saw the armorial bearings of a Noble, and the letter E.

'In her restless strivings she had turned over on her face on the edge of the bed, had drawn the end of the scarf into her mouth, and was in danger of suffocation. My first act was to put out my hand to relieve her breathing; and in moving the scarf aside, the embroidery in the corner caught my sight.

'I turned her gently over, placed my hands upon her breast to calm her and keep her down, and looked into her face. Her eyes were dilated and wild, and she constantly uttered piercing shrieks, and repeated the words, "My husband, my father, and my brother!" and then counted up to twelve, and said, "Hush!" For an instant, and no more, she would pause to listen, and then the piercing shrieks would begin again, and she would repeat the cry, "My husband, my father, and my brother!" and would count up

to twelve, and say "Hush!" There was no variation in the order, or the manner. There was no cessation, but the regular moment's pause, in the utterance of these sounds.

'"How long," I asked, "has this lasted?"

'To distinguish the brothers, I will call them the elder and the younger; by the elder, I mean him who exercised the most authority. It was the elder who replied, "Since about this hour last night."

'"She has a husband, a father, and a brother?"

'"A brother."

'"She has some recent association with the number twelve?"

'The younger brother impatiently rejoined, "With twelve o'clock!"

'"See, gentlemen," said I, "how useless I am, as you have brought me! If I had known what I was coming to see, I could have come provided. As it is, time must be lost. There are no medicines to be obtained in this lonely place."

'The elder brother looked to the younger, who said haughtily, "There is a case of medicines here," and brought it from a closet.

'I opened some of the bottles, smelt them, and put the stoppers to my lips. If I had wanted to use anything save narcotic medicines that were poisons in themselves, I would not have administered any of those.

'"Do you doubt them?" asked the younger brother.

'"You see, monsieur, I am going to use them," I replied, and said no more.

'I made the patient swallow, with great difficulty, and after many efforts, the dose that I desired to give. As I intended to repeat it after a while, and as it was necessary to watch its influence, I then sat down by the side of the bed. There was a timid and suppressed woman in attendance, who had retreated into a corner. Some thick old hangings had been nailed up before the windows, to deaden the sound of the shrieks. They continued to be uttered in their regular succession, with the cry, "My husband, my father, and my brother!" the counting up to twelve, and "Hush!" The frenzy was so violent, that I had not unfastened the bandages restraining the arms, but, I had looked to them, to see that they were not painful. The only spark of encouragement in the case, was, that my hand upon the sufferer's breast had this much soothing influence, that for minutes at a time it tranquillised the figure. It had no effect upon the cries: no pendulum could be more regular.

'I had sat by the side of the bed for half an hour, with the two brothers looking on, before the elder said:

'"There is another patient."

'I was startled and asked, "Is it a pressing case?"

'"You had better see," he carelessly answered; and took up a light.

*

'The other patient lay in a back room across a second staircase, which was a species of loft over a stable, a handsome peasant-boy – a boy of not more than seventeen at the most. He lay on his back, with his teeth set, his right hand clenched on his breast, and his glaring eyes looking straight upward. I could not see where his wound was, as I kneeled on one knee over him; but, I could see that he was dying of a wound from a sharp point.

'"I am a doctor, my poor fellow," said I. "Let me examine it."

'"I do not want it examined," he answered; "let it be."

'The wound was a sword-thrust, received from twenty to twenty-fours before, but no skill could have saved him if it had been looked to without delay. He was then dying fast. As I turned my eyes to the elder brother, I saw him looking down at this handsome boy whose life was ebbing out, as if he were a wounded bird, or hare, or rabbit; not at all as if he were a fellow-creature.

'"How has this been done, monsieur?" said I.

'"A crazed young common dog! A serf! Forced my brother to draw upon him, and has fallen by my brother's sword."

'There was no touch of pity, sorrow, or kindred humanity, in this answer.

'The boy's eyes had slowly moved to him as he had spoken, and they now slowly moved to me.

'"Doctor, they are very proud, these Nobles; but we common dogs are proud too, sometimes. They plunder

us, outrage us, beat us, kill us; but we have a little pride left, sometimes. She – have you seen her, Doctor?"

'I said, "I have seen her."

'"She is my sister, Doctor. They have had their shameful rights, these Nobles, in the modesty and virtue of our sisters, many years, but we have had good girls among us. She was a good girl. She was betrothed to a good young man, too: a tenant of his. We were all tenants of his – that man's who stands there. The other is his brother, the worst of a bad race."

'It was with the greatest difficulty that the boy gathered bodily force to speak; but, his spirit spoke with a dreadful emphasis.

'"We were so robbed by that man who stands there, as all we common dogs are by those superior Beings – taxed by him without mercy, obliged to work for him without pay, obliged to grind our corn at his mill, pillaged and plundered to that degree that when we chanced to have a bit of meat, we ate it in fear, with the door barred and the shutters closed, that his people should not see it and take it from us – I say, we were so robbed, and hunted, and were made so poor, that our father told us it was a dreadful thing to bring a child into the world, and that what we should most pray for, was, that our women might be barren and our miserable race die out!"

'I had never before seen the sense of being oppressed, bursting forth like a fire. Until I saw it in the dying boy.

'"Nevertheless, Doctor, my sister married. He was ailing at that time, poor fellow, and she married her lover, that she might tend and comfort him in our cottage. She had not been married many weeks, when that man's brother saw her and admired her, and asked that man to lend her to him. He was willing enough, but my sister was good and virtuous, and hated his brother with a hatred as strong as mine. What did the two then, to persuade her husband to use his influence with her, to make her willing?"

'The boy's eyes, which had been fixed on mine, slowly turned to the looker-on, and I saw in the two faces that all he said was true.

'"You know, Doctor, that it is among the Rights of these Nobles to harness us common dogs to carts, and drive us. They so harnessed him and drove him. They kept him out in the unwholesome mists at night, and ordered him back into his harness in the day. But he was not persuaded. No! Taken out of harness one day at noon, to feed – if he could find food – he sobbed twelve times, once for every stroke of the bell, and died on her bosom."

'Nothing human could have held life in the boy but his determination to tell all his wrong. He forced back the gathering shadows of death, as he forced his clenched right hand to remain clenched, and to cover his wound.

'"Then, with that man's permission and even with his aid, his brother took her away for his pleasure and diversion, for a little while. I saw her pass me on the road.

When I took the tidings home, our father's heart burst; he never spoke one of the words that filled it. I took my young sister (for I have another) to a place beyond the reach of this man, and where, at least, she will never be *his* vassal. Then, I tracked the brother here, and last night climbed in – a common dog, but sword in hand. – Where is the loft window? It was somewhere here?"

'The room was darkening to his sight; the world was narrowing around him. I glanced about me, and saw that the hay and straw were trampled over the floor, as if there had been a struggle.

'"She heard me, and ran in. I told her not to come near us till he was dead. He came in and first tossed me some pieces of money; then struck at me with a whip. But I, though a common dog, so struck at him as to make him draw. Let him break into as many pieces as he will, the sword that he stained with my common blood; he drew to defend himself – thrust at me with all his skill for his life."

'My glance had fallen but a few moments before, on the fragments of a broken sword, lying among the hay. That weapon was a gentleman's. In another place, lay an old sword that seemed to have been a soldier's.

'"Now, lift me up, Doctor; lift me up. Where is he?"

'"He is not here," I said, supporting the boy, and thinking that he referred to the brother.

'"He! Proud as these nobles are, he is afraid to see me. Where is the man who was here? Turn my face to him."

'I did so, raising the boy's head against my knee. But, invested for the moment with extraordinary power, he raised himself completely: obliging me to rise too, or I could not have still supported him.

'"Marquis," said the boy, "in the days when all these things are to be answered for, I summon you and yours, to the last of your bad race, to answer for them. In the days when all these things are to be answered for, I summon your brother, the worst of the bad race, to answer for them separately. I mark this cross of blood upon him, as a sign that I do it."

'Twice, he put his hand to the wound in his breast, and with his forefinger drew a cross in the air. He stood for an instant with the finger yet raised, and, as it dropped, he dropped with it, and I laid him down dead.

'When I returned to the bedside of the young woman, I found her raving in precisely the same order and continuity. I knew that this might last for many hours, and that it would probably end in the silence of the grave.

'I repeated the medicines I had given her, and I sat at the side of the bed until the night was far advanced. She never abated the piercing quality of her shrieks, never stumbled in the distinctness or the order of her words. They were always "My husband, my father, and my brother! One, two, three, four, five, six, seven, eight, nine, ten, eleven, twelve. Hush!"

'This lasted twenty-six hours from the time when I first saw her. I had come and gone twice, and was again sitting by her, when she began to falter. I did what little could be done to assist that opportunity, and by-and-by she sank into a lethargy, and lay like the dead.

'I released her arms, and called the woman to assist me to compose her figure and the dress she had torn. It was then that I knew her condition to be that of one in whom the first expectations of being a mother have arisen; and it was then that I lost the little hope I had had of her.

'"Is she dead?" asked the Marquis.

'"Not dead," said I; "but like to die."

'"What strength there is in these common bodies!" he said, looking down at her with some curiosity.

'"There is prodigious strength," I answered him, "in sorrow and despair."

'He first laughed at my words, and then frowned at them. He moved a chair with his foot near to mine, ordered the woman away, and said in a subdued voice,

'"Doctor, finding my brother in this difficulty with these hinds, I recommended that your aid should be invited. Your reputation is high, and, as a young man with your fortune to make, you are probably mindful of your interest. The things that you see here, are things to be seen, and not spoken of. Do you honour me with your attention, Doctor?"

'"Monsieur," said I, "in my profession, the communications of patients are always received in confidence." I was

guarded in my answer, for I was troubled in my mind with what I had heard and seen.

'I write with so much difficulty, the cold is so severe, I am so fearful of being detected and consigned to an underground cell and total darkness, that I must abridge this narrative. There is no confusion or failure in my memory; it can recall, and could detail, every word that was ever spoken between me and those brothers.

'She lingered for a week. Towards the last, I could understand some few syllables that she said to me, by placing my ear close to her lips. She asked me where she was, and I told her; who I was, and I told her. It was in vain that I asked her for her family name. She faintly shook her head upon the pillow, and kept her secret, as the boy had done.

'I had no opportunity of asking her any question, until I had told the brothers she was sinking fast, and could not live another day. Until then, though no one was ever presented to her consciousness save the woman and myself, one or other of them had always jealously sat behind the curtain at the head of the bed when I was there. But when it came to that, they seemed careless what communication I might hold with her; as if – the thought passed through my mind – I were dying too.

'I always observed that their pride bitterly resented the younger brother's (as I call him) having crossed swords with a peasant, and that peasant a boy. As often as I caught

the younger brother's eyes, their expression reminded me that he disliked me deeply, for knowing what I knew from the boy.

'My patient died, two hours before midnight – at a time, by my watch answering almost to the minute when I had first seen her. I was alone with her, when her forlorn young head drooped gently on one side, and all her earthly wrongs and sorrows ended.

'The brothers were waiting in a room downstairs, impatient to ride away.

'"At last she is dead?" said the elder, when I went in.

'"She is dead," said I.

'"I congratulate you, my brother," were his words as he turned round.

'He had before offered me money, which I had postponed taking. He now gave me a rouleau of gold. I took it from his hand, but laid it on the table.

'"Pray excuse me," said I. "Under the circumstances, no."

'They exchanged looks, but bent their heads to me as I bent mine to them, and we parted without another word on either side. Early in the morning, the rouleau of gold was left at my door in a little box, with my name on the outside. From the first, I had anxiously considered what I ought to do. I decided, that day, to write privately to the Minister, stating the nature of the two cases to which I had been summoned, and the place to which I had gone. I had

kept the matter a profound secret, even from my wife; and this, too, I resolved to state in my letter. I had no apprehension whatever of my real danger; but I was conscious that there might be danger for others, if others were compromised by possessing the knowledge that I possessed.

'I was much engaged that day, and could not complete my letter that night. I rose long before my usual time next morning to finish it. It was the last day of the year. The letter was lying before me just completed pleted, when I was told that a lady waited, who wished to see me.

'The lady was young, engaging, and handsome, but not marked for long life. She was in great agitation. She presented herself to me as the wife of the Marquis St Evrémonde. I connected the title by which the boy had addressed the elder brother, with the initial letter embroidered on the scarf, and had no difficulty in arriving at the conclusion that I had seen that nobleman very lately.

'She had in part suspected, and in part discovered, the main facts of the cruel story, of her husband's share in it, and my being resorted to. She did not know that the girl was dead. Her hope had been, she said in great distress, to show her, in secret, a woman's sympathy. Her hope had been to avert the wrath of Heaven from a House that had long been hateful to the suffering many.

'She had reasons for believing that there was a young sister living, and her greatest desire was, to help that sister.

I could tell her nothing but that there was such a sister; beyond that, I knew nothing. Her inducement to come to me, relying on my confidence, had been the hope that I could tell her the name and place of abode. Whereas, to this wretched hour I am ignorant of both.

'She was a good, compassionate lady, and not happy in her marriage. How could she be! The brother distrusted and disliked her, she stood in dread of him, and in dread of her husband too. When I handed her down to the door, there was a child, a pretty boy from two to three years old, in her carriage.

'"For his sake, Doctor," she said, pointing to him in tears, "I would do all I can to make what poor amends I can. I have a presentiment that if no other innocent atonement is made for this, it will one day be required of him. What I have left to call my own I will make it the first charge of his his life to bestow, with the compassion and lamenting of his dead mother, on this injured family, if the sister can be discovered.'

'She kissed the boy, and said, caressing him, "It is for thine own dear sake. Thou wilt be faithful, little Charles?" The child answered her bravely, "Yes!" I kissed her hand, and she took him in her arms, and went away caressing him. I never saw her more.

'As she had mentioned her husband's name in the faith that I knew it, I added no mention of it to my letter. I

sealed my letter, and, not trusting it out of my own hands, delivered it myself that day.

'That night, the last night of the year, towards nine o'clock, a man in a black dress rang at my gate, demanded to see me, and softly followed my servant, Ernest Defarge, a youth, upstairs. When my servant came into the room where I sat with my wife, we saw the man, who was supposed to be at the gate, standing silent behind him.

'An urgent case in the Rue St Honoré, he said. It would not detain me, he had a coach in waiting.

'It brought me here, it brought me to my grave. When I was clear of the house, a black muffler was drawn tightly over my mouth from behind, and my arms were pinioned. The two brothers crossed the road from a dark corner, and identified me with a single gesture. The Marquis took from his pocket the letter I had written, showed it me, burnt it in the light of a lantern that was held, and extinguished the ashes with his foot.

'If it had pleased GOD to put it in the hard heart of either of the brothers, in all these frightful years, to grant me any tidings of my dearest wife – so much as to let me know by a word whether alive or dead – I might have thought that He had not quite abandoned them. But, now I believe that the mark of the red cross is fatal to them, and that they have no part in His mercies. And them and their descendants, to the last of their race, I, Alexandre Manette, denounce to the times when all these things shall

be answered for. I denounce them to Heaven and to earth.'

A terrible sound arose when the reading of this document was done. The narrative called up the most revengeful passions of the time, and there was not a head in the nation but must have dropped before it.

Little need, in presence of that tribunal and that auditory, to show how the Defarges had not made the paper public, with the other captured Bastille memorials borne in procession, and had kept it, biding their time. Little need to show that this detested family name had long been anathematised by Saint Antoine, and was wrought into the fatal register.

And all the worse for the doomed man, that the denouncer was a well-known citizen, his own attached friend, the father of his wife, that the good physician of the Republic would deserve better still of the Republic by rooting out an obnoxious family of Aristocrats, there was wild excitement, patriotic fervour, not a touch of human sympathy.

'Much influence around him, has that Doctor?' murmured Madame Defarge, smiling to The Vengeance. 'Save him now, my Doctor, save him!'

At every juryman's vote, there was a roar. Another and another. Roar and roar.

Unanimously voted. At heart and by descent an Aristocrat, an enemy of the Republic. Death within four-and-twenty hours!

11

Dusk

The wretched wife of the innocent man thus doomed to die, fell under the sentence, as if she had been mortally stricken. But, she uttered no sound; and so strong was the voice within her, representing that it was she of all the world who must uphold him in his misery and not augment it, that it quickly raised her, even from that shock.

The quick noise and movement of the court's emptying itself by many passages had not ceased, when Lucie stood stretching out her arms towards her husband, with nothing in her face but love and consolation.

'If I might touch him! If I might embrace him once!'

There was but a gaoler left, along with two of the four men who had taken him last night, and Barsad. The people had all poured out to the show in the streets. Barsad proposed to the rest, 'Let her embrace him then; it is but a moment.' It was silently acquiesced in, and they passed her over the seats in the hall to a raised place, where he, by leaning over the dock, could fold her in his arms.

'Farewell, dear darling of my soul. My parting blessing on my love. We shall meet again, where the weary are at rest!'

They were her husband's words, as he held her to his bosom.

'I can bear it, dear Charles. I am supported from above: don't suffer for me. A parting blessing for our child.'

'I send it to her by you. I kiss her by you.'

'My husband. No! A moment!' He was tearing himself apart from her. 'We shall not be separated long. I feel that this will break my heart by-and-by; but I will do my duty while I can, and when I leave her, God will raise up friends for her, as He did for me.'

Her father had followed her, and would have fallen on his knees to both of them, but that Darnay put out a hand and seized him, crying:

'No, no! What have you done, that you should kneel to us! We know now, what you underwent when you suspected my descent, and when you knew it. We thank you with all our hearts, and all our love and duty. Heaven be with you!'

Her father's only answer was to draw his hands through his white hair, and wring them with a shriek of anguish.

'It could not be otherwise,' said the prisoner. 'It was the always-vain endeavour to discharge my poor mother's trust that first brought my fatal presence near you. Good could never come of such evil, a happier end was not in

nature to so unhappy a beginning. Be comforted, and forgive me. Heaven bless you!'

As he was drawn away, his wife released him, and stood looking after him with her hands touching one another in the attitude of prayer. As he went out at the prisoners' door, she turned, laid her head lovingly on her father's breast, tried to speak to him, and fell at his feet.

Then, issuing from the obscure corner from which he had never moved, Sydney Carton came and took her up. His arm trembled as it raised her, and supported her head. Yet, there was an air about him that was not all of pity – that had a flush of pride in it.

He carried her lightly to the door, and laid her tenderly down in a coach. Her father and their old friend got into it, and he took his seat beside the driver.

When they arrived at the gateway where he had paused in the dark not many hours before, to picture to himself on which of the rough stones of the street her feet had trodden, he lifted her again, and carried her up the staircase to their rooms. There, he laid her down on a couch, where her child and Miss Pross wept over her.

'Don't recall her to herself,' he said, softly, to the latter, 'she is better so. Don't revive her to consciousness, while she only faints.'

'Oh, Carton, Carton, dear Carton!' cried little Lucie, springing up and throwing her arms passionately round him, in a burst of grief. 'Now that you have come, I think

you will do something to help mamma, something to save papa!'

He bent over the child, and laid her blooming cheek against his face. He put her gently from him, and looked at her unconscious mother.

'Before I go,' he said, and paused – 'I may kiss her?'

It was remembered afterwards that when he bent down and touched her face with his lips, he murmured some words. The child, who was nearest to him, told them afterwards, and told her grand-children when she was a handsome old lady, that she heard him say, 'A life you love.'

When he had gone out into the next room, he turned suddenly on Mr Lorry and her father, and said to the latter:

'You had great influence but yesterday, Doctor Manette; let it at least be tried. These judges, and all the men in power, are very friendly to you, and very recognisant of your services; are they not?'

'Nothing connected with Charles was concealed from me. I had the strongest assurances that I should save him; and I did.'

'Try them again. The hours between this and tomorrow afternoon are few and short, but try.'

'I intend to try. I will not rest a moment.'

'That's well. I have known such energy as yours do great things before now – though never,' he added, with a smile and a sigh together, 'such great things as this.'

'I will go,' said Doctor Manette, 'to the Prosecutor and the President straight, and I will go to others whom it is better not to name. I will write too, and – But stay! There is a celebration in the streets, and no one will be accessible until dark.'

'That's true. Well! It is forlorn hope. I should like to know how you speed; though, mind! I expect nothing! When are you likely to have seen these dread powers, Doctor Manette?'

'Immediately after dark, I should hope.'

'It will be dark soon after four. Let us stretch the hour or two. If I go to Mr Lorry's at nine, shall I hear what you have done, either from our friend or from yourself?'

'Yes.'

'May you prosper!'

Mr Lorry followed Sydney to the outer door, and touching him on the shoulder as he was going away, caused him to turn.

'I have no hope,' said Mr Lorry, in a low and sorrowful whisper.

'Nor have I.'

'If any one of these men, or all of these men, were disposed to spare him, I doubt if they durst spare him after the demonstration in the court.'

'And so do I. I heard the fall of the axe in that sound.'

Mr Lorry leaned his arm upon the door-post, and bowed his face upon it.

'Don't despond,' said Carton, very gently; 'don't grieve. I encouraged Doctor Manette in this idea, because I felt that it might one day be consolatory to her. Otherwise, she might think "his life was wantonly thrown away or wasted," and that might trouble her.'

'Yes, yes, yes,' returned Mr Lorry, drying his eyes, 'you are right. But he will perish; there is no real hope.'

'Yes, He will perish: there is no real hope,' echoed Carton.

12

Darkness

Sydney Carton paused in the street, not quite decided where to go. 'At Tellson's banking-house at nine,' he said, with a musing face. 'Shall I do well, in the mean time, to show myself? I think so. It is best that these people should know there is such a man as I here; it is a sound precaution, and may be a necessary preparation. But care, care! care! Let me think it out!'

Checking his steps, which had begun to tend towards an object, he took a turn or two in the already darkening street, and traced the thought in his mind to its possible consequences. His first impression was confirmed. 'It is best,' he said, finally resolved, 'that these people should know there is such a man as I here.' And he turned his face towards Saint Antoine.

Defarge had described himself, that day, as the keeper of a wine-shop in the Saint Antoine suburb. Having ascertained its situation, Carton came out of those closer streets again, and dined at a place of refreshment and fell sound asleep after dinner.

It was as late as seven o'clock when he awoke refreshed, and went out into the streets again. As he passed along towards Saint Antoine, he stopped at a shop-window where there was a mirror, and slightly altered the disordered arrangement of his loose cravat, and his coat-collar, and his wild hair. This done, he went on direct to Defarge's, and went in.

There happened to be no customer in the shop but Jacques Three, of the restless fingers and the croaking voice. This man, whom he had seen upon the Jury, stood drinking at the little counter, in conversation with the Defarges, man and wife. The Vengeance assisted in the conversation, like a regular member of the establishment.

As Carton walked in, took his seat and asked (in very indifferent French) for a small measure of wine, Madame Defarge cast a careless glance at him, and then a keener, and then a keener, and then advanced to him herself, and asked him what it was he had ordered.

He repeated what he had already said.

'English?' asked Madame Defarge.

After looking at her, as if the sound of even a single French word were slow to express itself to him, he answered, in his former strong foreign accent, 'Yes, madame, yes. I am English!'

Madame Defarge returned to her counter to get the wine, and, as he took up a Jacobin journal and feigned to pore over it puzzling out its meaning, he heard her say, 'I swear to you, like Evrémonde!'

Defarge brought him the wine, and gave him Good Evening.

'Oh! Good evening, citizen,' filling his glass. 'Ah! and good wine. I drink to the Republic.'

Defarge went back to the counter, and said, 'Certainly, a little like.' Madame sternly retorted, 'I tell you a good deal like.' Jacques Three pacifically remarked, 'He is so much in your mind, see you, madame.' The amiable Vengeance added, with a laugh, 'Yes, my faith! And you are looking forward with so much pleasure to seeing him once more tomorrow!'

After a silence of a few moments, during which they all looked towards him without disturbing his outward attention from the Jacobin editor, they resumed their conversation.

'It is true what madame says,' observed Jacques Three. 'Why stop? There is great force in that. Why stop?'

'Well, well,' reasoned Defarge, 'but one must stop somewhere. After all, the question is still where?'

'At extermination,' said madame.

'Extermination is good doctrine, my wife,' said Defarge, rather troubled; 'in general, I say nothing against it. But this Doctor has suffered much; you have seen him today; you have observed his face when the paper was read.'

'I have observed his face!' repeated madame, contemptuously and angrily. 'Yes. I have observed his face, to be not the face of a true friend of the Republic.'

'And you have observed, my wife,' said Defarge, in a deprecatory manner, 'the anguish of his daughter, which must be a dreadful anguish to him!'

'I have observed his daughter,' repeated madame; 'yes, I have observed his daughter, more times than one. Let me but lift my finger –!' She seemed to raise it, and to let it fall with a rattle on the ledge before her, as if the axe had dropped.

'The citizeness is superb!' croaked the Juryman.

'She is an Angel!' said The Vengeance, and embraced her.

'As to thee,' pursued madame, implacably, addressing her husband, 'if it depended on thee – which, happily, it does not – thou wouldst rescue this man even now.'

'No!' protested Defarge. 'Not if to lift this glass would do it! But I would leave the matter there. I say, stop there.'

'See you then, Jacques,' said Madame Defarge, wrathfully; 'and see you, too, my little Vengeance; see you both! Listen! For other crimes as tyrants and oppressors, I have this race a long time on my register, doomed to destruction and extermination. Ask my husband, is that so.'

'It is so,' assented Defarge, without being asked.

'In the beginning of the great days, when the Bastille falls, he finds this paper of today, and he brings it home, and in the middle of the night when this place is clear and shut, we read it, here on this spot, by the light of this lamp. Ask him, is that so.'

'It is so,' assented Defarge.

'That night, I tell him, that I have now a secret to communicate. Ask him, is that so.'

'It is so,' assented Defarge again.

'I communicate to him that secret. "Defarge, I was brought up among the fishermen of the sea-shore, and that peasant family so injured by the two Evrémonde brothers, as that Bastille paper describes, is my family. Defarge, that sister of the mortally wounded boy upon the ground was my sister, that brother was my brother, that father was my father, those dead are my dead, and that summons to answer for those things descends to me!" Ask him, is that so.'

'It is so,' assented Defarge once more.

'Then tell Wind and Fire where to stop,' returned madame; 'but don't tell me.'

Both her hearers derived a horrible enjoyment from the deadly nature of her wrath and both highly commended it. Defarge, a weak minority, interposed a few words for the memory of the compassionate wife of the Marquis; but only elicited from his own wife a repetition of her last reply. 'Tell the Wind and the Fire where to stop; not me!'

The English customer paid for what he had had, perplexedly counted his change, and asked, as a stranger, to be directed towards the National Palace. Madame Defarge took him to the door, and put her arm on his,

in pointing out the road. The English customer was not without his reflections then, that it might be a good deed to seize that arm, lift it, and strike under it sharp and deep.

But, he went his way, and was soon swallowed up in the shadow of the prison wall. At the appointed hour, he emerged from it to present himself in Mr Lorry's room again, where he found the old gentleman walking to and fro in restless anxiety. Lucie's father had not been seen, since he quitted the banking-house towards four o'clock. She had some faint hopes that his mediation might save Charles, but they were very slight. He had been more than five hours gone.

Mr Lorry waited until ten; but, Doctor Manette not returning, and he being unwilling to leave Lucie any longer, it was arranged that he should go back to her, and come to the banking-house again at midnight. In the meanwhile, Carton would wait alone by the fire for the Doctor.

He waited and waited, and the clock struck twelve; but Doctor Manette did not come back. Mr Lorry returned, and found no tidings of him, and brought none. Where could he be?

They were discussing this question, and were almost building up some weak structure of hope on his prolonged absence, when they heard him on the stairs. The instant he entered the room, it was plain that all was lost.

Whether he had really been to any one, or whether he

had been all that time traversing the streets, was never known. As he stood staring at them, they asked him no question, for his face told them everything.

'I cannot find it,' said he, 'and I must have it. Where is it?'

His head and throat were bare, and, as he spoke with a helpless look straying all around, he took his coat off, and let it drop on the floor.

'Where is my bench? I have been looking everywhere for my bench, and I can't find it. What have they done with my work? Time presses: I must finish those shoes.'

They looked at one another, and their hearts died within them.

'Come, come!' said he, in a whimpering miserable way; 'let me get to work. Give me my work.'

Receiving no answer, he tore his hair, and beat his feet upon the ground, like a distracted child.

Lost, utterly lost!

It was so clearly beyond hope to reason with him, or try to restore him, – that – as if by agreement – they each put a hand upon his shoulder, and soothed him to sit down before the fire, with a promise that he should have his work presently. He sank into the chair, and brooded over the embers, and shed tears.

Affected, and impressed with terror as they both were, by this spectacle of ruin, it was not a time to yield to such emotions. His lonely daughter, bereft of her final hope

and reliance, appealed to them both too strongly. Again, as if by agreement, they looked at one another with one meaning in their faces. Carton was the first to speak:

'The last chance is gone: it was not much. Yes; he had better be taken to her. But, before you go, will you, for a moment, steadily attend to me? Don't ask me why I make the stipulations I am going to make, and exact the promise I am going to exact; I have a reason – a good one.'

'I do not doubt it,' answered Mr Lorry. 'Say on.'

Carton stooped to pick up the coat, which lay almost entangling his feet. As he did so, a small case in which the Doctor was accustomed to carry the list of his day's duties, fell lightly on the floor. Carton took it up, and there was a folded paper in it. 'We should look at this!' he said. Mr Lorry nodded his consent. He opened it, and exclaimed, 'Thank GOD!'

'What is it?' asked Mr Lorry, eagerly.

'A moment! Let me speak of it in its place. First,' he put his hand in his coat, and took another paper from it, 'that is the certificate which enables me to pass out of this city. Look at it. You see – Sydney Carton, an Englishman?'

Mr Lorry held it open in his hand, gazing in his earnest face.

'Keep it for me until tomorrow. I had better not take it into the prison.'

'Why not?'

'I don't know; I prefer not to do so. Now, take this

paper that Doctor Manette has carried about him. It is a similar certificate, enabling him and his daughter and her child, at any time, to pass the barrier and the frontier? You see?'

'Yes!'

'Perhaps he obtained it as his last and utmost precaution against evil, yesterday. Put it up carefully with mine and your own. Now, observe! I never doubted until within this hour or two, that he had, or could have such a paper. It is good, until recalled. But it may be soon recalled, and, I have reason to think, will be.'

'They are not in danger?'

'They are in great danger. They are in danger of denunciation by Madame Defarge. I know it from her own lips. I have lost no time, and since then, I have seen the spy. He confirms me. He knows that a wood-sawyer, living by the prison-wall, is under the control of the Defarges, and has been rehearsed by Madame Defarge as to his having seen Her' – he never mentioned Lucie's name – 'making signs and signals to prisoners. It is easy to foresee that the pretence will be the common one, a prison plot, and that it will involve her life – and perhaps her child's – and perhaps her father's – for both have been seen with her at that place. Don't look so horrified. You will save them all.'

'Heaven grant I may, Carton! But how?'

'I am going to tell you how. This new denunciation will

certainly not take place until after tomorrow; probably not until two or three days afterwards; more probably a week afterwards. You know it is a capital crime, to mourn for, or sympathise with, a victim of the Guillotine. She and her father would unquestionably be guilty of this crime, and this woman would wait to add that strength to her case, and make herself doubly sure. You follow me?'

'So attentively, and with so much confidence in what you say, that for the moment I lose sight,' touching the back of the Doctor's chair, 'even of this distress.'

'You have money, and can buy the means of travelling to the sea-coast as quickly as the journey can be made. Early tomorrow have your horses ready, so that they may be in starting trim at two o'clock in the afternoon.'

'It shall be done!'

'You are a noble heart. Did I say we could depend upon no better man? Tell her, tonight, what you know of her danger as involving her child and her father. Dwell upon that, for she would lay her own fair head beside her husband's cheerfully.' He faltered for an instant; then went on as before. 'For the sake of her child and her father, press upon her the necessity of leaving Paris, with them and you, at that hour. Tell her that it was her husband's last arrangement. Tell her that more depends upon it than she dare believe, or hope. You think that her father, even in this sad state, will submit himself to her; do you not?'

'I am sure of it.'

'I thought so. Quietly and steadily have all these arrangements made in the court-yard here, even to the taking of your own seat in the carriage. The moment I come to you, take me in, and drive away.'

'I understand that I wait for you under all circumstances?'

'You have my certificate in your hand with the rest, you know, and will reserve my place. Wait for nothing but to have my place occupied, and then for England!'

'Why, then,' said Mr Lorry, grasping his eager but so firm and steady hand, 'it does not all depend on one old man, but I shall have a young and ardent man at my side.'

'By the help of Heaven you shall! Promise me solemnly that nothing will influence you to alter the course on which we now stand pledged to one another.'

'Nothing, Carton.'

'Remember these words tomorrow: change the course, and no life can possibly be saved.'

'I will remember them. I hope to do my part faithfully.'

'And I hope to do mine. Now, good-bye!'

Though he said it with a grave smile of earnestness, and though he even put the old man's hand to his lips, he did not part from him then. He helped him so far to arouse the figure before the dying embers, as to get a cloak and hat put upon it, and to tempt it forth to find where the bench

and work were hidden that it still moaningly besought to have. He walked on the other side of it and protected it to the court-yard of the house where the afflicted heart outwatched the awful night. He entered the court-yard and remained there for a few moments alone, looking up at the light in the window of her room. Before he went away, he breathed a blessing towards it, and a Farewell.

13

Fifty-two

In the black prison of the Conciergerie, the doomed of the day awaited their fate. They were in number as the weeks of the year. Fifty-two were to roll that afternoon on the life-tide of the city to the boundless everlasting sea. Before their cells were quit of them, new occupants were appointed; before their blood ran into the blood spilled yesterday, the blood that was to mingle with theirs tomorrow was already set apart.

Charles Darnay, alone in a cell, had sustained himself with no flattering delusion since he came to it from the Tribunal. He had fully comprehended that no personal influence could possibly save him, that he was virtually sentenced by the millions, and that units could avail him nothing.

Nevertheless, it was not easy, with the face of his beloved wife fresh before him, to compose his mind to what it must bear. His hold on life was strong, and it was very, very hard to loosen; by gradual efforts and degrees unclosed a little here, it clenched the tighter there; and

when he brought his strength to bear on that hand and it yielded, this was closed again. There was a hurry, too, in all his thoughts, a turbulent and heated working of his heart, that contended against resignation.

But, all this was at first. Before long, the consideration that there was no disgrace in the fate he must meet, and that numbers went the same road wrongfully, and trod it firmly every day, sprang up to stimulate him. By degrees he calmed into the better state, when he could raise his thoughts much higher, and draw comfort down.

Before it had set in dark on the night of his condemnation, he had travelled thus far on his last way. Being allowed to purchase the means of writing, and a light, he sat down to write until such time as the prison lamps should be extinguished.

He wrote a long letter to Lucie, showing her that he had known nothing of her father's imprisonment, until he had heard of it from herself, and that he had been as ignorant as she of his father's and uncle's responsibility for that misery, until the paper had been read. He had already explained to her that his concealment from herself of the name he had relinquished, was the one condition – fully intelligible now – that her father had attached to their betrothal, and was the one promise he had still exacted on the morning of their marriage. He entreated her, for her father's sake, never to seek to know whether her father had become oblivious of the existence of the

paper, or had had it recalled to him (for the moment, or for good), by the story of the Tower, on that old Sunday under the dear old plane-tree in the garden. He besought her – though he added that he knew it was needless – to console her father, by impressing him through every tender means she could think of, with the truth that he had done nothing for which he could justly reproach himself, but had uniformly forgotten himself for their joint sakes. Next to her preservation of his own last grateful love and blessing, and her overcoming of her sorrow, to devote herself to their dear child, he adjured her, as they would meet in Heaven, to comfort her father.

To her father himself, he wrote in the same strain; but, he told her father that he expressly confided his wife and child to his care.

To Mr Lorry, he commended them all, and explained his worldly affairs. That done, with many added sentences of grateful friendship and warm attachment, all was done. He never thought of Carton. His mind was so full of the others, that he never once thought of him.

He had time to finish these letters before the lights were put out. When he lay down on his straw bed, he thought he had done with this world.

But, it beckoned him back in his sleep, and showed itself in shining forms. Free and happy, back in the old house in Soho, unaccountably released and light of heart, he was with Lucie again, and she told him it was all a

dream, and he had never gone away. Another pause of oblivion, and he awoke in the sombre morning, unconscious where he was or what had happened, until it flashed upon his mind, 'this is the day of my death!'

The hours went on; and the clocks struck the numbers he would never hear again. Nine gone for ever, ten gone for ever, eleven gone for ever, twelve coming on to pass away. After a hard contest with that eccentric action of thought which had last perplexed him, he had got the better of it. He walked up and down, softly repeating their names to himself. The worst of the strife was over. He could walk up and down, free from distracting fancies, praying for himself and for them.

Twelve gone for ever.

He had been apprised that the final hour was three, and he knew he would be summoned some time earlier, inasmuch as the tumbrils jolted heavily and slowly through the streets. Therefore, he resolved to keep two before his mind, as the hour, and so to strengthen himself in the interval that he might be able, after that time, to strengthen others.

Walking regularly to and fro with his arms folded on his breast, a very different man from the prisoner, who had walked to and fro at La Force, he heard one struck away from him, without surprise. The hour had measured like most other hours. Devoutly thankful to Heaven for his recovered self-possession, he thought, 'There is but another now,' and turned to walk again.

Footsteps in the stone passage outside the door. He stopped.

The key was put in the lock, and turned. Before the door was opened, or as it opened, a man said in a low voice, in English: 'He has never seen me here; I have kept out of his way. Go you in alone; I wait near. Lose no time!'

The door was quickly opened and closed, and there stood before him face to face, quiet, intent upon him, with the light of a smile on his features, and a cautionary finger on his lip, Sydney Carton.

There was something so bright and remarkable in his look, that, for the first moment, the prisoner misdoubted him to be an apparition of his own imagining. But, he spoke, and it was his voice; he took the prisoner's hand, and it was his real grasp.

'Of all the people upon earth, you least expected to see me?' he said.

'I could not believe it to be you. I can scarcely believe it now. You are not' – the apprehension came suddenly into his mind – 'a prisoner?'

'No. I am accidentally possessed of a power over one of the keepers here, and in virtue of it I stand before you. I come from her – your wife, dear Darnay.'

The prisoner wrung his hand.

'I bring you a request from her.'

'What is it?'

'A most earnest, pressing, and emphatic entreaty,

addressed to you in the most pathetic tones of the voice so dear to you, that you well remember.'

The prisoner turned his face partly aside.

'You have no time to ask me why I bring it, or what it means; I have no time to tell you. You must comply with it – take off those boots you wear, and draw on these of mine.'

There was a chair against the wall of the cell, behind the prisoner. Carton, pressing forward, had already, with the speed of lightning, got him down into it, and stood over him, barefoot.

'Draw on these boots of mine. Put your hands to them; put your will to them. Quick!'

'Carton, there is no escaping from this place; it never can be done. You will only die with me. It is madness.'

'It would be madness if I asked you to escape; but do I? When I ask you to pass out at that door, tell me it is madness and remain here. Change that cravat for this of mine, that coat for this of mine. While you do it, let me take this ribbon from your hair, and shake out your hair like this of mine!'

With wonderful quickness, he forced these changes upon him.

'Carton! Dear Carton! It is madness. It cannot be accomplished, it never can be done, it has been attempted, and has always failed. I implore you not to add your death to the bitterness of mine.'

'Do I ask you, my dear Darnay, to pass the door? When

413

I ask that, refuse. There are pen and ink and paper on this table. Is your hand steady enough to write?'

'It was when you came in.'

'Steady it again, and write what I shall dictate. Quick, friend, quick!'

Pressing his hand to his bewildered head, Darnay sat down at the table, Carton, with his right hand in his breast, stood close beside him.

'Write exactly as I speak.'

'To whom do I address it?'

'To no one.' Carton still had his hand in his breast.

'Do I date it?'

'No.'

The prisoner looked up, at each question. Carton, standing over him with his hand in his breast, looked down.

'"If you remember,"' said Carton, dictating, '"the words that passed between us, long ago, you will readily comprehend this when you see it. You do remember them, I know. It is not in your nature to forget them."'

He was drawing his hand from his breast; the prisoner chancing to look up in his hurried wonder as he wrote, the hand stopped, closing upon something.

'Have you written "forget them!"' Carton asked.

'I have. Is that a weapon in your hand?'

'No; I am not armed.'

'What is it in your hand?'

'You shall know directly. Write on; there are but a few words more.' He dictated again. '"I am thankful that the time has come, when I can prove them. That I do so is no subject for regret or grief."' As he said these words with his eyes fixed on the writer, his hand slowly and softly moved down close to the writer's face.

The pen dropped from Darnay's fingers on the table, and he looked about him vacantly.

'What vapour is that?' he asked

'Vapour?'

'Something that crossed me?'

'I am conscious of nothing; there can be nothing here. Take up the pen and finish. Hurry, hurry!'

As if his memory were impaired, or his faculties disordered, the prisoner made an effort to rally his attention. As he looked at Carton with clouded eyes and with an altered manner of breathing, Carton – his hand again in his breast – looked steadily at him.

'Hurry, hurry!'

The prisoner bent over the paper, once more.

'"If it had been otherwise;"' Carton's hand was again watchfully and softly stealing down; '"I never should have used the longer opportunity. If it had been otherwise;"' the hand was at the prisoner's face; '"I should but have had so much the more to answer for. If it had been otherwise –"' Carton looked at the pen and saw it was trailing off into unintelligible signs.

Carton's hand moved back to his breast no more. The prisoner sprang up with a reproachful look, but Carton's hand was close and firm at his nostrils, and Carton's left arm caught him round the waist. For a few seconds he faintly struggled with the man who had come to lay down his life for him; but, within a minute or so, he was stretched insensible on the ground.

Quickly, but with hands as true to the purpose as his heart was, Carton dressed himself in the clothes the prisoner had laid aside, combed back his hair, and tied it with the ribbon the prisoner had worn. Then, he softly called, 'Enter there! Come in!' and the Spy presented himself.

'You see?' said Carton, looking up, as he kneeled on one knee beside the insensible figure, putting the paper in the breast: 'is your hazard very great?'

'Mr Carton,' the Spy answered, with a timid snap of his fingers, 'my hazard is not *that*, in the thick of business here, if you are true to the whole of your bargain.'

'Don't fear me. I will be true to the death.'

'You must be, Mr Carton, if the tale of fifty-two is to be right.'

'Have no fear! I shall soon be out of the way of harming you, and the rest will soon be far from here, please God! Now, get assistance and take me to the coach.'

'You?' said the Spy nervously.

'Him, man, with whom I have exchanged. You go out at the gate by which you brought me in?'

'Of course.'

'I was weak and faint when you brought me in, and I am fainter now you take me out. The parting interview has overpowered me. Such a thing has happened here, often, and too often. Your life is in your own hands. Quick! Call assistance!'

'You swear not to betray me?' said the trembling Spy, as he paused for a last moment.

'Man, man!' returned Carton, stamping his foot; 'have I sworn by no solemn vow already, to go through with this, that you waste the precious moments now? Take him yourself to the court-yard you know of, place him yourself in the carriage, show him yourself to Mr Lorry, tell him yourself to give him no restorative but air, and to remember my words of last night, and his promise of last night, and drive away!'

The Spy withdrew, and Carton seated himself at the table, resting his forehead on his hands. The Spy returned immediately, with two men.

They raised the unconscious figure, placed it on a litter they had brought to the door, and bent to carry it away.

'The time is short, Evrémonde,' said the Spy, in a warning voice.

'I know it well,' answered Carton. 'Be careful of my friend, I entreat you, and leave me.'

'Come, then, my children,' said Barsad. 'Lift him, and come away!'

The door closed, and Carton was left alone. Straining his powers of listening to the utmost, he listened for any sound that might denote suspicion or alarm. There was none. Keys turned, doors clashed, footsteps passed along distant passages: no cry was raised, or hurry made, that seemed unusual. Breathing more freely in a little while, he sat down at the table, and listened again until the clock struck two.

Sounds that he was not afraid of, for he divined their meaning, then began to be audible. Several doors were opened in succession and finally his own. A gaoler, with a list in his hand, looked in, merely saying, 'Follow me, Evrémonde!' and he followed into a large dark room, at a distance. He could but dimly discern the others who were brought there to have their arms bound. The great majority were silent and still, looking fixedly at the ground.

As he stood by the wall in a dim corner, while some of the fifty-two were brought in after him, one man stopped in passing, to embrace him, as having a knowledge of him. It thrilled him with a great dread of discovery; but the man went on. A very few moments after that, a young woman, with a slight girlish form, a sweet spare face in which there was no vestige of colour, and large widely opened patient eyes, rose from the seat where he had observed her sitting, and came to speak to him.

'Citizen Evrémonde,' she said, touching him with her cold hand. 'I am a poor little seamstress, who was with you in La Force.'

He murmured for answer: 'True. I forget what you were accused of?'

'Plots. Though the just Heaven knows I am innocent of any. Is it likely?'

The forlorn smile with which she said it, so touched him, that tears started from his eyes.

'I am not afraid to die, Citizen Evrémonde, but I have done nothing. I am not unwilling to die, if the Republic which is to do so much good to us poor, will profit by my death; but I do not know how that can be, Citizen Evrémonde.'

As the last thing on earth that his heart was to warm and soften to, it warmed and softened to this pitiable girl.

'I heard you were released, Citizen Evrémonde.'

'I was. But, I was again taken and condemned.'

'If I may ride with you, Citizen Evrémonde, will you let me hold your hand?'

As the patient eyes were lifted to his face, he saw a sudden doubt in them, and then astonishment. He pressed the work-worn, hunger-worn young fingers, and touched his lips.

'Are you dying for him?' she whispered.

'And his wife and child. Hush! Yes.'

'O you will let me hold your brave hand, stranger?'

'Hush! Yes, my poor sister; to the last.'

*

The same shadows that are falling on the prison, are falling, in that same hour of the early afternoon, on the Barrier with the crowd about it, when a coach going out of Paris drives up to be examined.

'Who goes here? Whom have we within? Papers!'

The papers are handed out, and read.

'Alexandre Manette. Physician. French. Which is he?'

This is he; this helpless, inarticulately murmuring, wandering old man pointed out.

'Apparently the Citizen-Doctor is not in his right mind? The Revolution-fever will have been too much for him?'

Greatly too much for him.

'Hah! Many suffer with it. Lucie. His daughter. French. Which is she?'

This is she.

'Apparently it must be. Lucie, the wife of Evrémonde; is it not?'

It is.

'Hah! Evrémonde has an assignation elsewhere. Lucie, her child. English. This is she?'

She and no other.

'Kiss me, child of Evrémonde. Now, thou hast kissed a good Republican; something new in thy family; remember it! Sydney Carton. Advocate. English. Which is he?'

He lies here, in this corner of the carriage. He, too, is pointed out.

'Apparently the English advocate is in a swoon?'

It is hoped he will recover in the fresher air. It is represented that he is not in strong health, and has separated sadly from a friend who is under the displeasure of the Republic.

'Is that all? It is not a great deal, that! Many are under the displeasure of the Republic, and must look out at the little window. Jarvis Lorry. Banker. English. Which is he?'

'I am he. Necessarily, being the last.'

It is Jarvis Lorry who has replied to all the previous questions. It is Jarvis Lorry who has alighted and stands with his hand on the coach door, replying to a group of officials. They leisurely walk round the carriage and leisurely mount the box, to look at what little luggage it carries on the roof.

'Behold your papers, Jarvis Lorry, countersigned.'

'One can depart, citizen?'

'One can depart. Forward, my postilions! A good journey!'

'I salute you, citizens. – And the first danger passed!'

These are again the words of Jarvis Lorry, as he clasps his hands, and looks upward. There is terror in the carriage, there is weeping, there is the heavy breathing of the insensible traveller.

'Are we not going too slowly? Can they not be induced to go faster?' asks Lucie, clinging to the old man.

'It would seem like flight, my darling. I must not urge

them too much; it would rouse suspicion.'

'Look back, look back, and see if we are pursued!'

'The road is clear, my dearest. So far, we are not pursued.'

Houses in twos and threes pass by us, solitary farms, ruinous buildings, dye-works, tanneries, and the like, open country, avenues of leafless trees.

Out of the open country, in again among ruinous buildings, solitary farms, dye-works, tanneries, and the like, cottages in twos and threes, avenues of leafless trees. Have these men deceived us, and taken us back by another road? Is not this the same place twice over? Thank Heaven, no. A village. Look back, look back, and see if we are pursued! Hush! the posting-house.

Leisurely, our four horses are taken out; leisurely, the new horses come into visible existence, one by one; leisurely, the new postilions follow, sucking and plaiting the lashes of their whips; leisurely, the old postilions count their money, make wrong additions, and arrive at dissatisfied results.

At length the new postilions are in their saddles, and the old are left behind. We are through the village, up the hill, and down the hill, and on the low watery grounds. Suddenly, the postilions exchange speech with animated gesticulation, and the horses are pulled up, almost on their haunches. We are pursued?

'Ho! Within the carriage there. Speak then!'

'What is it?' asks Mr Lorry, looking out at window.

'How many did they say?'

'I do not understand you.'

'– At the last post. How many to the Guillotine today?'

'Fifty-two.'

'I said so! A brave number! My fellow-citizen here would have it forty-two; ten more heads are worth having. The Guillotine goes handsomely. I love it. Hi forward. Whoop!'

The night comes on dark. He moves more; he is beginning to revive, and to speak intelligibly; he thinks they are still together; he asks him, by his name, what he has in his hand. O pity us, kind Heaven, and help us! Look out, look out, and see if we are pursued.

The wind is rushing after us, and the clouds are flying after us, and the moon is plunging after us, and the whole wild night is in pursuit of us; but, so far we are pursued by nothing else.

14

The Knitting Done

In that same juncture of time when the Fifty-Two awaited their fate, Madame Defarge held darkly ominous council with The Vengeance and Jacques Three of the Revolutionary Jury. Not in the wine-shop did Madame Defarge confer with these ministers, but in the shed of the wood-sawyer, erst a mender of roads.

'But our Defarge,' said Jacques Three, 'is undoubtedly a good Republican? Eh?'

'There is no better,' the voluble Vengeance protested in her shrill notes, 'in France.'

'Peace, little Vengeance,' said Madame Defarge, laying her hand with a slight frown on her lieutenant's lips, 'hear me speak. My husband, fellow-citizen, is a good Republican and a bold man; he has deserved well of the Republic, and possesses its confidence. But my husband has his weaknesses, and he is so weak as to relent towards this Doctor.'

'It is a great pity,' croaked Jacques Three, dubiously shaking his head, with his cruel fingers at his hungry

mouth; 'it is not quite like a good citizen; it is a thing to regret.'

'See you,' said madame, 'I care nothing for this Doctor, I. But, the Evrémonde people are to be exterminated, and the wife and child must follow the husband and father.'

'She has a fine head for it,' croaked Jacques Three. 'I have seen blue eyes and golden hair there, and they looked charming when Samson held them up.'

'In a word,' said Madame Defarge, 'I cannot trust my husband in this matter. Not only do I feel, since last night, that I dare not confide to him the details of my projects; but also I feel that if I delay, there is danger of his giving warning, and then they might escape.'

'That must never be,' croaked Jacques Three; 'no one must escape.'

'In a word,' Madame Defarge went on, 'my husband has not my reason for pursuing this family annihilation, and I have not his reason for regarding this Doctor with any sensibility. I must act for myself, therefore. Come hither, little citizen.'

The wood-sawyer, who held her in the respect, and himself in the submission, of mortal fear, advanced with his hand to his red cap.

'Touching those signals, little citizen,' said Madame Defarge, sternly, 'that she made to the prisoners; you are ready to bear witness to them this very day?'

'Ay, ay, why not!' cried the sawyer. 'Every day, in all

weathers, from two to four, always signalling, sometimes with the little one, sometimes without. I know what I know. I have seen with my eyes.'

'Clearly plots,' said Jacques Three. 'Transparently!'

'Now, let me see,' said Madame Defarge, pondering again. 'Yet once more! Can I spare this Doctor to my husband? I have no feeling either way. Can I spare him?'

'He would count as one head,' observed Jacques Three, in a low voice. 'We really have not heads enough; it would be a pity, I think.'

'He was signalling with her when I saw her,' argued Madame Defarge; 'I cannot speak of one without the other; and I must not be silent, and trust the case wholly to him, this little citizen here. For, I am not a bad witness.'

The Vengeance and Jacques Three vied with each other in their fervent protestations that she was the most admirable and marvellous of witnesses.

'He must take his chance,' said Madame Defarge. 'No, I cannot spare him! You are engaged at three o'clock; you are going to see the batch of today executed. – You?'

The question was addressed to the wood-sawyer, who hurriedly replied in the affirmative: seizing the occasion to add that he was the most ardent of Republicans, and that he would be in effect the most desolate of Republicans, if anything prevented him from enjoying the pleasure of smoking his afternoon pipe in the contemplation of the droll national barber.

'I,' said madame, 'am equally engaged at the same place. After it is over – say at eight tonight – come you to me, in Saint Antoine, and we will give information against these people at my Section.'

The wood-sawyer said he would be proud and flattered to attend the citizeness. The citizeness looking at him, he became embarrassed, evaded her glance as a small dog would have done, retreated among his wood, and hid his confusion over the handle of his saw.

Madame Defarge beckoned the Juryman and The Vengeance a little nearer to the door, and there expounded her further views to them thus:

'She will now be at home, awaiting the moment of his death. She will be mourning and grieving. She will be in a state of mind to impeach the justice of the Republic. She will be full of sympathy with its enemies. I will go to her.'

'What an admirable woman; what an adorable woman!' exclaimed Jacques Three, rapturously. 'Ah, my cherished!' cried The Vengeance; and embraced her.

'Take you my knitting,' said Madame Defarge, placing it in her lieutenant's hands, 'and have it ready for me in my usual seat. Keep me my usual chair. Go you there, straight, for there will probably be a greater concourse than usual, today.'

'I willingly obey the orders of my Chief,' said The Vengeance with alacrity, and kissing her cheek. 'You will not be late?'

'I shall be there before the commencement.'

'And before the tumbrils arrive. Be sure you are there, my soul,' said The Vengeance, calling after her, for she had already turned into the street, 'before the tumbrils arrive!'

Madame Defarge slightly waved her hand, to imply that she heard, and might be relied upon to arrive in good time, and so went through the mud, and round the corner of the prison wall.

There were many women at that time, upon whom the time laid a dreadfully disfiguring hand; but, there was not one among them more to be dreaded than this ruthless woman, now taking her way along the streets. Of a strong and fearless character, of shrewd sense and readiness, of great determination, of that kind of beauty which not only seems to impart to its possessor firmness and animosity, but to strike into others an instinctive recognition of those qualities; the troubled time would have heaved her up, under any circumstances. But, imbued from her childhood with a brooding sense of wrong, and an inveterate hatred of a class, opportunity had developed her into a tigress. She was absolutely without pity.

It was nothing to her, that an innocent man was to die for the sins of his forefathers; she saw, not him, but them. It was nothing to her, that his wife was to be made a widow and his daughter an orphan; that was insufficient punishment, because they were her natural enemies and her prey, and as such had no right to live.

Such a heart Madame Defarge carried under her rough robe. Carelessly worn, it was a becoming robe enough, in a certain weird way, and her dark hair looked rich under her coarse red cap. Lying hidden in her bosom, was a loaded pistol. Lying hidden at her waist, was a sharpened dagger. Thus accoutred, and walking with the confident tread of such a character, and with the supple freedom of a woman who had habitually walked in her girlhood, bare-foot and bare-legged, on the brown sea-sand, Madame Defarge took her way along the streets.

Now, when the journey of the travelling coach, at that very moment waiting for the completion of its load, had been planned out last night, the difficulty of taking Miss Pross in it had much engaged Mr Lorry's attention. It was not merely desirable to avoid overloading the coach, but it was of the highest importance that the time occupied in examining it and its passengers, should be reduced to the utmost; since their escape might depend on the saving of only a few seconds here and there. Finally, he had proposed, after anxious consideration, that Miss Pross and Jerry, who were at liberty to leave the city, should leave it at three o'clock in the lightest-wheeled conveyance known to that period. Unencumbered with luggage, they would soon overtake the coach, and, passing it and preceding it on the road, would order its horses in advance, and greatly facilitate its progress during the

precious hours of the night, when delay was the most to be dreaded.

Seeing in this arrangement the hope of rendering real service in that pressing emergency, Miss Pross hailed it with joy. She and Jerry had beheld the coach start, had known who it was that Solomon brought, had passed some ten minutes in tortures of suspense, and were now concluding their arrangements to follow the coach, even as Madame Defarge, taking her way through the streets, now drew nearer and nearer to the else-deserted lodging in which they held their consultation.

'Now what do you think, Mr Cruncher,' said Miss Pross, whose agitation was so great that she could hardly speak, or stand, or move, or live: 'what do you think of our not starting from this court-yard? Another carriage having already gone from here today, it might awaken suspicion.'

'My opinion, miss,' returned Mr Cruncher, 'is as you're right. Likewise wot I'll stand by you, right or wrong.'

'I am so distracted with fear and hope for our precious creatures,' said Miss Pross, wildly crying, 'that I am incapable of forming any plan. Are *you* capable of forming any plan, my dear good Mr Cruncher?'

'Respectin' a future spear o' life, miss,' returned Mr Cruncher, 'I hope so. Respectin' any present use o' this here blessed old head o' mine, I think not. Would you do me the favour, miss, to take notice o' two promises

and wows wot it is my wishes fur to record in this here crisis?'

'Oh, for gracious sake!' cried Miss Pross, still wildly crying, 'record them at once, and get them out of the way, like an excellent man.'

'First,' said Mr Cruncher, 'them poor things well out o' this, never no more will I do it, never no more!'

'I am quite sure, Mr Cruncher,' returned Miss Pross, 'that you never will do it again, whatever it is, and I beg you not to think it necessary to mention more particularly what it is.'

'No, miss,' returned Jerry, 'it shall not be named to you. Second: them poor things well out o' this, and never no more will I interfere with Mrs Cruncher's flopping, never no more!'

'Whatever housekeeping arrangement that may be,' said Miss Pross, striving to dry her eyes and compose herself, 'I have no doubt it is best that Mrs Cruncher should have it entirely under her own superintendence. – O my poor darlings!'

'I go so far as to say, miss, morehover,' proceeded Mr Cruncher, with a most alarming tendency to hold forth as from a pulpit – 'and let my words be took down and took to Mrs Cruncher through yourself – that wot my opinions respectin' flopping has undergone a change, and that wot I only hope with all my heart as Mrs Cruncher may be a flopping at the present time.'

'There, there, there! I hope she is, my dear man,' cried the distracted Miss Pross, 'and I hope she finds it answering her expectations.'

And still Madame Defarge, pursuing her way along the streets, came nearer and nearer.

'If we ever get back to our native land,' said Miss Pross, 'you may rely upon my telling Mrs Cruncher as much as I may be able to remember and understand of what you have so impressively said. Now, pray let us think! My esteemed Mr Cruncher, let us think!'

Still, Madame Defarge, pursuing her way along the streets, came nearer and nearer.

'If you were to go before,' said Miss Pross, 'and stop the vehicle and horses from coming here, and were to wait somewhere for me; wouldn't that be best?'

Mr Cruncher thought it might be best.

'Where could you wait for me?' asked Miss Pross.

Mr Cruncher was so bewildered that he could think of no locality but Temple-bar. Alas! Temple-bar was hundreds of miles away, and Madame Defarge was drawing very near indeed.

'By the cathedral door,' said Miss Pross. 'Would it be much out of the way, to take me in, near the great cathedral door between the two towers?'

'No, miss,' answered Mr Cruncher.

'Then, like the best of men,' said Miss Pross, 'go to the posting-house straight, and make that change.'

'I am doubtful,' said Mr Cruncher, hesitating and shaking his head, 'about leaving of you, you see. We don't know what may happen.'

'Heaven knows we don't,' returned Miss Pross, 'but have no fear for me. Take me in at the cathedral, at three o'clock, or as near it as you can. There! Bless you, Mr Cruncher! Think – not of me, but of the lives that may depend on both of us!'

This exordium, and Miss Pross's two hands in quite agonised entreaty clasping his, decided Mr Cruncher. With an encouraging nod or two, he immediately went out to alter the arrangements, and left her by herself to follow as she had proposed.

The necessity of composing her appearance so that it should attract no special notice in the streets, was another relief. She looked at her watch, and it was twenty minutes past two. She had no time to lose, but must get ready at once.

Afraid, in her extreme perturbation, of the loneliness of the deserted rooms, Miss Pross got a basin of cold water and began laving her eyes, which were swollen and red. Haunted by her feverish apprehensions, she could not bear to have her sight obscured for a minute at a time by the dripping water, but constantly paused and looked round to see that there was no one watching her. In one of these pauses she recoiled and cried out, for she saw a figure standing in the room.

The basin fell to the ground broken, and the water flowed to the feet of Madame Defarge.

Madame Defarge looked coldly at her, and said, 'The wife of Evrémonde; where is she?'

It flashed upon Miss Pross's mind that the doors were all standing open, and would suggest the flight. Her first act was to shut them. There were four in the room, and she shut them all. She then placed herself before the door of the chamber which Lucie had occupied.

'You might, from your appearance, be the wife of Lucifer,' said Miss Pross, in her breathing. 'Nevertheless, you shall not get the better of me. I am an Englishwoman.'

Madame Defarge looked at her scornfully, but still with something of Miss Pross's own perception that they two were at bay. She knew full well that Miss Pross was the family's devoted friend; Miss Pross knew full well that Madame Defarge was the family's malevolent enemy.

'On my way yonder,' said Madame Defarge, with a slight movement of her hand towards the fatal spot, 'where they reserve my chair and my knitting for me, I am come to make my compliments to her in passing. I wish to see her.'

'I know that your intentions are evil,' said Miss Pross, 'and you may depend upon it, I'll hold my own against them.'

Each spoke in her own language; neither understood

the other's words; both were very watchful, and intent to deduce from look and manner, what the unintelligible words meant.

'It will do her no good to keep herself concealed from me at this moment,' said Madame Defarge. 'Let me see her. Go tell her that I wish to see her. Do you hear?'

'If those eyes of yours were bed-winches,' returned Miss Pross, 'and I was an English four-poster, they shouldn't loose a splinter of me. No, you wicked foreign woman; I am your match.'

Madame Defarge was not likely to follow these idiomatic remarks in detail; but, she so far understood them as to perceive that she was set at naught.

'Woman imbecile and pig-like!' said Madame Defarge, frowning. 'I take no answer from you. I demand to see her. Either tell her that I demand to see her, or stand out of the way of the door and let me go to her!'

'I little thought,' said Miss Pross, 'that I should ever want to understand your nonsensical language; but I would give all I have, except the clothes I wear, to know whether you suspect the truth, or any part of it.'

Madame Defarge had not moved from the spot where she stood when Miss Pross first became aware of her; but she now advanced one step.

'I am a Briton,' said Miss Pross, 'I am desperate. I don't care an English Twopence for myself. I know that the longer I keep you here, the greater hope there is for my

Ladybird. I'll not leave a handful of that dark hair upon your head, if you lay a finger on me!'

But, her courage was of that emotional nature that it brought the irrepressible tears into her eyes. This was a courage that Madame Defarge so little comprehended as to mistake for weakness. 'Ha, ha!' she laughed, 'you poor wretch! What are you worth! I address myself to that Doctor.' Then she raised her voice and called out, 'Citizen Doctor! Wife of Evrémonde! Child of Evrémonde! Any person but this miserable fool, answer the Citizeness Defarge!'

Perhaps the following silence, perhaps some latent disclosure in the expression of Miss Pross's face, perhaps a sudden misgiving apart from either suggestion, whispered to Madame Defarge that they were gone. Three of the doors she opened swiftly, and looked in.

'Those rooms are all in disorder, there has been hurried packing, there are odds and ends upon the ground. There is no one in that room behind you! Let me look.'

'Never!' said Miss Pross, who understood the request as perfectly as Madame Defarge understood the answer.

'If they are not in that room, they are gone, and can be pursued and brought back,' said Madame Defarge to herself.

'As long as you don't know whether they are in that room or not, you are uncertain what to do,' said Miss Pross to *her*self.

'I have been in the streets from the first, nothing has

stopped me, I will tear you to pieces, but I will have you from that door,' said Madame Defarge, and made at it. Miss Pross, on the instinct of the moment, seized her round the waist in both her arms, and held her tight. It was in vain for Madame Defarge to struggle and to strike; Miss Pross, with the vigorous tenacity of love, always so much stronger than hate, clasped her tight, and even lifted her from the floor in the struggle that they had. The two hands of Madame Defarge buffeted and tore her face; but, Miss Pross, with her head down, held her round the waist, and clung to her with more than the hold of a drowning woman.

Soon, Madame Defarge's hands ceased to strike, and felt at her encircled waist. 'It is under my arm,' said Miss Pross, in smothered tones, 'you shall not draw it. I am stronger than you.'

Madame Defarge's hands were at her bosom. Miss Pross looked up, saw what it was, struck at it, struck out a flash and a crash, and stood alone – blinded with smoke.

All this was in a second. As the smoke cleared, leaving an awful stillness, it passed out on the air, like the soul of the furious woman whose body lay lifeless on the ground.

In the first fright and horror of her situation, Miss Pross passed the body as far from it as she could, and ran down the stairs to call for fruitless help. Happily, she bethought herself of the consequences of what she did, in time to check herself and go back. It was dreadful to go in at the door again; but, she did go in, and even went

near it, to get the bonnet and other things that she must wear. These she put on, out on the staircase, first shutting and locking the door and taking away the key.

By good fortune she had a veil on her bonnet, or she could hardly have gone along the streets without being stopped. The marks of gripping fingers were deep in her face, and her hair was torn, and her dress (hastily composed with unsteady hands) was clutched and dragged a hundred ways.

In crossing the bridge, she dropped the door key in the river. Arriving at the cathedral some few minutes before her escort, and waiting there, she thought, what if the key were already taken in a net, what if it were identified, what if the door were opened and the remains discovered, what if she were stopped at the gate, sent to prison, and charged with murder! In the midst of these fluttering thoughts, the escort appeared, took her in, and took her away.

'Is there any noise in the streets?' she asked him.

'The usual noises,' Mr Cruncher replied; and looked surprised by the question and by her aspect.

'I don't hear you,' said Miss Pross. 'What do you say?'

It was in vain for Mr Cruncher to repeat what he said; Miss Pross could not hear him. 'So I'll nod my head,' thought Mr Cruncher, amazed, 'at all events she'll see that.' And she did.

'Is there any noise in the streets now?' asked Miss Pross again, presently.

Again Mr Cruncher nodded his head.

'I don't hear it.'

'Gone deaf in a hour?' said Mr Cruncher. 'Blest if she ain't in a queer condition! Wot can she have been a takin', to keep her courage up? Hark! There's the roll of them dreadful carts! You can hear that, miss?'

'I can hear,' said Miss Pross, seeing that he spoke to her, 'nothing. O, my good man, there was first a great crash, and then a great stillness, and that stillness seems to be fixed and unchangeable, never to be broken any more as long as my life lasts.'

'If she don't hear the roll of those dreadful carts, now very nigh their journey's end,' said Mr Cruncher, glancing over his shoulder, 'it's my opinion that indeed she never will hear anything else in this world.'

And indeed she never did.

15

The Footsteps Die Out for Ever

A long the Paris streets, the death-carts rumble, hollow and harsh. Six tumbrils carry the day's wine to La Guillotine.

As the sombre wheels of the six carts go round, they seem to plough up a long crooked furrow among the populace in the streets. Here and there, the inmate has visitors to see the sight; then he points his finger, with something of the complacency of a curator or authorised exponent, to this cart and to this, and seems to tell who sat here yesterday, and who there the day before.

Of the riders in the tumbrils, some observe these things, and all things on their last roadside, with an impassive stare; others, with a lingering interest in the ways of life and men. Some, seated with drooping heads, are sunk in silent despair. Only one, and he a miserable creature, of a crazed aspect, is so shattered and made drunk by horror, that he sings, and tries to dance. Not one of the whole number appeals by look or gesture, to the pity of the people.

There is a guard of sundry horsemen riding abreast of the tumbrils, and faces are often turned up to some of them, and they are asked some question. It would seem to be always the same question, for, it is always followed by a press of people towards the third cart. The horsemen abreast of that cart, frequently point out one man in it with their swords. The leading curiosity is, to know which is he; he stands at the back of the tumbril with his head bent down, to converse with a mere girl who sits on the side of the cart, and holds his hand. He has no curiosity or care for the scene about him, and always speaks to the girl. Here and there in the long street of St Honoré, cries are raised against him. If they move him at all, it is only to a quiet smile, as he shakes his hair a little more loosely about his face. He cannot easily touch his face, his arms being bound.

On the steps of a church, awaiting the coming-up of the tumbrils, stands the Spy and prison-sheep. He looks into the first of them: not there. He looks into the second: not there. He already asks himself, 'Has he sacrificed me?' when his face clears, as he looks into the third.

'Which is Evrémonde?' says a man behind him.

'That. At the back there.'

'With his hand in the girl's?'

'Yes.'

The man cries, 'Down, Evrémonde! To the Guillotine all aristocrats! Down, Evrémonde!'

'Hush, hush!' the Spy entreats him, timidly.

'And why not, citizen?'

'He is going to pay the forfeit: it will be paid in five minutes more. Let him be at peace.'

But the man continuing to exclaim, 'Down, Evrémonde!' the face of Evrémonde is for a moment turned towards him. Evrémonde then sees the Spy, and looks attentively at him, and goes his way.

The clocks are on the stroke of three, and the furrow ploughed among the populace is turning round, to come into the place of execution, and end. In front of it, seated in chairs, as in a garden of public diversion, are a number of women, busily knitting. On one of the foremost chairs, stands The Vengeance, looking about for her friend.

'Thérèse!' she cries, in her shrill tones. 'Who has seen her? Thérèse Defarge!'

'She never missed before,' says a knitting-woman of the sisterhood.

'No; nor will she miss now,' cries The Vengeance, petulantly. 'Thérèse!'

'Louder,' the woman recommends.

Ay! Louder, Vengeance, with a little oath or so added, and yet it will hardly bring her. Send other women up and down to seek her, lingering somewhere; and yet, although the messengers have done dread deeds, it is questionable whether of their own wills they will go far enough to find her!

'Bad Fortune!' cries The Vengeance, stamping her foot in the chair, 'and here are the tumbrils! And Evrémonde will be despatched in a wink, and she not here!'

The tumbrils begin to discharge their loads. The ministers of Sainte Guillotine are robed and ready. Crash! – A head is held up, and the knitting-women who scarcely lifted their eyes to look at it a moment ago when it could think and speak, count One.

The second tumbril empties and moves on; the third comes up. Crash! – And the knitting-women, never faltering or pausing in their work, count Two.

The supposed Evrémonde descends, and the seamstress is lifted out next after him. He gently places her with her back to the crashing engine that constantly whirrs up and falls, and she looks into his face and thanks him.

'But for you, dear stranger, I should not be so composed, nor should I have been able to raise my thoughts to Him who was put to death, that we might have hope and comfort here today. I think you were sent to me by Heaven.'

'Or you to me,' says Sydney Carton. 'Keep your eyes upon me, dear child, and mind no other object.'

'I mind nothing while I hold your hand. I shall mind nothing when I let it go, if they are rapid.'

'They will be rapid. Fear not!'

The two stand in the fast-thinning throng of victims, but they speak as if they were alone.

'Brave and generous friend, will you let me ask you one last question? I am very ignorant, and it troubles me – just a little.'

'Tell me what it is.'

'I have a cousin, an only relative and an orphan, like myself, whom I love very dearly. Poverty parted us, and she knows nothing of my fate – for I cannot write – and if I could, how should I tell her! It is better as it is.'

'Yes, yes; better as it is.'

'What I have been thinking as we came along, and what I am still thinking now, as I look into your kind strong face which gives me so much support, is this: – If the Republic really does good to the poor, and they come to be less hungry, and in all ways to suffer less, she may live a long time: she may even live to be old.'

'What then, my gentle sister?'

'Do you think that it will seem long to me, while I wait for her in the better land where I trust both you and I will be mercifully sheltered?'

'It cannot be, my child; there is no Time there, and no trouble there.'

'You comfort me so much! I am so ignorant. Am I to kiss you now? Is the moment come?'

'Yes.'

She kisses his lips; he kisses hers; they solemnly bless each other. She goes next before him – is gone; the knitting-women count Twenty-Two.

'I am the Resurrection and the Life, saith the Lord: he that believeth in me, though he were dead, yet shall he live: and whosoever liveth and believeth in me shall never die.'

The murmuring of many voices, the upturning of many faces, the pressing on of many footsteps in the outskirts of the crowd, so that it swells forward in a mass, like one great heave of water, all flashes away. Twenty-Three.

They said of him, about the city that night, that it was the peacefullest man's face ever beheld there. Many added that he looked sublime and prophetic.

If he had given an utterance to his thoughts, and they were prophetic, they would have been these:

'I see Barsad, and Cly, Defarge, The Vengeance, the Juryman, the Judge, long ranks of the new oppressors who have risen on the destruction of the old, perishing by this retributive instrument, before it shall cease out of its present use. I see the evil of this time and of the previous time of which this is the natural birth, gradually making expiation for itself and wearing out.

'I see the lives for which I lay down my life, peaceful, useful, prosperous and happy, in that England which I shall see no more. I see Her with a child upon her bosom, who bears my name. I see her father, aged and bent, but otherwise restored.

'I see that I hold a sanctuary in their hearts, and in the

hearts of their descendants, generations hence. I see her, an old woman, weeping for me on the anniversary of this day. I see her and her husband, their course done, lying side by side in their last earthly bed, and I know that each was not more honoured and held sacred in the other's soul, than I was in the souls of both.

'I see that child who lay upon her bosom and who bore my name, a man winning his way up in that path of life which once was mine. I see him winning it so well, that my name is made illustrious there by the light of his. I see the blots I threw upon it, faded away. I see him, foremost of just judges and honoured men, bringing a boy of my name, with a forehead that I know and golden hair, to this place, and I hear him tell the child my story, with a tender and a faltering voice.

'It is a far, far better thing that I do, than I have ever done; it is a far, far better rest that I go to than I have ever known.'